The Man Who Hunted Ice

Praise for The Man Who Hunted Ice

"This is a fun, exciting and fast-paced story that's loosely based in Ottawa—so of course it's a work of fiction. Because nothing this fun ever happens around here, unless it's the "Hamburglar Run." But Trevor does a masterful job of weaving Lorne's story, turning him into the Andrew Hammond of office vent cleaners. As a reporter, I would love to be in one of these scrums to ask Lorne some poking and prodding questions as he is suddenly thrust into the spotlight. A fun read on how celebrity status can change your life in a heartbeat."

~ Ian Mendes, *The Athletic*

"With a cast of unique and entertaining and often cantankerous characters, *The Man Who Hunted Ice* will appeal to fans of science fiction while also feeling strangely familiar to sports and pop culture fans."

~ Sean McIndoe, author of
The Down Goes Brown History of the NHL

The Man Who Hunted Ice

A Novel

Trevor Mahon

NON CANADA

Publisher's note: This book is a work of fiction. Names, characters, places and incidents are either the product of the author's imagination or are used fictitiously, and any resemblance to actual persons living or dead is entirely coincidental.

Library and Archives Canada Cataloguing in Publication

Title: The man who hunted ice / Trevor Mahon.

Names: Mahon, Trevor, author.

Identifiers: Canadiana (print) 20230446493 | Canadiana (ebook) 20230446531 | ISBN 9781989689554 (softcover) | ISBN 9781989689592 (EPUB)

Classification: LCC PS8626..A4174125 M36 2023 | DDC C813/.6—dc23

Printed and bound in Canada on 100% recycled paper.

Now Or Never Publishing
901, 163 Street
Surrey, British Columbia
Canada V4A 9T8

nonpublishing.com
Fighting Words.

We gratefully acknowledge the support of the Canada Council for the Arts and the British Columbia Arts Council for our publishing program.

For S.

Part I

Chapter One

As he zipped on his coveralls and pinned the lights to his shoulders, his foreman caught him by the arm.

"Do you have any shirts and ties?"

"What?"

"Shirts and ties."

He had to think about it.

"Yeah, a couple."

"They want you to start wearing them."

He looked at the foreman.

"In the ducts?"

"To work. And from work."

Air clattered in the vents.

"Just to work?"

"And from work. So—you got shirts and ties?"

"Yeah. One, I think. I'll have to check."

It had to be a joke. But the foreman still had Lorne's sleeve.

"Wear it tomorrow."

Lorne flashed his shoulder lights, first the left, then the right, then the left again. He did this at the beginning of every shift, even though he never used the lights. The foreman watched. Nobody else was around. If not for the watery glow of a pair of lamps in opposite corners, which burned a funereal purple, the two men would have been in darkness.

"Shirt and tie, shirt and tie, shirt and tie—"

Lorne droned the words as he paced across the room to a black square on the wall. He stumbled, which had the effect of transforming his chant into a rhythmic hum—*hmm-hmm-hmm, hmm-hmm-hmm*. The foreman stood at the door with his hand on the knob.

Reaching the square, Lorne hitched at the waist of his coveralls.

"How's the party today?" he said.

"Looks pretty dead."

Lorne peered into the square in an odd way, as if he were looking into a mirror and inspecting the corners of his eyebrows.

"Not quite," he said. "Not quite, not quite—"

He was about to say *I can see one of them right now*, but there was no point, because he heard the door shut. The foreman was gone.

Okay boys, he said to himself, *ready or not, here I come.*

And he disappeared into the black square.

CHAPTER TWO

It seemed funny that he should wear a shirt and tie to work when his coveralls did not even fit properly. That is what his wife said when he got home the next morning, at five past eight, and told her he needed to dress up.

"My coveralls are fine," he said.

"If you asked for the right size, they'd give them."

She may as well have told Lorne his penis was too small.

"I guess you'd like it if I was a fatass," he said.

"Of course not."

"Can you iron the tie for me."

He avoided the interrogative inflection with his wife.

"Sure, Lorny."

She had prepared eggs and olives for his breakfast, which was actually his dinner. Normally he ate from a TV tray in the parlour, but today he sat down at the kitchen table, his back resting against a loose splat. As he devoured the meal he stretched his legs. The air was deliciously cool against the clammy wool of his socks.

His wife came back into the room.

"I can't find your tie," she said. "I'll look again when I get home."

"Yeah."

She slipped on a limp baseball cap and pulled her ponytail through the gap above the fastener. A lock of her hair got caught.

Lorne, chewing, "Oh—Crick"—Crick was short for Cricket, which was her Christian name—"I have a hole in my—"

"I bet it has something to do with the Cancer Building," said Cricket.

"What?"

"Shirts and ties. Must have *something* to do with the Cancer Building."

"I bet it has *nothing* to do with the Cancer Building."

"I bet it *does*, Lorny."

Lorne glowered and returned to his eggs, tucking his feet under his chair. Cricket knew he would do that, just like she knew he would set his dishes in the sink for her to do when she got home, knew that his hands and feet would still smell after he washed them, and knew that he would fall asleep on the chesterfield in front of the television.

CHAPTER THREE

"You know," Lorne said weeks later, slipping an already-greasy tie over his head at the end of a shift, "I only wore a tie three times in my life before now."

He was speaking to Orinn, his foreman.

"Yeah?"

Lorne counted the moments out on his pinkie, ring, and middle fingers: "Mom's, Pop's, uncle's."

"Uncle's what?"

"Funeral."

"You never wore one to a wedding?" said Orinn.

"Wedding don't count."

Orinn was cursed with a mouth whose corners were naturally upturned, forcing on him a perpetual grin. People meeting him for the first time read openness and mirth in his expression. It would not take long for the cold tone of voice, and the joyless eyes, to sour their impression. His children's friends, in fact, liked him less than they liked another of their fathers who was a foul-mouthed alcoholic. Orinn was like an empty cookie jar. Lorne had learned this about Orinn long ago, but even he was still fooled now and then by the phantom grin.

"Nobody else ever invited me to one," Lorne said. "A wedding."

"Not even your own?"

Once in a while Orinn would say something funny like that, usually around Christmas. But not every Christmas.

"How much longer do I have to wear this?" said Lorne, tugging at the frayed collar of his shirt, which was pea-soup green. His fingers were covered in grime from the ducts.

"Longer," said Orinn.

In the purple watery light Lorne was sure he saw Orinn's teeth. It was difficult to tell whether the foreman meant to smile or to frown or something in between.

CHAPTER FOUR

The Cancer Building, so named because its central tenant was a medical research centre, was nineteen storeys high. It stood west of downtown and marked the unofficial edge of the city core. From a distance it appeared to be cylindrical, though this was an optical illusion; it was actually hexagonal. Late in the afternoon, when the sun struck the west-facing windows, the entire flank seemed ablaze. The structure housed fifty-eight businesses and eleven hundred workers.

During a heat wave the previous summer, the top ten storeys of the building had frozen solid. The ice had never thawed, and those upper reaches of its exterior remained sheathed in ice far into the following spring, long after the snows had melted. Until that catastrophe, almost nobody in the city knew what building superintendents meant when they talked about *moles*.

Lorne nodded off in front of the television almost every morning after returning from work. He never slept long. Before nine o'clock he would remove his socks and roll his pant legs up and scratch for half an hour. He would scratch his shins, his calves, and his thighs, and then spend ten or fifteen minutes on his feet. His hands had long ago ceased being itchy; all feeling had dried out of them. Every one of his fingers was covered in red-studded hashes.

Around eleven o'clock he would open a root beer. "Hello, you," he would say as he snatched the bottle out of the fridge. Once he downed it, he would return to the fridge for one more. "Now—where's your brother?"

When Cricket returned in the early evening, with her hair splayed out the back of her cap, Lorne would still be in front of the television, still with his pant legs rolled up. The chesterfield had a scrolling pattern that seemed to spring from either side of his back, like a pair of faded floral wings. Nothing in the world was as comfortable to Lorne as that couch. Sinking into its backrest, he looked like a little mustachioed child. He was five feet five inches tall and weighed one hundred and thirty-three pounds. He was shorter than both his father and his son.

While Lorne had all but destroyed the upholstery by sitting on it when he was still grimy from work, Cricket never failed, on finding him sprawled over the cushions, to say, "Oh, Lorny, the fabric—"

"Jesus, it's not like I'm sitting here in my coveralls."

"But you sweat through your clothes. Your oils—"

"My what?"

"Your oils, your body—"

"It's not like I'm sitting here *stark raving naked*—"

"If you'd just clean up a little first—"

"If you want me to sit here *stark raving naked*, I will! Leo used to sit up here with shit on his back..."

Leo—Leonidas—was their son, who had grown up and left home. Leo was the first of them to discover that Lorne was becoming famous.

CHAPTER FIVE

The previous summer, when Orinn had told him about the Cancer Building, Lorne was flabbergasted.

"Don't they have a guy?" he said.

By *guy*, Lorne meant a *cleaner*, which is how he and other *moles* referred to themselves. If anyone had ever called Lorne a mole to his face, Lorne might have slugged him with a greasy fist.

"Yep," said Orinn. "But he was sick."

Lorne was sitting on his bench, coveralls half on, his chest naked and violet in the thin basement light.

"Christ," he said. "How long?"

"Three days."

Lorne shook his head.

"Too long."

Orinn stood against the door jamb. He was smiling and not smiling.

"They're hoping to fix it," he said.

"Oh—*are* they, now."

"Yep. Sent in a whole mess—soldiers, even; firefighters, a bunch of scientists—"

"Oh—*did* they, now."

"If it's not too late, they'll probably—"

"It *is* too late," said Lorne, sliding one wiry arm and then the other into the sleeves of his coveralls. "It was too late yesterday."

"I guess they didn't know."

"They should've asked him."

"Who?"

"The damned cleaner, if he knew his ass from a rat."

Zipping up, Lorne rotated his shoulders two or three times to settle the coveralls in place. Orinn watched him. Lorne, he noted, always swelled his chest and arms when he suited up, as if trying to appear bigger than he was. One time he was standing behind Lorne as the cleaner was going through this puffing-up routine, and to amuse himself he mimicked Lorne's movements. But it did not bring him as much joy as he had hoped.

"The damned cleaner isn't a scientist," said Orinn.

"A cleaner knows more about it than scientists, if he knows his ass from a rat."

"I don't know about that. All I heard on the radio is they're hoping to save it."

Lorne made a dismissive gesture.

"It's a ten-storey corpse now," he said.

"Nineteen storeys."

"Sure, nineteen. A corpse is a corpse."

Lorne's building, the Sprill, was twenty-two storeys. He and Orinn were standing in the bowels of it, beneath seventy-five thousand tons of metal, glass and concrete. They may as well have been a couple of grubs burrowing deep in the earth. Only a small handful of the thousands of souls who worked above them during the day were aware of their operation, of the wispy man who arrived every night at a quarter to ten and used a coded knock to enter a door in an alley that most of them knew only as an escape route during fire drills.

Both of Cricket's parents were dead.

Her father was a kind man who died of mesothelioma when he was forty-nine years old. In his youth he had spent a summer working for his uncle's contracting outfit, demolishing ceilings and walls and inhaling millions of carcinogenic particles that had lain undisturbed for a century. Cricket helped her mother nurse him as his flesh fell away from his bones until, too weak to cough, he swallowed his own blood. And her mother passed a year later; Cricket turned nineteen a week after the funeral, and was already pregnant with Lorne's child. In earlier times, the mother's death would have been attributed to "misadventure." Two decades later, Cricket still sometimes referred to her mother as *Miss Adventure*.

A year or two after the deaths, when Cricket could talk about them without weeping, Lorne started making introductions in this way:

"I'm Lorne. This is Cricket, and I'm her husband and her parents."

He was four years older than Cricket.

"If your parents were still here," one of Cricket's friends said to her, "you'd never be with him, baby or no baby."

When the friend made this comment, the baby was twenty-one years old.

"That's just silly," said Cricket. "That's a silly thing to say."

"But it's true. Isn't it?"

Cricket chewed a corner of her cheek.

"Lorne would've really loved my parents," she said, eyes shining. "And they would've loved him."

She looked so wistful that the friend cut the interrogation short. The friend, it so happened, had married a lemon, and had long regretted it.

CHAPTER SIX

The earliest recorded occurrence of the ice phenomenon is from 1910, in the basement of a barrel-vaulted church in Algiers. The warden believed the appearance of ice along the cobbled floor to be a miracle. It is not clear whether he grew tired of the miracle once it spread over the entire floor. The church was demolished in the 1930s, long after it had ceased to be used.

In May 1945, during the Allies' partitioning of Europe, British soldiers discovered ice patches at both ends of Germany—one at the bottom of a cistern beneath a pile of frozen corpses, and one in the chimney of a small house that had been bombed to pieces. A corporal who undertook the delicate operation of removing the ice bloom from the chimney ended up losing a finger to frostbite.

"Burned by bloody ice," he told a medic. "What's next?"

A cottage in Mississippi froze solid in spring 1966. More blooms were detected and torched in the North Caucasus three years later. Archival evidence shows "phenomena" outside Vladivostok in 1971 and along the Yellow River a decade later that points towards the blooms; however, given the governing structures in the Soviet Union and China at the time, the claims have never been verified.

Scientists interviewed a Swiss man who for forty years had piloted a rope ferry on the Rhine in Basel. One night in 1947 the ferryman, seven or eight at the time, was awoken by flashes of silent lightning at the window. His brother slept soundly in the bed next to him. The ferryman crept to the pane to watch the marvels in the sky.

"The lightning was very far away but coming on very fast. It had been a hot, dry day. I did not want to wake up my father or Ralph [the ferryman's brother] so I moved like a cat. I never liked cats, any cats. I was at the window for maybe five minutes or six minutes, maybe seven... at dinner I had drunk two full glasses of milk and, now that I was awake and on my feet, I needed to relieve myself. Even now I always drink milk with dinner because of the calcium. Ralph never liked milk and he was the one who snored. Milk is bad for cats, too! Did you know that?

"I turned to the door and my eyes popped out of my head. The door frame was glowing like something from Mars. Little reddish pockets all around and spreading over onto the wall. It was the strangest thing—it was like the door was *looking at me*... Ralph slept through it all. Even when I got my father, [Ralph] slept the whole time we were trying to chip the creatures off the wallpaper. And it was very cold in the room even though it was summer. After fifteen minutes the room was misty with ice chips and hot air and we had to leave.

"I don't know what happened after that. We never went back to the house."

Ralph died years later in his sleep.

"He slept through his own death," the ferryman said. "Probably doesn't even know he's dead."

A teenager was the first to ask Lorne for his autograph. He approached the cleaner at a bus stop, told him he was a "big fan," got a picture and signature, and told Lorne he had beautiful penmanship. Lorne thought the boy was insane, and said so to a mother and young child standing nearby.

Lorne inherited his flair for penmanship from his father, a man who woke up at four o'clock in the morning every day of his life, including the day he was born. He and Lorne strongly resembled each other, though the father was ten inches taller, and was as bulky as Lorne was trim. In Lorne's mind, the old man carried himself as if he had attained his height through determined hard work. One time Lorne apologized for not being taller, and his father, not recognizing the remark for a joke, only patted his son's knee, as if to say *There's nothing we can do about that now.*

In the far corner of Lorne's childhood backyard, under a decayed cedar tree, stood a well that had been out of use for a hundred years. For whatever reason, successive generations of owners had neglected to fill it in. Lorne's father hauled him by the arm to the well and pointed into its depths.

"If you play around here," he said, "you might trip and fall in."

"So what?" said Lorne.

"So you'll fall down into the bottom and be dead."

"How deep is it?"

"Oh, seventy feet. Maybe eighty."

Lorne peered over the edge, feeling his father's grip tightening around his bicep. On the way back to the house, he asked his father whether anyone had ever fallen into the well.

"You bet they did."

"Did they get out?"

Lorne's father stopped.

"If you want to find out, you just play around there and see."

After that, Lorne was careful to go into the well only when his father was somewhere else.

When Lorne was nine years old, he was climbing around the well's upper masonry and felt a cold breath at his feet. The shaft was always cooler the lower he descended, but this time the air was icy, as if his feet were stuck in a freezer. Creeping down a few more feet and squinting into the gloom, he lost his footing and nearly pitched to the bottom; only by thrusting out all four limbs against the stone was he able to prevent a final fall. Panicking, he clambered up and out and dropped onto the dead leaves that ringed the mouth of the well. As he lay curled and sobbing, he thought about what his father had hinted about people tumbling into the black and never getting out.

CHAPTER SEVEN

One of Lorne and Cricket's neighbours, an elderly invalid, had subscriptions to several tabloid news magazines that she passed on to Cricket when she was finished with them. Cricket was a lightning reader and could breeze through a full magazine in ten minutes.

In one of the tabloids, Cricket read a short piece about chimney sweeps in eighteenth-century London, young lads whose work, it turned out, made them prone to cancer of the scrotum. Soot would accumulate in their scrotal folds and eventually kill them. The boys lived short miserable lives and died miserable deaths. The article quoted a researcher at an American university who went on about the lethality of carbon monoxide and described the sweeps' toils as if they were the last line of defence between earth and hell.

"Lorny, you're just like these boys!" Cricket told her husband, shoving the magazine at him. "They're like your ancestors... or they would be, if they'd grown up and had kids."

She meant it as a compliment, but Lorne did not look at her or the magazine.

Orinn had disliked Lorne when he first met him because the cleaner cut an unappealing figure. Something ferret-like in Lorne's features inspired occasional contempt in new acquaintances, especially when they made his acquaintance in poorly lit basements.

Along with jet-black thinning hair, Lorne had a pencil-thin moustache, two dark slashes on each side of his nostrils. He had a habit of twisting his lips, first one way, then the other, when thinking or listening or watching television. He was swarthier than someone who worked indoors ought to have been; a great-grandmother had, according to family lore, been Ojibway, but that had never been proven. As a child, Lorne's father once asked the woman—now long dead—whether she was an Indian, and she narrowed her eyes at him and said, "Do I *look* like an Indian?"

"I don't know," Lorne's father had said.

"If you don't know, you shouldn't ask."

Mr. Lorch did not ask his grandmother about it again. Nobody else in the family who had speculated on the woman's ethnicity was still living, and Lorne was not aware of this mystery of his ancestry.

CHAPTER EIGHT

In the ducts, Lorne stood upright, feet down, elbows pressed against metal. Above and below, all around him, was emptiness, darkness.

Use those shoulder lights, Orinn told him, at least once a week.

Don't need 'em.

He had wedged himself in the shaft, using his shoulders and elbows and thighs and knees and the outsides of his boots to pinion himself against the narrow walls. Every few moments he made minute adjustments. If he relaxed his body, he would fall. Depending on where he had lodged himself, he might drop a few feet before regaining his hold. But any longer descent and he might gather too much speed to check his pitch, and plunge five or six storeys, rattling down in blind terror, the debt of shattered bones and ruptured organs increasing with every moment. One could hardly use a climbing apparatus or other safeguard in such an environment. And if offered such equipment, he would have said *Horseshit.*

The shaft was as black as the bottom of an ocean, but Lorne, hovering in the darkness, looked around as if he were admiring a view of an African savannah. Sweat was smeared on his brow, his hands, his back, and his thighs, the perspiration always starting as soon as he zipped up his coveralls. He searched through the gloom until he made out the edges of the shaft enclosing his body. According to an optometrist, by now Lorne's eyes could see better in darkness than almost anyone's on earth. And the optometrist told him:

"At some point this is going to be very bad for you."

Not yet.

Lorne was peering around for something that most of us would never have been able to spot in such conditions. He knew it was there. As he shimmied up the chute he could feel a change in the air that had nothing to do with the building's cooling system. It was the same vague hint, almost a fragrance, of ice that had caught him off guard as a child when climbing in the upper quarters of the well. He sniffed the air and glanced up again.

Carefully, gingerly, he unkinked his muscles in a series of snake-like motions and wriggled another foot or two up the shaft. He stopped, inhaled, expanded his body against the metal. Sniffed once, twice; tilted his head back and looked up—

There you are, you little bastard.

Far up the shaft, near a perpendicular joint that Lorne passed by twice every night, was a tiny, faint phosphorescence, so thin and dull that it seemed as distant as a star.

You stay right there. I'm coming to get you.

As he prepared to squirm up the duct—as he readied his lungs to ascend into colder and colder heights—he recalled again that odd new rule about wearing a shirt and tie to work. Right there, teetering in a blackened shaft, he pictured himself wearing the "tails," as he referred to such mildly formal wear, on the job, in the vents. Crawling around in metal and oil with a tie dragging along the wall and—why not?—a watch and chain dangling from his belly.

He threw back his head and laughed. He laughed so lustily that his hand almost slipped.

Did you hear that, he cried, gaping up at the dim pinkish gleam far above his head. *I got to start dressing up for you boys now.*

When Lorne laughed deep in the ducts, the echoes of his voice raced through the skeleton of the building and sputtered out the vent grates. It made a sound like a host of goblins cackling in a cave. Although the night janitors knew what was causing the din, it made their blood run cold.

CHAPTER NINE

The Cancer Building's cleaner was not much suited to the job, and had come to it almost by accident. The previous cleaner, a custodian who made forays into the ducts only as needed, had been forced early into retirement because of arthritis in his hands; he could no longer grip a mop for long, let alone climb through the chutes hunting tiny pricks of light. The man who replaced him was slovenly, habitually late for work, and had extreme political views, which made him unpopular both at work and at home. And every January, the new man mapped out all of the sick days he would take over the next twelve months. It took several days of painstaking calculation; the point was to scatter the days in a manner that was optimal but seemingly random. At the beginning of last year, the cleaner had pencilled three days for himself in August, a Friday and the following Monday and Tuesday, which would give him a five-day weekend. He planned to spend those days at his brother's cabin an hour north of the city, fishing and drinking and playing Crazy Eights.

On the Thursday night before his little holiday, the cleaner, his wife, and his children fell ill with strep throat. He did not—could not—return to work for a week. By then, there was no work left. The Cancer Building was wormy with ice.

The superintendent announced that the building had died a "natural death," and nobody questioned his account. The little pink blooms were a rising problem in cities across Canada.

"We're working with our councillors to make sure this doesn't happen again," said the superintendent. "Our buildings will be protected."

Fascinated and alarmed by what had for decades been an obscure novelty, people contacted their local, provincial, and federal representatives to ask what was being done. A radio host speculated that the "disease" affecting city buildings could evolve into a full-scale disaster, destroying municipal infrastructure. One expert cited a report—which had already been debunked—warning that the phenomenon might be able to jump from masonry to human flesh.

In the fall, a sociology student at the city's largest university, grasping for an essay topic, landed on the Cancer Building debacle. Unlike the media, which reported the detail as incidental, the student zeroed in on the absent cleaner. Like most people, she assumed that "cleaner" meant "custodian."

"I don't get it," she told her boyfriend. "Are janitors supposed to mop inside the walls now?"

"I don't know."

No, it was not a janitor, she found out. Her landlord's niece, whom her boyfriend was sleeping with behind her back, had inside information.

"My uncle does maintenance for a building downtown. Bank building. They have a guy there nights and weekends."

"Doing what?"

"No idea. Whatever the guy in the Cancer Building *wasn't* doing."

The student thought the landlord's son was making the whole thing up. Ducts did not work that way, she said; that was only in movies. The spaces were too small. Nobody could slither into and around a heating system.

"They can in these buildings," the landlord's son told her. He had a condom in his pocket, visible through his tight black jeans.

"Why? Are the vents big?"

"Big enough. And the dudes are small."

Like jockeys, thought the student. Or chimney sweeps.

To gather more information, the student had a brief telephone call with the superintendent of the Sprill Building. The super did not mention Lorne by name, but said:

"Our guy hasn't missed a day in eleven years. And he's never fallen, never gotten a scratch on him..."

The student's boyfriend, who was sleeping with the landlord's niece, showed the essay to a friend who wrote for the university newspaper. It was printed in the next issue. Within three months, eleven thousand people read and shared the essay.

CHAPTER TEN

Later on, Lorne dumped snow on a boy's head, a gesture without malign intent. The episode made news across the country. How could a hero, the media asked, treat a child so shabbily? Had Lorch become so famous that the dictates of common decency no longer applied to him?

After the third or fourth threatening phone call, Lorne slammed down the receiver and turned to Cricket.

"What's with these assholes?" he cried. "I was only *joking* with the kid."

Cricket was cross-stitching.

"People don't always understand," she said.

"People are assholes."

When little Lorne felt the ghostly breath on his feet in the well, he leaped out, terrified, and wept on the grass. For a week he avoided the backyard entirely. Yet he was a very unimaginative child and found it hard to amuse himself. All he wanted to do was climb, but the only trees in the yard were stunted or dead or caked in sap. He did not mind the sap himself, but his mother hated it. She made Lorne do his own laundry whenever anything sticky or brown or bloody got on his clothes.

Time and boredom eventually prevailed, and Lorne made another descent. It was a damp day and the masonry was slick, so he wore gloves, something he rarely did no matter the season. For ten minutes he crept around the top of the shaft, resting now and then with his back against the stones and his legs, half bent, pressing against the wall across from him, sitting over the abyss. At one point he noticed a tiny depression in the mortar between two crooked stones. It took him a moment to identify it. A thumbprint—embedded in the rock by a mason over a century ago. A mason long vanished from the earth; yet his well still stood, and his thumbprint still held. To Lorne it was like discovering a fossil. He was staring at the thumbprint and wondering at the size of the man who made it when he again experienced a chill on the back of his thighs.

An urge to flee seized him, which he suppressed with a trembling effort. Very slowly he spread his legs and looked down into the darkness. He could no longer hear himself breathing.

What's that.

Mastering his terror, he slackened his legs and allowed his body to descend a couple of feet. As he repositioned his boots he could feel his thighs and calves getting colder. Down another foot he went, and another, and another, the blackness thickening around him. His breath licked at his cheeks. Up outside the well it was the full of summer, hazy, sultry; fifteen feet down, patches of frost twinkled in the gloom.

He sat there, holding himself aloft with the pressure of his little legs, glancing up at the small grey circle of light above, then back down into the depths. Another five feet down and it would be too dark to see a hand in front of his eyes. And he would never see the ice before it swept his feet from the stonework.

Is there water at the bottom.

Or bones.

Tremors of panic passed through his body. Something was below him—

There, there—he saw it, *right* there, not two feet under his buttocks, flickering as it caught the pale dregs of light in a way that distinguished it from the frost. It was of a hue he had never seen before, of a red that had gotten sick, a colour that had apparently crept out of the middle of the earth. Though Lorne's little frame blocked most of the remaining light, he could make out the thing's approximate size: about the circumference of a nickel, with irregular edges.

Shimmying around the well with his feet and haunches, Lorne descended again, slowly, spreading his legs so that they skirted the spot. He was reminded of a photo he had seen in a book on maritime disasters of a distress rocket falling from the sky towards the sea. The thing below him did not move, though its glow seemed to very gradually pulsate, waxing and waning like a dying Christmas light.

Lorne sat in that position for more than an hour, with his legs spread on either side of the rosy wonder, sitting on an invisible chair in a well from which nobody had drawn water since Victoria was Queen of the Commonwealth. Ice spread out from all sides of the thing. Every so often—it may only have been Lorne's eyes—the gleam would flare slightly, or bicker like candlelight, as if trying to make up its mind about something.

Cramping set in. Lorne reached out his toe and, with a fantastic show of courage, brushed it across the face of the glowing bloom. Nothing happened. He touched it with the sole of his sneaker. Whatever it was, it was about as thick as a leaf of construction paper. The light held steady. Was it breathing? Was it holding its breath?

He reached across and swiped at the thing with the tips of his fingers. He felt stone, nothing more.

You shit, he said. *You shitty little shit.*

Lorne scaled the wet stones of the shaft—slowly, with stiff legs—and flopped over the lip of the well onto the grass. His father had been securing a tarp to the top of the woodpile and caught him emerging from the deep, and happened to be wielding a flat stick of wood. As always, Lorne did not show any emotion during the spanking, but afterwards blubbered alone in his room.

Jarring him sooner than normal out of his grief was a pain in the index and middle fingers of his right hand. His father, he thought, must have glanced them with the stick. They were chapped and swollen, and now began to sting. Lorne did not know it at the time, but they were frostbitten. Frostbitten, on a day when his mother had opened the windows to an afternoon shower because it was too humid in the house.

CHAPTER ELEVEN

Three fans stood on the ceiling of the gymnasium of Lorne's high school, thirty feet above the floor. Cages were erected around the fans to protect the blades from errant basketballs and volleyballs. Still, over the years, about half a dozen balls had slipped through the wires of the cages and gotten stuck there, inspiring no small amount of jubilation from the athletes below. The balls sat aloft like clusters of eggs in a metal nest. Now and then a ball in the centre cage shifted or rolled from the wind of the blades, and a steady *ka-chunk ka-chunk ka-chunk* issued from above as the blades shaved at the ball's leather skin.

One lunch hour, with the gym full of students playing intramural volleyball, the *ka-chunk ka-chunk* began and would not quit. One of the balls was lodged fast, threatening to short out the fan motor.

"Lorny, Lorny!" cried several of the boys, rushing up to him in exaggerated panic. "The school needs you. Go! Go! Go!"

Lorne cackled and waved them away and told them they were a bunch of bastards. But as he was cackling and waving he was drifting towards a thin wooden ladder on the wall at half court that the pep staff climbed to hang banners. Soon other students were egging Lorne on, and he told them they were scrotum-sniffers and out of their minds as he whisked his way up the ladder, all three storeys, to a metal rafter that stretched across the ceiling.

"Go! Go! Go!"

"Shaddap—"

Hanging by his hands, he shimmied sideways along the rafter, kicking his legs as he went. From below he looked like a child. A gym teacher was present, but he did not care one way or another about the spectacle and pretended not to notice. Lorne avoided glancing down, even though doing so would have offered him a rare bird's-eye peek at the giant flaming bull logo painted on the court.

"Drop!" shouted someone.

Laughter.

"Your hands are slipping!"

"Jump, Lorny! I'll catch you!"

"You got a hole in your crotch, Lorne-o!"

It was the first time some of the younger students, the nines and tens, had ever noticed this dirty-looking boy with the torn pant hems who might, for all they knew, have been a janitor. He swung his body along the rafter so smoothly that some of them thought it was a performance, something the seniors had planned as a prank.

"Lorny, Lorny, your pants are falling off!"

"I can see your big cobra!"

"I can see your baby cobra!"

A roar went up when he grasped the cage. He reached between the wires but could not move the offending ball; he could only graze it with his fingers. The assembled chanted his name. More students, attracted by the din, poured into the gym through the north and south doors. Juniors were betting on whether Lorne would fall. Girls screamed as he dangled with one hand, pumping his other arm back and forth in the cage, labouring to free the ball. The spectators were beside themselves with excitement, thinking they were about to witness a student plunging to his death.

A new sound rippled through the crowd: the vice-principal had arrived and was pushing and slapping his way through the mass, knocking two or three students to the ground and bellowing up at Lorne—he did not know Lorne's name even though it was the boy's fourth year at the school—to *get down get down get DOWN.*

Lorne abandoned the mission and reversed course along the rafter. A mix of cheers and boos and laughter echoed unnaturally in every corner of the gym. Before he reached the wall he pricked his finger on the end of a screw and, instinctively, drew the finger into his mouth. A wild shriek went up as he swung back and forth on one hand while sucking the other. Had he fallen, the vice-principal later told Mr. and Mrs. Lorch, Lorne would have busted his head open on the hardwood like a watermelon, traumatizing everyone present and forcing the school to give passing grades to the entire student body.

Lorne was walking on air. He had descended safely and, while he failed in his quest, he was mobbed by the students before the vice-principal snatched him away. Everyone now knew he was a student, even if they quickly forgot about him. For a week he was the insane senior who had dangled from the gym ceiling. He was also suspended from school for a week, and narrowly avoided expulsion.

Two decades later, almost none of the pupils in the gym that day made the connection between the man who was suddenly famous for hunting ice in dark places and the boy who had swung himself across the rafters in a failed attempt to rescue a volleyball.

CHAPTER TWELVE

Cricket worked at a framing store south of downtown, along a trendy strip not far from the stadium. Lorne called the people who shopped in the area "stuck-ups." The only shopping Cricket did on the strip was for lunch on pay days, every second Friday. She would buy a leg of fried chicken and French fries and eat them on a bench in front of a small United church, regardless of rain or snow, to avoid stenching up her workplace.

A sister of Cricket's friend owned the store, and Cricket was its only employee. The business's motto was "If You Can Carry It, We Can Frame It!" Mostly the store framed photographs or paintings or awards, but also created displays for sports memorabilia, clothing, funeral urns, and taxidermy. Cricket only told Lorne about the strange jobs, which made him think her work was more interesting than it was.

One time a man brought a half-crumpled metal garbage can to the store.

"How much to frame this?"

Cricket peered inside the can.

"Are you serious?"

"Oh, I'm *damn* serious."

"Okee. And what sort of presentation were you thinking?"

"I want the can placed inside a frame so I can nail it up on a wall. Can you do that?"

"Yes, I think so. But the frame—so, we charge based on—"

"It'll be more than a regular frame. Got it. Can you do it today?"

"Um—probably, but—so, we also charge based on—"

"That'll cost extra too. Fine. I'll wait."

The customer, it turned out, had a teenage daughter who always forgot her one chore: bringing the garbage to the end of the driveway every Thursday for collection. He was going to hang the can up in a frame in the front hall with a plaque containing engraved instructions. It took Cricket an hour to frame the can. When the work was finished, the man pronounced it "adequate," and gave Cricket a ten-dollar tip.

"Sounds like an asshole," Lorne told Cricket, after she related the tale.

"He was actually kind of nice."

"I mean the daughter. Take the Christly garbage out!"

"Where'd he get frostbite?" said one of Lorne's sisters, across the dinner table.

Mrs. Lorch narrowed her eyes at her son.

"Were you sleeping in the freezer again?"

"No. I got it in the—the—"

"The *what*?"

Lorne could not look at his father.

"The—well, the *well*—"

From the end of the table Lorne's father shuffled in his chair, a sign of aggravation that Lorne would inherit.

"How'd he get frostbite in the *well*?" said Mrs. Lorch.

"I'll call somebody," said Mr. Lorch. "Tomorrow. Meantime—every one of you stay the hell away from that damn well."

The family ate in silence for a few minutes, even Lorne's mother, whom it seemed her husband had included in his injunction.

Lorne's sisters crooked their index and middle fingers as they ate, mocking their brother's injury. The tinkling of cutlery became oppressive. Finally:

"How'd you get frostbite, Lorny?" said his mother.

"I touched something."

"He touched something, Mom."

"What'd you touch?"

"I don't know. It was pink. Or red."

"It was pink, or maybe red, Dad."

His mother rolled a morsel of ham between her teeth.

"Did it hurt?"

"No."

"He said it didn't hurt, Mom and Dad."

"It didn't feel like anything," Lorne said.

Over his four years of high school, Lorne went on two dates. Neither ended the way he hoped. Both were with friends' younger sisters. He did not know it at the time, but each outing was a prank. In one case, the friend pranked him, as the younger sister was so introverted that she could hardly speak; in the other, a friend pranked his sister for borrowing his clothes without permission—setting her up with Lorne as a punishment.

Lorne and Cricket met at a church picnic when he was a few years out of school and flitting around as a menial worker, seeking a trade. Cricket was a junior in high school. Had they been contemporaries, Cricket would never have considered dating Lorne. By the time she entered grade nine at the same school, Lorne had graduated. The memory of his heroic climb across the gymnasium ceiling existed only in the minds of a few of the staff, and he had done nothing else to distinguish himself. No sign of his high school career—no trophy, no carved initials, no photos—remained.

Cricket had been something of an athlete, the sort who made several varsity teams but never as a starter, and so enjoyed the moderate amount of popularity that attends moderate success. Her grace never quite caught up to her height, but her bijoued eyes and quick shy smile attracted enough attention for her to forge a social life. In the trophy case across from the principal's office she grins out from a photograph of her junior soccer team, which won a bronze medal at the provincials. In the picture she is standing with a slight crouch because she did not want to look taller than a friend standing beside her.

When Cricket met Lorne, he was sporting the same moustache he had in his junior and senior years. The moustache never really thickened, and one of his high school teachers said it made him look like a villain in an old Hollywood movie. But Cricket was impressed by it, or, rather, she was impressed that an older man with a moustache showed interest in her. At the church picnic, Lorne asked whether she wanted lemonade, then sprang off to get some without waiting for her response; she noted how quickly he moved across the lawn, how he vaulted over a baby on a blanket and nearly stomped on a toddler's hand. He all but sprinted to the table with the pitchers and glasses. Later on he took second prize in the egg race, and he presented the egg to Cricket.

Lorne told Cricket all about the world, about the jobs he had been fired from, the best ways to get along in life. To her, Lorne was smarter than the prime minister. They drove around in the evenings in Cricket's parents' minivan, Cricket driving, Lorne hanging an arm or a leg out the passenger window and narrating the scenery. Her mother and father knew she was seeing a boy but died before they could discover it was the grubby journeyman who cut a scene at the church egg race. Cricket knew she was pregnant but had not worked up the courage to tell her mother before it was too late. She was nineteen and orphaned and expecting, and she was so scared that every night she thanked God for sending Lorne to her.

She never knew that all through high school Lorne's friends picked on him whenever the mood struck, or that he had been a D student, or that one time he tripped in the cafeteria and dropped his platter and food and a moan went around the tables but nobody even took the trouble to applaud, as they would have for anyone else. The fact that he was shorter than she was did not bother her at all; it became him much better than any showy display of height and muscles would have. To Cricket, a man who was secure enough to be short was worth having around.

Lorne was mediocre at sex, but Cricket had never slept with anyone else and considered him a genius at it. She believed he had far more experience than he actually did. On their first occasion, in the back of the van in a lane behind a shopping mall, she was so anxious at being found out a virgin that she burst into tears the minute she felt the cool night air on her thighs.

"No big deal," Lorne said, yanking at a sock that was snagged on his heel. "It's a piece of cake—"

"I'm gonna be really bad at this—"

The back seat smelled like turpentine.

"It's a piece of cake—"

They were quiet as she drove him back to his parents' house. She could not think of much to say and did not know whether it was proper to speak afterwards. As they slowed to a stop at a red light, she adjusted her baseball cap, which she had done at every light since losing her virginity ten minutes ago.

"Oh!" she said, fumbling for conversation. "By the way—what's an ice rat?"

"Eh?"

"Rats. You've told me about ice rats, but I never heard of them. What are they?"

CHAPTER THIRTEEN

A city worker came to inspect the well. The next day an official from the provincial health ministry arrived and took a sample.

"We just want to fill in the damn thing," Mr. Lorch told the health official.

"Got it," said the official, who wore thick rubber gloves and thick rubber pants. "First things first. How far down is it?"

He was looking at Lorne, so Lorne answered:

"Like—maybe seventeen feet? I think?"

The official frowned as if Lorne had placed *it* there himself.

"That's too deep and I don't have a harness," he said, peeling off a glove. "I'll come back tomorrow."

"Ah, Christ," said Mr. Lorch. "What's the holdup? What do you need?"

"I need to climb down into that hole and take a sample."

"How do you take a sample?"

When the official explained the operation and showed Mr. Lorch his scraping tool and jar, the latter set his hand on his son's head.

"Lorny can do that."

Lorne's neck buckled under the weight of his father's palm. He glanced up, scanning the old man's expression, searching for signs of a trap. But no—it was okay now. Lorne walked under the tangle of cedar branches and slipped into the mouth of the well while Mr. Lorch and the official posted themselves on either side. Lorne's pocket bulged with the jar and he carried the scraping tool in his teeth. The well's breath was marly and mildewy. As he descended with a smooth, light, spidery motion, the official glanced up at Mr. Lorch and raised his eyebrows.

The boy can move, the eyebrows said.

At one point Lorne had to negotiate a strip of ice just above the one he had encountered on an earlier descent. The walls were much thicker with it now. Stopping to think, and peering through the gloom that grew thicker with every foot he descended, Lorne sprang across the chasm and then sprang back—*bounce-bounce*—ending up five feet further down, to where a century's pressure had squeezed a couple of handholds out of the masonry.

"Stop showing off, Lorny," squawked Mr. Lorch.

The two men discussed the stonework; neither knew much about it, but each pretended he did. The official told Mr. Lorch there were a dozen other wells in the neighbourhood that he still had to inspect.

"How many wells?" cried Lorne, shrouded in darkness below.

"Keep your eyes on your work, Lorny."

Lorne did not expect to fall but wondered what the two men would do if he did. At almost the same moment, Mr. Lorch was thinking the same thing.

"Let us know if you need anything, Lorny."

"I will."

The boy's voice was far away now.

In the depths Lorne spotted a dull pink bloom on the stones by his waist and another, fainter one, opposite and lower down. A great crooked band of ice had formed around the walls and it was getting more and more difficult to keep his footing. He mashed the rubber tips of his shoes against every hold and used his elbows to brace himself. With another minute's shimmying he was face-to-face with one of those curious flat glowing bodies, perhaps the very one that had frozen his fingertips. It looked no more substantial, and was no thicker, than a dab of glowing paint.

"You almost done down there, boy?"

Scaffolding himself with his arms and toes and knees, Lorne worked the jar out of his pocket and slid the scraping tool from his teeth. The aftertaste made his skin crawl. He extended the tool towards the patch of pink-red as if he were about to thread a needle. It was very dark and he could just see the silhouette of the scraper hovering in front of the luminescent spot. Then it felt as if the tool had come alive and scampered over his palm, and he realized he had dropped it. He glanced down into the darkness, desperately trying to catch a gleam of its plummeting form. Five seconds, ten seconds; nothing. It was hopeless, and he knew he had to collect the sample with his fingers, because his father would never let him back into the well if he failed. From where he was perched, the voices of the men above him were tinny and garbled, as if sputtering from a dying radio.

Okay—okay—

Tongue in teeth, Lorne extended the fingers of his left hand—he felt he should protect the frostbitten ones of the right—and drew them towards the glow, closer, then closer still.

He stretched his arm until his mind started playing tricks on him, until he had thrust his hand so far that it was impossible that he had not touched the thing yet, as if the wall, even as his toes pressed into it, was receding into the far distance and the little glowing patch he reached for was as big as a star.

And even while he extended his arm, and wrestled with hallucination, his fingers began to grow numb. He was touching the little patch, over and over, squashing his fingertips against it.

Okayokayokay.

"Why do they call them 'rats'?" Mr. Lorch asked the official.

"Beats me. Why do they call rats 'rats'?"

"They should call them something else."

"I like 'rats.' Easy to remember."

Lorne scratched and rubbed and slashed at the gleam on the masonry until he nearly lost his footing and plunged into the void. He used all of his fingers. The thing did not move, and nothing of whatever it was composed of flaked off into his hand. Up above, in the tiny patch of sky, Mr. Lorch and the official were still nattering away. Once again Lorne began thinking dangerous thoughts about what lay below his exposed, tiny body. It occurred to him, as he scrabbled at the mocking glint in the stone, that he had not heard the scraping tool hit bottom. For all he knew, the tool was still falling.

"Godammit, Lorny, are you taking a sample of that thing or making love to it?"

It was the official who said this.

"Come up, Lorny," said the father. "It's okay."

Lorne was shivering with cold when he reached the top of the well and floated, courtesy of his father's huge hand gripping the back of his shirt, over the lip and onto the leaves. The official spied the empty jar.

"Where's the scalpel?" he said.

"I dropped it."

The official tucked the jar in his pocket and made a couple of notes in a book. He later had an administrative assistant write up a bill for the scalpel to send to the Lorches. But the assistant replaced the scalpel herself.

CHAPTER FOURTEEN

Within a few weeks biologists fanned across the Lorches' neighbourhood, creeping around homes and garages and sewer vents and drainage pipes and sheds and septic tanks and children's tree houses.

They were polite and full of apologies as they pushed their way past residents and told them not to worry but not to go into their backyard or run the water or turn out the lights. They would stick yellow cards on shed doors or well mouths, a signal that was alien to the protesting homeowners and never explained by the scientists. Over weeks and sometimes months more officials visited the spots and made hidden and arcane experiments. In two or three cases people were forced to move out, the city having condemned their properties.

What the scientists and health officials would discover over the next decade was that the new phenomenon was not new at all. It was very probably older than humankind.

We have one of those original scientists to thank for pulling much of the epidemiological research together. She was the one who made the final inspection of the well under the cedar canopy and signed the order to fill in the well with a special concrete-like goo developed by her lab.

The scientist also kept samples of dead ice rats, which were suspended in a transparent version of the same goo. All the specimens were round or slightly ovate, and ranged from pea-sized to one as large as a saucer. So far as the scientist knew, none of any other shape had ever been discovered. Many of her samples showed blushes where their pink-red bioluminescence had once glowed.

While the scientists did their work, Lorne followed along at a distance. Every time they attached one of the yellow cards to a pipe or well or drain, and then went away to gather reinforcements,

Lorne would squat motionless in a bush or up a tree, sometimes for hours, until the area was clear.

Then he would make his own inspection.

He had one chance at each site, because the biologists rarely left them untreated for more than a day. Several times he returned to a drain pipe, tagged only the night before, to find it sealed with hardened goo.

"Son of a bitch," he would say, the way his father did, snapping his hand up and down in a wild salute. "Son of a *bitch*—"

But he learned quickly and moved swiftly, and soon became an expert in reconnaissance and strategy. He could judge by the size of a site and the amount of tags in the area how long he had before the scientists came back to smother things out of existence. In four or five wells of the same vintage as his own, he found the little red-pink patches glowing at various depths. None was bigger than a quarter. Ice radiated out from each of them and dents and shavings on the masonry showed where the scientists had taken samples. In one of the wells he went down forty or fifty feet; whenever he reached what he thought must be the nethermost rat, he spotted another gleaming in the murk further below.

He wore gloves and tried to peel the things off the masonry. Once again it was like grabbing at a shaft of light. He approached the rats from every angle and with the most delicate dexterity. Before long he would grow frustrated, and the tips of his gloves would freeze. Out he went, heading for his next quarry—a shed somewhere, a pool house, the undergirders of a bridge a mile or two from home. Each time he met with the same intransigence, the things seeming to smirk at him in their unfluctuating radiance. Before long his glove would be as stiff as stone and he was forced to give up. Many evenings he bawled as he scrabbled up the cracked siding of his house and ducked back into his bedroom window. He slept in his clothes. His mother complained about his odour and demanded that he bathe more often, but he was already able to outrun her, especially in short bursts.

When the sociology student wrote her article about the cleaners, she called it "maybe the dirtiest job in the country." This was a bit of hyperbole, for which her professor scolded her. However, she was not far off. Lorne's occupation adopted some of the least palatable aspects of mining and janitoring and sewer scrubbing and was so obscure that no one had ever advertised for it and no one had sought it out. Lorne went from a custodian to a mole—a cleaner—by pure happenstance, because the Sprill Building's ducts needed a nightly sweep and he was willing to do it. During his first decade in the ducts, he was probably the only person in the world who considered himself lucky.

CHAPTER FIFTEEN

Lorne emerged from the back door of the Sprill, still fidgeting with his tie, into a bright, breezy morning. He was startled to see a large man in a windbreaker standing only a few feet away from him in the alley. The man stood with his hands in his pockets, as if he were in no great hurry.

Before Lorne could react, or even think of cocking a fist, the man made a show of stepping out of the way.

"Oh—excuse me," he said. "Pardon me—"

Lorne strolled past the man to the alley entrance. As he turned the corner, he glanced back and saw that the man was watching him.

The kooks are out early today.

Over the following weeks the man appeared now and again just as Lorne was finishing work. Sometimes he stood across the street from Lorne's bus stop for a few minutes before wandering off. Otherwise he posted himself near the mouth of the alley. After that first morning he was almost always reading a newspaper when Lorne came into sight. But one time Lorne caught him off guard, with the newspaper under his arm, and the man in the windbreaker made a fuss of rattling the paper open and pretending to read it. If Lorne had been looking, he might have noticed that it was the same newspaper every day.

This went on long enough that Lorne grew used to it. Whatever the man was, Lorne reckoned, he was not a threat. While tall and broad, he was too baby-faced for a thug. The man also wore a cap that was flattened at the top, and his hair spilled out the sides in a way that suggested it rarely met a comb. Before long, the man in the windbreaker began greeting Lorne with a nod, and Lorne started nodding back.

Around the neighbourhood, people sometimes called young Lorne "The Worm" or "Mole Boy".

"That kid," one neighbour, a church deacon, said, "looks like something the dog coughed up."

Lorne carried a haunted air about him, the hurry and impatience of a boy who could not find what he was looking for and who was driven to distraction by the search. At thirteen or fourteen years of age he sat at the dinner table across from his sisters in a state of stinky disarray, the scent of the low places where he spent his leisure hours hovering over the meal like a ghost whose presence the family could not drive off.

"Lorny," his mother said to him, "how many times do I have to tell you to wash before dinner?"

And the young adolescent, whose hair was striped with something green and whose shirt was stiff with liquid matter that had never before seen sunlight, let his cutlery clatter onto his plate. With an expression of mixed contempt and pain, he displayed his palms:

"I washed 'em! Both! With *soap*!"

The hands gleamed like beacons at the ends of his grimy arms.

"Lorny," his father said, scratching at his temple with the tines of his fork, "are we gonna have to put your food in a dog bowl? And you eat out in the yard like a mutt?"

"But I *did* wash! Both hands! Here, you just sniff 'em—"

Lorne's sisters, fed up with his foulness, slapped at his hands.

"This is why I can't have anybody over!" cried one.

"The whole house smells like *him* now," said the other.

Mr. Lorch still meted out punishment to Lorne for breaking the no-spelunking rule, making sure to do so at random intervals, hoping that would secure his son's attention. In the end he gave up. Lorne was getting too old to paddle anyway. During his last flogging, Lorne had chatted away to his father, asking him whether enough time had passed for the well in the backyard to be opened up again.

CHAPTER SIXTEEN

Lorne was a month into his new life in business-casual attire when his son forwarded him and his mother a link to the sociology student's article on cleaners:

Hey Moms and Pops HA! You seen this yet? It's pretty much about you, Pops. Did they talk to you about it? HA! They should of. I don't need any money right now. Work is busy but they dont always need me. Give you a call this week or the week after this week.

Cricket set aside a cross-stitch of a myna bird and within a minute had read the article twice through on her phone.

"Oh Lorny—"

It was the middle of the afternoon, and Lorne was slumped asleep against the back of the chesterfield in their tiny living room. The furniture in the parlour—the couch, two chairs, an end table, two lamps—was arranged in a semicircle, all of it touching except where a two-foot gap allowed for an exit to the kitchen. Lorne's mouth was open but he was not snoring.

"Hsst—Lorny—"

As usual, Lorne had missed his window to shower and go upstairs to bed, and had fallen asleep with his stockinged feet spraddled on either side of a crooked television tray. The tray, the only one remaining of a set of four, had belonged to Cricket's parents. Each tray bore a print of a star hockey player from the 1950s. The only one left was Gordie Howe, though neither

Lorne nor Cricket knew who that was. Years of use, years of spilled spaghetti and beer, had washed out much of Gordie below the neck. When Cricket set Lorne's plate on the tray, she always centred it on Gordie's smile, which was one of the only identifiable details remaining.

"*Lorny—*"

Out lashed the stockinged foot, glancing her knee.

"What? What?"

He always woke up as if he had been dropped into a cold bath.

"Lorny—"

"Eh? Eh? What you want?"

"You should read this. Leo sent it."

Lorne took the phone, scrolled through the story—he used his index finger rather than his thumb—and tossed the phone back, missing his wife's hand. He watched the phone bounce onto the carpet.

"Whoever wrote that's never been inside a duct, that's for damn sure."

"I think a girl wrote it," said Cricket.

"A *girl*? There you have it."

"Do you think this is why Orinn wants you to wear a tie?"

"Orinn doesn't want me to wear no tie. It's his boss told him that." The television tray jangled as Lorne folded it up; the legs no longer fit easily into the clips. "Though I don't know why Orinn shouldn't have to wear a tie if I have to."

Cricket scanned the article again, her mouth drifting into a smile.

"Did you read this part, Lorny? 'The men who ply this obscure trade are like characters that have stepped out of the pages of Dickens' London or Tolkien's Middle-earth to rescue us from a modern scourge.' How about *that*? That's you, Lorny—like a hero in a fairy tale!"

"What's the modern scourge?"

"Ice rats."

Lorne swished his palm through the air.

"Whoever wrote that knows squat about it."

"It's too bad nobody asked you about it."

Lorne shrugged.

"If they did," he said, fighting off a yawn, "I'd tell them to stick it up their arse."

CHAPTER SEVENTEEN

Lorne's building had a glass exterior that was a creamy azure on sunny days. It was completed in 1990, when Lorne was still in grade school.

Nothing was wrong with its predecessor, which had stood for sixty years, besides its brutalist appearance and a foreign owner who was constantly at odds with the city over his predilection for surprise rent spikes. The owner would telephone the mayor's office complaining of chest pains and paralysis in his arm and threatening to sue everyone on the municipal payroll. In 1987 the owner died—not of a heart attack, but in a bicycle crash that his family suspected was a suicide—and his daughter took up the quarrel with the city, including the chest pains and limp arm. When the building failed its next inspection, everyone's contingency was demolition. Yet a West German developer rushed in, and approval for a new office tower was passed by council in twenty minutes.

The ductwork in Lorne's building, if laid end to end, would stretch just over a mile. In some sections it was spacious, as much as two feet by two feet. At other junctures it was narrow enough that Lorne had to wriggle his way through in segments, like a worm: head, shoulders, abdomen, hips, legs.

Few of the thousand-plus workers who entered the building each day gave a thought to what was behind the walls. The mouths of the vents were singularities; what went on beyond them was none of the workers' concern. Had the interior walls been made of glass, like those of the exterior, these people might have gained an appreciation of Lorne's toils. They would have seen the burrow of ductwork running all around them like hamster tubes. Until Lorne became famous, many of the workers would have scoffed at the idea of anyone's passing into the vents at all, let alone squeezing through the entire mile in pitch darkness, six nights a week.

By the time Lorne left his mop behind and was entering the ducts of the Sprill at the beginning of every shift, scientists knew little yet about ice rats or why they materialized in warm places. They no longer seemed to be proliferating, as had first been believed when a series of discoveries—including the ones in Lorne's childhood neighbourhood—caught the media's attention years before.

People who did approach or touch the blooms ended up with frostbite, and occasionally a lost fingertip. On rare occasions a poor drunken soul was found frozen by a drainpipe on a mild fall morning, but such occurrences rarely made the news.

Inching through the shafts all night, cutting his callused hands on popped edges; that one time, five years back, that was a doozy—he was daydreaming, perhaps, not focused on the task—he missed a turn by a foot or two, and when he raised his head he sliced his crown on a screw. He had to drag himself halfway around the perimeter of the building with blood trickling into his mouth, snarling at two separate ice clusters as he shimmied past them, blooms that seemed to glow brighter than normal because, he was sure of it, they knew he needed a bandage and could not stop.

When he arrived home in the morning, the wound was still oozing blood and was covered with one of the tiniest bandages Cricket had ever seen.

"Well I didn't have time to do *brain surgery*," he told her as she fussed and tsk-tsked and dressed his cut. She'd had to clear away a layer of grease before reaching flesh. "There was rats in the tunnels, and I couldn't—"

"How many tonight?"

"Ah, not much. Eleven."

"*Eleven!*"

She gazed with wonder into her husband's eyes.

"Was it really *eleven*?"

"I already told you," said Lorne, fighting off a grin. "If you can't hear—"

"Wow. *Eleven.*"

Eleven was a lot, Cricket knew. Yet she knew enough to display astonishment no matter what the number. If it was eleven, it was something; if it was four, it was equally something; if it was one, well—it was amazing he was able to find it!

"Eleven. Unbelievable, Lo-lo. Eleven."

"*Eleven. Eleven.* What are you, a parrot?"

He could time his progress by the feel of familiar corners and conspicuous bolts. When he paused halfway up a six-storey shaft and removed the thick slice of bread and butter that Cricket had prepared for him, it was always between three and ten after three in the morning. He chewed with his mouth open and with his elbows close to his body. His feet pressed against the sides of the chute—as they had, years ago, in the well—and kept him from plummeting. The idea of taking his lunch elsewhere, in a less treacherous chute, never occurred to him. It was all about gravity. Who could eat lying flat on his stomach, or on his back, or curled up in a ball? To Lorne, balancing over an abyss while eating was the most natural thing on earth. He ate the bread slowly, and the noise of his smacking echoed up and down the shaft.

About once a week, while munching his lunch, he thought about the evening he lost his virginity to Cricket in the back of the van behind the mall. And just as often, as he ate, he recalled the day he lost his son's respect. His son had been only eight years old.

CHAPTER EIGHTEEN

Sheets of rain were falling. Lorne was hunkered under the lip of a wide eavestrough on the side of a row of townhomes.

His hair was dripping wet, and his banana-seated bicycle lay at his feet.

"Okay, I'm here. Show me."

A woman in a navy slicker stood beside him, holding a black umbrella high as if to shelter them both, though its canopy was positioned only over her own head.

"You want a ladder or anything?" Lorne said.

"I'm happy watching."

Lorne shrugged. In the next instant, he leaped five feet to grab the lower branches of an elm tree and scrambled up its trunk.

"Wait—"

Up the tree, sweeping towards the wall of orange brick and little arched windows, towards the Romanesque sweep of the eavestrough. He stood with his shoes on different branches that sank under his weight. The trough was several feet away and a full twenty feet above the rain-beaten grass.

"Hold on, now—"

She was out here as a favour to the boy's father, the man whose mouldering old well she had inspected a decade ago and from the shaft of which she had recovered her very first samples of *gelucelets*—ice rats. The fruits of those initial inspections had kept her busy and her laboratory funded ever since. During one of her visits to the well, shortly before ordering it filled in with the goo she and her colleagues were developing, she had made the boy's acquaintance.

"This here's Lorne," Mr. Lorch had said.

"Yeh," said Lorne.

Dirtiest child I've ever seen, she thought.

Hovering at the edge of the elm, on holds that his spectator below could not make out through the leaves, the dirtiest young man she had ever seen gazed up and down the eaves. It took him a moment. Rain thundered in the scientist's ears. At last—carefully—Lorne released one hand from its invisible grip on the tree and pointed at a spot just beyond his reach. The tree quivered.

"Oh, don't *do* that!"

"See it?" said Lorne, extending his hand, his tongue screwed into his cheek. "Can you see it?"

Drenched winds whipped their faces. She flinched; he did not. The earth where she stood was soft and growing softer.

"Can you *see* that," he went on.

"See *what*?"

Lorne, muttering curses, stretched a few inches further. Through bleary, blinking eyes, the scientist followed his arm, then his hand, then his index finger. Nothing. She rolled her gaze back along the eaves, passing the tip of Lorne's finger. And again. And a fourth time. Then—

"Oh!"

Her eyes locked; she felt them fix into place in their sockets.

"You see it?" bellowed Lorne, from above.

She knew from experience how easily one's eye overlooked them, how the luminescence and the colour, in tandem, were so brilliantly concealing, how they tricked even the keenest gaze if the gaze did not know exactly what it was searching for.

"I see it!" she said. "Where the brick meets the eaves—"

"Bingo bango!" cried Lorne.

She ran off in search of a ladder. All she found was a milk crate sitting at the end of a driveway. When she returned with the crate, she found Lorne's body lying twisted on the sodden lawn.

"Lost my grip," he said, chuckling through his teeth.

The scientist wanted to take Lorne to the hospital.

"None of that horseshit," he said. "Home."

"What if you broke something?"

"I didn't," Lorne said, in a voice bent with agony, though he was forcing himself to smile. "Just take me home. Dad said I'll *know* when I break something."

"I'll take an X-ray's word over Dad's."

"Dad's broken like *thirteen different* bones."

Mr. Lorch had a broken-bone story for any given activity, from mowing the lawn to screwing in a light bulb to folding up a lawn chair.

"I'm in deep shit if you take me to the hospital—"

"*I'm* in deep shit if you need a doctor and I—"

"Home, take me home, take me *home*—"

"ALL RIGHT, CHRIST, I'll take you home."

They drove in silence. The scientist stole glances at Lorne—not at his clothes, damp and muddy from his two-storey plunge onto the lawn, but at his hands: eighteen-year-old hands that looked as if they had been through a war, and not a recent war. It was as if he were wearing those of an uncle or a grandfather.

"How did you do that?" she said.

Lorne twisted against the seatbelt, searching for a position that his bruised spine would tolerate.

"Do what?"

"With the gelly, there."

"The—what?"

"The gelucelet."

Lorne's face was as blank as the sky.

"Oh," she said, "I guess you probably know them as *rats*—"

"Hey! Yah! Rats. Yah, that's what they're called."

"They're actually called *gelucelets*—"

Lorne looked at the scientist.

"Nah," he said, "they're called rats. Ice rats."

"Why do people call them ice rats? They don't look like rodents. They don't have whiskers, they don't move around—"

"I dunno. What should we call them—ice elves?"

"No, that's not—I think you're missing the—"

"Ice rabbits?"

"Never mind—"

"Ice rabbits is nuts! You want to call them ice rabbits—"

"Listen—what I want to know is how you peeled that gel—that *rat*—"

"Oh. It's easy—"

"—with your *bare hands*—"

"It ain't hard. I could've shown you."

"If you hadn't fallen out of a tree—"

"If I hadn't fallen out of the tree."

"I've tried before." The scientist made a scratching motion with her hand. "Almost lost a fingertip."

"It doesn't hurt if you know *how* to do it."

The scientist pulled onto Lorne's street. He had not directed her. She remembered where he lived from her visits to the well eleven years before.

"It's not hard," Lorne said. "It just takes a bit to learn. But when you do"—they had reached Lorne's driveway—"when you do, it's like... oh boy, it's like... it's like—"

His eyes were afire, almost ecstatic. It was the aspect of a young man who had never touched a woman but had discovered how to start a fire.

CHAPTER NINETEEN

Lorne approached the back alley of the Sprill on a crystal summer night. A light above the back door had gone out ages ago and never been fixed.

"Hi."

"CHRIST—"

"Oh sorry—did I scare you?"

A large figure loomed ten feet away, under a fire escape.

"Piss off," said Lorne.

"I'm sorry..."

A face flashed before Lorne like a struck match—or a glowing smartphone. The man, the one in the windbreaker Lorne had noticed hanging around the alley, held a phone just under his chin, as if he were about to tell a ghost tale. He was smiling a crumbly smile.

"Oh," said Lorne.

The man's face wavered in the grey light of the phone.

"How—how many do you think you'll get?"

"Eh?"

The man swallowed. "How many of the—the—"

"The—eh?"

"—the—*rats*. How many rats?"

Lorne gaped at the man's grey face.

"How do you know about that?"

"Oh," said the man, "oh *you* know, I've heard of it—"

"Heard of *what*?"

"Oh, you—you guys, the guys who... who..."

Lorne waited.

"Well—aren't you a—a *cleaner?*"

"Yah. That any of your business?"

"Well—no."

Lorne gave the man a glower and advanced towards the door.

"Give 'em hell tonight!" the man said.

Lorne rapped his code on the door and entered the building, the door clanging shut behind him.

A bet between online friends: two men, one in his thirties and one in his sixties, the younger with a few hundred followers, the elder with a few thousand. They communicated every day but had never met in person. A Sunday night of a slow news week, ten o'clock, a chat about horror movies. *The Thing* had scarred the thirtysomething as a child. His companion ranked *The Shining* above every other movie, horror or no, from the 1980s.

Greatest of all time, he wrote.

If The Shining *is better than any other 80s movie then it's 2nd overall to* The Thing

What's so scary about The Thing

The scene with the dogs in the barn when the dogs realize one of the other dogs is The Thing

Can't hold a candle to evil girl twins in Le Shining

More and more people, and a number of bots, chimed in. One commenter, considered a nuisance by everyone on the board, nearly sank the thread by posting a ten-part screed about *The Thing* and *The Shining* and all 1980s horror movies serving as metaphors for the *creeping crypto-fascism* that (per the individual) had *eaten away the genitals* of Western culture and that had placed every last person on the planet *in invisible bonds woven of strips of the skin of your wives and babies.*

The thirtysomething said, *Anyone else hungry for genitals?*

Oh me I am

Can I have some genitals with a side of genitals?

I grew up on the Prairies and my grandma cooked genitals over an open fire they popped in your mouth just like Pop Rocks candy

Has anyone ever frozen their genitals? Now THATS a horror movie

And the sixtysomething said, *Eskimos probably. It probably hurts them more when they thaw*

Yeah they have frozen balls those guys. Guys and dolls I mean

You said it not me

Eskimos and meat packers

And hockey players

Don't forget the guys who break ice on those ice breaking ships I can never remember what there called

Someone wrote, *What about those guys clean ice rats in the buildings downtown*

And the thirtysomething said, *??*

The sixtysomething said, *Holy shit forgot about those cats*

What ice rats

Whatta talking about

My uncle knows one of those guys the job is brutal

Not for the faint of heart or the highly educated

The best of the best

Who says the best and the brightest perished at Waterloo

Please can somebody tell me what ice rats are

Followed by: *If you want to discover where this new plague comes from you just walk into any government office in the West and ask to see where they keep them. They'll play dumb like all crypto-fascist police states and act like your best friend until they escort you out with one hand around your shoulder and one on a billy club and the last thing you'll see before you wake up at the bottom of the St. Lawrence is a big smile and stars and the raw eaten eyeless flesh of other victims of the police crypto-fascist state*

Followed by: *Piss off Ted*

At two in the morning someone provided a link to the sociology student's article on the Cancer Building and the cleaners. The story produced a sensation among the hundreds of people, both sober and drunk, who were now involved in the conversation. By three o'clock an enterprising soul had cobbled together a list of towers around the city that were rumoured to be rat-ridden.

How many rats do they catch a day

They work at night

How many at night

Something like 15 to 20

Holy shit for reals

Thats what the paper said

The thirtysomething man, who desperately wanted to go to bed, made an announcement: *Five bucks the Macdonald Tower gets sixteen rats tomorrow night*

I'm in

Me too

Ten bucks

Ten here

Five bucks they get only six

Twelve bucks for twenty boyo

The neoliberal crypto-fascist military complex has every last one of you in a snake pit of a demon sphincter

CHAPTER TWENTY

Sitting in the scientist's car in his driveway, writhing in pain from his fall, Lorne explained that a few months earlier he had been out "hunting"—searching for rats—on a dull, heavy spring morning. An acquaintance from school had been tooling around the neighbourhood on a bicycle and tagged along for a while, much to Lorne's annoyance. At last Lorne lied and said he had to go home for lunch.

"It's only nine-thirty," said the acquaintance.

"No it's not," Lorne said.

The other boy shrugged and pedalled off.

Lorne ducked through a lane between houses and huddled by a fence, watching the boy on the bike vanishing up the street. He rested his back against the crooked boards of the fence. The air was clammy and he could feel sweat under his arms. As he sat leaning against the fenceboards, he felt something cold on his back. It was as if, he later told the scientist, he were sitting in front of an open refrigerator in his underwear; the scientist told him the underwear part of the analogy was unnecessary. He found that parts of his jacket had stuck to the wood, and popped away in stages as he rocked forward. Turning, he discovered two thick blooms, one on top of the other, just above his head; ice was radiating from them in all directions. At once he was transported back to an earlier moment in his life, twenty feet deep in a bottomless well and face to face with a pink-red eye that was both alive and dead. The fear he had felt then, teetering over the chasm, came rushing back like a blast of air. He sprang to his feet as if leaping out of a nightmare. The neighbourhood was quiet. The things did not flare or stretch or move.

Two eyes, one on top of the other. Thick, plump, much *fuller* than he had ever seen before. *Newborns, maybe*, he thought, although he did not know how the things came into being, or whether they aged. All he knew was that these two specimens were large and evil-looking and—for all he knew—had very probably escaped from the hardened goo in the old well somehow and spent years hunting for him. In the immense quiet he thought he heard a faint crackling sound, as if the creatures were spreading their tendrils of ice, millimetre by millimetre, through the wood right in front of his eyes.

He felt the sound as a spoon scraping up and down his spine.

"You never forget that," he told the scientist. "Never."

"How big?"

"What?"

It was no longer raining. The wipers squealed over the windshield, and she flicked them off.

"How big were the gels?"

"Gels?"

The scientist thrust her tongue against her gums.

"The *rats*—"

"Oh—about this big."

Lorne held up his fist.

"Together?"

"No. Each."

The scientist pondered the steering wheel.

"Why didn't you report them?" she said. "Are they still there?"

"Hell, no."

He heard, he said, the ice boring into the fence. Until that moment the blooms, the rats, had been odd little wonders to him, like belly buttons or cuticles or armpit hair; since childhood, searching them out had proven a wonderful time-passer. Hunting rats had been as innocuous as fishing. Now, for the first time, the things seemed different, ominous—"bastardy," as Lorne put it.

He moved a step closer and felt, or thought he felt, a chill breath on his cheeks. It was clean and fragrant like mountain air. The little blots in the middle of the ice glowed with a strange dull light. He crouched, eye to eye with the upper bloom—

"Hey—"

The world seemed suspended; nothing moved. His fear left him as he bent forward until his nose nearly touched the larger rat.

"Huh!"

He had never noticed *that* before: it was hardly visible, hardly conspicuous, a flat tab, a sliver, like a pencil shaving that had been tucked in behind what in another creature would have been the shoulder.

"Hello," said Lorne. "Hello—"

And as he locked his eyes on the bloom, his fingers found the edge of the tab. The fingers tugged on the tab. The fingers did not freeze.

He gave the tab a quick tug.

"And two or three other tabs came out," he told the scientist. "In the corners."

"There aren't corners in a circle."

"They came out from the four corners like that first one, and then im*medi*ately they—so they went *back in*, and I had one and I grabbed the other—"

"*Which* other?"

"—and I got *just the edge* of a grip and I yanked that bastard *right off the goddamned fence.*"

The scientist stared at Lorne.

"And—and—*what?*" she said.

"And—the tabs folded up in my hand—like that."

Lorne curled the fingers of one hand, as if about to claw something.

The scientist and two research assistants would spend the next year attempting to use Lorne's technique to peel gelucelets all across southern Ontario. They made twenty-seven tries and failed every time. In the same period Lorne killed over one hundred rats. He injured his fingertips a dozen times and in a handful of others was nearly stumped by creatures that did not seem to have any exposed tabs. But if he waited, if he searched the blooms long enough, he ended up finding what he was looking for. He dug little holes in the earth with his heel and dropped in the dead rats—they lost their light and hardened almost immediately after being plucked—and buried them. And he kept a carved tally of his catches on the underside of the desk in his bedroom.

The patience and persistence he developed during that year would, later on, buttress him in his repeated bids to unhook Cricket's bra. Still, he wounded his hands on the hooks more often than on the ice rats.

CHAPTER TWENTY-ONE

When Lorne collected the rats from the walls of the ducts, he stuffed them into the zippered hip pockets of his coveralls. At the end of his shift he emptied the hard, disc-like corpses into a pail. Twice a week, depending on volumes, the rats were burned in a furnace.

One morning Lorne unzipped his coveralls and sat on a stool with his legs straddling the pail. His haul from yesterday and the day before still sat in a little pile at the bottom of the bucket. As he dug in his pocket for the five rats he had caught that night, a hand, purple in the basement light, darted across the pail.

"Did you count them?"

Lorne looked up and saw a rictus smile.

"Eh?"

"Did you *count* them?" said Orinn.

"There's five."

"How many?"

Lorne held the rats up like a hand of playing cards.

"One-two-three-four-*five*."

Orinn withdrew his hand and slipped a notebook out of his pocket. Lorne had never seen the book before; it had a ribbon bookmark dangling from its spine.

"What's that?"

Orinn snapped open a pen and made a note at the bottom of a page that was already covered in scrawlings.

"We need to keep track," Orinn said, folding the notebook up and dropping it back into his pocket.

"Keep track of what?"

"How many you catch."

Lorne puffed out his chest.

"Says *who*?"

"Says the super."

"And why's it any business of the super's?"

Orinn reached across the musty purple air and snagged Lorne's sleeve between his thumb and forefinger.

"He says we gotta do it and I need you to do it. Okay?"

Orinn left the room and his footfalls echoed in the corridor. Lorne sat on the stool with his legs splayed and he stared hard into the pail of dead ice rats, as if this was all somehow their fault.

He had an urge to kick the pail over, but he would have had to clean the mess up.

After the Lorches' son, Leonidas, was born, Cricket was unable to let him out of her sight. If Lorne held the baby even for a few minutes, Cricket was anxious, pacing around and nibbling her fingernails. Or she made a show of nibbling her nails; it seemed a natural accompaniment to the pacing, so she tugged on each nail with her teeth without actually puncturing the keratin.

"Just be careful," she would say, to no one in particular. "Be careful—"

"Dammit—you think I'm going to throw him around? Like a beanbag or—"

"You need to *really* support his head."

"I'm already supporting it with everything I got."

Lorne patted the baby on the crown with a knurled palm.

"Not so *hard*," said Cricket.

"Oh, come on! These things got skulls like cinderblocks—"

Yet Lorne would pat the little ball of cement more gently, and Cricket would return to pacing around the room and gumming her fingernails and changing the channel on the television without looking at it. After a few months, Lorne hardly touched the child except when it was in Cricket's arms, and even then he did little more than shake hands with it. On the rare occasions when the boy's crying woke Lorne in the night, Cricket was already whisking out of bed.

So for some Sundays, when Leonidas was several months old, Lorne took to sneaking out of bed before daybreak, stealing the baby from its crib, and spending fifteen minutes in the kitchen making what he believed to be giraffe noises to Leo, in the dark. The sound he uttered was nothing like that of a giraffe; he was confusing its call for that of a gazelle. He had discovered, by accident, that Leonidas was wonderfully serene at this hour of the day, and seemed delighted by these predawn excursions to the chair beside the old refrigerator, whose cool mint exterior and soothing buzz added to the effect. Lorne cooed and honked under his breath and the baby's eyes went rolling this way and that over his father's shadowy face. When Lorne spotted the first pale hues of dawn at the window, he returned his plunder to its crib and slipped like a serpent back into his own bed. Cricket would waken a half hour later to an alert and bubbly infant who tried its best to chirp an account of the strange creature he had visited with in the kitchen.

Lorne's aim was to create a secret language, a secret friendship, between himself and his son. During daylight hours he did not have a chance. Cricket kept the lad to herself, and the lad kept Cricket to himself, and Lorne just happened to flit around like a fly that was trying to find its way out of the house. Every so often, when he did not think Cricket was listening, he would mutter the jungle cries into his son's ear and monitor the little round face for signs of pleasure.

The last time he tried the language was on Leonidas's thirteenth birthday. The boy invited four friends over for gifts and cake, and during a round of horseplay one of the other boys' conical birthday hats stabbed Leonidas in the eye. The one whose hat had done the dirty work blubbered even louder than Leonidas, and Lorne kicked him straight out of the house, along with the other three boys, who were leaping around and screaming like they had just won the World Series. Nothing Cricket did could settle Leonidas, who was rolling around on the floor with both palms pressed into his eye, his party hat shooting off the back of his head.

Lorne pushed his wife aside, leaned over the boy, and made the gazelle sounds into his ear. He had to do it loudly, since Leonidas was wailing. Cricket stood by, astonished. Lorne wrestled with his son, who at thirteen was already taller than his father, and kept up the jungle sounds until Leonidas bawled so loudly and writhed so violently that there was no point in carrying on any further.

"What're you doing?" Cricket asked Lorne.

"Christ, I'm *trying* to help."

He was confident the trick would have worked if Cricket had not been staring at him and if the boy had not made such a scene out of a little piece of cardboard gouging his eyeball. The accident mildly, but permanently, damaged Leo's peripheral vision.

CHAPTER TWENTY-TWO

An aspiring artist, who had followed the online bets about the cleaners' takes, spent a week creating a graphic novel about the phenomenon. He copied the visual style, colouring, and dialogue of his favourite manga comics. The cleaners were made to look like brooding, muscular heroes, dressed in coveralls and masks and capes. By a fluke, one of the characters resembled Lorne, though with more meat and more chin. The characters lived in the ducts, swapped morbid tales, and spoke in a sort of duct poetry. Ice rats were red-eyed, prehistoric beasts that attacked the cleaners by pouncing from above and below and behind. In the novel, the cleaners kill the rats with shivs resembling small katanas. Everything, the entire cleaning universe, was skewed and blue-grey and ominous. The artist posted a link to the work on the same forum that had hosted the initial betting on the cleaners—

I cooked this up for fun check it out lol

Over the next forty-eight hours, more than sixteen thousand readers downloaded the book. People from as far away as Russia and Mongolia praised it, with one Kazakh writing, *I lauft my ass off. Is this a real thing? Or?*

Over the next week three separate media outlets contacted the artist for interviews. He agreed to each, thinking that the exposure would lead to steadier work. Yet the interviews went abysmally. The artist knew nothing about the cleaners and what they did or how the work was done, and could not bring himself to admit it. The final interviewer, from a city culture magazine, cornered him and asked, *Who were your research sources?*

I don't reveal the names of my sources.

The novel became an underground sensation, with images and snippets of dialogue making their way into memes in unexpected branches of social media. It even invaded city hall. During a debate about a proposed raise in transit fares, a councillor from a northwestern ward argued that any hike would *Scribble Arctic.* "Scribble Arctic" was a bit of nonsense one of the characters in the novel had used to describe an invasion of ice rats. In certain recesses of the Internet, "Scribble Arctic" had become everything from a political slogan to a cry gamers uttered when their avatars faced dismemberment. When the councillor finished his remarks, the mayor formally censured him: she had heard her teenaged son deploy the phrase as an ill-defined sexual innuendo.

Fans circulated hard copies of the novel, often crudely rendered by home printers. For a while, young boys read and reread the novel, and wrote their own fan versions. Cleaning ice rats supplanted all ambitions. One teacher reported that of eighteen boys in her fifth-grade class, fifteen now wanted to be cleaners when they grew up.

"I'm getting texts from parents—'My son wanted to be a doctor and now he and all his friends want to be janitors or whatever. What sort of curriculum are you teaching?' "

Two other boys wanted to become professional hockey players, and a third, who watched CPAC, wanted to be prime minister.

One boy who read the graphic novel was a star athlete at a middle school in the suburbs. Tall and limber, he excelled at every sport, and was a solid B student. His principal had already provided him with literature on athletic scholarship programs offered by two Ivy League colleges in the United States.

Some light reading material for you, the principal told him. *Have you ever been to Cambridge?*

My uncle played hockey for the Winter Hawks

I mean the one in Massachusetts, son
I don't have an uncle in Massachusetts
The Cambridge in Massachusetts
It's in Ontario
Harvard's not in Ontario
No Cambridge is

The boy was playing hockey against others two years older and baseball against others four years older. When he read the graphic novel—and he read it only once—he asked his father what an ice rat was.

Freaks. Nuisances, the father said.

Can I see one

So the father made a few calls and arranged for his son to meet a cleaner and put on gloves and hold some dead rats in his hands. A decade later, in the space of a single August night, Lorne would destroy both his and the boy's livelihoods.

CHAPTER TWENTY-THREE

After the Regatta that ended Lorne's career, someone etched *REMEMBER LORNE LORCH* into the parging of a strip-mall pizzeria in the city's south end. Someone—maybe the same person—tried to scratch the slogan into a cemetery wall in the same neighbourhood, but was chased away mid-scrawl, leaving only *REMEMBER LOR*.

Leonidas telephoned on Sunday afternoon, while Cricket was bringing a cross-stitch of a watermelon, along with two cups of tea, into the living room. She dropped the load and raised her phone to her ear.

"Hello, you—"

"Y'a Mom hi Mom!"

Lorne listened with increasing impatience as his wife answered a rapid series of questions: "Yes, yes—no! Well, yes, maybe; no—I think so? Yes. *Yes.* No. No, not at all. I don't think so, that's not a good idea... but maybe. Yes?"

Lorne's finger pecked at the remote, sneaking the volume up by degrees, until Cricket glared at him. He was planning his next strike when Cricket leaned towards him.

"He wants to talk to you."

Why the hell, Lorne mouthed.

Cricket shrugged and returned to her watermelon stitching.

"Ya," said Lorne, into the phone.

"Ya Dad hi Dad, ha ha!" said Leonidas. "Did you know you're famous? Ha, ha!"

Texts came in, from Lorne's sisters, from Cricket's boss at the framing store, from a cousin; a call from the neighbour who supplied Cricket with tabloid magazines, another from a young woman Cricket had babysat years before. Cricket had to switch her phone off. Lorne was sure it was a gag, but Cricket verified it online.

"It's right there," she said, pushing her phone in Lorne's face.

"That don't mean anything. Anyone can do that."

"This is the newspaper website."

"That doesn't mean nothing."

"It means *something*."

"It means nothing and it don't mean anything. Anybody with a computer can make something up like that."

Cricket read Lorne the page's mile-long URL, including indicating which letters were in upper case and which in lower case. Halfway through she got mixed up by the small typeface and started again.

"Dammit, I heard you the first time," said Lorne.

He snatched the phone from Cricket and stared at the screen. He scrolled up with an index finger, then down.

"Can you make it bigger," he said.

Cricket placed her thumb and forefinger on the screen and drew them slowly apart, expanding the size of the text.

"Not *that* much. I'm not *blind*."

It was in the Lifestyle section, of all places. Lorne could not understand that. It would be moved in the coming weeks; it would bounce around different desks before landing, to some pushback within the newsroom, in the Sports section. But that first evening, in the Lifestyle section of the city's major daily—a paper with a combined print and digital circulation of over two hundred thousand—the following appeared on the website at 4:51 PM local time:

Gelucelets Collection* – leaders, May 17–23

Lorch, Sprill Tower	17
Morena, Jumbo Data Building	14
Kravchenko, Macdonald, Tower 2	12
Dulka, Westerfeldt Insurance Building	8
Aquino, Front Street Blocks	7

*unofficial totals

Lorne said it was a great big bastard of a prank.

As he stepped off the bus downtown, underneath the cold empty lights of the office towers, he knew it was going to a bad night. The usual pre-shift serenity he felt on arrival had been replaced by a restlessness in all of his limbs. No doubt he would be hungry by ten o'clock; he would have to eat his wad of bread and butter early, leaving him famished in the last hours of his shift. It had hardly begun, yet already the night was a washout.

Entering the dim mouth of the alley he stopped short. The darkness had shifted, and the shadows were not where they were supposed to be.

"Eh—"

A flash from the black. Then another—and another, in front, behind, in the dusky margins—

"Congratulations, *Mr. Lorch.*"

Four figures, five figures, maybe more. He retreated a step. From the back of the alley came a popping sound. The sound repeated itself and got closer. He could not discern the noise or what it signalled, and he was terrified. But his night-notched vision distinguished no hostility in the faces before him. The popping sounds fell into a rhythm.

The figures were applauding.

In the vanguard were the larger man with the windbreaker and a little lollipop of a female friend, both holding illuminated mobile phones that swished about as they clapped. One or two others took photos one-handed, their flashes smearing Lorne's eyes.

"Great work, Mr. Lorch!" said the large man, giving Lorne a pat on the shoulder as he passed by.

"Seventeen of those things," said the woman, flicking a waist-length coil of hair from one shoulder to the other. "*Seventeen*. That's *amazing*—"

"Jesus *Christ* don't scare me like that again," said Lorne, scurrying through the cluster for the door. He banged on the sill, forgoing the coded knock.

"Give 'em hell tonight, Lorny!"

"Go, Lorch boy, Lorch, my man!"

"Thanks for what you do."

"Thanks for your service, sir!"

"Kick some icy ass!"

Lorne kept pounding on the sill until a custodian let him in. He made for the basement as if he were running for his life.

The custodian told Lorne that there were ice rats in St. Lucia, where he had grown up. But those rats, he said, were shaped like diamonds.

"That's the dumbest thing I ever heard. Rats are round."

"Not *these* rats, Lorny. Diamonds." The custodian used his index fingers to trace the shape in the air. "Diamond rats."

"Round," said Lorne.

The custodian drew a diamond shape again. Lorne countered with a circle.

PART 2

CHAPTER TWENTY-FOUR

Most of the correspondence arrived by post, since Lorne did not have an email address or a mobile phone. At first, Cricket read the messages to him in the morning, when he arrived home from work. After a few weeks, she suggested doing it in the evening instead, before he left for his shift.

"What the hell difference does it make?" Lorne said.

"It'll get you in the mood," said Cricket. She sat at the kitchen table wearing a baseball cap pulled low over her eyebrows.

"For what?"

Cricket winked. "To really give 'er."

"You don't think I give 'er?"

"Of *course* you give 'er."

"I don't need someone reading me no letter to make me give 'er."

"I'm going to read it anyway."

"I don't want to hear it."

"You don't have to listen."

Dear Mr. L. Lorch,

Ive never written a letter like this before but I have to say I read about you in the news a lot and of all the cleaners in the city youre by far my favourit. Do you know Aquino? You probably do. You're probably great freinds with him but I think hes shit and I think he cheats because theres no way he catches that many. Plus his building is way smaller and I know his wifes family and their a bunch of crooked crooks if I ever saw a crook. Anyway I was going ask for your autograph but I wont because youre probably too busy for it but if I ever see you in person I

hope youll give me an autograph and Id love to shake your hand. Thanks for keeping our buildings safe. Your all very brave and I think your all heros, even Aquino a little even if he cheats.
Yours truly
G. McCruddle

"Do you think Aquino cheats?" Cricket said.

Lorne was placing his wrapped lump of bread and butter in his coat pocket.

"Probably. But not the worst. Kravchenko—*he's* the worst."

"Oh really? Who says?"

"Orinn says."

"Who told Orinn?"

"I don't know. The super."

As Lorne moved around the kitchen, the floorboards blatted here and there under his feet. It was a Tuesday and he had donned his Tuesday shirt and tie and combed his thinning hair straight back from his brow. He scraped his fingers through one jacket pocket, then the other.

"Where's my tags?"

"On the fridge, where they always are."

The *tags* were taxi chits. Lorne no longer took the bus to work. Rising on tiptoe, he swiped a chit off the refrigerator and snorted his way out the back door.

Lou, Cricket's blue-haired boss at the framing store, would forward Cricket links to negative social media posts or insulting memes about Lorne, no matter how ridiculous or irrelevant they were.

Look at this one—what kind of yokel says this, she would write. And the post below Lou's text would read something like: *I'd be good at catching rats too if I looked like one*

Or: *"Lorch" is the sound my stomach makes after I eat spoiled clams*

Or: *The guy's a janitor and there's no such thing as ice rats you people need to do some research and critical thinking*

Lou condemned the postings but continued sending them. She told Cricket that people who said such offensive things should be *dragged into the street, shot, and pissed on.* Most of the posters, she added, were undiagnosed paranoid schizophrenics.

"How do you know that?" Cricket said.

"I can tell everything about a person by the way they write."

"Even in a meme?"

"*Especially* in a meme. You read enough of these things, you pick up on the nuances."

Lorne grumbled when Cricket read out his fan mail before he left for work, and told her she could stick it up her arse. Hours later, when he arrived home in one of his new shirts and ties, his face and neck sparkling with dust, he would repeat certain lines—

"What did that crazy lady say again—*You're by far my favourite*—did she really write that?"

"That's what she wrote, Lorny."

"You ever heard anything more ridiculous in your life?"

"I've heard *way* more ridiculous things."

Lorne lumbered around the kitchen, wondering aloud over and over what kind of lunatic would write such a pile of garbage. People had lost their minds, he said. They had too much free time. If they had *his* job, if they spent all night crawling around in the ducts of an office tower, they would not have the strength to lift a *finger* at the end of the day, let alone a *pen*—

"People appreciate what you do," said Cricket, keeping an eye on the bacon hissing in the plug-in skillet Lorne's parents had given them as a wedding present. "You never wrote a letter to anyone just to say—I don't know—'Good job, keep it up?'"

"Never had the time."

"Never had the time! You could do it right now."

"I could go sing to orphans now, too."

Minutes later, slumping his greasy back against the chesterfield, pulling his TV tray and breakfast closer, he turned to Cricket and sniggered.

"'Thank you for your service.' Where do you find these kooks?"

For Cricket, the compliment was less in the adulatory language of the letters than in the work involved in getting them to her and Lorne's mailbox. Composing, addressing, stamping, and posting letters involved an expense of energy and time that she was just beginning to appreciate. She had written dozens of letters in her life that never made it off her kitchen table. Any dimwit can write a letter, she thought, but it took a certain industry to actually mail it. How many more folks, she wondered, had penned fan mail to her husband and ended up being too lazy to walk it to the nearest post box?

One of the early letters was addressed to *Lorne Lorch—Cleaner.* The handwriting was large and balloon-like:

Mr. Lorch
I'm afraid I have no idea why people are making a fuss over you and your counterparts in your "field" as it were. We have firefighters and soldiers and police officers putting their lives on the line every day and yet you and your cohort of night crawlers are now being treated like the only thing keeping the barbarians from breaching the city gates. You owe it to the public to make a statement disavowing the attention you're receiving and urging citizens to channel their admiration towards those who actually merit it.

I am a retired bus driver and can think of no more ludicrous notion than that my fellow drivers and I should have had statistics printed in the newspaper on how many passengers we picked up and how closely we adhered to posted schedules.

Awaiting your prompt denunciation of this hysteria,
Barbet Fillonian

Cricket kept the letter from Lorne. At lunch that day, after framing a set of ribbons for a woman whose eighth-grade son had cleaned up at his school's track meet, Cricket sat at Lou's desk in the stockroom and composed a reply:

Dear Mr. Fillonian,
I'm disappointed by your letter because it doesn't sound like you have a good appreciation of what ~~Lorne~~ I do and how hard it is and how dangerous it is to put ~~Lorne's~~ my life on the line every night to keep hundreds of people in the building safe. I work really hard and I don't go boo about it and it's not my fault the newspaper writes about it.

You might want to walk a mile in ~~Lorne's~~ my shoes because ~~he's a~~ I'm a good man and I wouldn't ever write a nasty note like you did to a bus driver whose stats etc. suddenly appeared in the newspaper. And for that matter I think it's pretty silly to compare taking care of the menace that is ice rats to driving a bus for three or four hours. Have you ever got frostbite from your steering wheel? Ever had to crawl three storeys straight up in the pitch black dark without a safety net? Or do you sit on your fat ass and drive ten feet and stop and open the door and make sure everybody paid his fare and somehow you think that makes you a swashbuckler. I mean how much do you get paid for sitting on your ass all day and opening a door and saying Hi welcome to the bus do you have the right change? It sounds from your letter like you should of been an English teacher or something like that and it's not my ~~husband's~~ fault you're still bitter over your life choices. Why don't you go into the ducts one night with ~~Lorne~~ me and ~~he'll~~ HE'LL SHOW YOU just how easy his job is—then maybe you and him can go ride a bus together and if at the end of the night you think your job is harder than Lorne's well then I'll just eat every hat in my closet.
You, sir, are a skidmark.
(Sincerely)
Lorne Lorch

Cricket stopped changing the third-person narration to first-person when she realized she was never going to mail the letter.

Lou swung into the back room. "Crick, can you do a pair of baby shoes"—lowering her voice—"for a really *ugly* baby?"

"Yes, yes—"

"It's *really* ugly," said Lou. She was whispering, but her voice was not, it seemed to Cricket, as low as it ought to be. "I wonder if the daddy knows?"

"Knows?"

Lou shook her blue pigtails.

"Knows he's not the daddy."

"How can you know he's not the daddy?"

"The baby doesn't look anything like the mother."

Cricket chewed on this a moment.

"Well—does it look like the father?"

"How should I know that?" said Lou.

"What?"

"The father isn't even here!"

"So how do you know the daddy's not the daddy?"

Lou made an impatient gesture and turned back towards the counter.

"Sometimes, Crick-Crick, you're too thick-thick."

Cricket tore up both the letter from Barbet Fillonian and the response she had written to him.

Chapter Twenty-five

On the first of January, the papers and several other outlets published the final statistics for the previous year:

Gelucelets Collection – Leaders

Lorch, Sprill Tower	381
Kravchenko, Macdonald, Tower 2	326
Aquino, Front Street Blocks	319
Morena, Jumbo Data Building	311
Thiam, Sir Cooper Mauldin Plaza	304

Lorne was so far ahead that people across the city called and emailed and texted to ask whether the numbers were correct.

"They're calling you *Wayne Gretzky*!" said Cricket, beaming at Lorne over a saggy-looking sandwich.

"They might as well call me the Dwayne Gretzky of vacuuming," said Lorne, kicking out a leg and nearly knocking over his TV tray. "And you—the Dwayne Gretzky of hanging frames—"

"Oh, that's not what I do, Lorny—"

"—and Leo—the Dwayne Gretzky of baking Kaiser buns—"

"He does more than that. You know that."

Cricket found a copy of the newspaper article that compared her husband to Wayne Gretzky and taped it to the refrigerator door. Now and then she caught Lorne looking at it as he threw on his jacket or grabbed a taxi chit. He did not seem to be reading the clipping so much as verifying that it was still there. One morning he went so far as to rub his thumb over the page, smoothing its creases.

You slaughtered Kravchenko.

Lorne started; Cricket had stolen up behind him and spoken the words softly into his ear. He turned and scowled at his wife, even as a smile struggled at the corners of his mouth. He fought, but at last relented, and for a magical second he allowed pride to suffuse his features. Cricket was astonished at how soft and youthful his face became.

"Oh, hell," he said. "*Hell.* It's not like it's rocket science."

And Cricket wandered around the tiny green kitchen table as if she had been about to take care of something, and Lorne stood by the clipping, fixing his tie and murmuring *Oh hell, oh hell* again and again. Something about the way his back and shoulders sloped as he buttoned his cufflinks made Cricket want to do something for him, anything at all. But nothing came to mind. Nothing was needed.

Not twenty-four hours after the clipping went up on the refrigerator, a reporter telephoned to try to arrange Lorne's appearance at a child's birthday party.

"I think it'd be a blast," said Cricket. "And the *kids*! The kids would love it."

Lorne told Cricket the last thing in the world he wanted to do was play hired clown to a bunch of brats.

Now and then Lou asked Cricket for advice about how to handle her mother.

"Your mother's a sweet lady," Cricket would say.

"A sweet lady who tried to steal all my boyfriends."

"Well—"

"Do you know what it's like to be raised by a narcissist?"

"No."

"No, you wouldn't. Most people don't."

When Lou's mother called the store, Cricket's heart broke at the pitiful, hungry-sounding voice at the other end of the line. "A sad old woman," she told Lorne. But Lou would take the phone and ask her mother what the problem was, what was wrong now, what was it this time—*I don't have time for this, Mother, you know damn well how to use the microwave. The light switch isn't going to electrocute you. The mailman never said that and you know he didn't—*

"Just you watch," Lou would tell Cricket, hanging up. "She'll call in five minutes asking how to use the can opener."

And next Lou went on about how that was *it*, she was leaving, she was moving out. And over the next fifteen or twenty minutes, Cricket would gently talk Lou into giving her mother one more chance. It was terrifying to Cricket to think that Lou might one day leave her mother's house and ask to move in with her and Lorne.

Lorne was waiting for his order by the counter of a fast food restaurant.

"Wow, I can't believe they let *you* pay..."

A man stood a few feet away, shaking his head, his eyes like saucers.

"Eh?" said Lorne.

"The *lea*st they could do is give you a discount, like they do for firefighters and cops. Nurses, too. Even *nurses*."

"Eh."

A clerk rushed a cup of coffee to the man, who took it without taking his eyes off Lorne. He shuffled a step closer. He had a thick walrus moustache and wore a hockey jacket with TRAINER embroidered on one sleeve.

"What a world," he said. "What a world! Can you believe what a world this is? Why don't they just spit in your face and get it over with?"

Another cashier arrived with Lorne's order. The man with the walrus moustache pointed one finger towards her and another towards Lorne.

"You should be giving this guy his food for *nothing*. You should be thanking him for his service."

The clerk drifted back into a labyrinth of grills and fryers. Lorne wondered whether the man was the house lunatic, a wacko who wandered around inspecting tables and firing staff, as if he thought he was in charge.

"Gotta go," said Lorne.

"Hey—you bet," said the man. "Kill one of those little bastards for me."

At other times people nudged Lorne with their elbows and grinned at him, or winked at their children and said *That there is a man*, or called him *Lorchy* and told him to keep up the good work. These exchanges were often over before he understood what was happening.

CHAPTER TWENTY-SIX

Lorne's birthday was always a gloomy day because it meant Leonidas would be coming for a visit.

On the Sunday nearest Lorne's birthday, Cricket would prepare a tiny banquet of spare ribs, collard greens (memories of a great-aunt from Mississippi), scalloped potatoes, thin-sliced ham, hot olives, and ginger beer. Lorne could be counted on to slice the ham and provide the beer. Cricket would also set the little round kitchen table; she and Lorne only ate there on Lorne's birthday, Christmas Eve, Easter Sunday, and any time there was a solar eclipse. (Lorne had been paranoid about eclipses ever since a cousin of his had damaged her eyes by peeking through the curtains of her classroom during the solar eclipse of 1984. Their kitchen curtains were made of dark-hued cotton duck, and Lorne trusted them more than he trusted the gauzier ones in the parlour. He could, as Cricket suggested, spend eclipses in the cellar, but he said there was nothing to do down there.)

Cricket put on a navy summer dress with a pattern of white anchors and wore a baseball cap of the same colour, a prize from her work's lost and found. They would eat early, at half past three. At twenty-five past, Lorne started scooping greens onto his plate. Cricket lunged at the spoon.

"You can't start yet! Leo's not here."

"I'm hungry and it's my birthday."

"Come on, Lorny. It looks bad."

"No badder'n showing up late. It's *my* birthday, not his."

It was tradition that Leonidas always startled Lorne on arriving, and this time was no different: at twenty to four, he materialized behind Lorne's chair and slammed both hands on his father's shoulders. Lorne jumped, his thighs rattling against the table.

"Jesus Christ cubed, don't *do* that, boy!"

"Ha, ha, ha! Happy birthday, old man!"

"You know I hate that. I *hate* it—"

"Ha, ha, ha! You don't really hate it."

Leonidas was a tall slim fellow with long brown hair tied at the back of his head. Lorne said he dressed like a "punk," by which he meant "goth," because Leonidas usually wore untucked black button-down shirts and charcoal-coloured jeans.

"Lorny, don't be like that," said Cricket.

"Yeah, Dad, that's no way to welcome a guest. Ha, ha!"

Lorne shook his shoulders free of his son's large hands. The size of Leonidas's hands had always made him uncomfortable.

"You're late," said Lorne. "Sit down before it gets dark out."

Leonidas gave his father a playful smack on the back of the neck. Lorne stiffened like a servant abused in front of his family by a laughing lord. To his mind, Leonidas was always taking these sorts of liberties. And to his mind, it went back to the day when Leonidas was eight years old and lost all respect for his father.

Cricket settled everyone in and removed her cap.

"Special occasion, Mom?"

"What's that?"

"You took your bucket off. Ha, ha!"

Cricket swept her hair, which was standing straight up from her brow, to one side.

"I always forget one thing."

"And it's always your hair, Mom. Ha, ha!"

The trio ate loudly. Sweat broke out above and below their eyes. Every adjustment they made on their chairs knocked them against the table and jiggled the china. Leonidas talked incessantly, filling them in on everything he had been up to, which sounded impressive to Cricket but not to his father. He was working as an apprentice baker at a grocery store. Lorne said that he had never known an apprenticeship to go on as long as his son's had.

"Ha, ha! Well, Dad, it's not the apprenticeships of *your* day," said Leonidas, plowing his greens around his plate with a fork. "I'm not making candles here."

"So when, then," said Lorne, "do you become a master?"

"This isn't the sixth century, Dad. Ha, ha!"

"Oh, Lorny—"

"Is your master even a master? Are you apprentice to another apprentice?"

Cricket cracked Lorne's knuckles with the handle of her butter knife.

"It's okay, Mom," said Leonidas. "He's the birthday boy. He can be grouchy all he wants."

"I'm not being grouchy."

"He's not being grouchy, Mom. Ha, ha!"

Midway through the meal it dawned on Lorne that the three of them were not spread evenly around the table, that his and Leonidas's chairs were set closer together than they were to Cricket's. It was not that he did not like his son or objected to being near him, but it did not seem necessary for them to be elbowing each other over their plates. Employing his tablemates' conversation as a screen, Lorne started working himself and his chair away from his son, seesawing and bumping along as discreetly as he could. Leonidas was telling his mother about a colleague who had dropped a rack of pies and Cricket was laughing so hard that the clasp of her necklace popped open. Lorne continued seesawing until he rocked too far and brought his chair down heavily on the floor. His wife and son went silent and stared at him. Lorne was about to say *Damn chair doesn't work on my birthday dammit* but at the critical moment his mouth and his throat went dry, betraying him now just as they had a decade and a half ago, which had caused Leonidas to lose all respect for him.

The family played a round of Cheat in the little parlour, which Leonidas filled to exploding with his nonstop chatting and laughter. Cricket destroyed the men at the game, having by far the best poker face among the three.

"Maybe she's cheating, Dad. Cheating at Cheat. Though that would mean she's *not* cheating. Ha, ha!"

"Whoever invented this game should have his tail cut off," said Lorne.

"I really like this game, Lorny."

"Of course *you* like it. You're good at it."

Leonidas won the next game and they gave it up; though they kept the lights low and the curtains partially drawn, it was warm enough in the parlour that the cards were sticking to their hands. Lorne then opened his presents. Cricket got him a set of undershirts for work, a pound of chocolate, and a magazine of barbecue recipes. The Lorches' barbecue was broken and had not been used in five years, but Lorne loved reading the recipes and looking at the pictures.

Leonidas presented his father with a scrapbook of media clippings about Lorne or that mentioned Lorne's name.

"Do you like it, Dad? Ha, ha! It took me almost twelve minutes to put it all together."

Lorne flipped through the pages.

"So much horseshit," he said.

"We should put the one from the fridge in there," said Cricket. "The one where they call you Wayne Gretzky."

"Way ahead of you, Mom. It's already in there."

Cricket gathered up the empty cups and Leonidas carried the tray for her into the kitchen. Leonidas was patting around for his phone and wallet when a weird bark sounded in the parlour. A moment later Lorne appeared in the kitchen looking like he had stepped in a puddle.

"This guy," he said, holding the scrapbook open and tapping his finger on one of the clippings. "Can you *believe* this guy!"

"Who—you?"

"No! Kravchenko—"

Leonidas inhaled through his teeth.

"Yeah, Dad, ha, ha! You're mentioned, right there at the bottom—"

"I know I'm *mentioned*, Leo. But the whole story's about Kravchenko."

"Yeah, he's an interesting unit. Did you read it?"

"I stopped reading when I saw his name."

"He's talking about opening up a school. Ha, ha! Did you read that?"

"A school? What—like he's a professor, now?"

"Ha, ha! No, not that kind of school. A camp. Like hockey school! Camps, Dad, you know? For kids."

Lorne stared at his son, then at the clipping.

"That doesn't sound right to me," he said.

"Oh! Yes!" said Cricket. "I heard something about that on the radio... I didn't know it was one of the cleaners doing it."

"Doing what? Camping? With little boys?"

"It's not like *that*, Lorny—"

Leonidas pointed to the bottom of the article.

"Says right there, Dad. A training camp! Kravchenko's gonna give kids pointers on catching ice rats, ha, ha!"

"That's the stupidest thing I ever heard," said Lorne. "What the—listen, you can't just get a bunch of kids together like that. Where's he gonna get the rats? He gonna draw them on the wall?"

While it took him months to secure the required permitting, Kravchenko held his first camp the following February, during cleaning's slow season. He took twenty young people from across the city through their paces in a back arm of the Macdonald Plaza's Tower 2, which he had cleaned for eight years. The kids learned to track and collect ice rats, though only on the final day was each child allowed to peel an actual living specimen from the mouth of a vent by the boilers—and only after donning coveralls, gloves, and masks.

The awards Kravchenko handed out at the end of the week were for "Best Attitude," "Most Punctual," "Team Player," and "Most Obedient" (he would drop the last from subsequent camps, not because of its hints of totalitarianism but because his wife told him it was interchangeable with "Best Attitude"). However, at the end of the last day, he took a tall, slim boy aside and said, "Scantland, you got better at this in one week than I did in my first year."

"Okay, thanks."

"I'd give you one medal but then I have to give you all medals."

"Thanks."

We have already described this boy, Scantland: the star middle-school athlete whose principal recommended that he pursue scholarships in hockey or baseball. After his week at Kravchenko's camp, he quit both sports. And while he missed the last six weeks of the hockey season, he still ended up leading his team in scoring.

CHAPTER TWENTY-SEVEN

The Front Street Blocks, a stone complex south of downtown, housed a mishmash of legal firms and industry associations and government offices. It comprised three eight-storey buildings, standing shoulder to shoulder and connected by glass tunnels at the third and sixth floors. The windows were as narrow as loopholes in a Spanish castle. From the street the structure was cold and grim-looking; on wet days, rain streaked the stone in irregular bands, giving the stones a dirty, splattered appearance. It was the kind of place even pigeons barely bothered to haunt.

An infestation of ice rats in the ducts and along the back walls in the 2000s required the conversion of some custodians to rat-hunters. The only one who showed ability was Aquino, a rake-thin transplant from the Philippines. Within three years he was the only one left; the others had either quit or been injured. He worked longer hours than Lorne or Kravchenko or any of the others. His fans, and more than a few journalists, considered this perfectly fair, no more a bending of the "rules" than the powder that Thiam (Sir Cooper Mauldin Plaza) used on his hands for gripping, or the night-vision goggles it was rumoured Moreno (Jumbo Data Building) wore in the ducts.

Like most of his counterparts, Aquino rarely fell ill; even when he was sick, he, like the rest, scorned the notion of a night off. Yet in July of the second year of stats-keeping, he went out to Bubbly's, a chain roadhouse, with his family for his brother's birthday. He and the brother shared an order of Hawaiian nachos. The dish contained scallops, which Aquino had never eaten, and to which, he would discover, he was allergic. For three days his body turned itself inside out. He shivered and sweated for twenty-four hours and then slept for another twenty-four. In the depths of his fever he shrieked about ice rats and hallucinated that they were invading his bedroom; the family had to wrestle him away from the wall, where he was clawing at phantom blooms, and back into bed.

During the first two days of Aquino's fever, frantic texts and calls passed between the unsleeping superintendent and the maintenance managers of the Front Street Blocks. In their desperation the managers contacted a handful of personnel agencies, looking for anyone who had experience hunting ice rats. Their own maintenance staff refused, even under threat of suspension, to climb into the ducts, all afraid of freezing to death. Nobody could be found to do the work. The superintendent considered driving to Aquino's apartment and shouting at him in bed, telling him he needed to get back to work or else Kravchenko was going to leap past him in the standings. An inspector suggested that they bring in a substitute cleaner from a smaller building. Yet no other super, even one who ran a three-storey and largely ratless building in the west end, would free one up for duty.

Fans who were used to spotting Aquino on his walk to and from the office grew alarmed, and then suspicious, when he went missing. They contacted the media, which contacted the superintendent. A press agent from parts unknown was brought in and briefed. She gave the following statement at 2:45 PM on the second day:

> *Mr. Aquino is on a brief previously planned vacation and will return to his duties shortly. The Front Street Complex has put measures in place to prevent any impacts on the health and safety of the public. Have a nice day.*

Late on the second night, one of the foremen climbed from a desk into a vent on the seventh floor, with a mind to sweep ten or twenty feet of the ducts. He was forty, not much older than an average cleaner, but both impatient and out of shape. From conversations with Aquino he knew that he should sniff the air in the ducts for suspicions of ice. His nose, however, was not the informed machine that the cleaners' were, and all he inhaled was dust. As he crawled further into the wall he broke into a coughing fit. Light leaked past his shoulders from the vent behind him, but he could see almost nothing. It did not take long for him to give up. In attempting to reverse, his coveralls bunched up against the narrow duct perimeter. He was not stuck, but he thought he was.

Jesus Murphy get me OUT OF HERE.

His boots were only two or three feet from the mouth of the vent.

Jesus H. MURPHY.

A technician had to pull the foreman out by the ankles, and the latter's hip was torn by a screw Aquino was always clever enough to avoid.

"We need that asshole back in the ducts pronto," the super told the foreman. "Send him medicine, send him grenades—get his ass back here."

The super paced around, knocking now and then into janitors, mounting ladders and cupping an ear to vent grates, and every few minutes monitoring the ambient air temperature. The walls were colder than normal, he was sure of it; those little shits were migrating through the entire system, and they were going to destroy the building like a virus.

By late afternoon of the third day the super—bloodshot, unshaven—lay sprawled over his desk with all the blinds drawn. He had been awake for forty-four hours and thought he was having visions; he noticed a hand sweeping back and forth across his face and a clattering voice rising up from the bottom of the sea and saying over and over again, "He's here, he's back, he's HERE—"

Aquino, still on fire but ready for battle, was at that moment shimmying in the walls between the third and fourth floors of the east building. Foreman, techs, and custodians, followed by the groggy superintendent, raced from vent to vent, squashing their lips against the grates and calling and shouting and banging as if they were prisoners watching one of their own rappelling down the outside wall to freedom. At every vent they said the same thing:

"Seen anything, Scoot?"

A scratching in the darkness, a faraway voice shuddering against the metal: "Haven't found any parties. No parties yet, guys."

He called the clusters of rats *parties* just as Lorne did, even though the two men had never met or shared any war stories from the ducts. At each *no parties* the men outside the grates whooped and cheered and pounded one another on the back. Their elation was violent. The relief was almost too much for their souls to bear, these workers who had done their rounds over the past forty-eight hours with the ghost of the Cancer Building at the top of their minds, who watched the walls and windows and elevators for insidious sprinkles of ice that could breed behind the walls and stop up the elevators and choke out the exits, consigning everyone in the building to a frozen grave. The men and women stayed all night, taking turns, leaving the wastebaskets full and the floors unswept. The superintendent wept with joy when, on the top floor of the building, he met Aquino's shadow-streaked grin at a ceiling vent—

"Three parties, Superman. In my backpack now. Everything good."

"You're not shitting me? Everything good?"

"No shitting. Everything good."

Aquino was pale and his brow and cheeks were shining. Somehow he had made his round only four minutes slower than usual.

"Okay, okay, good," said the super.

"Down now, Superman."

And Aquino, moving like a squirrel, turned himself around in that tiny space and began his long descent down shafts and chutes in the dark. He found one more rat on the sixth floor that he had missed on the way up. While he had the central and west buildings still to sweep, when he emerged from a vent on the ground floor, the workers mobbed him and in their ecstasy nearly tore him to pieces.

CHAPTER TWENTY-EIGHT

The final statistics for the second year:

Lorch, Sprill Tower	411
Aquino, Front Street Blocks	344
Kravchenko, Macdonald, Tower 2	315
Thiam, Sir Cooper Mauldin Plaza	297
Dulka, Westerfeldt Insurance Building	272

Aquino's partisans, aware of an *incident* in July but not its specifics, circulated a rumour that he had been working with a broken vertebra and that the injury had cost him the scoring title. When they told Aquino this, crowding alongside him as he walked to work, he laughed and shook his head as if it was the craziest thing he had ever heard. Yet he did not deny it. They told him that Lorne Lorch won the title by default and that Lorne Lorch could not have done up Aquino's zipper.

"I like Lorchy," said Aquino. "Big Lorchy's my favourite."

A large man in a windbreaker now sometimes slipped in with the other fans and walked a while with Aquino. He never said much. If someone paid Aquino a compliment, the man nodded in agreement. But if one of the disciples said that Aquino was better than Lorch, the large man would shake his head.

"No, sir," he would say. "With all due respect, nobody's at Lorch's level. There's Lorch and then there's everybody else."

The other fans watched for the man and heckled him whenever he showed up. He took the jeering with calm forbearance, with the clear-eyed, almost wistful serenity of the martyr, of the man whose belief is his shelter and whose faith needs no defending. Aquino smiled at the man in the windbreaker as easily as he smiled at everyone else. Yet the smile was always a little bigger.

Lorne finished first the season after that. The media referred to him as the first three-time winner of the "crown," though as yet there was no crown, or trophy, or ceremony.

Lorch, Sprill Tower	381
Aquino, Front Street Blocks	300
Kravchenko, Macdonald, Tower 2	300
Morena, Jumbo Data Building	286
Brathwaite, Pegasus Icon, Tower C	254

Vicious bickering developed between Kravchenko's and Aquino's camps when these totals were made public. Each side claimed the other had rigged the statistics, that their own man was the "true second." While Kravchenko understood the protocol of listing their names alphabetically due to the tie, he disliked seeing his own below Aquino's in the standings. It annoyed him to think that anyone skimming the column might skip the totals and assume he, Kravchenko, had come in third.

The second-place tie miffed not only the two cleaners and their fans, but also a growing community of gamblers. This underworld, born on social media sites and for a while relegated to university dorms, was spreading its tentacles across the entire city. Betting on the cleaners was officially prohibited and illegal. The field was unlicensed, the counts unverified, and the "league" unofficial. Yet by the end of that third year, fully a third of city councillors were betting at least occasionally on nightly and weekly results.

Stories—legends—circulated that showed how the racket was maturing. A woman left her husband because he spent all of his free time shuffling from building to building, asking bewildered office workers for tips and rumours about the men who swept through the ducts each night. A vice detective told a reporter—"on background," she later claimed—that daily transactions were reaching into the low six figures. Three individuals wearing fake beards roughed up a grocer in the bathroom of his own store over an unpaid debt; on their way out, one of the goons tipped over a pyramid of lemons and advised the grocer, "That'll be *you*, next."

The grocer, rearranging his spectacles and clutching at his torn collar, did not understand.

"What, the lemons?"

The goon stomped on a lemon and waved his hand at the grocer.

"*That's* you."

"If you only needed one lemon," cried the grocer, "why'd you have to ruin my display?"

In the first week of January, a man vanished from his home in the city's western suburbs. His body was found a week later in a storm reservoir. The death was treated as suspicious, but no charges were laid. Some time later the man's wife discovered their children's college fund and their personal chequing account were empty. Her husband had bet the farm on a specific final configuration—Morena finishing the year above Aquino but below Kravchenko. The widow told a detective that her husband probably committed suicide, and said only an idiot would believe Morena could beat Aquino in the ducts.

CHAPTER TWENTY-NINE

Orinn announced that Lorne was getting a raise.

"What for?" Lorne said.

"You're the first three-time winner of the Cleaners Cup."

"Eh?"

"And the super says you deserve a raise."

"Eh?"

Orinn's mouth was smiling without his consent.

"He wants to make sure you're happy here."

When Lorne told Cricket about the raise, she started to sing "Hail to the Chief" until he told her to shut up.

"I haven't got a raise in three years," she said.

"I hope I don't have to fill out any forms or anything."

Now and then Orinn would drop a hint, share a rumour, that Aquino had collected thirty rats in four days last week, or that Morena had moved up two spots in the standings. A year or two earlier, Lorne was content to chuckle it off and say that the poor bastards must be getting the whip. Now he would stop dressing, or undressing, and stare at his foreman.

"Who says he got thirty?"

"He says. Kravchenko. Kravchenko's people."

"Kravchenko couldn't peel thirty in *ten* days. Not even if it was raining rats."

"The super said so."

Lorne reached for his boots, knocked the soles together, and set them down again.

"And supers never lie?"

Orinn's mouth went flat.

"I'm telling you what I was told. It's no biggie, Lorny. Kravchenko's still far behind you."

"I don't care where he is."

"Then what's the problem?"

"There's no problem."

"Don't worry about Kravchenko. He's a bum."

"I know he's a bum. I just never heard so much about a bum in my life."

Orinn took Lorne by the sleeve. "Hey," he said, "you know what they call the guy? They call him 'Cutthroat.'"

"Eh?"

"Cutthroat Kravchenko."

"Why? Did he kill someone?"

"It's a nickname. Like Dulka's."

"What's Dulka's?"

"'The Duke.'"

Lorne bent down to his boot laces.

"'Dulka the Duke,'" said Orinn. "Because his—"

"I get it, I get it! And it's the stupidest thing I ever heard."

Although Lorne did not, as a habit, speak brusquely to his boss, Orinn was not surprised at the man's tone. A little distance had grown between them in the last month, when unofficial stats showed Aquino nosing his way up the collection ladder at what appeared to be a faster pace than Lorne's. The super told Orinn the owner was asking about it.

Like to know if Lorch is sick or anything, the super said. *Just wondering, you understand.*

I'll ask him.

That was easier said than done; in all the years Orinn had supervised Lorne, he had kept out of his cleaner's business, because the cleaner did his business. There was no point in telling Gretzky to pass more or Picasso to paint better. Lorne was a machine that never needed oiling. As far as Orinn was concerned, his sole task when it came to Lorne was to ensure the man arrived for work on time and did not expire in the ducts. For a long time, which was soon to end, no foreman in the city had it as good.

Lorny boy, he had said. And Lorne's ears pricked up, because the foreman never called him *Lorny boy*.

What.

What's today's take, Lorny boy?

Without taking his eyes off Orinn, Lorne gestured to the pail at his feet.

Six.

Mind if I have a look?

Orinn took up the bucket and swept his hand around inside. The dead rats, faintly stubbly to the touch, clacked against one another.

Six, said Lorne again.

Six.

An odd little word, *six*, when spoken with unintentional emphasis in a purple-lit basement. Orinn grinned and stirred the rats as if they were the last possible things he expected to find there.

Six, said Orinn.

Is that a problem?

Orinn set the bucket down. He could feel the rumble and tumble of the enormous furnace system as if it were beating in his blood.

Nope, he said. *I know you're peeling everything in there.*

Had Orinn not been so eager to exit the basement, he might have heard, in the wake of these phosphorescent words, the shuffle and scrape of a small man in too-big coveralls rising to his feet.

I know you're peeling everything in there

It was the first time Orinn had ever laid hands on Lorne without laying hands on him.

CHAPTER THIRTY

Lorne was headed for the mailbox to drop off a birthday card for one of his sisters, a card that Cricket had bought, signed and stamped. Crossing the street two back from his own, a block that badly needed repaving, he mounted the sidewalk and stopped short. The street was quiet and nobody was about, but a piece of the scenery did not fit. It was as if a drawer had been left unshut somewhere. He backed into the street again and surveyed the houses in front of him. Then he scanned the lawns, the sidewalk, the curb—

Right there, the drain, the aperture that should have been black with nothingness—a faint twinkle, a moon in the clouds. A face.

Lorne approached the drain and dropped on one knee. The drain opening was a foot and a half long and three inches tall.

"Hi, there."

"Hi."

It was a boy, maybe eight years old.

"Everything okay in there?"

The boy stood, or sat, or hung, back from the opening. Lorne could only make out his brow, eyes and nose.

"Yeah."

"Need any help?"

"No."

"How'd you get in there?"

Lorne glanced around him. Smoke billowed lazily from a chimney down the block; otherwise the street was absolutely still.

"Come on, now," he said to the eyes and nose. "We need to get you out."

"I can get out."

"How'd you get in?"

A pause.

"You won't tell anybody?"

"Not if you tell me right now."

The boy's eyes did not blink as he outlined the location of his ingress. Lorne did not know exactly where it was, whether it was near or far. From the boy's description, negotiating it involved an accordion-like sequence of stretching and squeezing.

"You won't tell?" the boy said.

"If you promise you can get out by yourself, I won't tell."

"I promise."

Lorne rose, a little stiffly, to his feet. There seemed no obvious way to mark the end of the exchange. He wavered a moment.

"Say," he said. "What exactly are you—"

He caught himself. The man and the lad gazed at each other. Nothing in the latter's eyes showed that he had any idea who Lorne was. Yet it was as clear as a rainbow what the boy was up to.

"Oh—"

Behind Lorne, across the street, the front door of a bungalow swung open and a couple of girls, nine or ten and dressed in matching mauve raincoats, trooped outside. They sniffed around the front yard with their feet in the way children do when sent outside without a purpose.

"Oh, okay—"

Lorne saw the eyes in the drain roll away from his own.

"Okay, there, sonny—you have a good one, now."

So they *did* still do that, Lorne thought, pacing away down the street. Cleaning—hunting, as he called it—was still something children played at, just as Lorne had all those years ago. The wondrous game endured; Kravchenko's "cleaning school," and others now opening across the city, had not managed to destroy it. Kids still strapped on their shoes and their gloves and went diving into sewers just for the thrill of it.

Lorne walked home on air. Kravchenko could stick his school up his ass. As long as there were rats in the world, there would be people who did not give a damn about scoring races and cleaning cups—or whatever the hell it was called—and simply loved to hunt the little bastards. Lorne related this happy discovery to Cricket, though he did not tell her about the girls in the mauve jackets, because he had not noticed them.

"What was that the other day," Lorne later said to Orinn, peering into the black square in the basement at the beginning of a shift, "about Kravchenko?"

"What about Kravchenko?"

"What did you say they call him?"

It took a moment for Orinn to catch up.

"Oh. 'Cutthroat.'"

"Cutthroat?"

"Cutthroat Kravchenko. Maybe it's spelled with a 'K,' I don't know."

Lorne was clutching the edges of the square and pulling himself towards and then pushing himself away from it, as if preparing for a skydive.

"What a dumb name," said Lorne.

"Do you want to know what yours is?"

"My what?"

"Your nickname."

"I don't give a horse apple."

And Lorne leaped into the square.

"The Torch," said Orinn, shouting into the blackness after him. "You're *Lorch the Torch...*"

Lorne never admitted it, but he liked the name, even if it made no sense.

CHAPTER THIRTY-ONE

Lorne was stripping off his coveralls and telling Orinn what a pain in the arse that big rat, there, the one at the bottom of the pail, had been—

"It was like trying to peel goddamn drywall—"

Orinn was standing at the door of the basement room, not quite in and not quite out. He nodded and grimaced as Lorne went on about the big bastard of a rat. But he remained at the door, hovering. At last Lorne told his boss that the big rat was dead if he wanted to, you know, wander into the room and have a look. When Orinn still hesitated, Lorne slapped his hands onto his thighs.

"What's the problem?"

The air system mumbled like a giant clothes dryer.

"Lorchy—"

The faintest shadow played on the floor near Orinn's feet. He was not moving, but the shadow was.

"Lorchy—"

Lorne rose just as two figures stepped into the room. Orinn made a show of signalling to the arrivals to keep their distance.

"—these guys just have a couple of questions for you. Two minutes, that's all."

"Questions?"

"Yeah, questions."

The shorter of the two figures leaned over the bucket.

"About what?"

"Tonight's take."

"Eh?"

The figures were in front of him now, their backs to the lamp, their phones glowing a creamy blue. The blue clashed with the ambient purple. Neither of the apparitions introduced themselves.

"Hi, Lorne," said the shorter one, a woman with square spectacles and an asymmetrical lump of wavy hair. "How many tonight?"

"How many what?"

"Gels."

"Gels?"

"Rats," said Orinn, standing a little apart.

"Eh? Five—"

"Good. How were the ducts?"

"What do you mean?"

"Anything unusual, any challenges, obstructions—"

"What?"

"—or was it a standard clean?"

Lorne looked at his foreman.

"Go ahead, Lorchy," said Orinn.

"Yeah," said Lorne, the word crunching like glass between his teeth. "Standard."

"Five gels. Yesterday you got—you got—six, I think, was it? Six?"

"Six," said the woman's counterpart, a young man with a wispy beard.

Lorne could see an acoustic wave on the woman's phone spasming as it snatched at their voices.

"Is this part of a trend, maybe?" said the woman.

"Are you seeing fewer—" This from the young man, who stopped and lowered his head; it was not his turn. "Sorry—"

"No, go for it," said the woman.

"Thanks. Lorny—Lorne—are you seeing fewer gels in the ducts?"

"What the hell do you mean?"

"Well," said the man, "yesterday you caught six gels."

"You mean rats?"

"Rats, yes. Today you got five."

"So what?"

"That's completely out of his control," said Orinn.

"So that's one less—fewer, sorry—one fewer than yesterday."

"Were there only five in there?" broke in the woman. "Or are you saying you only *got* five?"

Even in the gloom Orinn could see—almost feel—Lorne's body expanding, as if someone were blowing it full of radon.

"I already told you he got everything in there," Orinn said. "He always does."

"We just want to hear it from him," said the man, scratching at his beard.

The creamy-blue screens of the phones trembled a few inches from Lorne's nose. Orinn held his breath. There was no telling how Lorne might react, given that any irritation he was feeling towards the invasion of privacy was no doubt compounded by the confusing nature of what was happening. Yet amazingly, Lorne mastered himself, seemed to understand—if hazily—what was going on.

"It goes up and down," he said.

"So that's it, then? Only five gels in the whole system tonight?"

Orinn could see the set of Lorne's jaw.

"Only five."

"Okay, great," said the woman.

"Terrific," said the man.

They asked Lorne a few more questions—did he have a shoulder injury, an upper-body injury of some sort? No, nothing. Any rodent rats, spiders? Just one rat; he never saw many of the little bastards, thank Christ. What was his favourite chocolate bar? Oh, Christ—KitKats, probably. How did he feel about Kravchenko's take last night, which was the same as his own? Kravchenko could catch *fifty* rats as far as Lorne cared. Orinn interjected several times and was ignored several times; at one point, when the male reporter asked Lorne about the temperature in the ducts, Orinn said, "You don't have to answer that—he won't answer that—"

"It's just right," Lorne said. "That's what the temperature is."

"Have you ever considered starting at the *top* of the building instead of the bottom?"

"If you have questions about strategy," Orinn said, "you should be asking *me*."

"Makes no difference," said Lorne.

"Have you ever tried it?"

"Yah."

After making a quick inspection of the rats in the pail—were they always round like that, were they always that size?—the reporters left. Lorne, still half out of his coveralls, slumped back onto the bench and wiped the night's grime from his brow. Orinn was not prepared for silence; he had expected an earful the moment the two of them were alone.

"So," he said, reaching a hand to the cleaner's sleeve—but, this time, retracting it— "you know the old saying: 'It's easier to ask for forgiveness than for permission.'"

Lorne resumed shuffling out of his uniform, then glanced up at his foreman.

"Is that the end of it?"

Orinn said probably not.

And he departed before Lorne could become angry, and without filling in the tally ledger. It was one of the few times Lorne filled in the ledger himself. His glorious penmanship was quite easy to make out, embowered as it was within Orinn's columns of chicken scratch.

CHAPTER THIRTY-TWO

It is true that no cleaner had died of exposure to ice rats. But it is not true that a cleaner had never died in the ducts.

A few years before Lorne's time—before he had even taken up a mop at the Sprill Building—hunting ice rats in office buildings underwent a metamorphosis. For the previous fifteen years, when rats had been discovered in those structures, scientists and technical experts had been called into service. As the worldwide outbreak diminished, so did volumes in the ducts. A few enterprising custodians had already begun peeling, or attempting to peel, the few enterprising rats that remained. These pioneers lost some fingers and more than one got temporarily stuck. Yet they elaborated the principles of the field whose pinnacle Lorne would reach a few years later. They worked in obscurity and retired into obscurity, or disability, or early death. They did not receive hazard pay, nor were they entitled to special benefits. When they injured themselves in the ducts they had to keep it to themselves; the building insurance did not cover such eventualities, and foremen were terrified of lawsuits. So the men quietly went about their work in splints and bandages and under the influence of whatever painkillers they could afford. They rarely spoke of rat-hunting, even to their loved ones, because it was just another unpleasant part of the job.

Around the time Lorne was hired as an evening janitor at the Sprill, a man about his own age and size and complexion was performing the same function in a nine-storey building west of the city core. The structure, square and flat-toned, had in the late 1990s been evacuated for some months due to constellations of rats appearing in regular cycles. At one point the entire building had been tarped over in the manner of a circus tent while workers from the provincial health ministry fought a tenacious and ultimately victorious battle against the rats. By the middle of the next decade, all traces of the terrible occupation had disappeared. The edifice was repaired and retrofitted with materials that would, it was hoped, stave off future invasions. For the most part, the retrofits were successful. Yet once in a while, perhaps every six or eight months, the janitor passing near a vent would catch a fragrance of winter that was to his foreman like the odour of a corpse.

Yah, the janitor would say, *okay, fine, okay*

And he would remove his belt—he did not like wearing a belt in the ducts—and put on a fresh pair of latex gloves, which would have earned him ridicule from Lorne. No matter where the scent issued from, the janitor always entered a ceiling vent on the fifth floor. It required standing on tiptoe on the desk of a vice-president of something or other. The janitor was careful not to upset any of the articles on the desk surface, though the vice-president always sensed that something was wrong, that someone had been standing on the desk, when he arrived for work the next day.

On his last night on earth, the janitor sprang into the ducts from the vice-president's desk and squirmed around to orient himself. He let his eyes grow accustomed to the cramped darkness. Only one path presented itself, and he followed it, moving in a snail-like motion.

Think it's on the eighth, a foreman called.

Yah, chief, I think so.

Maybe the ninth—smells maybe higher, said the building's other night custodian, a cousin of the man in the ducts.

For two hours the proto-cleaner slumped through the building's heating system, back and forth, up and down, his movements audible every now and again as a gentle rumble in the walls and ceilings. The cousin covered their work on the floor. Once in a while he heard a squeak or pop, and he would shout:

Still enjoying yourself in there, Pops?

He called the man in the ducts *Pops* because the man in the ducts was two years older.

Having a ball, Pops would answer. *Water's fine.*

The cousin went about his and Pops' rounds for another hour. While he worked, the cousin revolved in his mind a puzzle from a movie he had seen at the theatre with Pops and a few mutual friends. At a key point in the film, the heroes had to place exactly four litres of water on a scale but were given only a three-litre and a five-litre jug to fill. Just as the heroes were solving the puzzle, Pops leaned over and asked the cousin if they could trade seats, because he could not see over the hat of the man in front of him. The cousin, who was three inches taller than Pops, consented, but in changing places he missed the solution to the jug problem. Now as he pushed his mop trolley around the empty spaces of the building the cousin was trying to solve the puzzle. Several times he made it to within a step of the solution before giving up. He flip-flopped between beginning with the three-litre jug and with the five-litre jug. *Fill up three, pour three into five, fill up three?... Fill up five, pour five into three, pour three into three, pour five more into five...* The answer, he knew, was right in front of him. Yet rather than getting more and more irritated, the cousin grew more and more tickled, as if whatever was just beyond his reach was too ridiculous to get mad about. He was like a squirrel attempting to climb a bird feeder and tumbling down over and over again. *Fill up three, pour into five, pour back into three... dammit, dammit you silly bastard hee hee fill up five pour into three you bastard*

The cousin never solved the puzzle. He was muttering *three into five five into three* and chuckling and mopping at a jelly stain on the tiles of the ninth-floor kitchenette when his supervisor stuck his head in the door.

Hey how's our boy? said the cousin.

The supervisor shook his head.

No? Where is he?

I came to ask you that.

Ask me what?

Where is he.

The cousin was going to make a joke, tell the supervisor that Pops was probably having a nap in the ducts. But he was aware that the supervisor would not understand, that he would then have to reassure the supervisor that Pops was *not* actually sleeping in the ducts, and that he—the cousin—had been making a funny on the company dime. He did not want Pops to get in trouble. So he said:

He's in the ducts somewhere I think.

As soon as he was alone again, the cousin left his mop and made a catlike dash around the floor, stopping at each vent.

Popsy, Popsy, he called, as quietly as he could, cupping his hands around his mouth. *Yo Popsy Pop—*

He made his way from floor to floor, creeping from pool to pool of night lighting.

Popsy Pop

As he slipped through the elevator lobby on the second floor it occurred to the cousin that he had not heard any creaking from the ducts in an hour, maybe two. He stopped, and gazed up at the ceiling. His face was steeped in the pink of the EXIT sign by the stairwell. Pops, the cousin knew, had rarely been sick in his life and could launch his five-foot-six-inch body up and grab the rafters in their uncle's garage. One time he had swiped a pear out of his sister's hand and slam-dunked it in a playground basketball hoop. He had never played sports because the family did not have a car and his father refused to allow his son to mooch rides.

Fifty minutes earlier, in fact, Pops had followed his nostrils to a slanting shaft on the third floor. There he discovered an ice bloom in a dip, a sort of shallow well, in a corner. It proved impossible to scrape the rat out with the edge of his boot, so he turned himself upside down and wedged himself into the trough. After some flailing and after tearing the glove on his right hand, he managed to peel the rat with his left. At the moment the rat came unstuck from the metal, it died—as did its bioluminescence, the only light in that quarter of the ducts. Whether Pops became dizzy or disoriented is unknown; his cousin and a day custodian found his body twelve hours later, still upside down in the trough, with the rat fast to his frozen left hand. The coroner declared the cause of death to be asphyxiation.

Was he a heavy smoker, the coroner asked Pops' cousin.

Not a heavy smoker.

Not a heavy smoker or not a smoker at all?

He was a light smoker.

Okay, good, said the coroner.

He made some notes.

Does that matter? said the cousin.

The coroner thought about it.

Not really.

The third floor was sealed off that morning and an ambulance arrived without its flashers on and the rumour around the other offices was that a refrigerator tube had burst and sprayed Freon around the kitchenette. That was the tale Lorne heard through the janitors' grapevine, although he did not give it a moment's notice. A community newspaper reported Pops' passing—he had been active in the church—but gave almost no details. The family did not know how to explain the death, so they told people that Pops had had a stroke at work.

The building is no longer in use, but has not yet been demolished.

CHAPTER THIRTY-THREE

KitKat chocolate bars started showing up in the Lorches' mail and on the front step. Sometimes they were wrapped in messages that said:

Enjoy Mr. Lorch!

or

Great minds think alike!

Cricket showed Lorne the bars. He believed it was only a coincidence that people were mailing him his favourite chocolate bar.

"A broken clock's right once in a while," he told Cricket.

"Twice a day."

"Eh?"

"A broken clock's right twice a day."

"Twice? Then how in hell's it broken?"

Later that night, in the ducts, Lorne wondered what time it was and remembered the saying: *A broken clock's right twice a day.* After scanning a full day's passage of time in his mind, then verifying his count, he stopped crawling and said:

"Goddamn it, she's right. That's *right!*"

He was ten feet from a vent grate when he said this. A custodian, passing near the vent with a waste bin, heard him.

Weird son of a bitch, the custodian reflected.

Someone from the KitKat company reached out to Lorne about endorsing the chocolate. Lorne refused, telling the representative he sometimes ate Hershey bars.

When Cricket next talked to Leonidas on the phone, she told him about the KitKats.

"Ha, ha, Mom! It's 'cause it was in the paper."

"What was?"

During that first media scrum in the basement with the two reporters—an event that had morphed into a daily occurrence—Lorne had been asked what his favourite chocolate was.

"Oh Christ," said Lorne. "They actually *wrote* that?"

Cricket missed the write-ups of those early briefings because they were posted on the websites of local magazines she had never heard of. It was only after the daily newspaper started printing segments that she paid attention.

"So fine, dandy—I said I like KitKats," Lorne said, peeling the wrapper off one of the bars. "Big whoop."

"It is a big whoop. Your fans really like you."

"They're a bunch of damn lunatics."

Someone sent an empty KitKat wrapper with a note reading:

I sent the chocolate to our local EMTs because they're REAL heroes

Cricket discarded the note and the wrapper.

An email to Cricket's personal account:

Dear Cricket,
Please pass this on to Lorne. Just wanted to let him know how great he's been cleaning lately and I hope he's keeping safe and sound. The others guys can't touch him. They need to really make a Cleaners Cup and not just talk about it, because your trophy case would be filling up with cups.

Has Lorne ever thought about shifting his hours a bit? I guess it's maybe not up to him, it's probably Orinn or the general manager. But I read something about the cleaners catch twice as many rats between nine and midnight than they do the whole rest of the night. That's what I read. Some of the other guys already work earlier hours, which is probably the only reason why they're keeping within a hundred of Lorne during the year. Otherwise he'd leave them in the dust right? But I guess Lorne catches what's in there, no matter when he starts. Just wanted to pass the suggestion along in case somebody was interested. Lorne would know better than me.

Say hi to Lorne for me please. I guess I was the first of the "tailgaters" and he has been kind enough to speak to me now and then.

Thanks Cricket,
Laird

Lorne had no recollection of the name or the circumstances described in the letter.

"How does he know *your* name?" he asked his wife.

"I guess he guessed."

Cricket was aware that people in the city knew her name, because it had appeared in print a number of times beside Lorne's.

On Lorne and Cricket's anniversary that year, Lorne wanted to send his wife flowers. Usually they shared a takeout meal and exchanged cards, or at least little notes. In recent years Lorne's messages had gotten shorter and shorter: last year he had simply written *Happy a-versry Lorne X* on a sheet of paper from a notepad. This year he leafed through the Yellow Pages to find a florist, but they all looked the same to him, and Orinn had once told him florists were crooks.

After Cricket left for work on the morning of their anniversary, Lorne, instead of going to sleep, sneaked out and visited a flower shop two kilometres from home. The florist, a smiling Romanian woman, showed Lorne arrangements he had never heard of and did not bother trying to pronounce. Lorne liked the idea of roses but was flabbergasted when the florist told him how much a dozen cost.

"Let me think about it," he told the florist.

"You can buy six only," the florist said. "Or—three."

Back home Lorne wrote *Have a good avrsy love Lorne X* on the blank back of a window washing advertisement, and he and Cricket ate Chinese food before he left for work. As he slid through the ducts he brooded over the state of a world where something as stupid and useless as a rose could cost so much money when they grew for free in the goddamn shit-covered earth.

After the end of the third season, some of the cleaners were rumoured to be in rough shape. In their efforts to finish the year strong, a few had worked through sickness and injury.

"Which guys?" Lorne asked Orinn.

"Kravchenko."

"Bah—what, did he break a nail?"

"Broke his rib."

"Who says?"

"They says."

Lorne asked his usual two reporters, the man and the woman, about it.

"Broke two ribs," said the woman, adjusting her square-rimmed glasses. "What do you think about that?"

"I think it must've hurt."

A third reporter, standing behind the familiar duo, uttered a little bark, a laugh. He had only started attending scrums the week before.

"What's that?" said Lorne, looking at the new man.

"Oh nothing, nothing—nothing at all."

"How'd he do it?" Lorne asked the reporter with the glasses. "Break his ribs?"

"Kravchenko? He didn't say."

"Funny a guy never stops talking about himself would suddenly stop talking about himself just after he talked about himself."

"This is all off the record, guys," said Orinn, standing away from the group, near the lamp, with his arms crossed.

The square-framed glasses shimmered in his direction.

"Lorny didn't say it was off the record."

"Did you ask him?"

"Lorny—was that on the record, or off? It sounds like it was on."

Lorne set his hands on his hips.

"Hell, okay, fine. Off."

"You should say so *before*hand," said the third reporter.

After the trio left, Lorne turned to Orinn.

"Who was that guy?"

"Just another cluck," said Orinn.

"Is he lord and master of the record?"

.

In the middle of December, Kravchenko had slipped on mop water on the back stairwell of Tower 2 of the Macdonald Plaza and rolled down half a flight of steps, cracking two ribs and breaking his left wrist. After having a custodian fix him with tensor bandages, he worked his full shift in the ducts, passing out twice from the pain.

Morena developed shingles on his arms, which made it almost impossible for him to grip anything. Dulka—The

Duke—played out the final weeks of the season half-blind, apparently having gotten a sliver of metal caught under an eyelid. Aquino looked "ragged." Another cleaner or two were seen to be limping or stiff-backed. One quietly retired, or at least no longer showed up for work, and was replaced. A gladiator mythos was springing up around the cleaners: they were an unbreakable bunch, and nothing could stop them from getting the job done. Police officers, firefighters—even soldiers—took days off when they were hurt. To the public, if a cleaner did not show up for a shift, he was probably within pinching range of death.

Yet nobody reported on the constellation of scars on Lorne's chest or the burns he received on his finger from the toaster or the ache that had appeared in his right shoulder. He plugged away and bore his minor hurts without complaint and won the race by the usual wide margin.

A phenom, they called him, *the Michael Jordan of the ducts*.

But Kravchenko—he was a *warrior*.

"Christ," Lorne said. "I don't know why these guys don't just go to the doctor and keep their damn mouths shut about it."

Morena, the Jumbo Data Building's cleaner, gave his scrums in a hallway on the ground floor, near the men's washroom. While he was shorter than all of the reporters, his hair always stood straight up after a shift, making him appear taller than he was.

Regardless of the weather, he appeared for the scrums in shorts and a baseball jersey that had belonged to his father.

"What's tonight's take?"

"Four."

"How were the ducts?"

"Ducts are good."

"Two's a bit low for a Thursday. You got four last Thursday. Are you finding fewer rats?"

"I'm just doing the best I can," said Morena, bumping one fist onto the other. "I'm keeping my nose to the grindstone. All in, every corner. I'm just keeping at it."

"Aquino got eight tonight."

"He's a great cleaner. I'm just keeping at it, all in. Checking every corner. All I can do is all I can do."

Aquino's scrums were livelier because his post-shift ritual included swilling two cans of beer.

"Morena's good," he told his reporters, sitting against a painted brick wall outside a boiler room of the Front Street Blocks. "Morena's okay. Good cleaner. I like Morena."

"How are you feeling?"

"I'm feeling the best ever."

"How were the rats tonight? Sticky?"

"Sticky. Sticky fellows."

Kravchenko was fond of answering questions with parables. In the early days this quirk delighted journalists, but as the stories got longer and more abstruse, few of the assembled stuck around for the moral. Kravchenko made some of the tales up as he went along.

People who spotted Kravchenko on the street were always surprised at how small he was. It was the same with every other cleaner: as more and more attention was given to their exploits in the ducts, the more the contrast deepened between their size in the public mind and the amount of space they took up on a bus seat.

CHAPTER THIRTY-FOUR

To whom it may concern

Jerry told me I should write this out and it would get to the right hands. So here I am. I dont expect much will come of it as our family has suffered blow after blow after blow after blow after blow after

Lorne was able to make out the script, but he was so irritated by these opening lines that he pretended he could not. Cricket, already in her parka and ballcap, standing over Lorne and his TV tray with the eggs and bacon and olives, took the note and read it rapidly through. Random phrases escaped her lips, as if some sprite were playing with a volume knob just inside her mouth:

"...'Just a terrible terrible year'... stocks, something about stocks... raccoons, I think—raccoons in the eaves? I think it's raccoons... okay... okay, a grandpa died, then a grandma, I think... now here, it looks like—I think someone got cut from a baseball team... okay, yeah, they got cut from the ball team but they were 'clearly the better catcher'... it goes on and on like this, Lorny...

"Now it says the son, I guess, I *think* it's the son—son is sick, has been sick for months... 'broken-hearted,' it says... but—okay, Lorny, here it is, it's talking about you... you're his favourite. Whose favourite? I guess the son's? Yes, here it is—" Cricket's lips did not move but her jaw worked from one side to the other as she devoured the next five or six lines. "—okay, I think—I *think* what he's saying is his son's been sick for a while and has been following you in the news. You're his favourite cleaner... he writes stories about the two of you catching rats in the ducts. He wants to be a cleaner... His father says, 'He wouldn't last two seconds, but it's all he wants to do.'"

"Sounds like a maniac," said Lorne.

Cricket zipped through the rest of the letter, then folded it over and dropped it on the TV tray.

"He wants to meet you."

"Who?"

"The kid. The son."

"Oh, Christ. What's he got?"

Cricket scanned the letter again.

"It doesn't say. It sounds serious, though."

"AIDS, probably. Christ."

A Sunday afternoon, a fresh, gleaming blanket of snow; it had been ages since Lorne had seen such whiteness, as the snow along his own street was always ash-coloured from salt and mud. As the car rolled to a stop, the cab driver let out a whistle.

"They better tip you well, Lorny," he said. "Looks like money ain't the most of their problems."

"Doesn't look like a place for dying kids," said Lorne.

The cabbie peered up through his windshield at stone and gleaming gables.

"If I could pick," he said, "I'd probably want to die here, too."

Before Lorne had finished knocking at the front door, a man in a blue sweater vest hauled him inside by the arm. He seemed to have been talking before Lorne arrived:

"—just leave those boots there yes okay thank you... bag, yes, bring the bag, bring it all in, he's... not to make too much noise, we step light if we can because... daughter, *this is him, this is him*, wave to her, just wave, she won't bother you... oh! Sorry, watch it, did I do that? I always... oh, darn it, sorry, my wife trips on the stairs too... always quiet, just quieter please... around here... found it all where it used to be, if you can believe that—"

At the end of a long, squeaking hallway on the second floor, the man—still pulling Lorne by the arm—finally came to a halt. He placed a finger over his lips and opened a door so slowly that Lorne thought it must be rigged with explosives. They entered a room whose blinds were half-drawn, and what sunlight was on hand stretched halfway up a twin bed, halfway up a pair of legs.

The man, the father, dug his nails into Lorne's arm.

"Sweetie—"

The father's voice was soft, tentative.

"Sweeeetie—"

"Enh—"

His silver hair twinkling in the fresh light of the bedroom, the father gestured at Lorne to advance.

"Sweeeeetie—I have a wonderful surprise for yooouuuu..."

The bedroom was kitted out like that of any boy's, with a vivid orange colour to the walls, a laundry hamper topped by a basketball hoop, closet doors folded open, and a badly painted homemade bed that was, Lorne guessed, supposed to resemble a boat, or maybe a race car. A figure with long legs sat on the bed, its back cushioned at the headboard by three or four thick pillows. Everything on the bed was orange: pillows, sheet, coverlet, and patient. Yes, the patient: he was in a pair of coarse orange coveralls. His legs reached nearly to the end of the mattress. When the patient turned his head, Lorne saw a beard that dropped almost to the patient's chest.

"Sweetie," said the father. "Swee-tie—"

"Oh—what?"

"How are you feeling—"

The sick boy's—sick man's—face had dragged past his father's and now rested on Lorne's. For an interminable time the patient stared at Lorne through languid, bloodshot eyes.

"Hi," said Lorne. "Nice to meet you—"

An astonishing change took place in the man on the bed. His mouth opened wider than Lorne thought a human mouth could, and a deep blush stood out on the cheeks above the beard.

"Holy Christ," the patient croaked. "Holy *shit*—"

"*Language*, Sweetie—"

"Holy f—holy—holy—!"

The man's stockinged feet bounced up and down on the mattress. He did not smile—he was too stunned—but the unmistakable light of ecstasy suffused his features.

"Ah—how's it going?" said Lorne.

Sweetie glanced at his father and then at Lorne, understanding that something extraordinary was happening but not able to manage it all in his mind. His coveralls were nearly identical in hue and make to those Lorne wore in the ducts. A coincidence, Lorne thought, until a minute later he spotted the sewn-on breast patch that read L. LORCH. For a second or two, Lorne wondered whether the man on the bed had stolen his uniform.

"Oh, that," said the father, stationing himself by the foot of the bed. "It was a Christmas present—he wanted one just like yours."

The patient beamed up at Lorne.

"Just like yours," he said, fiddling with the name patch. "Is it like yours? I mean *just* like yours—"

"Sweetie, we've been over this—"

"I want to know it's just like his!"

The father made a mute appeal to Lorne.

"Oh—yah," said Lorne. "It's just like mine."

The patient threw his arms up and howled with pleasure. Then:

"Do you have a number?"

"What?"

"Do you guys wear numbers?"

"Where?"

"At work. In the HVAC or wherever."

"Ah—no, we don't."

"They should, shouldn't they, Sweetie?" said the father, dropping his hands into his vest pockets. "What number do you think our guest should take?"

The patient's brow contracted.

"I don't know... I guess something high, but not... something below a hundred, but not—oh! Hey—how about ninety-nine!"

"That's pretty good," said the father. "But I can think of one better."

"Really?"

"Really."

"What is it? Eighty-eight?"

"No."

"Sixty-six?"

"I'll give you a hint about the number. It's a low one."

"Nine?"

"A low *one*," repeated the father.

Lorne felt as though he had been thrust into the middle of a badminton game without being given a racket. He could now sense the presence of other people in the room, but could not take his eyes or ears off the exchange between Sweetie and the father.

"A good, low *one*," said the father. "A low—"

"Oh," said Sweetie finally. "Oh! OH! ONE!"

"Yes—!"

"ONE! NUMBER ONE!"

The patient, despite his sickliness, had a strident, window-rattling voice.

"Okay, Sweetie, okay, don't excite yourself," said the father.

"Yes, yes, bring it down, dear—"

That was someone else, a sister, behind Lorne.

"Number one! That's it! Number ONE—!"

A chair was whisked beside the bed and Lorne was whisked into it. The father raised the blinds another foot and the winter afternoon light streamed over the patient's features. Lorne noticed that Sweetie's coveralls were made of a thinner fabric than his own, and were definitely not authentic; they would not have lasted a week in the ducts. But he did not say so.

"I brought you a couple of things," said Lorne. "Orinn gave 'em to me—"

The patient quaked.

"Orinn—!"

"You know Orinn?"

"Yeah—he's your coach, right?"

"Eh?"

"Your foreman," said the father.

"Oh. Yep."

"I know *all* those guys," said Sweetie. "One time I saw Kravchenko's foreman, Salter, at the peelers—"

"Listen to Mr. Lorch, Sweetie."

Lorne unzipped the duffle bag and drew out a pair of shoulder lamps for the sick man to add to his coveralls, a pad of Sprill Building stationery, and a picture of Lorne from a post-shift scrum, which Lorne had autographed in the car on the way over—

"Your signature is sick," the patient said, admiring the photo.

Lorne ignored the remark, since he believed it to be an insult.

"How about some pics, guys?" said a voice. It was the female reporter with the square glasses. Lorne did not recognize her at first because she was not standing in a basement bathed in purple light.

"Pictures!" said the father, sweeping around the bed. "Yes, let's have some pictures, if Mr. Lorch is okay with it."

"Oh—sure."

Mobile phones filmed and photographed Lorne and Sweetie and the father and the sister—the sister wore a wedding ring, but looked as though she lived in the house with her parents and sick brother—and one or two other people who buzzed into the frame. Sweetie talked nonstop. He asked the cleaner to take him through a typical day, asked whether he followed the stats, told Lorne he had read everything ever written about him.

"That's great," said Lorne. "Thanks."

Once the photos were finished, the chatter in the room died down. The reporter nodded at Lorne.

"Well, Swee—well, son," Lorne said, stirring his hand inside the duffle, "I guess I got one other thing here for you."

"You do?"

As if he were alone in the room and had discovered something of interest only to himself, Lorne pulled from the bag a small purple-grey disc with jagged edges. A thrill rippled through the group in the bedroom. Someone gasped. The female reporter assumed Lorne was making a show of it, because he held the rat up to the light and turned it around like some baroque sommelier. Yet he was doing so only because he discovered he had taken a different one from the pail two nights ago than he meant to; he remembered them all, every last one, by shape, texture, and size.

"This here," said Lorne, to Sweetie, "I'm really not supposed to do this, so don't you tell anybody—"

Sweetie was enthralled. The questions tumbled out of him like marbles down a staircase—where did he get it? Which floor? Was it a hard one? What colour was it when it was alive? Lorne told him that it was one of the bastards he peeled on Friday, a group of real sons of bitches.

"Oh, wow!" said Sweetie, holding the rat aloft. "Wow—"

He was out of bed now and bouncing like a child, dancing around with his new treasure, while his father and sister and another woman who may have been his mother but was possibly also a neighbour hopped around with him, trying to cajole him back into bed. A scent of baby powder filled the room and Lorne thought he saw motes of it in the sunbeam that invaded the window. He noticed that Sweetie's coveralls were a size too tight, just as his were a size too large.

"Oh, wow, wow," Sweetie said, breathless, allowing himself to be pushed back on top of his coverlet. He wriggled back into a sitting position, still clutching the rat, his knuckles white. "Wow, wow, wow, I've never *never* seen one of these things..."

And Sweetie rambled rat-a-tat about how nothing on earth would ever beat getting his very own ice rat. He said he might never get married or win the lottery or have sexual congress with a woman and he would still die a happy man.

"Okay," said Lorne.

Part 3

Chapter Thirty-five

After more than a decade of perfect attendance, Lorne's streak came to an end. He did not break any bones like Kravchenko, or contract food poisoning like Aquino, or get hit by a bus, or staple his hand to a wall. He woke up at five o'clock in the afternoon on a Thursday and the walls and dresser were fooling around. He thought it was because he had overslept by twenty minutes, and so the daylight seeping under the blind was twenty minutes older. In any case, the room was moving. Lorne lay with his eyes open and the room was twisting back and forth. When he got to his feet, the twisting got worse.

Crick, he yelled. *Crick! Something's wrong with the damn dresser*

Cricket had just arrived home from a wild day at Lou's framing store. The maid of honour for an upcoming wedding needed fifty garlands of flowers framed in a variety of shapes; they were to form letters spelling out *Congrats Adriana and Giacommo* (the groom's name, in fact, was spelled with only one *m*, and the maid deliberately misspelled it because Giacomo had made a pass at her at the stag and doe). By the time she finished the job, which took most of the day, Cricket's cheek and hands and sweatshirt and baseball cap were stained with pollen dust. Her face was still yellow when she came bucking up the stairs to answer her husband.

"The room's moving," Lorne told her. He was wearing a pair of grey long underwear that had served as his pajamas since high school.

"What's that, Lorny?"

"The room's moving. Spinning."

He spread his arms to each side as if reaching for some invisible support. He was not incensed or afraid, only annoyed at the conduct of the walls.

"Sit back down," said Cricket.

"How'm I supposed to when everything's going 'round?"

Cricket helped him onto the mattress.

"I need a new bed," he said.

"Yes, you do," said Cricket, shoving him onto the pillow more roughly than she meant to. "Tell me what you see."

"The room's moving. Whirling."

"Did you hit your head?"

"Christ, I hit my head every night in the ducts."

"You should write it down."

"Write what down?"

"If you get hurt at work, you need to document it. I dropped a flower pot on my toe last year and I had to write a phone book before Lou'd let me get some ice. Lawsuits."

"Oh, that's all for lawyers and shit. I'm fine."

"But you said the room's spinning!"

"*Yes*, the room's spinning, and my bed's spinning, and I need to use the shitter and I damn well need a new bed—"

The couple referred to the little bedroom—it had probably been used for appalling purposes by earlier tenants—as Lorne's, and the bed as Lorne's, and everything else as Lorne's. In the morning Cricket shut Lorne's blinds and opened Lorne's closet. This was habit, rather than household policy. Lorne accepted that all of these things were as much Cricket's as they were his. He had inherited this tendency from his father; Mr. Lorch went out of his way to claim everything that lay in the house or on the property at any given time. That included anything his children bought for themselves with job money, so long as they lived under his roof.

"I'm worried you're hitting your head too much," said Cricket.

"Bah! I been hitting my head for years."

"But the room wasn't spinning for years, either, Lorny."

As his head sank further down, the wings of the pillow folded around his ears in a fleecy embrace. The pillow cover was pistachio green except for the blot of brown where his hair and cheeks had stained the fabric. He closed his eyes.

"Can you feel the room spinning now?"

"No, it's—just kind of waving."

"Waving?"

"Like we're on a boat."

"How many fingers am I holding up?"

"I don't care. Fifteen."

Over the phone, a doctor diagnosed Lorne with a mild concussion.

"Tell him to take a couple days and not watch TV," the doctor told Cricket. "And nothing else—no phones, computers, anything."

"He doesn't have a computer. *Or* a phone."

"Yes, yes, exactly! That's the idea."

Lorne missed two days of work. The superintendent managed to pull two custodians from another building who had occasionally gone into the ducts when needed. They did not do a great job, but they each brought in a couple of rats, enough to keep the building out of danger. Orinn cancelled the post-shift scrum on the first night; on the second, he forgot to give the same order, and twice the usual number of reporters showed up.

"Is something wrong with Lorny?"

"No."

"Is Lorny here?"

Orinn struggled to flatten his mouth. "Why don't you guys write about something important?"

"This *is* important."

"People have a right to know!"

The super himself, in a polo the colour of a fire engine—he sported bright polos all year long—slipped into the room and was in front of the reporters almost before they noticed.

"I've just received word," he began, enunciating as if he were speaking to a huddle of nursing home residents, "that Lorne Lorch will be absent from work today."

"No shit," whispered someone in back.

"Where was he yesterday?"

"Absent."

Because of the nocturnal nature of the work, the assembled journalists spent a moment discussing whether "yesterday" meant "today."

"Two shifts—he missed two shifts," said the super. "But he'll be back tomorrow. Tomorrow, yes. Upper-body injury, nothing serious."

"How serious is the upper-body injury? And whereabouts on his head is the upper-body injury?"

"The injury isn't serious. And all we can say is it's upper-body."

"But it's above the neck—in the headal region? Can you confirm that?"

"I can't confirm that."

"Can you confirm that the headal region is above the neck?"

Chortles. Orinn tried to frown, but the corners of his mouth would not co-operate.

"I can confirm that on *most people* the head is above the neck."

"Good, good," said the reporter, pretending to scribble furiously, as if the phone in his hand was a notebook. It was the same reporter, Folknall, who had scolded Lorne about the importance of clarifying what was and was not off the record. He was older than the others, stocky, and wore a five o'clock shadow that looked groomed. Though he could not have said why, Orinn guessed that the man had once been much fatter.

It was early in the season—very early; after three seasons, three full years, people had come around and knew not to panic. Nobody placed bets on what they read and saw in January, because there was no future in shorting a horse that had barely left the gate. Yet something astonishing was afoot: Lorne was not leading the scoring race. He was third, behind Dulka and Kravchenko, with Aquino only a couple of rats behind him.

On Lorne's first scrum back after his upper-body injury, a reporter asked him whether he was "concerned" about his position in the standings, and whether a couple of days here and there might not jeopardize his drive to become the first four-time winner of the Cleaners Cup.

"The what?"

"The Cleaners Cup. It's—"

"Oh, Christ," said Lorne, "I don't care about any of that. All I'm doing is peeling those little bastards from the ducts."

"How's your upper-body injury?"

"It's great."

"How upper is it?"

"I don't know," said Lorne.

Most of the questions that week were about Lorne's injury and whether he was disturbed or exasperated or horrified that he was not leading the scoring race this late into the season. One of the newspapers took the "I don't care about the Cleaners Cup" quote and framed an op-ed around it. Those words, per the editorial, were those of an admirable human being, a hero in our midst whose only aim was to serve the commonweal and protect his fellow citizens. Lorne was compared to everyone from George Washington to Cincinnatus to Batman.

Lorne would catch up, and win the Cup a fourth time.

At a hardware store, Lorne was on his way to the cashier with a tube of caulking when a man with a big checked parka and big checked smile recognized him. Big fan, he said, *big* fan; what a pleasure, my kids'll never believe this, I won't even ask for a picture, Lorny, I know you're a busy man, *busy* man. The way the man waved his arms about, the way he stood too close, Lorne expected at every moment to be folded into the man's embrace. No autograph, no picture, the man did not want anything. But before he released Lorne—*I'll let you on your way, Lorny*—he said:

Now—no more sick days, Lorny, okay? I got you, but Kravchenko's nipping at your heels.

The following week a woman pushing a carriage with sleeping twins told Lorne he needed to be at work *every day*. Lorne was about to defend himself to the woman, but she looked as though she had not slept in a week.

CHAPTER THIRTY-SIX

A winter festival; little golden snowflakes in the sunshine. Children were playing hockey on an outdoor rink, mostly boys and a few girls, the girls a little older than the boys. It was cold and bright. A tall man leaned over the boards in the corner, shielding his eyes from the sky. He had, without anyone's asking, assumed the role of referee. Now and then he snapped out a call—*Hey! Hey! That's a trip... Hey! Watch that rough stuff, there... she don't have the puck, you can't block her, that's interference y'know...* The children ignored him, though he timed the penalties on his watch and banged his palm on the inside of the boards when the two minutes had expired.

Ice sculptures stood all around a square: horsemen, teddy bears, a large mobile phone, the Parliament Buildings, a Porsche, a three-headed dragon, and others, all somewhat limp and humped from a thaw the day before. The horseman's sword was a wet noodle; the teddy bear's legs had all but vanished, as if the bear were sinking into a bog. Bunting and streams of flags stretched from corner to corner. An overcaffeinated voice on a public-address system was calling egg-and-spoon races.

Cricket brought Lorne to the event because she needed to be outside and see people and because she knew he loved fresh maple candy. He made a big fuss all the way there and told her he hated sweets and that there were two million better things he could be doing with his time. Yet he put on his nice hat and buttoned his coat up and rode the bus with her to the festival, picking at bits of down that had escaped her parka and fallen on her jeans.

All types of sweet things were burning in the square, filling the air with sheets of cinnamon and molasses and brown sugar. Lorne's nostrils caught the scents and he skipped ahead like a horse that had jumped the traces. Cricket was in line at the candy apple wagon when Lorne came bounding towards her with a chunk of khaki-coloured fudge in his hand the size of a shoe.

"Don't bother with that garbage," he said, gesturing at a nearby child who was lapping the syrup off an apple. "You can have some of this."

"I want a candy apple," said Cricket.

"This is better."

"No way it's better."

"Jesus Christ, you're hopeless."

He wandered off with his fudge. Stray flecks of snow landed on his treat and he immediately bit them off. He never licked anything, even ice cream. *Licking* was for infants and old women. Men did not lick; they bit, and bit hard.

Hey!

He ambled through the square, adjusting his wool cap and gnawing at his fudge.

See that? Did you see that guy? That's

Trades—a couple of men near the egg races were talking trades. Aquino for Dulka, straight up—was that nonsense? Or genius? What about Lorch for *both* Aquino and Dulka? This was a common thing now, not so much in the newspapers as on social media: hypotheticals, scenarios where Lorch and one of the other cleaners swapped buildings. Lorch for those two *and* Kravchenko? Lorch *and* Kravchenko for the rest of the top five? And prospects—there were *prospects*, now, creeping into the wider discussion. Thiam, the Sir Cooper Mauldin Plaza cleaner, had dropped out of the top ten and did not look like he would make it back; a young janitor at the Sir Cooper was showing promise, a boy with narrow shoulders who could roll himself into a ball the size of a turkey. Apparently he had already been in the ducts, serving as Thiam's understudy and (though Thiam was probably too dim to realize it) probable successor. And then Kravchenko had brought a kid from his training camp into the ducts at Tower 2 one night, to show the lad the ropes, give him a taste of the big time. *Scantland*, he told reporters, *you remember this name*. Scantland went into the ducts with Kravchenko and slipped around him and ahead, collected all but one rat, and finished an hour quicker than his teacher...

The two men near the egg race were jawing about trades and prospects as Lorne whisked past in his twenty-dollar hat and buttoned-up jacket, and they were already primed for it—

Hey!

That was Lorchy!

Heads snapped up around the square.

Yo—see who that *was?*

Cricket, too; the hardcore among them knew her almost as well as they knew Lorne. The young man who handed her the candy apple, dressed in a straw hat and 1890s moustache, whispered: *I'd give you this for free, Mrs. Lorch, if my boss wasn't looking.*

People were startled at how much taller she was than her spouse.

Hi fellas

Hey there guy!

The kids in the hockey game, swooping around the rink like herons, called to one another without giving up the chase—

That's Lorny Lorch guys!

Is that The Torch?

Hey Mr. Lorch hey!

Boys were now following him through the trampled-down snow, paying him compliments, patting him on the back. *You're my favourite cleaner by FAR. You're the best in the world. Yeah Mr. Lorch yeah!*

Hi boys. Nice to see ya.

Lorne was finally figuring out how to speak to the public. Less was more, which suited him well. They asked how many rats he caught the night before, and were any of them big suckers or were they all little suckers. A lad with a crooked mouth strolled along holding Lorne by the belt, as if he had adopted the man as his guardian and would go wherever the belt led him. And as Lorne walked through the festival, Cricket was at his side, though separated from her husband by a little body or two. She lost her candy apple holding the hands of two of Lorne's admirers, one of them nearly an adult. *Hey there Lorny great work you rock there guy*. Every ten feet brought a fresh spray of flattery, and snow fell and twinkled in the shifting sunlight of the afternoon. Cricket caught her husband smiling. *We better go*, she thought. *He won't be able to hold that for long...*

Doubling back now, following their leader, Lorne's little army streamed past the hockey rink. The game was half alive and half dead, with some of the players skirmishing for the puck and others gawking or leaning over the boards at the parading spectacle of which Lorne and Cricket formed the nucleus. A shot went wide of the net and plunked against the frozen wood of the boards.

No raising it

THAT'S TWO MINUTES THERE SON

At the near boards stood—wobbled—a little tow-headed boy about six or seven. Lorne must have noticed him long before any of the others did. The mass of boys and girls and a few man-children drifted towards the rink, towards the edge of the red line, where the tow-headed boy was resting a shoulder against the boards.

Oh—Lorny, don't—

Lorne scooped up a mound of grainy snow and dumped it over the little boy's head.

A roar went up. The boy, who had not seen Lorne's approach, staggered on his skates, dropping his stick, and clutched at the top of the boards. He blinked up at Lorne through a tiny avalanche of still-tumbling snow, shock flickering in his eyes. Cricket, too late, grabbed Lorne's sleeve.

Lorne winked at the boy.

"Nice hat, son," he said.

A second roar, this time of laughter: the boy recognized his assailant. He seemed to grow taller and wider, like some lowly creature that had burrowed its way up out of the earth and was now blinking into the sun. For a moment, the enraptured boy and his idol were alone in the universe. The bigger lads whacked the boy on the back and tousled his hat with their big rough gloves and grinned in his face with their ugly breath. And while they mobbed the wobbly little boy, he scrubbed the snow from his face and looked at its dregs on his mittens as if the flakes were made of silver.

Nice one, Lorny, ha!
You gave it to that kid, hey?
Cute, cute—I love it!
That little bastard sure got his!

Cricket's arm did not leave Lorne's, even as he scrawled out autographs in his gorgeous hand and the fudge on his knuckles stained everything he signed. People said it was a beautiful thing, this knight who toiled all night in unimaginable places so that the city would not turn to ice as it slept—it was beautiful to see him and his spouse strolling about a winter festival, arm-in-arm, just like a couple of regular folks. The self-appointed referee, the tall man in the corner, was laughing and pounding the boards and telling the tow-headed boy he needed to keep his head up.

CHAPTER THIRTY-SEVEN

The superintendents, under pressure from the media and elements of the public, floated alternative points systems for cleaning. Bigger rats could be worth more than smaller. Those caught later in the night, when the cleaners were wearier, might bring a bonus. Such changes would require more oversight, perhaps a governing body, maybe even referees.

"Where would the refs go?" Orinn asked his superintendent, who was wearing a sapphire-coloured polo shirt.

"The basement. Or maybe in the ducts."

"In the ducts?"

"Yes."

"So you'd pay somebody to crawl around behind Lorne all night, with what—with a pen and paper?"

The super shook his head.

"It'd be the governing body paying them. They couldn't be on the building payrolls. It'd look bad."

Orinn was playing with a tape measure, drawing the tape out a couple of feet and letting it rattle and hiss back into its case.

"You know what I think?" he told the super.

"What?"

"I think this is just a way for the other guys to pick up points on Lorny."

Before getting to the night's take in the vents, the reporter with the square glasses wanted to know:

"Did you throw a snowball in a kid's face?"

Lorne squinted at her—not just with his eyes, but with his head, shoulders, and body.

"What?"

"Someone said you threw snowballs at a little boy."

"Who said that?"

"I got texts from people."

"I never threw a snowball at no kid. Who told you that?" Lorne asked.

"A couple people," said her colleague, the male reporter, who had shaved his wispy beard.

After making the rounds on social media, the tale had found its way into *City Throb* magazine. The author of an article had it "on good authority" that Lorne had dumped snow on a toddler's head, and wrote that *This writer has no idea what would possess an adult mammal like Lorne Lorch to pick on a small child. There must be—this writer hopes there is—an explanation that hasn't made itself explicit.*

"I don't like to ask, Lorny," said the reporter with the square glasses. "I know you wouldn't do something like that without a good reason."

"Do what without a good reason?"

"Throw a snowball at a little kid."

"How far away were you when you threw it?"

"What was the texture—hard? Powdery? Did it crumble, or—"

"Obviously hard," said another reporter. "You can't throw a powdery snowball hard enough to give *anyone* a black eye, let alone a three-year-old."

"Oh, come *on*," said Orinn, standing at the back, his rictus-like smile pulled tight. "The kid was way older than *three*."

"How about it, Lorny?"

"Did you mean to give him a shiner, Lorne-o?"

Lorne was shaking his head and with each question his head shook faster and faster until his hair was flying out at the temples.

"I never threw no snowball," he said. "And for Christ's sake, he wasn't a *baby*—"

"So how old was he?"

"Oh hell—I don't know. Ten? Eight?"

"Did he have a moustache?"

This was from Folknall.

"Yah," said Lorne, "and it was thicker than yours."

"Lorny, are you saying you didn't throw the snowball?"

"That's what I'm saying."

"But how'd the kid get the black eye?"

"I never saw a black eye. All I did was dump a bit of snow on him. I was fooling around, for crying out loud. Jesus *Murphy*..."

"Those guys," Lorne said to Orinn after the scrum, as he reefed the knot of his tie into place. "Have you ever heard so much horseshit?"

"I know you didn't hit the kid on purpose, Lorny. I told the super."

Lorne stopped.

"The super?"

"He asked me about it."

"Well—Jesus."

Lorne threw on his jacket. It was a cold morning, but he did not button it up.

"It wasn't like what those clucks said. I just dropped some snow on his head."

Kravchenko was asked about it at one of his own scrums.

"I like Lorny. I like him a lot, you know? But you know what—you know what—Lorny knows where the ice goes, and it goes in the bucket"—here Kravchenko nudged the wooden chest at his feet that held his rat corpses—"not in a kid's face."

Cricket had read the story in *City Throb* about the episode but did not tell Lorne about it. She spent most of the next week lodging anonymous complaints to social media companies whose users had shared inaccurate or exaggerated versions of the incident.

This user, she wrote about one blogger, *must be expelled from your platform for telling lies, or face legal action. This isn't a joke. You will face a class-action lawsuit.*

She received a swift response:

I'm sorry I'm not responsible for the content on the site I'm just the webmaster sorry

What are you master of then? Cricket asked.

Sorry if you have a comment about functionality or design I'd be happy to assist

She posted comments accusing other cleaners and their foremen of cheating, their superintendents of crooked activity. When asked by users whether she meant cheating in terms of "miscounting rats" or "committing adultery," she said it was at least one and probably the other.

On the first of February Aquino was ten rats ahead in the race, and Kravchenko and Lorne were tied. Oddsmakers knew Aquino's lead was vanishingly small and would not hold. By the end of that month Lorne would take the lead and keep it. That was no surprise. Except to the most fervent partisans of the other two cleaners, it was folly to think anyone could keep pace with Lorne over 365 days. Kravchenko and Aquino, and Morena, and Dulka the Duke, and the scrubs who filled the rest of the field, they sometimes missed rats, sometimes spent hours on rats that had no intention of coming loose, sometimes showed up for work drunk or hungry. They could be clumsy.

Dulka, after six years of plying the same ducts at the Westerfeldt Insurance Building, sometimes got lost in them; once he fell through a vent onto a conference table, stupefying a knot of forensic accountants who were pulling an all-nighter on a client's latest bankruptcy.

CHAPTER THIRTY-EIGHT

"Lorny—phone."

"Bring it here."

"It's the land line."

Lorne could not remember the last time he had used the hump-backed telephone that sat on the kitchen windowsill. For years it had hung by the kitchen door, but at some point the fixture had come loose, and Lorne never bothered reattaching it.

Cricket left the receiver on its side, so it was facing Lorne as he entered the kitchen. As if the phone saw him coming, a scratchy noise—actually a nostril exhale from the caller—issued from the speaker.

Lorne took up the receiver.

"Yass?"

"Mr. *Lorch*—?"

Lorne had never heard the voice before, but he somehow recognized it. It was not the accent so much as the emphasis, the careful way the caller uttered Lorne's name.

"Yass."

"This is Mykyta Kravchenko."

"Okay."

A pause, then a low chuckle.

"Do you have a minute?"

"Okay—a minute."

Lorne was bent awkwardly over the table. Kravchenko sighed through his nostrils.

"I hope you don't mind the call," he said.

"Not yet."

Kravchenko chuckled again. Lorne rested his free hand on the table, which tottered under his weight.

"How's your old pinto?" said Kravchenko.

"Eh?"

"Oh—your *bean*, your head."

"It's fine."

"Okay, okay. Good."

Lorne wondered how Kravchenko had learned about that.

"I'm calling," Kravchenko went on, "about the snow."

"What snow?"

"The snowball. The kid."

"Oh, Christ," said Lorne, moaning. "Are you kidding me? You, too—"

"No, no! No, Lorny—"

"I never threw a snowball at a kid. Not since *I* was a kid—"

"Oh, I know. My daughter was there. She saw it, Lorny—she said you were just being a joker."

"I was just playing around, and people who *weren't even there* started to—"

"I know, Lorny, I know. I had the same thing."

"Eh?"

"I got hell for something too. A year ago, at one of my camps. One of the kids was acting like all horse, horsing, horsing around, right? And I say, 'Look, Charles, if you keep it up, I will make you push a dead rat across the basement floor with your nose.' Then this *other* boy, who was even worse than Charles, says, 'I think I could push a dead rat with my nose faster than Charles.' Where they got their ideas! Who said it was a race? But this other boy, the worse boy—the worst boy, Lorny, he really wants to push the rat across the floor with his nose and he says we have to time him. Okay, sure, I time him, right? I time this worst boy with a stopwatch. He's actually fast. The kids are jumping and cheering him, I time him, he does a pretty good job. But some of the parents arrive to pick up their kids, and they see this little pig doing this and they say I run a *concentration* camp, not a *cleaning* camp! Can you believe that?"

"Oh."

"It was in the newspaper I make kids sniff rats and push their noses around. For three weeks. Then it went away. You remember? I told the reporter the kid *asked* to do it, but he said, 'If the kid asked to shoot himself in the head, should I say 'Okay, here's a gun? Here's a bullet—let me load it for you?' It was the pits, Lorny. The pits."

"Okay."

"So what I mean to say is I *feel* you, Lorny."

"Great."

"You never heard about that? It was on the news one night."

"I don't watch the news," said Lorne. "I don't read that stuff. I just do the job."

"Seriously?"

"Seriously. I'd rather be in the ducts than in the damn papers."

"Are you serious with me right now?"

"Yah."

"You *like* the ducts, Lorny?"

"Sure. Why not? Don't you?"

A pause.

"It's a job," said Kravchenko. "It's money. Not much, but money. But hey—there's lots money around, right?"

"If you say so."

"The bookies and all that. Hey, Lorny, I need to quit and go into bookie business, right?"

"Listen, I got to go."

"Oh, sure, sure, Lorny. Say, Lorny—it's nice to see your voice, if you know what I mean."

"Okay."

"And no hard feelings, but I think I win the Cup this year."

"Do you."

"I think I win the Cup," Kravchenko went on, "and no hard feelings, I'm your biggest fan—I think Aquino comes in second. But just by a bit, Lorny. Like by five, six rats. That's just this year. And I tell you a secret: I got a kid coming up who's gonna give you a run for the money *every* year. You should see him, Lorny. But this year *I* win. Not him, me. This year. I like you, Lorny. Okay, Lorny—"

He hung up without saying goodbye.

CHAPTER THIRTY-NINE

Dropped off on a dead, frigid night for his shift, Lorne hustled into the back alley behind the Sprill. The silver-hued light above the door, long burned out, had been replaced. This was a courtesy to Lorne, to protect him from being startled by tail-gating fans.

Still, Lorne jumped when the wall near the door moved. Laird—Cricket's recent correspondent, Lorne's first fan and the only one to brave the night's winds—was standing against the concrete wall.

"Hi there, Lorny," he said.

"Christ—okay—"

Lorne made for the door.

"Oh—wait—"

"What?"

Laird stepped away from the wall. He wore a down-filled overcoat and, despite the lick of the wind, only earmuffs, no hat. His hair was as rumpled as ever.

"I hope you don't mind," he said, "but I have something important to say to you. It's not just me—some of the others have been saying so, and they wanted me to tell you."

Laird ran his hand—gloved, leather—over his cheeks and mouth.

"Just a suggestion," he added.

"What is?"

"Well, we—oh! Wait." Laird reached into the inside of his coat, fished around a moment, and produced a KitKat bar. "This is for you—from all of us."

Lorne did not take the bar.

"I have to get to work."

"Oh—just, you know, Lorny, I just wanted to—this was just what we think... take it or leave it. But we think—*I* think—*I* think—*we* think—"

"Jesus, Mary and Joseph *what*?"

"—well—we think you—you *might* want to—you know—*reverse*."

"Reverse? Reverse what?"

"Oh your—course. Your... oh heck, I don't know what you guys call it, I don't know, I wouldn't know... start at the top, I mean. Start there, and work down."

The silver light above the door somehow made the alley feel even colder than it was. A gust of wind bounced Laird's hair up and down.

"Start at the *top*?" said Lorne. "Why in hell would I do that?"

"Oh, I know! Crazy, right? It's just an idea, Lorny—"

"I start in the basement and I finish in the basement—"

"Oh, I know. It's just—I don't know if you've—well, now, so—so *Aquino*, he's actually—"

"Aquino—!"

The flame touched the powder. Lorne exploded, giving his first and greatest partisan a lecture from cellar to attic. Who said he should change his order of operations? Had any of them ever spent a night in the ducts, any ducts? Had any of them ever peeled a rat with his bare hands? How many Cleaning Cups, or whatever the hell they were called, had any of these jokers ever won?

None, that's who!

Laird took his medicine, nodding or shaking his head where appropriate, holding up his hands in a gesture of surrender, every now and then breaking in with a *Yes Lorny!* or an *I know, Lorny!* Finally, Lorne, having repeated over and over that he by God knew how to do his own by God job, reached for the back door.

He paused.

"If you think you're so smart," he said, turning on Laird, "why don't *you* do it?"

Laird stiffened.

"Do what?"

"Do my job. Clean."

"Why don't *I* do it?"

Lorne swept his hand towards the door.

"Be my guest. You and the rest of 'em."

"Oh, no, no, Lorny—"

"I can bring you in right now. I'll give you a uniform and lights and gloves. You can give it a try and show me how it's done."

Laird's arms hung at his side. He looked like a boy who had missed the school bus.

"I couldn't, Lorny—"

"Why not?"

"Well—I can't."

"Why?"

Laird thrust his palms towards Lorne.

"My hands're too big!" he said, with the trace of a whimper in his voice. "*I'm* too big. You see? Look at them. Look at *me*. I don't fit!"

"You can fit if you try hard enough—"

"No, Lorny. It's like—it's apples and oranges—"

"Apples and watermelons. You can fit a watermelon into the same space you can fit an apple if you squeeze it hard enough."

Laird was in despair.

"I've tried. I've *tried*, Lorny, I wanted—I'm sorry, I keep calling you *Lorny*, Mr. Lorch... The thing is I *can't fit*... I tried in three different buildings, I tried a drainpipe, I tried everywhere. I tried, I really did—"

"Blah, blah, blah. Yah, your hands're big. Then find something else to do, pal. Work with your hands. Get a job, son! *That's* your problem, you have nothing to do. Get a job and no more horseshit."

Laird's hands were still extended towards Lorne. He withdrew them.

"Oh, it's not that," he said. "I do have a job."

"Oh yah? What do you do?"

"I consult."

"You do what?"

"I'm a consultant."

Laird told Lorne the name of the consultancy and was surprised that the cleaner had never heard of it. Lorne asked what a consultant did, and at the end of a long explanation from Laird, he wondered aloud how that all could possibly be worth an office and a paycheque.

"I don't know what to tell you," said Laird, grinning joylessly. "Guess I've fooled them."

For the first time, Lorne noticed the quality of the other man's clothes—the heavy overcoat, the spotless leather gloves, the pants that agreed so well with Laird's fluffy contours. Even the earmuffs, something Lorne had for some reason always associated with poverty, were of a soft, shiny charcoal hue, crisp and sharp enough for parade dress.

"Mr. Lorch—"

"Christ, you don't have to call me *Mister*—"

"But I shouldn't call you 'Lorny.'"

Laird advanced a hand, and the KitKat, bone-hard now in the freezing air, peeked out from his leather glove. Lorne took the bar.

"You don't have to eat it," said Laird. "It's just in case."

"I'll eat it."

"I'm sorry I tried to tell you how to do your job."

"It's fine, I don't give a—"

"But I wouldn't like it if you told me how to consult! I don't *think* sometimes. I really don't. My wife says so. *You think too much about things that don't need thinking*. That's *exactly* what she says. She said it to me last night. You know what, Mr. Lor—Lorny? I'm going to tell the others it's none of their business—*our* business—how you roll in the ducts. Who cares if Aquino's ahead of you? It's not like it's *July*. Or *March*. It's *February*."

"Yah," said Lorne.

"Goddamn it, Lorny, it's *February*!"

"Yah. February!"

"Right, Mr. Lorny?"

"God*damn* it, it's *February*!"

Laird turned and made a deferential show of rapping on the back door for his idol. *I'll never understand these maniacs*, Lorne thought, as a custodian crunched the door open.

He ate the KitKat for dessert, wedged and hovering in a vertical chute near the top of the building. The sweetness of the chocolate in the utter darkness, after the fatty mass of bread and butter, hit his brain like a shot of whiskey.

That's some tasty shit

Still—he wished Laird had not given him the KitKat. Every time the wrapper crinkled in his pocket he thought of the other man—the *consultant*—and he did not want to. When Laird admitted that his hands were too big, his body too big, to fit in the ducts, his expression was exactly the same as Leonidas's on the day the boy lost all respect for Lorne.

CHAPTER FORTY

Lorne shuffled in from work and let himself down onto a kitchen chair. He no longer went straight to the chesterfield and the TV tray; a stop, a slump, at the table was now as much a part of his post-work routine as the eggs and olives he devoured with his short legs spread wide in front of the television. Cricket was already in her parka and the eggs were crackling in the pan.

Lorne had carried the scent of sour frost into the house. Cricket was concentrating on flipping an egg whose yolk had flattened and was beginning to run. It took her a moment to realize that something in the kitchen was different.

Lorne had spoken.

"Sorry, Lorny—what?"

A pause.

"Oh—I said it was a hard one."

Every night was always the same, regardless of how many rats Lorne caught or how awful the weather was or how he was feeling. The night was a night, the job was a job. For him to admit it had been a *hard one*, Cricket knew, was like anyone else saying *I lost three fingers*. He was sitting a little apart from the table, with one palm resting on his thigh. It was the same attitude he took every morning in the same chair at the same time. But now—was it always like this, and Cricket was just now noticing?—he looked like something that could not feed itself, that would starve unless someone was around to open a can of food.

Cricket worked away at the eggs and opened the jar of olives while the sizzling grew more and more violent in the pan. When she carried his plate of dinner-breakfast through the kitchen door into the little dim parlour, Lorne got up and followed her like a dog. She set the plate on the tray, angled the tray so he could slip around it into his spot, and set it up against his belly. He began with the olives, plucking one at a time with his crabbed fingers.

Have a sweet sleep, she told him.

She gently slid a finger along the peeling surface of the tray.

At the end of a morning scrum, the reporter with the square glasses told Lorne she smelled something funny in the building. Lorne usually ignored small talk, and he ignored this comment—until the reporter added:

"It smells *cold* in here."

"I don't smell nothing," said Lorne.

The reporter who formerly wore the wispy beard said he smelled something, too.

"You've all probably caught the cold," Lorne said.

"Ha! 'Caught the cold.' Is that on the record, or off?" said Folknall, grinning from the back of the scrum. Lorne noticed for the first time that Folknall's hair was long, hanging down below his jawline. It made the reporter's head, Lorne reflected, look like a squash.

"I don't care. I can't smell anything."

Lorne was telling the truth. He could not smell anything because he had, without realizing it, caught the cold.

The following evening, when Lorne arrived at the back of the Sprill, the superintendent was standing in the alley. Before Lorne could ask what was going on, the super was marching around to the far side of the building, beckoning him to follow. They entered an alley so narrow that the super had to walk with his torso swivelled to prevent his shoulders from rubbing on the walls. A door was propped open with a broken cinder block. Despite the heavy mucus in his nostrils, as soon as Lorne's nose passed the threshold, it sniffed ice.

It was a Saturday, so the building was mostly vacant. The super brought Lorne to the fifth floor and past the offices of two different businesses, a small accounting firm and a larger analytics company, and then through a series of doors and around a series of corners. As solid as Lorne's spatial awareness was in the ducts, it was quick to desert him in unfamiliar floor space. Had the super suddenly turned and ordered him to double back to the stairwell, he might not have been able to find it.

Lorne was filled with dread. The day was just beginning to fade outside; the Saturday evening traffic five storeys below reached him through the glass like the echo of waves on a distant beach. The super turned a final corner and stood facing what looked like a fountain cut into the stucco wall. For an instant Lorne thought it was rather handsome, an ornament that suited the lighting and the softened hues of the walls on either side. But even as his mind struggled to identify what he was looking at, his stomach contracted. He was not gazing at a fountain. He was gazing at a cataract of ice, vomited from a vent on the wall.

"Jesus Christ. Jesus *Christ*—"

He said the name over and over even though he thought his lips were shut.

"Exactly," said the superintendent.

A small squad in uniforms that looked like hazmat suits were buzzing around the ice. Lorne was transported back to the little weed-choked backyard of his youth, and the well, and the health officers who visited in their strange costumes and poured the strange choking substance down the mouth of the well—the terrifying subterranean nothing in which he had spent so many happy hours.

"We need to shut down for a day or two," the super said.

"Jesus—Jesus—Jesus—"

"It's a safety thing."

"Jesus Christ—"

"So I need to ask—do you think you might've missed anything else in there?"

The question shattered Lorne's trance.

"Eh? What—"

The super was a head taller than Lorne, and the collar of his lime-green polo stood out above the collar of his parka. The man had an utterly expressionless face. But Lorne could tell by the way the super spoke, by the way the words sounded slightly chewed up, that he was displeased.

"I mean if you missed one, or two, or however many—I need to know if you maybe missed more."

"Where's Orinn?"

"He's not here."

"I wanna talk to Orinn."

"Lorny, I need to know if you missed anything."

"I need to talk to Orinn."

Lorne wandered around like a man in a blizzard, asking men or women in white suits what the hell they were doing, what the hell was happening. Getting no answers, he threatened to enter the ducts from the far side of the building and attack the ice-vomit from the rear. The woman leading the rat task force dismissed the idea with a wave of her rubber-gloved hand.

"It's too risky," she said, "and it's too late. We need to spray, and if I need to invoke the Health Act to do it, I'm invoking the Health Act."

The Sprill closed for two days while the task force treated the damage and liquidated the offending rats. The worst part for Lorne was the sight of a trio of gum-chomping HVAC technicians arriving with their idiotic hoses and absurd-looking tools, summoned to help the task force in ways Lorne could not.

CHAPTER FORTY-ONE

When Lorne returned to the job later that week, his cabbie, one of his regulars, greeted him with a sober expression.

"Lorny," he said, drawing away from the curb without so much as glancing in the mirror for oncoming traffic, "you're my favourite cleaner in the whole city, and my wife and kids never shut up about you. My boy wears coveralls to school and gets his ass beat. But Lorny, Lorny, you can't miss things like that. You just can't. It's bad. I hate Kravchenko with every fibre, Lorny. But the guy doesn't mess up."

He went on to tell Lorne that he, the cabbie, had a clean driving record, but that did not mean he was allowed to run over strollers or plow through storefronts because he was having a bad day. Lorne sat in the back seat like a smouldering volcano.

Given how fast news of the incident travelled across the city, and how many people took the liberty of tut-tutting Lorne about it, Cricket found him less irritable than she expected. He went about in a fog, like a man who had been slammed over the head with a frying pan.

At breakfast—dinner—one morning, he blurted out that there could not have been more than three rats, three little rats probably no bigger than the tip of his pinkie finger.

"Oh, Lorny, Lorny," said Cricket, "it wasn't your fault. You had a cold—"

"I know I have a cold. And I'm saying there couldn't have been more than three."

In fact, there had been four rats, but not the "dozens" that had been reported. In any case, it was impossible for the task force to make a tally, because there was so much ice.

Leonidas telephoned his father.

"Well, Dad—ha, ha!—I read about your little Crystal Palace at work."

"It's all a load of bull," Lorne told him.

"What happened?"

Leonidas had been told that the entire building had frozen solid and that giant jagged pieces were flaking off and shattering onto the sidewalks below.

"Where'd you hear that horseshit?" cried Lorne.

"Ha, ha! Don't get upset, Dad. Just giving you the word on the street."

"You should find a street that isn't so stupid."

Cricket, seated on the arm of the chesterfield, jabbed Lorne's arm.

"Ask him how work's going," she whispered.

Lorne ignored her.

"Is the kid all right?" said Leonidas.

"What kid?"

"The snowball kid, the one you clobbered. Is he out of the hospital yet?"

"Jesus, boy—"

Leonidas said he was just repeating what he was hearing at work, and what his girlfriend's friends were telling her. Lorne did not know which fire to put out first: the ice cataract on the fifth floor, the snowball, Leonidas's jackass friends, the girl's jackass friends—

Cricket, eyes goggling, poked Lorne again:

"Did he say he's got a girlfriend?"

Lorne poked her back until she retreated from the chesterfield.

"Nobody went to no hospital, boy. It was nothing, it was less than nothing—"

"Okay, Dad! Ha, ha. It's just one of the meat guys said—"

"Tell the meat guy to stick it up his ass. Tell all the meat guys to stick it all up their asses—all of it!"

Lorne thrust the phone at Cricket and got up and paced in a circle in the tiny parlour. Without thinking, he yanked down the blinds and covered the room in darkness. For a moment, just a moment, he needed to not exist.

Cricket asked Leonidas about his new girlfriend.

Folknall wrote a column about the debacle in *City Throb* that was picked up by the city's major newspaper. He downplayed the severity of what had happened, letting his readers know that they were acting like a bunch of blue-haired grandmothers screaming and jumping up on chairs because a mouse had skittered across the floor. Yet he also wrote that nobody who had even a passing interest in rat-hunting could fail to realize that "the sun is setting" on Lorne's dominance in the Cleaners League.

In the end there was no scene, no reporters. The super spoke to him as if they had already discussed the matter and were meeting now just to make it official. Neither of them even sat down. That was probably because they met in a stairwell. The lighting was terrible, but it was better than that of either the super's office or the basement room with the purple lamp.

As always, he listened, smiling, to what the super was saying. There was no point in arguing. It may not have been fair—the super came close to acknowledging this—but there was no justice in the ducts.

No justice—just ice.

If the super had had his way, he would not have done it. Or, at least, he might have waited a little longer. The man brought many fine qualities to the job and had done so for years. The super telephoned a couple of his favourite reporters to tell them, off the record, that he was losing a good man. He did not say so during the next morning's on-the-record press conference. What he said instead was this:

"Given our recent struggles in the ducts and in interacting with the fanbase, management believes a reset is needed in terms of short- and long-term hunting strategy. With this change, we take full responsibility for our recent performance and expect real results beginning this week. The Sprill Building has a glorious history of success in the Cleaners Cup and we intend to continue that tradition for years to come. We have room for many more championship banners in our atrium, and our fans can look forward to those spaces being filled in the coming years."

While an actual Cleaners Cup was under construction at a trophy store in the city's south end, nobody had manufactured any championship banners.

The important thing was to do something, anything. Too many people had written letters to the newspapers, too much venom had been spilled on social media. Tenants of the building were complaining, demanding renegotiations of their office rental rates. Whether the super liked it or not, whether the owners accepted it, rat-hunting touched all facets of running a commercial building. Something had to be done.

Lorne arrived for work and found himself alone as he pulled on his coveralls and tested the snap-on shoulder lights he never used. A utility belt and an old toque that had always sat on an overturned crate in the corner were gone. Nobody but Lorne would have noticed them missing, would know they belonged to Orinn, who had taken them home after being fired.

CHAPTER FORTY-TWO

It was raining. Lorne had the television on in the little parlour, and as usual had the volume so loud that it could be heard in the street. Leonidas was sprawled on the kitchen floor, trying to make a replica of London Bridge out of erector blocks. The telephone rang. Leonidas was not allowed to answer incoming calls because he always squashed his lips against the speaker, making anything he said unintelligible to whoever was calling. Cricket stepped over him, answered the phone with a singsong "Hel-*looo*?"

The caller spoke for a full thirty seconds before Cricket had a chance to cup the receiver and bellow:

"TELEPHONE, LORNY."

And Leonidas parroted:

"DADDY... TELEPHONE, DADDY."

Lorne trudged into the kitchen and grabbed the phone.

"Yah."

Once again the caller did all of the talking. Lorne barked back:

"Silvio—Silvio—listen—hey *listen*—"

He was startled by three sharp raps behind him, at the storm door. In the next instant a stocky man in jeans and denim shirt stomped inside, letting the door bang shut behind him.

Lorne still held the telephone to his ear.

"Silvio—"

He spoke this both to the telephone and to the man in denim, who stiffened and turned his ear towards the parlour.

"Dammit, Silvio—"

As Lorne slapped the phone onto its cradle, Silvio cupped his hands over his ears and jabbered at Lorne in a low voice, as if it were impossible for him to be heard over the television.

"Christ! Knock it off," said Lorne, storming into the parlour and twisting the TV volume down so hard that Leonidas thought the knob had popped off the panel into his father's hand.

Even with the TV muted, Silvio's hands were still over his ears, and his lips were moving but not making a sound. Leonidas thought the performance hilarious, and laughed into the backs of his hands. He did not want Silvio to see him laughing, because he was afraid of his neighbour. Silvio, for his part, was fond of Leonidas, but his booming, bearish greetings always rang out like gunshots in the boy's ears.

"Silvio, cut that crap—"

Silvio continued miming his argument, gesturing helplessly towards the parlour and the television. The two men stood over Leonidas. Finally Silvio's voice returned, mid-sentence:

"—oh, Holy Mary Mother of *God*, it's a miracle, Lorny—I can *hear* again!"

"Okay, you made your point—"

"... I'm not making a point, Lorny. I'm not joking. My ears hurt. They *hurt*. Look at that—hey, Leo—is my ears bleeding?"

"Oh come off it—"

"I won't. It's rude, Lorny. These walls"—Silvio placed a hand on the drywall just above Leonidas's head—"these walls? Paper. Paper, Lorny. You got paper. I got paper. But I respect my neighbours—"

"I respect *my* neighbours, Silvio, but it's a two-way street—"

"I just *said I* respect my neighbours."

"And I say it's a two-way street—"

Silvio leaned down to Leonidas:

"You believe this guy? You believe your old Pop-Pop? Talk some sense into your old father, Leo, I'm *begging* you—"

"His father already got *plenty* of sense," said Lorne.

"Ha, ha!" said Leonidas. "Ha, ha!"

A sheet of rain battered the door. It seemed a signal, announcing that Silvio's time was up. He grabbed the door handle.

"You're a nice guy, Lorny, but you need to get your hearing checked. Do it for me. Do it for the greater good."

And he was gone, through the hissing storm door, down the steps, around the short, fat fence, running for cover like a man chased by a tiger. His departure was so swift, so immediate, that Lorne hardly had time to register it, let alone offer a rejoinder.

"Boy, he's in some mood today," said Cricket.

"Christ yeah."

All in all, very little harm had been done; Lorne and Silvio drank beer over the back fence as often as they battled over TV noise. But this one was different. In the instant after Silvio had said *You need to get your hearing checked* and absconded through the storm door, Lorne had swallowed. Not just swallowed—he gulped, audibly. His throat was dry, that was all. But he knew that Leo had seen it and heard it. Leo had seen his father gulping.

That damn boy, Lorne reflected, back in the parlour on the chesterfield, peering towards the kitchen door. *Dammit, that damn boy, why'd he have to look just then... why'd I have to eat them damn biscuits make my throat all dry?* He might have asked for a glass of water, but that would have been even worse: it would have been like asking for a bathroom break in the middle of a blitzkrieg. *Damn boy was looking right at me; why couldn't he kept his eyes on his damn blocks.*

Lorne sat and stared at the mute television until Cricket poked her head into the room.

"He didn't say you can't have *any* sound," she said.

"He can go straight to hell," said Lorne. "I'm not doing this for *him.*"

The family ate a late lunch together in front of the television, Cricket and Leonidas wedged into a chair together and sharing a tray, Lorne sprawled on the chesterfield. The father shot glances at his son. Leonidas ate his sandwich without taking his eyes off the television. Lorne played around with the remote control, every now and then raising or lowering the TV volume by a notch or two, watching his son's reactions. While Cricket frowned at Lorne several times, Leonidas never turned his head. It was abnormal, Lorne knew, for someone not to look at the person with the remote control when the person with the remote control was being a jackass. It was suspicious, like someone not flinching after an explosion.

Lorne made similar tests over the next few days, but it was no use. Leonidas acted as if nothing had happened and that he had not noticed Lorne's gulp. It was a very sad and grouchy week for Lorne. The boy had seen his father in a weak moment and Lorne knew he would never catch back up.

Decades later, at Leonidas's wedding reception, an obnoxious uncle of the bride followed Leo around telling him that nobody could join the family unless he pinned him—the uncle—in a wrestling match. The uncle had wrestled in high school, forty years and sixty pounds ago. Leonidas, in a suit and tails, was in a knot of people, including his new wife, Arlen, the best man, a couple of bridesmaids, the mother of the bride, and Lorne. The uncle came pushing his way in.

"C'mere, boy," he said, with a stretched, blotchy smile. "Now I told you once and I'm tell you now—let's get this over with. C'mon, it won't hurt you. I promise your daddy nobody'll hurt—"

"Go *away*," said Arlen, punching the uncle in the back of the neck. Lorne winced at the punch, but the uncle did not.

The uncle then turned to Lorne and said he would never *really* hurt his son and that it was *really* all in good fun, and also that he won a bronze medal (it was actually a white ribbon) at his school's wrestling meet in 1978.

"A medal, eh?" said Leonidas. "Ha, ha! That's terrific."

"Only one guy beat me," said the uncle, "and he won the provincials." The boy who beat the uncle was actually trounced at the regionals and never made it to the provincials.

"Oh."

Leonidas continued humouring the uncle, who alternately prodded and patted his new nephew-in-law. Lorne stood next to his son slurping a beer, the foam of which had already spilled on the cuff of his suit jacket.

"You know what *I* think?" said the uncle at last, flinging an arm around Leonidas. "You know what *I* think?"

"Ha, ha! I sure don't."

"I just say you'n me, we just shake and call it, Leo, boy. Between me and you." The uncle plunked his hand on Leonidas's shoulder and gazed earnestly into his eyes. "Between us, Leo—I actually *paralyzed* a man once. Turned him paraplegic. You think I'm kidding? You ever see the guy walk? You should see the guy walk now? You seen him? Can't walk straight. Years ago and he can't walk right. Totally paralyzed—"

Arlen punched the uncle again, this time in the side of the neck. The uncle seemed to expand, as if he were being filled with air. He kneaded Leo's shoulders and got heavier and heavier and said over and over again how he had paralyzed a boy a long time ago and was afraid of what he could do.

Leo, though slightly tipsy, knew exactly what the situation called for. And he didn't waste a moment. Turning to face the uncle, he made a show of gulping.

It was a grand gulp, and everyone in the group laughed, except for two. One was the uncle, who shook his head as if in disbelief, as if he were hearing his own story for the first time. The other was Lorne. The most famous man at the wedding was sent back to a rainy afternoon and a loud television and a neighbour who would not mind his own business.

That boy, he thought, squeezing his beer glass. *Waits twenty years to stick it to his old man. And on his damn wedding day!*

CHAPTER FORTY-THREE

In the spring after Lorne had taken his third Cleaners Cup—a trophy that was soon to come into actual existence—builders descended on a vacant corner a few blocks south of the Sprill.

They broke ground while the soil was still hard. It was a quiet build, taking over a year and a half to complete. After eight months the frame was already taller than any of the surrounding buildings. Letters to the editor called the building an eyesore and a noise nuisance, and complained that the public had not been suitably consulted before construction began. One man, who sounded about fifty years old, went on the radio to declare that he had recently shared his first kiss in the vacant lot on which the building was being erected, and that it was a shame the kiss was being buried under "billions of tons of concrete."

When completed, the structure was forty-five storeys high, by far the tallest in the core. It was called the Chunce & Chimbly Tower, after the elderly partners who had funded it; however, owing to its gleaming, concave shoulders and a helm-like radio box sitting at its apex, it was swiftly nicknamed Sir Gareth, after an obscure Knight of the Round Table and, less importantly, Mr. Chimbly's late and unknighted brother.

The builders incorporated the most cutting-edge anti-rat measures, including coating the ducts with a film that—as per provincial health officials and the city's task force—would make it "less habitable" for the little bastards, and more difficult for them or anything else to cling to the metal.

For a couple of years the treatments worked. On average, technicians discovered and removed a rat about every three weeks. The rats were small and their bioluminescence washed-out, as if the organisms themselves were malnourished. Provincial and federal officials went into the ducts to take samples. One scientist got lost in the ducts and had to be guided out by a custodian, and another hurt his elbow slipping on the slick metal. Yet because the duct system had been modified and widened for such purposes, not a single individual got stuck.

"I could pitch a tent in there," said one official, crawling out of a vent—a wonderfully large vent, which could be unfastened from either side. "Absolutely gorgeous."

"Any rats?" a colleague asked.

The scientist shook his head and looked almost wistful.

"No," he said. "Not even a fly."

Scantland, Kravchenko's young protégé, was vaguely aware of the construction of the Chunce & Chimbly Tower. One of his friends' older brothers worked at the site setting girders and liked to text photos of himself dangling from the building's edge. A cousin was also part of the electrical team, and complained every time he visited the Scantlands about how slow and stupid the other electricians were.

Now well into his teens, Scantland often posted photographs of himself on a social media platform called Dropcuster. Now and then he ventured an opinion on current events or politics. Such as:

My thoughts and prayers go out to all the Israelies (sic) *and Palestinians*

Or

My heart breaks for the victims of the shooting and their families

Or

It's better to light a candle than scream at the darknss

He would superimpose these comments over photographs of himself, and add a fake background. The backgrounds were boilerplate, taken from the Dropcuster stock, and included a wildebeest-choked African savannah, the planet Jupiter, the House of Commons, and the assassination of Lee Harvey Oswald.

We should all think of the words of Dr. Martin Luthor [sic] *King*

That last message ran over a close-up photograph of Scantland, the text running between his nose and mouth, like a pencilled-on moustache. The background, which he had chosen quite at random, was a building under construction at night, lit up with safety lights, giving it a spooky, spacy quality. The building was, in fact, the Chunce & Chimbly Tower, better known now as Sir Gareth, which a friend's brother helped build and a cousin helped electrify and which Scantland himself would come to know better than almost anyone alive.

Kravchenko cautioned him not to be controversial in his postings:

One race post, one sex post, you say something bad about some retarded kid—that's all the reporters, all anybody wants to talk. You remember Lorne Lorch? Beating up that kid in the snowbank? His foreman got fired.

Okay.

The foreman got fired and never found another. Nobody hires him. He's black.

Black?

Ball. He got blackballed. You don't want to get blackballed ever, kid.

When the first rat was discovered in Sir Gareth, the superintendents—like the owners, a pair of brothers—tried to keep it a secret, but they were unsuccessful. Dozens of people rallied in front of the structure, carrying signs with slogans like *Let the People Decide* and *Humans are Better than Rats*. It was the biggest demonstration at Sir Gareth until the building's final night, two years later.

Lorne and Cricket's son was married and living in a townhome in the eastern suburbs, a slightly larger house than theirs.

Before he permitted the young couple to submit their offer, Lorne inspected the air system, the back shed, and the basement for rats. Leonidas marvelled over how his father could still wriggle into small places, sometimes sideways, sometimes upside down. For Arlen, Leonidas's wife, watching rat-cleaning's first superstar in action was a marvel. She had been a Lorne booster from the early days. When Leonidas, the tall, chuckling pastry man at the grocery where she worked, told her on their third date that Lorne was his father, she thought he was teasing her; she told him he was the meanest person in the whole bakery department. When Lorne met his future daughter-in-law, he was most impressed by her teeth, which were as clean and strong-looking a set as he had ever seen.

Lorne's rat inspection took longer than the actual house inspection, which was conducted by a young man in work boots and phones and pagers. At one point the inspector opened a narrow linen closet door and was peering inside when he heard muttered cursing from somewhere in the ceiling.

"Can you please ask your father to hold his questions till I'm done?"

"He's not my father," said Arlen. "He's my father-in-*law*."

"Please—no more questions."

"Okay, okay, ha, ha! I'll tell him—if I can find him."

A few minutes later Leonidas tracked Lorne's position to the ceiling above the upstairs corridor, just between the main bedroom and bathroom.

"Hey, Dad! The inspector said no comments, ha, ha!"

From behind the stippled ceiling:

"I didn't give him any *comments*, I only—"

"No talking, then. Ha, ha!"

Leonidas heard scratching as his father continued on his way.

Both Lorne and the inspector gave passing grades to the house. Although the inspector was cold to Lorne during the process, once he put his pencil and phones and pagers away he asked for an autograph and photo.

When the couple was alone, Arlen shook her head.

"Your dad's a wolverine," she said.

"Ha, ha! Yep—he's something, all right."

But while only one of Leonidas's eyes worked properly, he noticed things that Arlen did not. However swiftly Lorne moved in ducts or in other small spaces, he seemed to move a little slower outside of them. His hair was paling a little at the temples and a slight paunch had appeared at his middle. Yet it was the ginger way Lorne sat himself down in the foyer, the way he rocked ponderously forward to tie his boots, that made Leonidas want to jump in and tie the laces himself.

Lorne was unimpressed with the Chunce & Chimbly. He would not call it by its proper name or even by its nickname.

"Looks to me," he told Cricket, "like a big ol' glass cock."

On his taxi commute into the core, or his three-minute walk between the taxi and the alley behind the Sprill, Lorne seldom looked up, and usually only to check the sky for weather. Now the upper reaches of Sir Gareth—with towering mirrored shoulders and silver radio cabin—flashed sunshine at him from above. Though it was almost half a kilometre away, it still loomed twice as tall as most of its neighbours. Lorne thought it was unnatural, too much, out of place.

CHAPTER FORTY-FOUR

A city in Uruguay, amused at the brouhaha around *alimañas de hielo* up in Canada, occasionally sent gifts to the cleaners. Lorne had received a beautiful wool cardigan from Montevideo, though it was too big for him; the Uruguayans overestimated the sizes of the men who plied the ducts. Cricket ended up using the cardigan as a pajama top on cold nights.

A couple of Canadian university students were backpacking through Quebrada de los Cuervos National Park when one of them, attempting to leap a creek, sprained his ankle. A family picnicking in the same area brought the pair back to their wide, cool bungalow to feed them and put them up for the night. The students spoke just enough Spanish and the family just enough English for remedial communications between them. During a late dinner the children gaped at the students, having never seen anyone eat so much.

The patriarch's brother, an influential member of the Treinta y Tres city council, paid the students a visit, asking them questions about orders of government in Canada. When the students' civics knowledge proved deficient—they were studying psychology and film, respectively—the councillor quizzed them on climate, hockey, the Royal Canadian Mounted Police, and two or three comedians that the guests were too young to have heard of. The councillor nodded along at each bungling answer. Then he lit up:

"Hey—those guys, you know, those guys in the walls—"

He pointed to the walls and repeated the same in Spanish. A dozen Uruguayans jumped out of their seats or clapped their hands and chattered rapidly, gesturing at the walls and ceilings. The students thought their hosts had gone mad. One of the young Uruguayans, a lean fellow with the beginnings of a moustache, crouched down, waddling about and plucking invisible rats off invisible walls.

"—those guys, you know? They live in the, the, *qué, qué*, the *pared*, the little ices, they chase the little ices—"

The male student, sitting on a couch with his ankle elevated, had lost the thread completely. His companion, though, listening to the musketry of Spanish and English and watching the teen with the moustache scraping at the walls, as last snapped her fingers.

"Cleaners? Like—what's his name—Larry? Lorne?"

"Lorne Lorch," said the male student.

The family exploded with joy.

"Yé, yé, yé, that's the boy! That's the boy! Lorny Lorchy!"

After the excitement Lorne's name had inspired, the male student could hardly admit that he was a fan of Xiong, Morena's young successor in the Jumbo Data Building. But he was able to answer a number of the councillor's questions about the *gran deporte*. The family and the students drank Rocha Tannat wine and ate tortas fritas and stayed up until after midnight talking about ice rats and Lorne Lorch and the Cleaners Cup. The hosts did not seem to tire, except for the children, who fell asleep one by one in strange poses around the floor.

"Eh, now," said the councillor, perched on a footstool and rocking back and forth, "what does it look like?"

"What's what look like?"

"*La Copa*," said the councillor's brother. He stood swaying behind the councillor.

"Whut? Oh—the Cup. He means the Cup. The CLEANERS CUP," said the female student to her boyfriend, as if his grasp of English was as unsteady as his grasp of Spanish. She, without malice, sometimes spoke to him in public as if he were hard of hearing.

"Oh—no," said the male student, "no, it's not a *real* cup—"

"Eh?"

"They just call it that. You know, like... you know how a car racer gets the pole position? But it's not like he gets a *pole*, or something."

"No CUP?"

The others picked up the lamentation:

"NO Cup?"

"Sorry, no," said the student, grimacing.

"NO CUP... no *Copa*, no *Copa*, no, no, no!"

While his family squealed and mourned and said *No Copa No Copa* like people who had lost loved ones at sea, the councillor texted an acquaintance of his, a senior bureaucrat in a larger city that, it so happened, was an unofficial sister city to Lorne's. Sharing the terrible news, he added, *Is there anything you can do? I mean I feel sorry for these poor buggers who don't even get a trophy to kiss.*

Early next afternoon a tiny trophy store a couple of neighbourhoods away from Lorne's house received an urgent call and commission from the office of the *alcalde* in a city in Uruguay. Inside ten minutes—though there would be much back-and-forth and quarrelling over detail in the weeks to come—the shop owner's fifteen-year-old son had sketched out a bowl design.

When the Cup was finally unveiled, Uruguay disowned it. The *alcalde* of the sister city wrote an anonymous online review of the trophy shop, accusing it of shoddy customer service and recommending a competing shop he had discovered in the Yellow Pages. Locally, however, *City Throb* compared the trophy favourably with the Stanley Cup, and Folknall called it "the world's best laurel for one of the world's sketchiest sports." Photos of the gleaming bowl appeared in all of the major newspapers and magazines. A graffiti artist rendered it in silver paint along the back alley of the Sprill, where Lorne passed it every day on his way to work.

While there was no formal presentation of the trophy to Lorne, his name, as repeating champion, was engraved on it several times. The plates on which his name appeared would eventually be removed and a new one added before the debacle of the Summer Regatta a few years later.

After it was pointed out to him the first time, Lorne never again noticed the Cup painting in the back alley of the Sprill.

"What a waste of money," he told Cricket.

"What—the paint?"

"No. The stupid trophy!"

Cricket said she had no idea where the actual Cup was, but that it rightfully belonged on top of their television set. Lorne told her it would make the TV catch fire.

"Well—we need a new TV anyway," she said.

Amazingly, Lorne laughed. Then he coughed, as if his hard little body were punishing him for it. He was soaking his elbows in ice water.

The Cleaners Cup was kept in a glass display at City Hall.

The two brothers who ran the Chunce & Chimbly brought in four cleaners over two years. They made the hires as discreetly as possible. None of the cleaners was or had been a custodian or technician, and none of them turned out to be good at the job.

Given the size of the building and the amount of ductwork to cover, the cleaners often worked staggered shifts. At the time, Sir Gareth was not considered a member of the Cleaners League, and there were no rules against more than one man working the ducts. In spite of the efforts of the cleaners, in spite of as many as three men sweeping the chutes and shafts, the occasional rat managed to bloom. The anti-gel substance coating the metal was useful only—apparently—in preventing clusters of the creatures, not in eliminating them entirely. Instead of patches of three or four rats here and there, singles sprang up several feet apart, like little radioactive footprints.

The rat pandemic of earlier decades had trickled into a minor nuisance in most parts of the world. Across Asia, Europe and North Africa the rats had been mostly eradicated. Only a single rat had been found in all of Oceania, and that was in the 1960s; paleobiologists estimated that the worst outbreak in the region took place in western Australia more than twenty thousand years ago. In some places, the mandates of rat-based task forces were winding down without any plans for extension. The international community was moving towards an era in which it no longer faced the possibility of urban glaciation. A new survey of the outbreak published by a popular science writer appeared in the History section of bookstores, rather than under Science or Current Affairs.

Other leagues and Cleaners Cups had sprung up around the world under a variety of guises. In just as many underworlds, dozens of gamblers were murdered and a multitude received bruised kidneys. As in Lorne's case, doughty or otherwise unlucky souls who went into the ducts sometimes became celebrities. A man in Nairobi took the Kenyan version of the Cup for five consecutive years, and a year after retiring told a news outlet that he had not had to pay for a single meal in all that time. In Indonesia a husband-and-wife team almost singlehandedly eliminated the rats from their village, and now ran the village council.

CHAPTER FORTY-FIVE

As mentioned, Morena, one of Lorne's early competitors, had left the cleaning business. He was replaced by the dynamic young Xióng in the Jumbo Data Building. Xióng was not the first cleaner to have his coveralls custom-made or to wear a number: Kravchenko's aunt had sewn his ugly pea soup-green uniform, and Wilton, a B-division cleaner, wore the number 45 on his shoulders as a tribute to the year of his late mother's birth. Yet Xióng was the first to get any media attention for a tailored uniform and for sporting a number—2—on his back.

Morena was a couple of years younger than Lorne when he retired. In fact, he did not exactly *retire*: he simply left, telling his foreman he did not want to do the job anymore.

But Alf, the foreman told him, *how are you gonna live? Where you gonna work?*

I'll find something, don't worry your pretty little head.

What Morena managed to find, thanks to a senior civil servant who had grown up in Morena's neighbourhood and was a quiet booster of his, was a monthly disability pension for knee problems "developed wholly or in part by activities in HVAC-related work." Morena also—discreetly—took odd carpentry jobs, and made pocket change fashioning terrifying-looking rocking horses.

If he did not gain loads of money in retirement, Morena did gain peace of mind. Two weeks before his announcement, he had read a story about eighteenth-century chimney sweeps in London and their high incidences of testicular cancer. It was the same story Cricket had read years before in a tabloid magazine.

When he read about the cancer, Morena felt his testicles tingling, and was overcome with nausea.

The balls always come first, he told his wife.

By now the Chunce & Chimbly—Sir Gareth—had two cleaners left. One of them quit around the same time as Morena.

The one who remained was six feet tall and weighed almost two hundred pounds, making him a giant in the field. He would never have been able to squeeze himself into the Sprill ducts or most others across the city. Only thirty years old, he had some talent at sniffing out rats, though he carried a dangerous impatience into the ducts. If he spent more than a few minutes on a single rat, he ended up scraping and clawing at it with his gloves and tools until it cracked to pieces. That not only left a mess on the metal, but doubled (per some research, tripled) the likelihood that more would bloom from the particles he left behind. It was like lopping off the stem of a dandelion without pulling up the root.

A couple of times the cleaner—Knarb—missed a rat, sometimes the same one in consecutive shifts. When a foreman reminded him of how perilous this could be to the safety and integrity of the building, Knarb said:

"Yah, and I left the toilet seat up at home, too. I guess I'm supposed to be Mister Perfection 24/7, I guess?"

Around that time, a movement was afoot on social media and in other quarters to have Sir Gareth inducted into the Cleaners League.

"What's that guy," Knarb asked the foremen one night, "Lord? The champ. What's-his-nuts—"

"Lord—?"

"The guy who gets all the rats."

"Oh—Lorch."

"Lorch, that's the clown. Lorch!"

"Yeah, he's—"

"I bet you scrotes ten bucks apiece I'll beat him tonight," said Knarb, pushing past his supervisors and zipping his coveralls up to the middle of his chest. "It's gonna be a bloodbath. Maybe when I'm done in here I'll go over to Lord's building and finish *his* shift for him. Ya-ha-ha—!"

If Knarb had not missed a juicy rat only twenty feet from the entry vent—a rat the foremen smelled as soon as they entered the basement that evening—he might have been allowed to carry on as usual. After all, he did find six rats that night, and the fat one was all that he missed. He had his strengths as a cleaner and could cover a lot of ground, but he was too much of a freight train. The job called for meticulousness, and Knarb lacked anything resembling that quality; he sometimes arrived at work with dental floss still hanging from his teeth.

Scantland turned eighteen and graduated high school. While it had been years since he had picked up a bat or a hockey stick, a dozen colleges and universities had offered him athletic scholarships. His parents opened and read every offer, allowed themselves a moment to dream of what might have been, and discarded them.

Presiding over a series of training camps, Kravchenko was astonished at Scantland's compulsive training, the boy's obsession with finding and peeling every atom of every rat from the ducts. Scantland never gloated; he hardly ever smiled. His compeers learned, as teammates had years earlier, that he was not one for celebrating. In hockey, when he scored goals, he had never thrown his arms in the air or handed out high-fives. Instead, he turned around and hustled back towards centre ice for the faceoff, stick dragging behind as if it could not keep up, his buck teeth set hard, a blank, idiotic look on his face. Compliments were lost on him, as were most attempts at conversation. Some of the campers disliked him because they thought he was a snob. Yet when confronted over his aloofness, he seemed so surprised that it was impossible for an accuser to continue the attack. After a few years he was a ghost at the camps, a prodigy, someone who did what he wanted when he wanted. The other campers knew without being told that he was not to be disturbed.

The foremen did not seek out Kravchenko. They received a text from him at three o'clock one morning:

I heard you looking for help

A few hours later, one of the foremen replied:

Who is this howd you get this number

I have a guy for you.

An interview, or rather an inspection, was set up for later that week in a small boardroom in the Chunce & Chimbly. Kravchenko answered most of the questions the foremen put to Scantland. The young cleaner sat with his legs spread wide, his eye roving about the room, fixing on the vents, giving the air an odd sniff. To the foremen, he looked about fourteen years old, with his overbite, the sandy-blond hair spraying out under his cap, and the way he could not stop his knee from jogging up and down. His cheeks were still studded with pimples, and it was evident that acne scarring would probably mark him for life.

Kravchenko, in a natty shirt and tie, had his pitch prepared:

"He works first week—free," he told the foremen.

"We can't do that."

"Why not?"

"Liability."

"Okay, okay. So—he doesn't work free," said Kravchenko. "But if he's not good—*zip, zoop*—you throw him out."

As he said this, Kravchenko made a strange motion with his fingers, as if zipping a sweater up over his head.

"Zip, zoop?"

"Zip, zoop."

One of the foremen asked whether Scantland had a Social Insurance Number.

"Yes," said Kravchenko. "Yes, he'll get one."

"He's got one or he'll get one?"

"Yessiree, boss."

The following Sunday night, at half past one, Knarb was slinking through one of the wider tunnels on the thirty-seventh floor. He had not found any rats. As he crawled along, peering through the gloom, he felt an unusual vibration, a murmur, in the metal.

What the Christ

He cocked his head to listen, his hair brushing against the overhead wall of the duct. There it was again—far away but clear, as if the metal were whispering. He sat still for a minute or two. The muttering continued.

Knarb was just about to shout, to drum the metal with his hand. But then it hit him:

Oh, shit, the kid. Tonight? That was tonight...

The foremen had told him about a "sweeper," someone who would follow him into the ducts as an assistant, a sort of personal janitor, someone to pick up the litter he dropped behind him as he worked. It suited Knarb fine. Now he could leave apple cores and empty Pepsi cans and sandwich wrappers throughout the two kilometres of ductwork, and they would be gone the next time he passed by.

CHAPTER FORTY-SIX

The Regatta would take place in the middle of August. Lorne's new foreman, Mallard, a man with a honey-coloured beard and a voice that was often too low for Lorne to make out, forgot to tell his cleaner about it.

One of the scrum journalists asked Lorne where he would be cleaning on Regatta Day.

"Here on earth," Lorne told the woman.

Like the rest of the journalists, she was used to comments like this.

"Very funny, Lorny," said the reporter. "You know what I mean."

"Nope."

"The Summer Regatta. You're entered—obviously?"

"Of course he is," said someone else.

Folknall, as always, was somewhere at the back, and Lorne could hear him giggling. *Always laughing*, Lorne thought. *Even when there's nothing to laugh at.*

"Of *course* he's entered," said Mallard, the foreman, sounding offended. "You think there'd be a Regatta without him?"

"What the Christ is the Regatta?" said Lorne.

"Oh, it's a rowing contest, Lorne-o," said Folknall. "I bet you'll be great on the water. You got the look of a master sculler."

And Folknall squatted and mimed vigorous rowing, puffing heavily. When he stopped, it took him a moment to catch his breath.

"Fine," said Lorne. "Don't tell me. No shits given here."

Scantland chose the number 100 because—*well, why not?* There was no rule saying uniform numbers could not have more than two digits. There were no rules about uniform numbers at all.

The chemical coating inside the Chunce & Chimbly ducts, a synthetic designed to make it harder for rats to attach themselves to the metal, also altered the creatures' hue. Instead of the pink-red phosphorescence the cleaners were used to, the gelucelets that appeared in the bowels of Sir Gareth were greenish, like untreated pool water.

Knarb had never hunted rats before, so he did not know the difference. For Scantland, however, it was an adjustment. One morning the young sweeper climbed out of the ducts and, on his way out a back door, smelled ice from a vent on the wall. He had missed one, somewhere. He pulled on his still-damp red-and-black coveralls with the number 100 on the back and crawled back into the guts of the building. It took him three hours to find it: a little flat nickel of a bloom wedged into the corner of the metal at a joint on the fortieth floor. After emerging again, not having ever failed before, the young man sobbed for twenty minutes behind a trash bin in an alley.

During Scantland's first few weeks at work, the duct system had seemed an enormous labyrinth, a corkscrew leading to darker and darker nowheres. Though he never admitted it to Kravchenko, Scantland carried a cell phone with him during his shifts; at certain moments, especially when he could not detect the vibration of Knarb's movements a twisty kilometre away in the darkness, he felt anxious, like a child lost in a department store. Even using a light he often went astray, and once or twice nearly panicked when he thought himself trapped. At these times the discovery of a candy bar wrapper left behind by Knarb—a sign that another human had passed along the same endless tunnel—was like a beacon in the wilderness. After work he sometimes fell asleep in the back seat of the car as his father drove him home. His absence from Dropcuster spurred alarm among his followers, and his DMs were full of comments like *Are you dead* and *Where are you* and *I can help you if you need help.* He spilled a glass of cranberry juice in the kitchen and laughed maniacally until his parents screamed at him to stop. Time away from the ducts went by like a rocket; time at work was interminably long. Once or twice he sat in the ducts with his head between his legs and his eyes closed, pretending that he was somewhere else, someplace in the world with warmth and sunlight and other human beings. One glum morning it struck him that he could not remember the last time he had had an erection.

Yet slowly, as weeks passed into months, the duct system became a little shorter, began to make sense. Scantland started to pinpoint the fertile areas, where rats were more likely to bloom. As in other buildings, other systems, there were dead spaces, where rats almost never appeared; these he could sweep through rapidly, scanning up and down, right and left, without stopping, and in doing so cover twice the space that the older guard ever did—the older guard, who would have found the idea of hurrying through any space at all appalling negligence.

What Lorne and the others would have approved of, however, was Scantland's eschewing of gloves.

In the big boys, Kravchenko had told him, *you don't wear gloves unless you have good, good reason. In my academy, okay, we don't want kids losing fingers. But you don't see hockey players wearing full cages in the NHL, okay? That's sissy stuff.*

Scantland hit his stride after about three months. It was just as well, because Knarb quit around the same time. The foremen were not surprised. They knew Knarb was not a man to hold jobs for long, and it was clear he was getting bored. One morning he emerged without a single rat, telling the attending foreman it was like a "graveyard" in the ducts. Scantland emerged two hours later with a sack clattering with a half dozen hard dead discs.

The following evening, the foreman said to Knarb:

"You didn't find any rats and the kid found six."

"No he didn't."

That was how Knarb handled criticism or controversy: he denied that anything was wrong. This actually worked for him about half the time. He did not state his denials angrily, or sarcastically, as he often stated his opinions or fast-food orders. When he said *No he didn't*, it was as if he were telling you a secret, something he was sharing with you alone, and possibly at a risk to his personal safety. *He never found those six rats. That waitress never sat on my lap. This is not my truck. I found that money. Your sister made that up.*

Knarb peeled parts of two rats, two the night after, and then never showed up for work again. The foremen texted him:

Are you giving your notice

Later that day, a reply from Knarb's phone, written by a girlfriend:

Yeah hes giving his notice. Because he thinks he can make loads of $$$ doing daytime trading because he thinks hes a finance genius and not a godam bum

"I guess we need a cleaner," one foreman said to another.

"Nope. We already got one."

CHAPTER FORTY-SEVEN

After the Regatta, people said—still say—that Lorne was far cannier than he presented in the media, that you could only believe a quarter of what he said. Oh, Lorny, you know, he *tracked* everyone, he knew *everything* about his competitors. He had a whole *team*, they said, probably an operations department, keeping tabs on every other cleaner. *Don't believe that stuff, that hell-if-I-know, I-don't-give-a-rat's-ass-about-it... Lorch is a master politician!...* On one of the blogs, which received so many visits and comments after the Regatta that its server crashed, people started referring to Lorne as Darkheart, the Lord of Darkness, The Evil One, The Evil Lorne Lorch, Lorne the Evil Lorch, and Linn Litch the Rat-Cleaning Bitch.

Lorch the Loser knew his reign was over before we did and he burned his crown rather than hand it over to the rightful heir

My cousin knows Kravchenko personally and he said Lorch went to a training camp five years ago and saw Scantland there and he probably hatched it all right there

Somebody rigged the lottery for him. 100%

Can you imagine somebody being that petty?

Can you just imagine

My kid used to wear Lorch coveralls to school. I just threw them out

I set my coveralls on fire just like Lorch set everything on fire

Flushed em down the shitter and I didnt care how much the plumber cost

Never meet your heroes boys and girls

Couldnt beat a kid! so he burns everything down!!!!11

Unexpectedly, Orinn formed part of the primary broadcast team on Regatta Day. As hordes of people descended on the Chunce & Chimbly at half past four in the morning, his studio partner asked him, on the air, what the hell was happening.

"You know something," he said, his rictus smile brushing against the microphone of his headset, "anything at all. It's Lorny. Anything at all could be happening in there."

A couple of fans, back-alley tailgaters, presented Lorne with a wheel of Parmigiano Reggiano cheese.

"What the Christ is this?" said Lorne, fumbling with the cheese.

"Complimenti of a-Luigi, at a-Piazzo and a-Brothers-a," said one of the fans. Lorne recognized her as Laird's friend, the girl with the long thick ponytail.

"Who?"

"A-Lu*i*gi!"

"What for?"

"For-a Monday night-a!"

Lorne tried to tuck the cheese under his arm.

"Is this a gag?"

Hell, no!" said the other fan, wearing a raincoat despite the clear night sky. "It's for your dozen."

"What dozen?"

Lorne had already forgotten; he was not the sort to dwell on his accomplishments. It was a facet of his personality that the media had explored at length. That equanimity—bordering on indifference—was why, according to his partisans and admirers, he was so consistently great at the job. On the other hand, supporters of other cleaners held that *too much* composure was no great thing, especially for a rat catcher. *You want 'em calm but not too calm*, one columnist wrote, *just like you don't want a bomb defuser or a bullfighter to be too relaxed*. Per this other camp, Aquino and Kravchenko always came in second, yes; but they were far more compelling figures. Sure, an *automaton* like Lorne might endure longer than most other cleaners—but automatons, machines, were not known for innovation, spontaneity. A man who did a job without passion or creativity was less likely to improvise his way out of unfamiliar situations, out of trouble...

"Aquino, you remember, right?" said the first fan, the young woman. "He caught twelve one night, Lorny. Few months ago."

"Twelve what?"

Laughter.

"Well—*bastards*," said the woman. "*Bastards* is what you call them, Mr. Lorch."

A pause.

"Oh—rats?"

"Yeah."

"I never heard that. Aquino got twelve?"

"It was probably a mistake," said the woman. "He never got more than seven, eight before."

"He got nine once," said the second fan, the one in the raincoat.

"Not a chance."

"He did!"

Behind the two fans was another handful, gathered around a portable gas oven and turning over sausages and hamburgers on the grill. Some wore orange coveralls with various numbers on the back; others wore orange T-shirts or waved orange pennants. Lorne found it all a little too orange. And as the two fans argued over Aquino's personal best, the wheel of cheese got heavier in Lorne's arms.

"I don't see where the damn cheese comes in," he said.

"Oh! Right. So—Luigi gave Aquino a wheel of cheese just like that one. For catching twelve rats."

"Compliments of Luigi. He called it a 'dozen-cheese,' or something."

"Well—"

"It's like a hat trick," said the man in the raincoat. "Except you get cheese instead of hats."

Lorne had no idea what to do with the wheel.

"Okay, okay, fine," he said, toting his bulky reward past the tailgaters to the door, ignoring their greetings and back-slaps. "Tell Lucio thanks."

"It's *Luigi*—"

"Okay, fine—"

Scantland wore number 100. Xióng, another youngster, would change his to 969; he had begun with 2, but too many people, including a retired NHL star, told him it was a "brutal" number.

Lou, Cricket's boss at the framing store, said that Lorne needed to choose a number. Lou still dyed her hair blue, but she now wore it in a bob.

"Numbers are the trend," she told Cricket. "That's where the winds are blowing. Lorne doesn't want to be left behind, does he?"

"He doesn't like numbers."

"Why not?"

"I don't know. He thinks they're unlucky. 'Numbers are for saps.'"

"All *I* know is what I read online and what people tell me. And people are saying it's weird."

"Who's saying it's weird?"

"People."

"Who?"

Lou dug around in her apron for her phone before spotting it on the counter, beside three dead tulips that Cricket had been attempting to work into a cedar-trimmed display box. Thumbing her away through a social media site Cricket had never heard of, she positioned the phone in front of her employee's face.

"Just read one or two of these—"

Cricket held the phone inches from her eyes and started running through the comment section with an index finger. To Lou, it looked like Cricket was scrolling without reading; she could not believe a human being could digest text so fast. A shadow appeared on Cricket's face.

"Who—"

Flip

"—are—"

Flip

"—these—"

Flip

"—these—"

She was stuck on *these* for several more flips of the finger—

"—these—these *arse—arse—arse—*"

"Arse—?"

"—arseHOLES—"

"Oh, you can't take those personally, Cricks," said Lou, resting her arms on the counter. "It's just what people are saying about Lorny. I figured you'd want to know."

Cricket monitored all the main blogs, personalities, and sites having anything to do with the Cleaners League. She had missed this one completely. As she surfed around the site and browsed the article titles, she saw that many of the stories had hundreds of comments. One story, titled "The Five Fakest Things About Cleaning," had over a thousand. Other titles were "Russian Scientist Says 'Ice Rats' Are Completely Harmless," "Xióng's Ex-Girlfriend Tells All," and "Half of City Cleaners Born in Other Cities."

"'Aquino: Cleaning Titan, Tax Cheat,'" Cricket read aloud.

"Oh yah," said Lou, still hunched over the counter. "You should read that one. Aquino's a creep. They even call him that—Creepino. I do a lot of research on this. They call Aquino horrible things, racist stuff. Thank God Lorny's white!... Or wait—didn't you say he's part Indian?"

Cricket was scrolling and reading at a frenzied pace. When a customer came into the shop, an elderly man with a box full of rabbits' feet that he wanted mounted on a board like piano keys, Cricket wandered away, into the back, her eyes and finger glued to Lou's phone.

Later that week, Leonidas telephoned his father to tell him he needed to choose a number.

"Ha, ha! Everyone keeps asking me what number you are, Dad."

"Tell them to mind their own damn business."

"That's what I tell them, ha, ha! But they get riled up about it. The guys at work aren't gonna stand for it."

"What guys?"

"The bakery guys. Ha, ha, they give me a hard time!"

"Christ. Do they?"

Leonidas had been discussing the issue with his wife, who was pregnant with their first child. Together, the couple came up with a choice of three numbers, and asked Lorne to choose his favourite.

"Arlen says she's okay with whatever you pick," said Leonidas. "But she wants you to give special consideration to 11."

"Why 11?"

"Ha, ha! It's how long her parents have been married."

"Eleven years?"

"Yeah, ha, ha!"

"How old are they?"

"Oh—God knows."

The other numbers Leonidas submitted were 1 and 360.

"I'll give it some thought, dammit," Lorne told him.

"Ha, ha! That's great, Dad. I'll tell the guys."

A dozen fans milled around the mouth of the alley, a few bouncing on their heels to keep warm. They greeted Lorne with shouts of *There he is! Lorchy the Torchy!* By now he recognized all of them. The little woman with the waist-length ponytail saluted Lorne, military-style, and then cackled into her mittens. A pair of brothers, maybe twins, always in matching toques (one hat threadbare and torn, the other smooth and clean), called out *Lorny old lad!* Someone was cooking bratwursts and elk burgers on a portable gas stove. The smell of meat and beer activated Lorne's salivary glands.

"Hi! Lorny!"

It was Laird, standing just outside the alley. Waving at the cleaner with one hand, he fumbled with something on his shoulder that looked like a small sack of potatoes.

"Oh—yah."

"How's it going?"

"Still alive. Thanks for the KitKat—"

"Oh, it was *nothing*, nothing at all."

Laird's voice sounded smothered. Lorne figured it was from diffidence, since the fans all knew they were not supposed to bother him before a shift.

"How're the rats treating you?" said Laird, almost whispering.

"About the same."

"That's great, great—"

The sack on Laird's shoulder moved, and then moaned.

"What the Christ—"

"Sorry Lorny—give me a minute here—"

Laird bent and then straightened his legs, jiggling his load higher on his shoulder.

"Long day," he said. "I was hoping she'd stay awake to meet you, but it doesn't look like it."

"What *is* that?"

"That? That's my little one," said Laird, giving the sack—his daughter—a pat. All Lorne saw was a bundle of clothing. "A future cleaner! We need more ladies in the ducts, eh, Lorny?"

Lorne moved around the larger man and stared up into a little brown hood. A kitten-like face was squashed sideways against Laird's shoulder, the lips twisted in uneasy sleep.

"How old is it?"

"Two next month," said Laird, and then added, "she."

Smoke from the barbecue spiralled up into the night.

"Hell," he said, "I didn't know you were—"

"Oh yes! My wife's a big fan."

"Really?"

"Really. This—" Laird gestured into the alley, into what Lorne's tailgaters called the Tunnel of Champions "—is where we met."

Before entering the ducts, Scantland, clipped and uniformed, would pace a series of semicircles around his chair, balling and unballing his fists, every so often glancing at the baseball cap on the seat. His breathing would become deeper and his exhalations louder until he was snorting like a bull. Nothing was stranger than hearing those fearsome noises issuing from the skinny slouching kid who, moments earlier, was saying *Hi sir* and *Thank you sir* to the foreman on duty.

After a few more gesticulations, Scantland paced the perimeter of the room, breathing deeply, snorting, and running a hand along the walls.

How's the weather in Vancouver, boy?

What's the news in Timbuktu?

Think I might get a sex change—what do you think of that?

As the boy finished his hand-painting, his breathing became shallower, more rapid. Once these and all other pre-game rites were accomplished, he would stand bolt upright, pluck his cap from the seat, pull it onto his head backwards—

Give 'em hell in there, boy.

At this final boost from the foreman, Scantland would return to earth.

You bet.

CHAPTER FORTY-EIGHT

Every cleaner, from Lorne and Aquino to newcomers like Xióng, had his own particular gait, as it were, in the ducts. Because they worked solo and in the dark, it was impossible for anyone to analyze or contrast how they moved. They were ghosts in the deep.

For example, the public was not aware that Dulka, who had a reputation as a brawler, was by far the most graceful ductman. The Duke was not even aware of this himself. If he ever thought about it, he must have reckoned that all of his counterparts glided through the shafts as smoothly as he did, tumbling silently head-over-bottom, whisking around corners like a prowling fox, rolling eight or ten hours without creaking a single joint in the metalwork.

Aquino was a cross between a fox and a squirrel, scuttling as often as he sailed. Lorne was a turtle—but a relentless one.

Scantland, on the other hand, advanced through the ducts like something from the distant past, like a blind, unhearing creature that operated on naked instinct. After several months inside Sir Gareth he could detect green-tinted rats from dozens of feet away, sometimes even around corners. He was developing, or rather perfecting, his own collection method: in plucking a rat, rather than carefully feeling for one of the subtle flat extensions that Lorne used to gain a purchase and begin a peel, Scantland attacked the organisms with a queer slashing motion of both arms, fast but light, moving first diagonally and then horizontally. As the green luminescence flared in an ecstasy of panic, the slashes became faster and faster. Now and then the young man moaned or chanted, though he did not realize this himself, and was surprised to learn that he could be heard outside the vents. In its last agony, the rat would gleam brightly enough to be seen outside any nearby vent. At that moment, the climax of the operation, Scantland would slump back against the opposite wall of the duct, watching the rat's light fade to black.

By this performance, in some inexplicable way, he was able to wound the rat before peeling it. The wounding made the creature easier to grip, as its limbs all extended at once. After the rat's light had gone out, Scantland had no more trouble prying the thing from the wall than he would peeling the sticker off a banana skin. Kravchenko, initially startled by his protégé's technique, said it was like *a sorcery*, and referred to the process as "my boy's little séance."

After each peel Scantland needed about a minute to recover, like a hockey player returning to the bench after a shift. But as soon as the minute was up he was off again, skittering through the ducts.

When Scantland emerged at the end of his shift, he always had a faraway look in his eyes, as if someone had just shaken him awake. Only when he removed his ball cap did his reverie dissipate. He deposited his catch in a chest, threw on a jacket, and departed. As he walked out, he gave his report verbally to whichever foreman was on duty.

Unlike Lorne and the others, whose minds were on breakfast and chesterfields as soon as they shed their coveralls, Scantland never stopped sniffing for ice.

A few months into his tenure at the Chunce & Chimbly, he was strolling the back corridors towards the exit. A foreman was behind him, scribbling down Scantland's report. Just before turning a corner, the foreman crashed into his charge's back; Scantland had stopped short.

"What is it, boy?" said the foreman, not without irritation, as he picked up his pen from the floor.

"Can you smell that, Blue?"

Scantland referred to the foremen by colour, though the colour did not appear to match any aspect of his bosses' physical or mental appearances. *Blue* was of Sri Lankan descent and wore a black work shirt and army-green pants.

"Smell what?"

Scantland, nose in the air, wheeled in a full clockwise circle, then again counter-clockwise. He thrust his long arm towards the ceiling.

"I got them all," he said to Blue. "I know I did. *All* of them."

"That's great."

"But I still smell them."

"Probably on your fingers."

Scantland gave his hand a twice-over with his nostrils.

"Maybe. Smells more like Doritos, though."

He rolled up his coat sleeve and scratched his wrist. Blue caught a peek of the flesh there. It was red, rashed.

"Everything okay in there?"

Scantland followed the foreman's eye.

"Oh, yeah, sure," he said, rolling the sleeve back another inch and displaying the naked skin. Blue peered more closely. The shaft of a thin black arrow, its head pointing towards Scantland's palm, was visible on the flesh.

"Oh Jesus," said Blue, glancing sideways at the arm. "You even old enough for that?"

"Eighteen," said Scantland.

"How many you got?"

"Just this one."

Rolling his sleeve back down, Scantland beamed at Blue.

"Got it two days ago," he said. "I got ideas for others."

"Okay, great," said Blue. "Why an arrow?"

"Oh, that's private—"

Scantland's head jerked up. He snuffed the air, making a sound like a snorting bull.

"There—right there!—"

Blue ducked, glancing over both shoulders:

"What? Where?"

"Is there an ice machine around here?"

"No."

Scantland stared at a ceiling vent.

"Is there a hockey rink nearby?"

"I told you two days ago, boy—the nearest one's a mile west of here. You need to wash those damn fingers after you work!"

The cleaner took a last couple of whiffs.

"Weird," he said. "Freaky."

"Go smell some gasoline," said the foreman. "Clean out your sinuses."

Blue watched Scantland stroll down the hall and out into the morning sunshine. It occurred to him that the young man, aside from a bit of dirt on his cheeks, looked as fresh at the end of a shift as he did at the beginning.

CHAPTER FORTY-NINE

Months before the Regatta, tickets appeared online on resale sites, and at prices that caught the attention of the mayor's office.

"What're the tickets for?" she asked an advisor. "You can't stick bleachers inside vents."

"You can put them everywhere else," said the advisor.

"Where everywhere?"

"On the street, near the buildings. Rooftops. People are already planning parties."

"I hope they have permits for these parties."

Incidentally, her remark—"I hope they have permits for these parties"—became a long-running catch phrase between the advisor and her friends.

"Me, too," said the advisor.

The Regatta would be a city-wide affair, with several divisions competing throughout the major districts. It was to be something of a carnival, the beginning, it was hoped, of an annual tradition. Private entities, especially the building owners, were organizing the event and taking care of promotion and advertising. The city and province stepped in to regulate ticket prices and betting and, not least of all, party permits.

Fans were already parading the uniform colours of their favourite cleaners. They wore coveralls over their parkas in the street and on Fridays in the office. Two girls got into a fistfight at a high school because each was wearing an Aquino black-and-beige and each accused the other's of being a knockoff. A director at a think tank was reprimanded for arriving at a stakeholder meeting in the red, green and white of Farooqi, a middling cleaner whose freestyle rap videos had won him a wide following online. *Lorch 3:16* signs popped up now and then at hockey games and support meetings.

Once or twice Lorne spotted fans wearing plain orange coveralls, sometimes with LORCH emblazoned over the breast or across the shoulders and some random number—77, 97, 150—down the back.

"I don't get these maniacs," he said to Cricket.

"Oh, you know—it's the same as people who wear hockey sweaters on game days."

"I don't get that either."

"People like to show their support."

"Weird people."

"*You're* weird, Lorny."

A pause.

"Maybe," he said.

And though the process of laughing had never come easy to him, Lorne chuckled.

During breaks at Lou's framing shop, Cricket folded herself over her phone in the stockroom. She would sit slumped in Lou's rolling chair, phone between knees, head bent over the screen. For a time Lou thought Cricket was texting somebody, probably a lover.

In fact her employee was combing the boards of various cleaning blogs and responding to any negative comments about Lorne:

S.O.M. [Sad Old Man] *going to the Big Event this summer gonna be a bloodbath for S.O.M.*

SEEMS TO ME YOU'RE THE SAD ONE. YOU EVER TOUCHED A RAT

Lorch is shit

SEEMS TO ME IF ANYONE'S SHIT IT'S YOU

Tax cheat Philipino [Aquino] *will destroy S.O.M. and all of Commie's* [Kravchenko] *stable*

I WOULDN'T BET ON IT SIR

Screw all of them send them back to their country their wastes of meat the Torch is a joke

YOU'RE A JOKE MY GOOD MAN

ANYONE CAN TALK SMACK FROM BEHIND A KEYBOARD. EVER TRIED WALKING A MILE IN SOMEONE'S SHOES?

HOW MANY RATS DID YOU CATCH IN YOUR LIFE. I DIDN'T THINK SO

She spent her half-hour lunch battling it out on comment boards, and battling it out at other times, between household chores and errands, with a growing list of foes on social media. At one point, she came across a social media account purporting to be Lorne's own. She was going to complain, but the author so well captured her husband's brusque tone and use of "bastard" as a catch-all noun that she thought the profile a fitting tribute, and let it stand.

Lorne's old scientist acquaintance, the woman for whom he had first demonstrated his peeling technique, was retiring from her role as editor-in-chief of a trade journal. She had told her employer she wanted to spend more time with her grandchildren.

"I never heard you talk about grandchildren," one of the junior editors told her.

"I talk about them all the time."

Another editor, passing by, overheard.

"She means *the little shits*," he said.

The junior editor snapped his fingers.

"Ah, okay! I never knew the *little shits* were your grandkids."

"What did you think they were?"

"I don't know."

Her last day in the office was the last day of March, which delivered the year's first thunderstorm in the morning and in the afternoon a spray of sleet. A navy-uniformed courier delivered some documents to her; as she signed the receipt, she noticed a shock of bright orange at the courier's throat.

"What's that?" she asked him. "Is it Happy Hour?"

"What? Oh, this—"

The courier set his scanning device on the desk. He then unzipped his uniform to the waist and pulled it open, Superman-style, from both sides. Underneath the uniform was a full set of imitation Lorch coveralls. They did not have Lorne's name stitched over the breast; instead, a large silhouette of a torch swept diagonally from left shoulder to right hip. The workmanship was abysmal and the torch was peeling off the fabric. Yet the courier's expression was as ardent and steely as if he were displaying an Olympic medal.

"What's that?" said the scientist.

"I'm a Torch guy."

"What's that? A cult?"

"He's the man. Torch is the *man*," said the courier, rezipping.

"If you say so."

"Don't tell me you never heard of the Torch!"

"Which one is the Torch?"

"Lorny Lorch."

A thin light appeared in the scientist's eye.

"Now that you mention it, yes, I *have* heard of the Torch."

The courier grinned, an expression that struck the scientist as artificial, as the man was thrusting out his chin to an unnatural extent. He took up his scanner in one hand. With the other, he rubbed two fingers against his thumb.

"I'm putting fifty bones on Lorchy."

"Huh."

"How many bones're you dropping?"

"Bones?"

He asked her whom she was betting on, and under what system.

"Why would people bet on cleaners?" she said.

"Why would people bet on cleaners? Why do they bet on horses? Or golfers? Little white balls in a casino?"

A several-years-old phone book was among the jetsam the scientist was discarding as she cleaned out her office. After the courier left, on a whim, she looked up Lorne's name, and found his number listed.

Surely, she thought, *he's changed it by now, or removed it from—*

"Yah?"

"Mr. Lorch?"

"Yah."

"*Lorne* Lorch?"

"Yah—"

It was late afternoon, and he had just woken up. His voice sounded older than she expected. It took a couple of tries before she made him understand who she was. But when his memory finally clicked—

"Oh, yah—hey, Doc!"

She asked how he was doing, how he felt, where he stood in the scoring race. *No idea*, he said; *they're not putting 'em out this year.* This was, he had been told, to drum up interest and suspense for the *event* taking place in August, the *big bowling show or whatever.*

"And how're you, Doc?" he said.

"Retiring today."

"Eh?"

"Yep. Packing it in."

"Did they throw you a party or anything?"

"No, I told them not to. But I got a plaque."

"A plaque. Well, shit, a plaque."

"Yes, a plaque."

"Huh."

They talked a little about rats and wells and the early days of the rat pandemic. Lorne snorted hearing again of the rainy afternoon long ago when he dangled from an eavestrough and showed her how to snag an ice rat.

"I thought you broke your back," she said. "Actually, maybe you did."

Lorne snorted again.

"Christ, it hurt—bad," he said. "I couldn't walk right for a month. Lost some feeling in my arm, too. But I don't think I broke it."

"I still don't understand how you can grab those things with your bare hands. It doesn't make sense."

"It does if you know what you're doing."

"Same as you can't put a fire out with your hands."

"I can."

"No, that's nonsense, you—"

"I can! Ask Cricket."

"Who's Cricket?"

"I can put a candle out with my fingers. *And* with my eye!"

"And your fingers haven't all fallen off?"

Lorne examined his digits, wiggling them back and forth. Some had lost their range of motion. A ring finger was stiff. They looked as if each one had been scavenged from a different corpse and stapled to the edges of his palms.

"They're all there," he said. "And they're still good enough. Maybe a little sore sometimes."

"Aren't we all."

The scientist told him that while the rat pandemic was in decline, it was not necessarily over; as far as anyone could tell, it was simply in remission. She compared the situation to the Holocene epoch, a steady state following—and possibly preceding—glaciation.

"That's great," he said. "That's good news, eh?"

"Yes, Lorny," she added. "For you, that's probably good news."

CHAPTER FIFTY

Cricket scrolled and scrolled through her phone with her index finger, at home, on breaks at work, in queues, on the street, in the grocery store. At times she disappeared into the kitchen and shut the folding door to the parlour. The door was made of vinyl and badly needed patching. The thwapping noise it made on being stretched shut reminded Lorne of younger days, when a six-year-old Leonidas pulled it open and closed, saying:

Begin scene!

followed by

End scene!

Holed up in the kitchen with her phone, Cricket typed, furiously, with both thumbs and both index fingers. The motion was very odd, like that of an insect or a crustacean. Sometimes Lorne could hear the tapping from the parlour, and he would shout:

"Jesus H. Christ, are you *texting* or are you *tap dancing* in there?"

In early April, on one of Lorne's rare days off—granted, now and then, after several consecutive days of a zero cull in the ducts—Cricket spent three hours at the kitchen table. She left

Lorne in front of the television in his jeans and a collared half-zip sweater bearing the logo of a city junior hockey team, a gift from the players. He never layered, never wore a T-shirt under his sweaters, and so was always colder than he needed to be. He sat with his arms crossed glowering at the television, as if daring it to entertain him. At lunch Cricket emerged with a ham-and-cheese sandwich and a can of sparkling water; the latter was a recent preference, introduced to Lorne by a reporter.

"Our stomach linings corrode as we age," the reporter told him. "You need to be gentle on it."

"My stomach's fine."

"You can have stomach cancer and feel fine."

"I don't have stomach cancer."

"You could. You could have cancer everywhere without knowing till it's too late."

Something about the slim green can beckoned to Lorne's short stumpy fingers, and he appreciated things that "worked," such as sparkling water, which effervesced, as compared to tap water, which did nothing. Now he drank a can a day, usually after waking up in the afternoon. Whenever Cricket went on a grocery run, he asked her to *get a little more of the bubbly shit.*

He hardly grunted when Cricket placed his lunch in front of him. It was another hour before the folding door shot open and she appeared again to collect his dishes.

"I can take it," he said, bolting forward on the chesterfield. "I can do it—"

"You sit there," she said, grabbing the dishes. "I don't have anything else to do."

But the can and plate sat on the kitchen table beside her as she spent another hour tapping away on her phone. The television droned away on the other side of the folding door. When she finally finished, she closed her eyes and laid her head on the table. Her eyes prickled, as if she had gotten soap in them.

A while later she joined Lorne in the parlour, sitting in her chair a little apart from his. Lorne was watching *The Shawshank Redemption.* Though he disliked the movie, every time it was on

TV he watched it to the end. Cricket sat there for several minutes before he turned to his right and saw her rubbing her eyes. He returned to the movie. The protagonist—"Shawshank or whoever"—was in solitary confinement.

"I hate this part," she said.

An instant later the wild hues of a Golden Age musical shimmered across the screen. Cricket thought the station had changed movies mid-stream, and was about to make a crack about it. Then she saw Lorne's hand on the remote.

"Oh, you didn't have to turn it, Lorny."

"Doesn't matter to me."

"But you don't have to turn it to *this*. Isn't that cop show on you like?"

"Nope. Not till evening."

"You should record it."

"Bah."

Neither Lorne nor Cricket cared much for musicals, but they watched this one until the credits finished rolling.

Later on, when Lorne was asleep, Cricket went to the cellar for a couple of potatoes. When she got there, she discovered that the preserves pantry was shut.

For years one of the pantry doors had been impossible to shut, and always stood ajar, like a dislocated jaw. Cricket had long given up on trying to close it. Lorne told her the cupboard was useless anyway, and not worth the time and expense of repairing it. Yet the cupboard was the only piece of furniture Cricket had salvaged from her parents' puny estate. As a child she used to climb into the bottom space below the shelves, usually empty but for the occasional jar, and read her mother's *Ellery Queen* magazines by flashlight. The inside of the pantry smelled like newspapers and dead peaches and long-ago autumns. She had encouraged a young Leonidas to use the same hiding place, although without the mollifying influence of nostalgia, the cupboard seemed to him a dark, stinky prison. After the boy had grown and moved out, on an idle evening after Lorne had left for work, Cricket made an attempt to fit herself into the cupboard, as she had as a child. She nearly succeeded, but found that she could not bend her neck enough to pack her head in with the rest of her body. It was a great disappointment, missing by an inch or two a trip to the distant past; and a minor disappointment, discovering that she was no longer as flexible as she had once been.

Lorne told her over and over that her parents would have laughed at her for keeping the mouldering old pantry, told her he was surprised their ghosts had not haunted her over it.

"I'd haunt the shit out of you," he said. "Every night. *Throoowwww it awwwaaaayyyyy...*"

"I know."

"I can buy you a new one. You pick it out, I'll buy it. I told you. You don't have to lift a damn finger."

"I know, Lorny."

Now she was down in the cellar and Lorne was asleep and the entire space was different because the pantry door had been shut. For a horrible instant Cricket thought Lorne had taken the old one to the landfill and replaced it without her permission, without her even noticing. But the smell of dead peaches, the pantry's breath, still hung before her in the dusty dark air. The cedar was the same cedar as before.

Lorny—

A musical; another musical had been on the TV while Cricket typed away on her phone in the kitchen. Lorne did not understand the point of musicals and never watched them. But he had put a musical on, and not the Busby Berkeley one he and Cricket watched together. Another musical; he had put on a musical...

... And when she went to gather his dishes, he was sitting in the same position in which she had left him, arms folded, legs out, glaring at the TV. He did not appear to have moved; he hardly looked alive. Yet leaving the musical on and the volume up, he had devoured his lunch, stolen down to the cellar, found the scatter of his tools, and somehow—despite a want of skill—fixed the pantry door. It took him eighteen minutes when he had always given up after five. Not only did he fix the door, but he rearranged the jars of preserves and jams by age and fruit. They stood there before Cricket like a Christmas display. Her lips, then her tongue, went numb.

Lorny—

The name failed, crumbled into atoms behind her teeth.

She never thanked Lorne, because that would only have annoyed him. But the next morning, when he arrived home from work, she had added a slice of toast to his usual eggs-and-olives morning supper. And Lorne had never seen so much jam piled on a single slice in his life.

One of the foremen, Red, asked Scantland how often he hunted. It was a random question, like asking a fighter pilot how close to the ground he could fly.

"Hunt?"

"Rats."

"All night," said Scantland, gesturing at the vent opening from which he had just materialized.

"No—*hunting*, son. *Playing*. You understand?"

"I don't *play*."

"Like Lorch used to do, remember?" said the foreman, scratching and wrinkling the cotton of his shirt. "He used to go down wells, up towers... cisterns, I don't know... toilets? Outhouses? He went everywhere. He found rats *everywhere*."

Scantland had never ducked into a drainage pipe on his way to school, or been sent to the principal's office for creeping around in the janitor's closet, or sniffed for ice in the middle of a eulogy.

"Lorch went looking around for rats?" said Scantland.

"Yep. Still does, I heard."

"Outside the ducts?"

"Yep. Don't you?"

Scantland looked almost surprised, as if he had never considered the idea.

"Nah—not really."

Even on hot days, Scantland wore a light jacket to cover his arms. The foremen, he knew, would tease him, as he had gotten several more tattoos and was working on a sleeve for his right arm. The designs were both Eastern and Western. He had spent hours after work online, browsing tattoo sites and symbols and researching the meanings of various scripts and images. There was a profile of Confucius (though it more closely resembled Mao), a black bear-panda hybrid (whether intentional or not), a yin and yang, Roman numerals relating to important dates in his life, blood-tipped tulips, a political slogan (*Don't tread on me*), and two sugar skulls, one on each bicep.

Kravchenko advised him not to display the tattoos until the sleeve, at least, was finished.

"We get you a shot in a magazine," Kravchenko said, "they'll want you in a tank shirt, top, as soon's they see you have tats. You can't take a shot with half an arm, right?"

"What?"

"Half an arm. Your tats. It's only half."

"Oh."

Scantland deferred to Kravchenko and did not show his tattoos in public. He did post cliffhanger comments on social media, and added photos on his Dropcuster page in which he appeared in an overcoat hugging himself, with a grin and an eye drawn to his covered arms. It was obvious to most of his followers—growing more numerous as word spread of his talents as a cleaner—what he was hiding. Captions like *If these arms could talk* and *A picture tells a thousand words* and *My body is a canvas* were not difficult to riddle out.

CHAPTER FIFTY-ONE

The Westerfeldt Insurance Building, southwest of downtown, was the hub of a complex dominated by art studios and dental clinics. It was one of the stateliest of the Cleaners League buildings. The structure was only a dozen years old and sported a greenhouse on its roof.

Dulka—the Duke—was a long-time ductman who had in younger days worked for a number of construction outfits. He burned too many bridges and spit on too many foremen; at thirty-two, he found himself blacklisted from one end of town to the other. He was forced to take menial work in the Westerfeldt, watering plants and kicking radiators. Nobody ordered him into the ducts. He went in one day on a whim, when the custodian who normally performed the service did not show up for work.

He had a reputation as a rebel, although that was due mainly to scuffles with over-eager fans, ones who stuck their hands in his pockets in the hopes of finding a souvenir rat. With scant remains of hair that he had never attempted to style, his flannel shirts, his pot belly, and his consistent use of the word "youse" during his scrums, he built a fanship among those who thought Lorne too sour and Aquino too pretty and Morena a loose cannon. A bachelor, he was an unlikely heartthrob to certain middle-aged married women who saw him as a more high-spirited version of the men their husbands had become. The letters that cohort of admirers wrote to him tended to be exceptionally graphic. While he liked to play with reporters and hint at the occasional tryst and a distant secret marriage, he was actually a virgin. The only woman he had ever made out with was a former—and at the time retired—high school biology teacher.

Folknall explicitly, and others implicitly, referred to Dulka as a "mid-carder": a talented cleaner who belonged in the League but who would never challenge Lorch or Aquino or Kravchenko for the Cup. Twice Dulka had finished fourth in the scoring race. The year before the Regatta, he came in sixth. Folknall wrote an article calling Dulka "The Duke of the Second Division," which, the writer boasted, had spurred threats from Dulka partisans against the reporter and his magazine.

"I can't control what youse guys say," Dulka told a scrum outside the Westerfeldt. "It's not up to me. I catch all the rats I see. If youse see any I'm missing, well—well—I'd like to know about it—"

Dulka's foreman gave him a vote of confidence and told him the standings, the Cup, everything, was a lot of "horseshit," a favoured term in the cleaning world.

"Yeah—horseshit," Dulka said.

"Lorch wins because his shack is full of rats. This one isn't."

"It's all horseshit."

Fans wrote to share similar sentiments, reminding Dulka that a few years back he was laid up for a week and a half with salmonella and ended up missing third place by only a handful of rats. The Westerfeldt was near a power station, they said, which, they believed, somehow made things harder for him. The energy-efficient layout of the ducts was a nightmare. The public transit he took to work was often delayed. Dulka had a partially club foot, and they reminded him of that, too, writing of it in tragic tones. He was one of the few cleaners who answered his mail, or tried to answer. To most of the letters, he responded simply with:

You bet. Thanks

Behind the scenes, the Westerfeldt super told the foreman that an "adjustment" to the roster might be worth exploring, given that the roster was only one man and had not changed in eleven years. Dulka sensed something was up, and decided to act. In the early months of the Regatta year, from January to March, he stopped eating red meat and drinking beer every day. He took a forty-five-minute walk in the late afternoons, before his shift started. His grocer teased him about his carrots, cucumbers, eggplants, and tomatoes—

"Where's my man's jerky?" the grocer said, gaping at the vegetables in Dulka's basket as if they were so many severed heads. "Where's my man's hamburger? What's all this, what's this orange jerky? What's this green jerky? Where's my jerky jerky?"

Dulka howled at *jerky jerky*.

Water, lots of water, walks, the odd pushup, the odd set of crunches, forcing himself to go to bed hungry—*just an experiment*, he told anyone who noticed. *Attacking the ol' beer gut, since it's always attacking me.* Within nine weeks Dulka was a belt notch smaller. While his *steam*, as he put it, felt about the same, he no longer felt bloated after a meal. His joints ached less. In the ducts he could move farther without tiring, and he recovered a little more quickly after a rest. On the fifteenth of March he weighed himself and was astounded to discover that he had lost twenty-four pounds. He told his brother the news.

"I could lose you fifty pounds of fat," said the brother.

"I know."

"By chopping off your head."

"Sure."

As we already know, the media were not compiling scoring lists that year. The Cleaners Cup would now go to whomever won the Regatta. This change worked in Dulka's favour. For the first time in years, it only mattered that he collected every rat he saw, not how many the other cleaners were peeling. Some days the foreman did not even bother counting Dulka's take.

The list of competitors for the Regatta would not be finalized until May, but it was taken for granted that Dulka would compete with Lorch and the others in the elite Masters Division.

Cricket found out before Lorne did.

"Have you ever met Harley?" she asked him one morning, as he tore into his eggs and olives.

"Who?"

"Dulka. Harley."

"Harley Dulka?"

"From the Westerfeldt."

"Oh," said Lorne, chewing loudly, rescued just in time from irritation. "Yeah. I mean—no. Never met the guy."

While he ate, Lorne was reading the folded-up Vehicles section of the newspaper, even though he had never learned to drive. He looked forward to Wednesdays because it was the only day on which this supplement appeared. The glossy sedans and SUVs tickled him as the shiniest of shiny things.

"You know how I know his first name?" said Cricket.

Lorne shrugged and the newspaper ruckled between his fingers. "Guessed?"

"No. From his mother."

Peering over the top of the newspaper, Lorne saw Cricket bent over her phone. The look on her face was unusual; it was stern and sober, but glowing with a strange light.

"How from his mother?"

"Just read her statement online. Dulka's dead."

"What—!"

Cricket read on.

"No, no, sorry—not dead. Not yet. 'Critically injured.'"

Lorne was up and at her shoulder before the scattered leaves of his newspaper drifted to the parlour floor.

"Fell," Cricket said, reading from her phone. "Slipped down a shaft, fell... four storeys... no, five..."

"Jesus—"

"... coma. Wow, he really—"

"When?" said Lorne.

He was trying to read the text, but Cricket was scrolling too quickly.

"Night before last."

Lorne's mouth hung open.

"Jesus—"

"He's not dead, Lorny. Critically injured."

The tone of Cricket's voice did not match the gravity of the moment.

"It's not funny," said Lorne.

"I never said it was."

For a few minutes the dusty, dim, closed little parlour was silent except for the sound of Lorne's breathing and the whisper of Cricket's finger swiping against the display of her phone. At last:

"How?" Lorne asked. "I mean, Christ, it's not like he's a rookie—"

"He slipped. Lost his grip, they think."

One bend of the Westerfeldt ducts, at the fifteenth floor, led to a forty-one-foot vertical shaft that Dulka could only navigate by shimmying with his shoulders and thighs against the walls. In that way, it was like the long chute at the Sprill where Lorne sometimes ate his bread and butter while puffing out his body against the metal.

Dulka maneuvered up and down this section twice a night, and had done so thousands of times. It posed him no more trouble, indeed no more thought, than a crevasse a mountain man skipped over on his morning rounds. For someone with wide shoulders, it was even less of a challenge. But Dulka was a man who had lost twenty-four pounds, whose shoulders were perhaps a hair slimmer than they had been, and whose overall strength might have dropped accordingly, not by much, but just by enough.

At five past three on a Tuesday morning, one of the night janitors at the Westerfeldt heard what sounded like a "whoosh, like an airplane went past the building." He stopped, listening for an explosion, or for any other excuse to evacuate. But after that initial roar the building was quiet. The custodian proceeded on his way, swishing his mop back and forth, the soles of his shoes occasionally squeaking on the floor. Five minutes, maybe ten minutes later, it struck him that the building was too silent. Something had switched off or gone out. At the end of another five minutes—

"Where's my boy?—"

When he stuck his head into a vent and listened, he could hear from somewhere in that nine hundred and forty metres of ductwork a moaning, almost a mewling, that chilled his blood.

Across the city, at every scrum, reporters asked cleaners what they thought of Dulka's accident, what they thought had happened, and whether they thought the catastrophe would affect their own performance in the ducts. *Do you think you could slip, too? Do you worry about dying?* Lorne tried to be firm, telling his scrummers it would be irresponsible to speculate on such things. But his voice was smaller than usual.

"We're just praying he's okay," he said.

"Are you and Mrs. Lorch religious?"

"What? No."

Lorne told Cricket over and over that it was Dulka's own damned fault. It was every cleaner's duty, he said, to protect himself in the ducts. There were drops, spikes, pieces of jagged metal; you were upside down, backwards, in darkness. Not all men were made for peeling rats, he said. And since cleaning had become a competitive sport, the pressure to work faster and faster had made the vocation much more dangerous.

"Nobody's got your back in the dark," Lorne said to Cricket. "*Jesus* don't go into the ducts with you. It's just you."

In the following days, whenever Cricket mentioned the accident, Lorne silenced her. He did not want to hear about it anymore.

Cricket never told Lorne, but her first thought after reading about Dulka's misfortune was that it would increase Lorne's odds of winning the Regatta. It was not as if she had wished the accident on Dulka. But she *had* heard there was going to be prize money, and their refrigerator was almost twenty years old.

CHAPTER FIFTY-TWO

One of Scantland's two thousand Dropcuster followers dared him to do a shift blindfolded.

Ha ha, Scantland replied. *That would be funny. But it would also be irresponseble I wouldn't ask you to do your job blindfolded*

The follower said:

I am legally blind and I do my job blindfolded every day dude

Whats your job my good sir

I'm an accountant

Scantland was not sure whether to believe the man, but told him he always gave his *people* the benefit of the doubt. After a friendly back-and-forth about the challenges of being a blind man in chartered accountancy, Scantland repeated his assertion that accepting the dare would be irresponsible.

I'll give you $500, the blind accountant wrote.

LOL you're persistent my good sir Ill give you that. But I gotta go. Thanks for the convo everybody

A minute later Scantland sent a direct message to the accountant:

Make it $750 and you got a deal

An hour passed. Then:

$650 Half up front

Scantland texted the accountant back just as he strolled into Sir Gareth for his evening shift.

Okay but I need the 1st 350 dollars in the next 10 mins

The accountant thought Scantland was playing a little in asking for a more than half up front. Scantland was very poor at math. He also had no idea how a blind man could send texts. If the boy had bothered to tell Kravchenko about the exchange, his mentor would have warned him away from what was, in all likelihood, a grifter or some other species of criminal.

Yet the accountant was an accountant, and he was legally blind. Five minutes before "puck drop," as some of the foremen called it, Scantland received a money transfer for $349.99. A moment after stepping into the ducts at the bottom of the Chunce & Chimbly, Scantland tore sections of electrical tape from a roll in his pocket and blacked out his eyes, taking care not to seal his eyebrows. After a few adjustments—his lids struggled against the tape, so he managed to fashion small patches with the non-adhesive sides facing in—he was on his way.

The process was difficult at first, and within ten minutes Scantland wondered whether he had made a mistake. He became disoriented, and once or twice he knocked his head loud enough to make an echo. For twenty minutes he was a rookie again, overwhelmed by the enormity of his arena and its byzantine layout. For a moment he considered giving up and removing his blinds. Squatting on his heels, taking a minute to regroup, he slapped his face with both hands and said *You are not a rookie you can smell and feel and you are better than some stupid old blind man.* He had a year's worth of experience in the guts of this building; he, not a blind accountant, owned these ducts. And almost without realizing it, he was moving again, tripping along in spite of his own caution, his nose and hands his beacons in the darkness. Now and then an old friend appeared: a loose screw he felt and recognized, a wide stretch where he could spread his arms like wings, the sound of a floor buffer whirring beyond a vent whose pilot, a custodian, moved through the building at a clockwork pace. After an hour, when the air conditioning blasted on and Scantland's knees grazed a familiar quarter-sized hole on the eleventh floor, the cleaner observed that he was only five minutes behind his usual clip.

Piece of cake, he said to himself. *Should've asked for more cash.*

Hours later, on his way down, he had a minor scare. His attention drifting for a moment, he swept a hand forward for purchase and it landed into nothingness. Off course by only a few feet, Scantland had nearly dropped head-first into a ten-foot shaft; a fall that, while not fatal, would have been unpalatable.

He sailed through the remaining floors and finished his shift a few minutes early, making sure to remove his blinds before he emerged from the exit vent and met his foreman. He had collected six gelucelets. Only one gave him any trouble, causing a slight burn on the tip of his thumb when he misjudged its position by a millimetre or two.

The experience was so exhilarating that he had to restrain himself from spiking his bag of rats like a football.

The foreman looked horrified.

"What the Christ happened to your *eyes*?"

"Oh—my *eyes*. My *eyes*..."

The skin around them was pink and raw from the tape.

"Yeah, your *eyes*. You got pinkeye?"

"Eh—no—"

"Allergies?"

Scantland dropped his sack.

"Oh, yeah—okay. Allergies."

"Which ones?"

"Oh *every* one."

He dropped the bag of rats and moved towards his leather chair to begin the process of undressing. Seating himself, he stopped, nose in the air.

His brow clouded.

"What?" said the foreman.

"I got everything," Scantland said. "I got every last one. But I can still smell it."

"Jesus, boy, your nose is probably drunk with it. Surprised you can smell anything else."

For a day or so the accountant balked at paying the balance of the bet, asking for proof that Scantland had cleaned the entire ducts blind. A standoff ensued. Scantland shared the problem with a few trusted friends and they advised him he should go straight to the police. It gnawed at him and caused a couple of poor sleeps, even though he was $349.99 richer than before. Kravchenko had always cautioned him about "chiselers" and told him that nobody in your life, not your mother or father or wife or kids, is as nice to you—*at the first*—as a chiseler. Suppose this accountant, presuming he was an accountant, presuming he was blind, started telling people Scantland was a moron? How would that look to Scantland's fans on Dropcuster?

Scantland considered publishing his private text conversation with the accountant on his Dropcuster page. As he was crawling inside Sir Gareth's sternum, mulling these and other recourses, his phone pinged in his breast pocket:

Okay dude, I've talked to some people. They say I should trust you. So I'll send the rest of the money in the morning. Congratulations.

Scantland texted back:

K thx

Word somehow leaked about the bet, and got back to Scantland's mentor. Kravchenko reamed out his protégé, then went to the media and called Scantland a "young ass," though he allowed that the feat had been incredible.

"Don't take any more bets," he ordered Scantland. "Next they tell you, 'Do it in two hours,' or 'Do it without pants,' or 'Do it in a woman's dress.' Don't become performing circus. Don't be a clown for them... never, never, be the clown."

CHAPTER FIFTY-THREE

A month or two before the Regatta, a new face appeared at the back door of the Sprill. At first, Lorne thought the man was "off" somehow, possibly insane. This was because every night the man offered Lorne a sprightly greeting:

"Whutsup, Chiefy?"

"Oh."

That was the first two nights. On the third, the man smacked Lorne on the shoulder like an old friend, and wished him a good night in the ducts.

"Who the hell *is* that guy?" Lorne asked Mallard, the foreman.

"Wills."

"And who the hell is Wills?"

"New guy."

Wills was a little taller than Lorne but about as slim, with a café-au-lait complexion and short black hair. A serial hummer, with a pleasant baritone voice.

Weirdo, Lorne thought.

After Lorne scored twelve rats twice in a month, Luigi stopped sending him wheels of cheese. Luigi sent word that he did not want to burden his *favourite cleaner of all cleaners* with too much cheese. Instead, on days where Lorne or any other cleaner captured a dozen rats, Luigi discounted his Monterey Jack by ten percent.

Lorne noticed that the elbow was out in Cricket's jacket. He wanted to buy her a new one, but he was afraid of picking the wrong style. He called Leo and asked him about it.

"I don't know why you're all worked up about this, Dad," his son told him. "Mom'll love anything you get her. She'll probably wear it to sleep. Ha, ha!"

"I'm not buying her pajamas, I'm buying her a coat."

"Ha, ha! Well, I know she likes turquoise. She told me that once—she said her favourite colour was turquoise. Ha, ha! I had to look it up. Turquoise!"

Lorne asked how to spell *turquoise* and went to a store he knew that sold winter coats. The clerk did not recognize him. When Lorne asked about turquoise jackets, the clerk said turquoise only worked against certain complexions.

"What season is your wife?" she asked Lorne.

"I have no idea what you're talking about."

"Has she ever had a draping?"

The clerk told Lorne he was a bright summer. In fact, he was more of an autumn than a summer. Lorne said he would come back after asking his wife what damn season she was.

In the meantime, he asked Leonidas if he would stitch up his mother's jacket. Leo did, sneaking over to the house on his lunch break, still wearing the double-breasted jacket he wore as a pastry chef at the grocer's.

Wills sometimes stood in the corner of the basement room during scrums, smiling and winking whenever he and Lorne made eye contact.

"Hey Chiefy," he would say to Lorne, after the reporters had filed out. "Beauty in there tonight—beauty."

Lorne's ear caught the barest hint of an accent, but he could not narrow it down to a hemisphere.

"Oh."

"Keepin' 'em down, Chief. Keepin' 'em down. Beauty stuff."

"Okay."

One evening, Wills, after opening the door for Lorne—and also giving a smile and wave to the tailgaters, Lorne's fans, in the alley—proceeded down the corridor with him, then accompanied him through the stairwell door and down into the bowels of the Sprill. He kept a step or two back of Lorne, and as their footsteps rang on the metal stairs, Wills hummed a tune the cleaner identified as a Stevie Wonder but was actually a Jay-Z. When they reached the basement room, Wills continued inside and stood by in the purple light of the lamp. He hummed, milling around, looking at the ceiling and walls while Lorne, keeping an eye on him, dressed for his shift. Mallard drifted in; he and Lorne nodded at each other, but the foreman made no mention of the other man in the room.

At last Lorne, zipped and clipped, approached the black square. He crouched and peered into the darkness. Straightening up again, he backed into something solid.

"Hey—"

He turned, and his shoulder bumped against Wills' chest.

"Oh sorry there, Chief—did you want me to go first—?"

"What?"

Mallard advanced with a grimace, as if he had just watched Lorne spill a bowl of soup.

"Yes, yes, Lorny," he said, "yes, okay, this is okay—"

"What's okay?"

Wills stood by with his palms on his gut.

"This," said Mallard, gesticulating from one man to the other. "This—I forgot to tell you—"

"Tell me *what*?"

"Wills is supposed to shadow you."

"Shadow me *where*?"

Mallard pointed at the black square.

"Oh no—NO—not in a million years," said Lorne, blocking the square with his body, spreading his arms and legs like a starfish. (Mallard and Wills both noticed that one arm did not reach as high as the other, and that getting into this position seemed to cause Lorne some discomfort.) "I don't need a nanny in here to—"

"No, no, Lorny, not a nanny," said Mallard. "This is just Wills—"

"I don't give a shit what you call him, nanny or not—"

"—no, Wills here, he's... no, Lorny, it's not what you think—"

Lorne's eyes fell on Wills.

"It's not what you think, Lorny. He's not here to monitor you. He's there to learn."

"Learn what?"

"How to clean."

"I'm the cleaner here."

"Yes, Lorny, you're the cleaner here." At that moment the grim agony in Mallard's smile reminded Lorne of Orinn's. "You're the cleaner and you'll *be* the cleaner."

"Damn right. Damn *right*. I'm doing it—I'm doing it, I'm gonna be in the tournament—"

"The tourna—oh, yeah, the Regatta. Yeah, Lorny, of course, of *course*, you're our man—"

"I don't need help."

"Nobody said you did."

"I'm going in here by myself."

"Lorny, listen—Wills won't be in the way. I promise, Lorny. He's just there to watch."

"I don't like people watching."

"Lorny, look—you saw what happened, right? You know what just happened to another guy, right? We all know, right?" Lorne's mouth twisted, but he did not respond. "The Westerfeldt's in a shitload—a boatload of shit now, a boat full of *shit*, because they lost their guy, and none of the janitors want to go in the ducts. They think they'll get mangled too. Can you believe that? The guy works twelve, thirteen years, he gets mangled *once*, and now it's an unsafe place?"

Was his own damn fault, Lorne wanted to say.

"... Now, listen, just what if something happened to you? Now, now, Lorny, don't get mad—I'm not saying you'd ever slip or fall, like that shithead Dulka. But suppose something *else* happened? Things happen, Lorny, and it's nobody's fault... a panel gives way, or I don't know... a fire. Or, heck, Lorny, you could get hit by a bus, or a meat truck... hell, an air conditioner could drop out a window..."

Lorne did not believe anything like that could ever happen to him. If it ever did, he said, he would hunt down and murder every HVAC worker in the city.

"At some point you'll need a rest, Lorny. Oh, I don't mean today, or next week, or next month. But you won't be doing this forever. Right? You agree with that much? All the super's saying—"

"The super!"

"—is that maybe it'd be a good idea to take a day or two, once in a while. Just here and there. Give your bones a rest, you know?"

Mallard looked at Wills, who was grinning.

"Like Babe Ruth," Wills said.

"Who?"

"Babe Ruth. Baseball player, big fat guy who hit home runs."

"And you think *you're* Babe Ruth?" said Lorne.

"No, Lorny," said Wills, "you are. I'm just here to be Babe's legs."

Mallard snapped his fingers.

"That's exactly it. Babe's legs."

"I don't know what in the Christ you two are talking about."

Mallard explained how younger players sometimes subbed in for Ruth late in games so he could conserve his energy over a long season.

"They called the subs *Babe's Legs*, or some shit, because they carried Ruth in the—"

"I don't need any *carrying*," Lorne said.

"Nobody said you did, Lorny. But you just ask Babe Ruth about it—he'd tell you it was the greatest thing on earth. Whenever he wanted a break, he just carted his fat ass to the bench and watched the rest of the game. This was the greatest ballplayer ever, Lorny. If he could do it, anyone can."

"Tell me you never wanted to just kick your feet up and let someone else jump in and take care of what was left, Lorny. You just tell me that."

"Christ, I don't know—"

"I won't touch a thing," Wills assured Lorne, resting his hand on his heart.

"You won't even know he's *in* there," said Mallard.

CHAPTER FIFTY-FOUR

Lorne reached his cab at twenty minutes past eight o'clock. The air was already moist and it was going to be what he called a *stinker.* He would probably sleep away the day on the chesterfield in the parlour with the curtains drawn. Besides the cellar, that was the coolest spot in the house.

He found his cab snatched.

Sitting in the back seat, with one leg and buttock hanging out, was a young construction worker. The worker was arguing with the driver, one of Lorne's regulars, a big Egyptian lad who was pursuing an engineering degree in Canada and living with his brother's family. The men mirrored each other, pointing their fingers and jerking their heads in concert, as if they had met ahead of time to choreograph their quarrel. The worker wore his hard hat backwards and it bumped against the ceiling of the car.

"Out, sir, out, I'm sorry out out out—"

"Whyncha drive? You don't have a fare, guy!"

"I told you I have fare, I have fare—"

The cabbie spotted Lorne, and his face lit up.

"—here he is, I told you! I told you! *That* fare. Right there *that* fare—"

Waving through the window at Lorne, the driver made a series of helpless gestures towards the interloper occupying the seat behind him.

"What's happening, Reggie?"

The cabbie's name was not Reggie, but it sounded like Reggie to Lorne, whose pronunciation was always poor when it came to names that were not Anglo-Saxon.

"This sir trying to take your ride for him*self*," said Reggie. "Can you believe that, Big Man? You work all night and this guy steal your ride—"

"I never stole any ride," said the worker. He was wearing a crinkled orange shirt with two bars of yellow reflective tape, and the tape was coming off the fabric at both ends. "You can't *reserve* a *cab*—"

"You *can so* reserve a cab—"

"No, you have to call ahead. That's the rules. Otherwise it's fair game." The worker turned to Lorne. "Did *you* call ahead, guy?"

"Eh?"

The worker repeated his question, miming the shape of a phone by his ear.

"What? No," said Lorne, "I never—"

"Then you never reserved it, guy."

"He *did* reserve it," said Reggie, by now halfway out of the driver's seat. "Don't you know who Big Man is?"

"I don't care if he's Jesus Christ Almighty if he didn't call ahead. Rules are rules!"

"I get sent wait for him two, three times a week. So *some*body reserve. I don't just wait here for fun."

"But *he* didn't reserve. For shit's sakes, nobody around here knows the *rules*—"

At last Reggie ceased arguing and got out of the car, shutting the door and hitching up his pants as if he were about to go for a walk. The construction worker said it made no difference to him, he was already late and already in shit and would sit there all damn day if that was what it took. Both seemed prepared for a lengthy standoff.

"Oh, hell," said Lorne, "it's okay, Reggie. I can grab another one."

Reggie tossed his hands on top of his head.

"No, *no*, Big Man, this is your ride—"

"It's fine, Reg."

The cabbie shook his head as if everything he had ever believed in was coming to an end.

"It's not fair, Big Man!"

"It's okay."

"It's injustice, Big Man, it's the worst injustice of all—"

During this exchange the worker was watching Lorne. He removed his hard hat and craned forward in the seat.

"Ha!"

Reggie and Lorne turned to look at him.

"Oh, Christ," said the worker, "*I* see. *Now* I get it!"

He swung out of the cab, his steel toes plonking on the asphalt. Standing up, adjusting the strap of his hard hat, he glowered at Reggie and Lorne.

"I get it now," he went on. "I get it."

"You got what?" said Reggie.

The worker, hat in hand, made a wide, sweeping bow.

"I didn't realize whose cab I was *stealing*," he said. "Look who it is! It's royalty in disguise! The monkey suit almost fooled me. *Almost*. But you're a duct guy, eh? Holy shits and giggles, it's my lucky day. In you go, sir. Please"—the worker pulled the door wide and gestured towards the seat—"by all means, take my seat. I'm sorry I soiled it, your highness. Please, sir. Please—"

"Blah, blah, blah," said Reggie, drawing open the driver door. "Don't pay no attention, Big Man. He's no class."

"Oh, I'm class," said the worker. "I'm *real* class. I'm the classiest! Please, sir. Please—this is a great honour. Please step on my toe. Kick me in the nuts. It would be the greatest moment of my life. I could get a tattoo on my sack—'Aquino kicked this.'"

"He's not Aquino," said Reggie. "That's Lorne the Torch!"

"My mistake! *I'm* not a torch, so I don't get a cab. I don't even have a home. I thought I was having a bad day because my girlfriend kicked me out and I don't have anywhere to sleep. But God works in mysterious ways... he takes away my girl and my roof but I get the honour of giving up a cab to Mr. Jesus Christ Almighty who works in the furnace—"

Rolling away from the curb a few moments later, Reggie told Lorne not to pay any attention to the worker. "I see that guy around, he's always like that. I was his girl, I'd throw him out every day."

The worker made a teacup-sipping motion at Lorne as the cab doubled past. Peeling back the sleeves of his button-down shirt and loosening his tie, Lorne sighed through his teeth.

"One day," he muttered, "I won't have to wear this damn getup anymore."

In the preceding hours, Lorne had peeled four rats: two on the eleventh floor, one on the fourth, and one on the twentieth. During much of the shift he felt as solitary as he always did. But he was not alone. It was almost irritating; he wanted Wills to bumble and stumble and make a nuisance of himself, so that he could tell Mallard never to let the man in the ducts again. Yet Wills proved as unobtrusive a shadow as a shadow. More than once Lorne glanced over his shoulder and called Wills' name, thinking the new man might have fallen behind, gotten lost:

"Wills—*Wills*—"

"Right here, Chiefy—"

The voice always seemed nearer than it should have.

As Lorne felt and worked and peeled, he sometimes held his breath and listened. Occasionally he made out the sound of Wills' breath at a careful distance. At other times there was no sign that his shadow was nearby. On his descent through the ducts, at around the ninth floor, an odd unease pecked at Lorne as he was wriggling down a narrow shaft:

This is weird. He's weird to be in here

And then:

Am I weird? This is weird. Am I weird

The ducts had never bothered him before. They were his office and his playground. His mission was clear and critical: if he did not crawl through a kilometre-plus of tubes and tunnels every night and clear them of ice rats, the whole building, and the tens of millions of dollars it was worth, could crumble into pieces. There was nothing *weird* about that, about his being there or doing the job.

Yet having another person gliding along behind him in the dark, observing, waiting, looking around, maybe running fingers along the metal for dirt and grease—that was odd, it was *weird.* Nobody in his right mind would crawl through ducts for nothing. Lorne had something. Wills apparently had something, but it did not exist right now, at this moment, and so he had nothing. It was unnatural to be in the ducts without doing anything but looking.

"You still back there?"

"Still here, Chiefy."

At a spot where the duct opened into a joint, Lorne rolled himself up and turned around, so that he was facing the direction from which he had come. About twenty feet away the gloom, so smooth there, wrinkled a little, and then morphed into the shape of a face. Though barely lit by a trickle of light from a faraway grate, Wills' grin was like a half moon in the night sky.

"Scooch up here," said Lorne.

Wills shuffled forward, making much more use of his fingertips and hips than Lorne had expected. *He hasn't lost his shit yet,* Lorne thought. *Not afraid in here. That's good.* At this point in the duct system, the passage was so narrow that all four walls pressed against both men's bodies. Lorne had heard stories about some of the younger cleaners, fresh out of the academies, who, hitting the "streets"—what Lorne called an actual paying duct job—panicked deep inside buildings, found themselves lost, stuck, afraid. On a couple of occasions janitors or off-duty cleaners, or even retired cleaners, had had to enter the ducts and talk the poor buggers out. It was not a job for everyone, and it had occurred to Lorne that it was probably not a place or a job for anyone.

When Wills was within a few feet, Lorne asked him how it was going.

"Glorious, Chiefy."

"Pretty dark, eh?"

"You got it."

Lorne squirmed his hard little shoulders against the walls. The metal rumbled softly.

"*Tight* in here, ain't it?"

Wills squirmed in turn.

"Sure is, Chiefy."

"Sometimes I have trouble breathing in here. You?"

Sniffing deeply, Wills shook his head.

"No problem here, Chiefy."

Wills was smiling at Lorne. Beneath the smile seemed to be another smile, one Lorne could not make out.

"Okay," said Lorne.

He stared into Wills' eyes for several seconds without blinking. Wills stared back.

"You smell that?"

"Smell what?"

"Smell something?"

"No way, Chiefy," said Wills. "It wasn't me."

"You really don't smell anything?"

"Nope."

"You see anything?"

Wills looked left and right, up and down. Then right, left, down and up.

"Just dark, Chiefy."

Lorne told Wills to close his eyes and smell, *really* smell, demonstrating how to clear the nostrils with a snuffing exhalation and then draw in a deep, thick *pile* of air until the lungs pressed against the ribs. Wills mimicked Lorne's technique, then again, then a third time. After each repetition he opened his eyes and stared about. Lorne waited.

At last:

"I don't know, Chief," said Wills. "I smell *some*thing, but I don't know what. Like *metal* but *not metal.*"

Lorne put questions to him: was the smell sharp, or dull? Sweet, or sour? Did it tickle his nose or scrape it? Wills answered as best he could. Lorne gazed at him with an elflike light in his eyes.

"What, Chiefy?"

"Don't you see it?"

"See what?"

Lorne frowned.

"I'm glad you're only here to watch," he said, "because you sure as hell can't see a rat right in front of your face."

"What—you?"

"Eh? *No*, not me—"

Lorne jerked his head towards the wall of the duct, just next to Wills' cheek. A tiny pink glister stood on the metal. The rat was so dull that it took Wills a moment to make it out. When he did, his eyes flared.

"There he is!" he said. "Okay, Chiefy. Okay, good eye—"

Wills stared at the rat as if it were a nugget of gold.

"Pretty neat, eh?" said Lorne.

"Oh, beauty, beauty."

"Little bastard—"

Lorne demonstrated his peeling technique for Wills, alternately talking his shadow through the steps and muttering curses under his breath as he worked the penny-sized rat off the metal. Once he had collected it, he popped it into Wills' hand. Wills flinched, thinking the creature would burn him. Lorne snorted.

"They don't burn you when they're dead," he said.

Wills watched the light draining from the creature.

"I never woulda saw it myself," said Wills.

"They're hard to see if you got *day eyes*," Lorne said. "Takes a while for the eyes to go night-like. That, and a year or two of practice."

"Impressive, Chiefy."

"Impressive, eh?"

"Impressive."

When he found the other three rats, Lorne subjected Wills to the same test of the senses. *The guy is blind*, he thought. *Couldn't see a rat if it was sticking between his teeth*. He started teasing Wills, saying it was a damn shame a man with such a nice-looking nose did not know how to use it. With every new rat and every fresh peeling, his ribbing grew jollier. Taking the last rat of the night, a little after four o'clock in the morning, he told Wills that his homework was to sleep for a week in a meat locker. Wills said he looked forward to it.

When Lorne crawled out of the black square in the basement, Mallard, waiting on Lorne's bench, leaped to his feet.

"Hey—hey! How was it?"

"Fine."

"Where's Wills?"

Lorne glanced back over his shoulder.

"Oh, him? I don't know. Lost him hours ago."

"What!"

"It's every man for himself."

"Lorny, you can't just leave a—"

Just then, Wills pulled himself out of the ducts behind Lorne, grinning.

"Boo!" he said.

"Jesus, guys," said Mallard, his ginger beard bouncing up and down. "Don't never do that. That's not funny."

After the scrum, which Wills observed from a corner before drifting out with the reporters, Mallard asked Lorne for a report.

"Nobody died."

"How'd Wills do?"

"He didn't get stuck."

"He wasn't trouble?"

Lorne shrugged.

"Didn't get stuck."

Privately, however, Lorne thought Wills had done quite well. The man had remained serene even in the tightest, darkest stretches of the ducts. He had kept up but not gotten in the way. And, most important, he had not been a pest. Lorne feared being stuck in the walls with a chatterbox; however, the younger man only spoke when spoken to, and kept his humming to a minimum, even during the deadest hours of the night.

Wills, for his part, was satisfied with his performance. He had been ordered by the superintendent, via Mallard, to do nothing to upset or antagonize Lorne, which is why he pretended he could not see or smell the rats.

CHAPTER FIFTY-FIVE

Lorne arrived home on a rainy April morning and found that Cricket had already left for work. His eggs and olives were ready but getting cold, and his tray was still folded up behind the chesterfield. It took him a minute or two to figure out how to unfold and clip it into position. By the time it was ready, he was so hungry that he ate standing up, holding the plate in one hand and dipping into it with the other.

Much later, when Lorne woke from his daytime slumbers at half past six, he was still alone. He looked up the number of Lou's shop in the phone book, and when he telephoned, Cricket's recorded voice announced that the place was closed. He made himself a pre-shift sandwich out of lunch meat, then prepared a thick slice of bread and butter for his midnight lunch in the ducts.

Cricket had left him a note, but he had not read it; he had wrapped his sandwich in it. When he returned home the next morning, Cricket was there. She told him they needed a lawyer and that Lou knew one, a friend of a cousin. The lawyer—small world!—knew the lawyer of the Vancouver-based party who was threatening legal action against Cricket.

"Jesus H. Christ," said Lorne. "What the hell *legal action* what the hell—?"

The Vancouver lawyer was representing an anti-cleaning blogger, one of the ones Cricket had discovered through Lou. Cricket ascertained that the blogger was co-proprietor of Boiled Ogopogo, a microbrewery specializing in lagers and IPAs. Due to an ice rat outbreak five or six years ago on the microbrewery's premises, the property manager had temporarily employed a cleaner. Unlike Lorne, that cleaner was lazy and delighted in disgusting stories, which in his many idle moments he shared with the microbrewers and other businesses operating within the facility. The brewers grew to despise the cleaner and, thanks to cherry-picked and anecdotal research, the entire cleaning field. Soon our microbrewer was blogging under the name "Peeler of the Rat Peelers" with a signature sign-off, "Hunting the rats who hunt the rats."

The blogger mentioned Lorne now and again in his posts, usually dismissively. As far as he—The Peeler—was concerned, Lorne was just one more huckster in a rabble that included Kravchenko, Aquino, Dulka, a few in Vancouver and other major cities, and a handful of foreigners. That was enough to infuriate Cricket—that Lorne was considered the equal of a chump like Dulka. Cricket posted a couple of nasty anonymous comments and moved on. Then The Peeler wrote a two-thousand-word article about Lorne.

Calling him the most overrated of all cleaners and a man whose skill set disqualified him from every other profession besides "resurrection man," the blogger stated that even in terms of the modest salary that Lorne made—which was higher than that of most of his peers—he was the most overpaid person in human history. The article contained clickable graphs and statistics that were supposed to prove this assertion. Comparing Lorne's income to inflation-adjusted wages of leech collectors, mudlarks, plague gravesmen, whipping boys, and political advisors, The Peeler sketched out a competent argument that Lorne's market value was exaggerated.

Cricket wrote out a long draft email demanding corrections and retractions, and then condensed it, line by line. In the second draft she exhorted The Peeler to remove the offending article and issue an apology. In the third she enjoined the blogger to shut down his blog entirely. The more drafts she composed, and the shorter the email got, the angrier Cricket became.

In the end she did not send the email. She instead posted a single comment on the blog. Rather than add it to the dozens of replies below the article about Lorne, most of which agreed with

The Peeler that Lorne was a fraud and a joke—she would get to those people later, she told herself—she watched and waited for the next new article so she could be the first to comment. Two days later, The Peeler published "Would a Mouse Be a Better Cleaner Than a Cleaner?"

The first comment, from "Babywipes1492," read:

A mouse would be better at ANYTHING then a cleaner

The second, from "AyatollahOfBirdSeed":

No … cleaners would never be able to make their way out of a maze even with cheese at the end

The third, from "Beetle1":

You should go brew some more shit tasting beer Chris. I heard you're not allowed around small children. Not surprised you have it in for people who actually contribute something to society you fat lazy eyed piece of shit

When Cricket visited the blog later that afternoon, she saw that her comment had been deleted. It was obvious, however, from the sixty or seventy comments that followed that it had created a sensation. Whether from discretion or other reasons, neither The Peeler's proper name nor occupation was typically alluded to on the blog or its boards. The comments under Cricket's deleted one were full of speculation about the moderator's identity; one or two people, without realizing it, identified him outright.

What's this about small children?

Satisfied, Cricket deleted her own profile from the site and from a related site under which she employed the same username. *I bet he doesn't write any crap like that anymore!* she thought.

Within three weeks the letter arrived from the lawyer. It accused Cricket of libel and threatened legal action.

Jesus Jesus Jesus, Lorne said. *Jesus Jesus—*

He said *Jesus* for ten minutes, until Cricket warned him that his mother could hear him and that she would have to answer for Jesus on behalf of her son.

During the first phone call with Lou's cousin's friend, a lawyer with noisy nostrils, Cricket expressed astonishment that The Peeler had identified her.

The lawyer laughed.

"It's your IP," he said, over the phone from his office. "You might as well have called yourself 'Cricket Lorch, wife of Lorne Lorch, whom this article is about.'"

"Really?"

"Don't you know about IPs?"

"No, I don't," cried Cricket. "I don't know *anything* about that."

"You found out who *he* was. How'd you do that?"

"Well—well, it wasn't hard—"

Cricket had recently read every story The Peeler had posted over the past three years, including comments, and took note whenever he mentioned anything, however vague, about his personal life. She did not sleep for twenty-eight hours while performing these searches, and Lorne never noticed because his eggs and olives and other meals arrived at his TV tray on time. Seven or eight clues and some corroborating research was enough for Cricket to make the connection between *The Peeler* and *Chris, Founder and Head Brewlover, Boiled Ogopogo Inc.*

"So," the lawyer said, exhaling through his teeth. "You know you can't just call someone a pedophile, right?"

"I didn't call him that."

"It's implied."

"He can imply anything he wants."

"Implied *what* now?" said Lorne, trying to mash his ear against Cricket's head, which was mashed against her phone.

"Implied nothing," said Cricket.

"You implied everything, Mrs. Lorch. You doxed him—you published his identity without his consent, with malicious intent—"

"I never did that."

"It's implied, Mrs. Lorch."

Cricket sucked her teeth.

"Sounds to me like you can say someone implied *anything* and take them to court."

"If you do it properly, yes."

"This is all a bunch of horseshit," said Lorne. He could not hear what was going on, but he was sure it was horseshit.

"I'm going to tell you what you need to do," the lawyer told Cricket. "And you need to do it. Immediately. Okay?"

"Okay."

"Here's what you do. You issue a public apology to the blog and the moderator *without naming names*—"

"His name, or my name?"

"*His* name."

"But I got to give *my* name?"

"Yes."

"Why?"

"Because you need to show contrition. Humility, okay? That's your ticket out. I'll talk to his lawyer... tell him you value your privacy over everything and that this is gonna destroy you, just shatter you emotionally—"

"It *is* going to destroy me."

"Jesus, can't you put the speaker on!" said Lorne. "Shatter what?"

"You offer the apology—*I* offer the apology, I mean, on your behalf. We'll dangle that. If he kind of comme-çi-comme-ça's it, you offer—*I* offer—anger management courses, a voluntary ban from social media, the regular works."

Cricket's mouth puckered into a tiny slit.

"I don't need anger management courses."

"I'm not saying you're the kind of lady to break jars or put your head through doors, like some of my other clients. But you need to keep a lid on your lid when you're online. And *don't* call people pedos unless they're convicted pedophiles."

After a long silence, Lorne surmised that it was his turn to speak:

"Fine, dandy, we'll do what you said."

"I want to hear it from Mrs. Lorch."

"Fine," said Cricket, stonily. "Whatever."

The following evening, when Lorne was at work, the lawyer called back. Good news: the public apology was going to clinch it. Cricket said she would get to work writing it. No, the lawyer told her; I've already written it. I'll text it to you and you sign it with your finger. Easy peasy, he said. And, he added, that'll be the end of it, *as long as you keep your damn mouth shut and never ever use the P word again.*

The apology appeared on The Peeler's blog two days later, with Cricket's name—along with a description of her relationship to Lorne—emblazoned beneath it. As the lawyer recommended, Cricket did not read the hundreds of comments the apology generated, or visit the blog again. The lawyer told her she had developed a *reputation*, and that the next blogger might not be stupid and egotistical enough to be satisfied with an apology.

For the next week Lorne was grilled about the episode during his post-shift scrums. The lawyer gave him canned lines that he used poorly, and not in the correct order. The super materialized in a bright orange polo to announce that the incident had been addressed and that further questions were a waste of everyone's time.

"Mr. Lorch and his lovely wife are moving on with their lives," the super said.

"And they're getting darn good at it," said Folknall, from the back.

"Good at what?" said Lorne.

Mallard kneaded his beard with his fingers.

"Good at moving on," said Folknall. "Right? This pedophile thing they're moving on from. Before that, they were moving on from shoving the toddler's head in the snow—"

"Now, come on, Folks," cried Mallard. "You and I both know that's—"

"Are you talking to *Folknall*," said a younger reporter, "or to us?"

"Who's us?"

"Is it 'folks' or 'Folknall'?"

"It's either Folknall or it's everybody."

Lorne turned to Mallard.

"If I have to put up with this much longer," he muttered to his foreman, "it's fifty-fifty I drop dead of a stroke before summer."

CHAPTER FIFTY-SIX

In May the Chunce & Chimbly held a long-delayed opening ceremony. The block in front of the structure was closed to traffic and set up with bleachers, including theatre-style rows of chairs for VIPs.

The morning sun blazed high on the glass façade of the building and glanced off Sir Gareth's immense shoulders. Pedestrians on their way to work or to other errands stopped to listen to the mayor, the ancient-looking Messrs. Chunce and Chimbly, the provincial member, the city councillor for the downtown district, and others give speeches about the *New City* and the *City of the Future.* "Imagine a skyline of knights gleaming in the light of the setting sun," said the mayor, beads of microphone static riding the waves of her voice. "Imagine our city as a trade and commercial and high-tech and cultural and athletic and artistic and political hub. If you close your eyes you can see it.

"Please—close your eyes. Do you see it?"

A breeze feathered the scalps of the assembled. Traffic mumbled on adjacent streets. The three dozen VIPs, along with the bleacher folk and some passersby, shut their eyes tight. They pictured all manner of things. Some saw a bright, polished cityscape and flying cars. Mr. Chimbly dreamed of the face of a former partner who years ago had tried to blackmail him, and ended up ruined. The mayor herself imagined a long street of Sir Gareths, and a much larger crowd in front of her, a better-looking crowd.

"Isn't it beautiful?" she said.

The spectators murmured, shuffled, sighed. Someone hiccupped.

"Thank you for taking the first step on the journey with me."

"Think I'm getting off here," said one spectator.

The mayor reminded everybody to have a slice from one of the Camelot-inspired sheet cakes sitting on a table by the stage, and then called Mr. Chunce up for a "special announcement."

Mr. Chunce, a man of medium size and build and a ramrod posture despite his eighty years, clumped to the rostrum and gripped the microphone as if he had been hunting it all morning.

"You are aware," he began, in a marbly voice, "Mr. Chimbly and I consider this little pile of bricks to be our baby, or at least the favourite of all our children. And like any good parents, like many of you ladies with your babies, we would do anything to protect our baby. We want to keep her strong and healthy. Babies, you know, are prone to all types of sickness—colic, whooping cough. Parasites, too. *Worms.*" (Booing.) "Yes! Parasites. This glorious pile of bricks behind me? It's no different than any other baby. It's healthy, my friends, the very picture of health. But it's not immune to everything. It's not immune to *everything*. No—it may be safe from colic, and polio, and *gas*, and whatever else, but guess what? *You* know. *You* know. Don't you? *You* know what sickness our buildings suffer from." (Mixed applause and boos.)

"We've found a nurse for her, did you know that? A nurse—actually a young man of exceptional abilities, whose job it is to scrub the ducts of our bouncing baby girl to keep her clean of disease—of the *one and only* disease—those little icy *menaces* that plague all the best buildings of our city, and, sadly, sadly, this one here, the best we've ever had—"

"Piss on them!" cried someone. By now there were a few hundred people about.

"—yes, the best," went on Mr. Chunce. "Of course, it's not all bad. Not at all! The little buggers—I mean, the little *parasites*—can hardly get a foothold in our marvellous pile of bricks. We took every precaution science and experience could offer, and we've been successful. We're only finding, what, one or two of the buggers a week?"

The two superintendents, standing off to the side, nodded their assent. They knew, but did not say, that just last night Scantland had plucked ten rats and had not stopped sniffing until he was out of the building and halfway down the street.

Mr. Chunce went on about how nasty and ridiculous ice rats were and how politicians might make more of an effort to eliminate them from the face of the earth rather than dreaming up ways to raise taxes and attack business owners. Behind him the mayor wore an iron smile and flicked an invisible lock of hair behind her ear.

Eventually, after some criticisms of progressivism and "eco nuts who'd be happier if the entire globe was a ball of ice again," Mr. Chunce drifted towards his point.

"The Chunce & Chimbly—'Sir Gareth'—hasn't been part of this 'League of Cleaning,' or whatever you call it." (Boos.) "That's right, boo! Boo! And you've let us know, haven't you? Boo! Boo! You've written us so much about this our office can hardly keep up."

"Open Gareth to competition!" bellowed a city councillor.

"Scantland's a beast!"

"Give beast a chance!"

"Okay, ha, yes," said Mr. Chunce, "yes, yes, we know. We're not illiterates here. We read all your letters."

"Scantland rules!"

"We read your letters and listened to your telephone calls," Mr. Chunce went on, now strangling the microphone with both hands. "And we've settled it. It's settled. Folks, at long last, it's *settled*."

Silence. The clouds passed overhead. Even the traffic on nearby streets seemed to hold its breath.

"Sir Gareth," said Mr. Chunce, "is entering the lottery for the Summer Regatta. Signed,, sealed, delivered. We're entering our pile and our lad in—"

The crowd did not merely *roar*. It *shrieked*. Mr. Chunce tried to finish, but the din drowned him out. People on the rostrum jumped up and down, making a sound like thunder. The mayor applauded and backed away towards the steps, ducking pieces of cake and paper plates that the overexcited throng was now tossing into the air. At the back of the crowd, just behind the bleachers, a man pushing a toddler in a stroller tore his shirt half off and pounded his chest with his fists.

Those who were not screaming and tearing off their clothes were texting friends and colleagues to tell them Sir Gareth had entered the Regatta lottery—the upcoming draw that would determine where each Masters contestant would compete, since the organizers had decided it would be "spicier" to have each man moving about in unfamiliar ducts. High above, the building's head and shoulders gleamed so incandescently in the sunshine that they could have cracked the sky.

"Wonderful, wonderful," the mayor said, shaking hands with Mr. Chunce, who beamed and nodded and murmured *Holy buggers these people.*

Across the street, on top of a fifteen-storey building, a man and a woman in hard hats were running a tape measure across the length of the roof. Well-connected individuals in the city's political and business spheres, having learned the news, were already looking to reserve front-row seats for the Regatta. These same people would be among the first to flee the scene on Regatta night, as a mob crashed its way up the Chunce & Chimbly to the twenty-eighth floor.

CHAPTER FIFTY-SEVEN

"Only Sauvignon blanc," Folknall said, pouring out glasses for Lorne and himself. A pearl of the wine splashed onto Lorne's fingers. "Nothing else, nothing better. You like wine?"

"I don't know," said Lorne.

"Even if you don't," said Folknall, "you'll like this. It's *proper* wine." He rubbed his thumb over the logo on the bottle and launched into a lengthy history of the vintner. All Lorne would recall later was that the wine was from California and that it bothered one of his fillings. The two men were at a wine bar in the west end that had once been a martial arts gym. Lorne wore one of Cricket's baseball caps because he did not want to be recognized or bothered. Yet it seemed that Folknall, presiding over their table as if emceeing a banquet, was doing his best to say Lorne's name as often as he could.

"You look for this bottle at the store, *Lorny*," he said. "You share it with all those other *Lorches*. Are the *Lorches* a big *wine* family?"

Lorne said the Lorches were neither a big family nor a wine family.

"Well, nobody ever said *Lorne Lorch* minces his words," said Folknall, simpering, banging his hand on the table.

"Nope."

In the wake of the embarrassment over Cricket's legal trouble with the blogger, Mallard, Lorne's foreman, had arranged this outing with Folknall. Or, more accurately, he was the one who told Lorne about the outing; it appeared that more influential forces within the Sprill hierarchy had organized it. Folknall had chosen the time and place and even offered to drive Lorne, though Lorne insisted on a taxi. Mallard had not given Lorne any instructions besides "be nice, ask him lots of questions about himself... thank him for the nice things he's written—"

"He wrote a bunch of shit about me," Lorne said.

"I know, but don't focus on that."

By the time Lorne arrived and found him on the upper balcony, Folknall was already uncorked and unbuttoned. No server could pass their table without the journalist's giving him or her a high five, and without Folknall then muttering to Lorne that the server was an asshole or a moron. (A couple of the female servers, however, were "dedicated as shit"; only one employee in the whole place actually "knows his stuff, knows shit-all about wines.") Most of the time Folknall had to reach so far to deliver his fives, high or low, that his torso ended up parallel to the floor, his long hair dangling beside his cheek like a string of weeds on a boat propeller.

"So tell me," he said, rocking back up to a sitting position, "how's everything?"

"Good."

"Feeling good?"

"Good."

"How's your family? How's the weather?"

"Everything's fine—"

"How's your *wife* doing? Laying low, what? Don't blame her. You know," Folknall said, holding the already-half-empty bottle of Sauvignon on his palm like a trophy, "I only drink on Tuesdays. Never on the weekend."

"Oh."

"So—your wife? Crickety-crackety?"

"She's fine."

A queer smile appeared on Folknall's face.

"Fine, eh? She's *fine*. Now, listen, Lorny—she did kind of shit the bed, Lorny. I know she's your wife. But she kind of shit the bed... just a little. She squeezed just a little shit on the bed."

"Hey—"

"You gotta admit she shit the bed, Lorny."

"She didn't shit nothing."

Folknall held his index finger and thumb a speck apart.

"Just a little?"

Lorne made an impatient sound with his throat.

"Well, maybe she did a little. But she shit it for *me*."

"We-ell!" Folknall clasped his hands together above his head like a prizefighter. "That's a horse of a different colour, isn't it? May she shit in *many* beds for you." Taking a long sip of wine, he licked the corners of his mouth. "In all honesty, Lorny, I half-expected you'd bring her tonight."

"Who?"

"The missus."

"Why would I?"

"Oh, no reason... it doesn't matter to me," said Folknall. He raised a hand for a high five to a server who was far out of range. Then he tilted far back in his chair, peering through the dim light of the bar at the server's retreating figure. "Hey—do you think that guy's a man or a woman?"

Lorne turned to look.

"That one," said Folknall. "Oh, shit, he's going downstairs. He or she. You wouldn't believe how many of 'em come through here, Lorny. And I'm the only one who seems able to tell."

Lorne, cupping his wine glass with both hands, took a taste of its contents. It was the first time in his life he had ever drunk white wine, although he had had red twice before. The Sauvignon tugged at the corners of his jaw.

"Is that not glorious?" said Folknall.

"Sure."

"Is it not?"

"It's really good."

They were ten or fifteen minutes into the conversation before Lorne remembered the list of questions Mallard had provided him to put to Folknall. Mallard had written a dozen down, but Lorne could only recall three: the third ("Beatles or Stones?"), the eighth ("What was your first job in the field?"), and the ninth ("What do you think of the Ebola virus?"). There were other ones, better ones, but Lorne did not want to bring the list out and read from it, even discreetly. Since he knew nothing about Ebola and always got the Beatles mixed up with the Monkees, he put number eight to Folknall:

"What was your first job? Did you like it?"

The reporter grinned.

"Congratulations, Lorny Lorchy," he said.

"For what?"

"That's the first question you've ever asked me about myself."

"Oh—uh—"

"I ask *you* questions all the time. I've asked you over a thousand questions, probably. Right? That's probably right, I'm not even kidding. A *thousand*, Lorny!"

"Yah—well, I think—"

"And here, finally, after how many years—how many years? I don't even know—you finally asked me a ques—" Folknall bolted forward again, his body all but flopping over the table—"look, *that* guy right there, look! Dude or dudette?"

Again Lorne turned to look.

"Who?"

"Guy or gal? Quick, now."

"Jesus, I can't see—"

"My name isn't Jesus. Wait—what do you *mean* you can't see?"

"It's dark in here."

"You work in the dark, Lorny!"

"Yeah, but—it's not the same. That's darker dark... there's too much light in here."

Lorne gestured at the low track lighting on the ceiling and at the candle on their table, which was bickering back and forth.

"There's too much light in this dark."

Folknall laughed and slapped the table.

"A light dark," he said. "Lorny, you should be a philosopher. I should write this. I should write this down..."

A server approached with a bottle of Prosecco. Lorne noticed that the server, who wore a pink button-down shirt with the sleeves rolled up, made a wide arc on her way to the table and approached from behind Folknall. The reporter nearly jumped out of his seat when she said

"COMPLIMENTS of the house, Mr. Lorch!"

"That from Randy?" said Folknall, grabbing the bottle and inspecting the label. "That's decent. That's decent, Lorny. You're in good hands. Randy knows how to pick 'em, Lorny."

"How much is it?" said Lorne.

Folknall's hand came down on the table again.

"It's *free*, you silly bastard!" he said, cackling. "Tell Randy thanks, dear—from *both* of us."

To compensate for his tipsiness, Folknall sat as straight as he could, and spoke with gradually increasing volume, as if to someone on the other side of the bar. A couple came by the table for an autograph, and Lorne obliged while Folknall scrawled his own name on a napkin and placed it in his pocket "in case of emergency." Lorne then listened to Folknall go on about how poorly constructed basketballs are. Sensing he needed to act, Lorne interrupted:

"Listen," he said, as Folknall swept his hand at a passing patron whom he had mistaken for a server. "I was wondering if I could ask you a favour—"

"NAME... IT..."

Lorne would have liked to use Folknall's first name, to create an air of camaraderie, collegiality. But he did not know what it was.

"It's just my *wife*," he went on, "and I get you have to write your stories or whatnot, fine and dandy... I don't want to tell you how to do your job—"

Folknall was staring at Lorne. His expression was both closed and open, as if he had just noticed he was not alone.

"That's your job, okay... okay now, I don't mind if you talk about me, or say dumb shit or anything like that about *me*. But if you could keep Cricket out of it—if you could just... you've already talked about it, okay, fine, that's done. You talked about her thing with the internet or whatever. I just want you to know—"

"KNOW... *WHAT*... LORNY."

"Just—just that I'm trying my best out there, all right? Christ! I'm not trying to hurt anybody. But Crick, now—she never signed up for any of this. She feels like cat shit about all this. I know you gotta write what you gotta write, you sell newspapers, or magazines. Or something. But we had a... it's been a bit of a go lately. That whole thing with the kid and the snow—that was just messing around, I never threw no kid in a snowbank, or punched any kid in the face. And this thing, with the internet or whatever... it'd just be a—a—" Lorne stumbled on the word *favour*, since Mallard had told him not to frame the request as a favour—"just a—a *nice thing*, to both of us I mean, me and Crick... if you could just lay off the thing with the... the guy on the internet, the whole mess there..."

The reporter was cradling the empty bottle of Sauvignon blanc in the crook of one arm and picking at the label. His lips flickered in an odd way.

"Hey—"

Folknall looked up.

"You all right?" said Lorne.

Folknall grinned, but his eyes were fuzzy.

"You know something?" he said, his voice quiet now.

"What?"

"You're the best cleaner of all time."

"Oh."

"In any country. The *best.*"

"Okay."

"Of *all time.*"

"Aw, that's just—"

"And you know what else? I used to hate you, Lorny," said Folknall. "I mean I *really* disliked you. Disliked your guts."

"Okay—"

"My stepmom," said Folknall, "now—*that* was a woman never drank. So why'd she drink at the funeral? I'll never know. She shouldn't have. It was a bad idea. We shouldn't drank this," he said, rapping the bottle's label with his finger. "We shouldn't. I don't know why we did."

Lorne suddenly remembered that his mother's favourite Beatle had been Ringo, but by then it was too late to bring it up. Folknall's eyes were floating in their sockets.

After an hour, and a pair of bottles, the two men stood up to leave. The act of rising seemed to sober Folknall.

"You're the best cleaner," he whispered to Lorne. "*The* best. Okay? Okay? You heard me. I'm telling you that to your face, Lorny. This is me—this is my mouth—these are my lips. Respond, please. Can you see my lips moving?"

"Yah—"

"My lips see you and they say—*they* say, Lorny—you're the best cleaner who ever walked this earth."

Folknall reached his arm out to pat Lorne's shoulder, but he was too far away. So he made a swatting motion with his hand.

"But you need to start *acting* it, Lorny. Okay? You need to start acting the part."

A week later Folknall wrote a piece about the wheel of cheese phenomenon, saying that collecting a dozen rats in a night was no great accomplishment. *If one kid's parents lay out twelve Easter eggs and another's lay out six, the kid who gathers twelve shouldn't get a prize—though maybe his parents should—for loving their child more than the other child's parents love him.*

He called Lorne a big fish in a small pond and wrote that cleaners were no more deserving of praise than a pair of dice after being thrown. Yet he did not mention the incident with Cricket and the microbrewer, then or again. Mallard told Lorne he must have been *as smooth as silk* with Folknall.

"I guess," Lorne said.

Chapter Fifty-eight

Massive, he thought. It's massive. He could spread his arms out wide like wings and just touch both walls. In some parts he could nearly stand up and walk.

But he did not like this place. It was too damn quiet. The Sprill was noisy, it buckled and groaned. It had a soul. The Sprill spoke to him, checked in on him, during the night. This place was like a giant fake palm tree.

One sound alone was audible to Lorne, though it barely registered at the edge of his hearing. He thought it was a printer, or some other office machine, buzzing on the other side of the wall. Yet it seemed to follow him from floor to floor. Only before daybreak, as Lorne was squeezing his way towards his and Sir Gareth's doom, did he recognize it as the noise of thousands of people becoming unglued at the same time.

While he was in the ducts, Scantland's girlfriend, Bear, would text him:

Hy babe

Catching anything tonite ???

Sometimes she asked for photos. He sent shots of the rats he had clapping in his sack, or of rats still glowing grey-green on the duct wall, or of himself giving a victory sign. She posted these on her Dropcuster and other social media pages. Since the Chunce & Chimbly had been entered in the Regatta, Scantland had gained thousands more followers. Conspicuous in his photos were the sideburns and handlebar moustache he was working on, and which Bear retouched and thickened before posting the pictures online.

On both shoulders of his coveralls, just below the flashlights, Scantland bore the logo of an energy drink company. The business had hired Scantland and a couple of young NHL superstars to endorse its brand.

The buildings around the Masters towers sold tickets to the Regatta. A pair for a window facing the Sprill Building went for $150; facing the Westerfeldt, $130; facing Sir Gareth, $270. Non-window seating was far cheaper. The discrepancies in price were puzzling; what went on in the ducts of the nine major buildings would be invisible to in-person spectators. It was assumed that window seats, and rooftop seats, were more expensive because they would provide a view of the masses of fans expected in the streets. People were paying a premium for a better look at other people.

The city council issued several strong statements against unlicensed betting, but more than half of the councillors put money on the Regatta. The mayor made a token bet on Lorne of five dollars. She then had her husband put twelve hundred dollars on Scantland. A couple of bookies were rumoured to have fled the city with sizeable loads of cash. Some of the building superintendents received telephone calls from gentlemen who, in thick Belarussian accents, politely requested tours of the premises. High-tech and government offices posted notices that business-casual attire was required of all employees, and that "athletic paraphernalia and other partisan colours are only to be worn in the office on designated Fridays."

The prizes and jackpot for the Regatta were announced on the first day of summer.

For the Masters Division, which Lorne would be competing in, the award was $50,000, along with a nice blazer and dinner for two at an upscale Irish restaurant. In a press conference, the mayor outlined the complicated formula the organizers were using to reconcile the variation in takes that might result from buildings of different sizes. Social media was quickly afire with conspiracy theories about how the calculations favoured different structures and different cleaners. That evening the mayor posted a comment on her official account:

> *The mathematics are sound and have been rigorously vetted by a variety of experts in several fields, including engineering, kinesiology, climatology, human biology, and our own Gelucelet Task Force. None of the cleaners will have an advantage over the others, nor will any be disadvantaged. We are confident that all of the cleaners in the Masters and other divisions will be competing on an even playing field and that their performance and results will be judged as equitably and accurately as possible.*
>
> *We look forward to the first of what we expect to be many exciting and memorable Regattas.*

Due to Sir Gareth's size compared with the other Big Nine buildings, its easier-to-traverse ducts, and a host of other factors, its rats would be equivalent to 0.96 Sprill rats, 0.95 Jumbo Data rats, and 0.98 Westerfeldt rats. As it turned out, these calculations would be obliterated in the chaos of Regatta night.

All rats are equal, Folknall wrote, *but some have more whiskers than others.*

Lorne was having trouble sleeping, so one morning he moved to Leonidas's old twin bed, covering himself with a drool-hardened old throw from his son's closet. Unlike the pantry door in the basement, the closet door had always worked perfectly, folding open and shut without a sound. It was one of the few things in the drafty old townhome that had never broken down. Sprawling on the coverlet, Lorne reached behind his head and tried the doors again, idly, rolling them open and closed.

Jesus, he thought. *Kid slept on this plank for years? Why didn't he say something?*

Squirming around on the mattress, Lorne pulled his son's old throw over him and folded and unfolded the closet door behind his head. He would repeat this motion, he told himself, until he fell asleep. It was better than counting damned sheep. His arm continued drawing and pushing on the little spool-shaped knob without the least trouble, without his fingers cramping. The movement was rhythmic, pleasant. He had been tallying up each open-and-shut but soon lost his count. Still his arm moved in that mechanical motion like a frond in a breeze.

...Now his ear caught a measured buzzing noise in the distance. It was quiet on the street at that time of day. The sound must, he decided, be coming from the closet door; he must have overworked or worn out the track system. But then the buzzing stopped. Lorne's arm wafted back and forth, back and forth.

The sound resumed. Lorne's arm swayed back and forth over his head but he could feel his elbow settled against his temple. The motion had come apart somewhere. The buzzing stopped and started several more times and he could feel a light wind from the window sprinkling his face. It smelled like freshly mown grass and mulch and compost. Lorne was annoyed that his opening and closing the closet door had upset its tracking and he wondered why he did such a stupid thing just because he could not sleep. He would have fallen asleep long ago if not for the bloody squeaking and his arm refusing to tire for some reason as it rolled the door back and forth again and again but his elbow was fastened to the side of his head and something in the whole operation did not fit—

A blast from outside: planks of wood dumped on the ground somewhere nearby, behind someone's house. Lorne started, bolted, dashed downstairs. The clock above the kitchen sink showed twenty-five minutes past four.

CHRIST

The phone was ringing—*that* was the buzzing he had heard while grappling with sleep. He rushed to the kitchen, still tangled in Leo's blanket, and seized the telephone receiver.

"Hello what—?"

It was Lou.

"Lorny! You got the big one, hey?" she said.

"Eh?"

"You got the big one."

"What big one?"

"That's a full plate for you, Lorny. How great is that? Everybody thinks it's gonna be too much—well, that's what people are saying *online*. But they don't know you like I do—"

"Is Cricket there?"

"No, she left ten minutes ago—oh! I guess you were probably asleep? I forgot you sleep all day. You never heard?"

"I'm not asleep—"

"I'll let Crick tell you. She was real excited, Lorny."

Lou hung up.

Cricket arrived home five minutes later, breathless.

"You got the big one," she said, panting. "Sir Gareth."

"The what?"

The Regatta lottery; it had taken place that afternoon, and had been broadcast live on television. Nine buildings, nine cleaners, *stuffed in a sack*, as Folknall wrote, *and pulled out at random—or so we're led to believe by the powers that be.* Somehow, despite a multitude of questions over the past weeks in his scrums, despite Cricket's anxiety, despite the delivery boy having scrawled *GOOD LUCK IN THE LOTTERY TODAY LORNY I HOPE YOU GET THE WESTERFELDT* on the newspaper, Lorne had forgotten all about it. He had slept through the city-wide frenzy of Lottery Day.

"The Chunce. For the Regatta. They drew today, and you got the Chunce. The Chunce, Lorny! The big one!"

"Oh, Christ. Of course I did. Where the hell is the Chunce?"

Cricket reminded him that the building was only ten or so blocks from the Sprill, that its head and shoulders were easily visible above the structures around it. Since his eyes were more often on his feet than on the sky, he sometimes forgot Sir Gareth existed at all.

Mallard asked Lorne if he was "okay" for the Chunce & Chimbly.

"Sure," said Lorne.

"It's a big-ass building. Isn't it?"

Mallard was peeling an orange. Lorne disliked the smell of oranges and despised how sticky they were.

"If you want to go in my place," he told Mallard, "be my guest."

"No, no, Lorny—it's not that. I just don't want you to think you *have* to do it. You're the all-time champ. That comes with certain, ah... privileges."

"Eh?"

"I'm just saying it's a big-ass building, and I guess kind of slick inside. In the ducts. Slippery. We can appeal, you know, we can ask for—"

"I don't slip," Lorne said.

While sleeping through the Regatta lottery under his son's old drool-stained throw, Lorne lost one of his biggest fans.

It was Sweetie, the young man with the mysterious ailment Lorne had visited a couple of winters before. Sweetie was the first person Lorne had met who wore the now-ubiquitous replica coveralls with the LORCH patch on the breast. On the day of the Regatta lottery, just before the names were drawn, Sweetie died.

The family kept the death a secret, although they did inform the reporter with the square-rimmed glasses. They asked her not to share the news with anyone, including Lorne. The request was not easy to fulfil, since the reporter felt Lorne ought to know about Sweetie's passing. Ultimately, she respected the family's wishes. A private service took place at the house and no notice was printed online or in the newspaper. (An aunt had started composing an obituary, but as Sweetie had not accomplished much in his life, she gave up rather than embellish.)

It's a shame, the aunt confided to a friend. *I wish more people could know. Lots would've offered their sympathies, at least.*

Oh yes, the friend said. *Lorne Lorch himself might have come to the funeral.*

He would have. I met him when he visited. Such a nice man—much nicer than people say.

The reason the family did not want a fuss made about the death, and why they did not want Lorne to find out, was because of the manner of the young man's passing. Officially, they advised a few close relatives and friends that he had died "suddenly, after a brief illness." That was not entirely inaccurate. The young man had died in an embarrassing way, and the family did not want anyone to find out.

Sweetie was cremated in his orange coveralls.

CHAPTER FIFTY-NINE

Bakers turned out *Regatta éclairs* in nine different colours, representing those of the nine Masters cleaners. Summer travellers from Europe and Africa and the Far East extended their vacations at considerable cost. No hotel rooms would be available during Regatta week for a one-hundred-kilometre radius. At lunchtime office workers sat outside, munching sandwiches and looking up at the buildings around them, as if waiting for something to happen.

The cleaners kept low profiles. Their fans avoided bothering them, and the occasional slight or outburst was forgiven by foremen and supporters and wives and children and mothers and fathers. Post-shift scrums were clipped and short: in some cases, cleaners answered only one or two questions before pushing their way through the reporters and out the door, muttering to themselves. Foremen brought in architects to brief the men on the unfamiliar structures they would work on Regatta night. The deputy mayor, who had lived in Oklahoma's tornado country as a teenager, said the sky above the city was turning green, a green so thick it was almost invisible.

Two weeks out, Lorne felt good. His back was not bothering him much and his hands were steady. He collected ten rats one night. One of the rats was the size of a drink coaster, and he peeled it with one hand.

Come here, you

As he crawled through the ducts he spoke to the rat's corpse, which he named Terrence.

How's that rub-a-dub treating you, Terrence, lad?

You had a good life, Terrence, ol' bean, ol' bastard

When Terrence slid deeper into Lorne's pocket:

Terrence you touch my balls and I'll slap your face

At the end of his shift Lorne fired the ten rats one by one into the collection bucket, winding up each time like a baseball pitcher. He went home and sat down in front of the television, where his eggs and olives were waiting for him. Cricket, running late, came crashing through looking for her baseball cap and nearly tipped Lorne's tray over.

"Jesus, Crick—"

She had several caps, and about once every two weeks they all seemed to vanish just before she left for work. Nothing upset her more than not being able to find a cap. Rushing around, plunking her head against the wall to peer behind the couch, crawling on all fours under the kitchen table, she was like a hen who had lost a chick. Lorne ate and listened to her thumping around upstairs. The thumping stopped for a moment; fast footsteps came clattering across the ceiling, then down the stairs, and at last Cricket darted through the room, her face blotchy, hair flying, jacket hanging off her shoulders—with a red cap aslant on her head.

"Bye, Lorny!"

He heard the storm door croak open out back.

"Crick!"

A pause.

"What?"

Her voice was thinner, already outside.

"Oh—just—"

"Gotta go, Lorny—eat your eggs before they're cold—"

He had not been able to tell her what he wanted to, and it left him in a cold mood. He watched television and slowly ate his eggs and popped olives into his mouth. The television was muted. An old rerun of *Hammy Hamster* was on. Lorne had loved watching the show as a child and, as an adult, found it immensely calming. The anthropomorphic rodents were amusing enough, but the constant trickle of a stream in the background was like a warm bath in Lorne's ears. Leonidas had never liked the show as much as Lorne had, but he loved it when Lorne imitated the guinea pig's bombastic voice:

Looks like your mother's... BUUURNing the MEEEATloaf again...

The notion struck him in the kitchen, as he dropped his plate into the sink and placed his fork (he never used a knife) in his empty cup. The fork clanked around in the cup, and the noise reminded him of what he wanted to say to Cricket as she rushed out with her hair flying and her cap screwed on sideways:

I might retire one day you know. I probably will retire. And I'll probably retire before you do. So maybe you should show me how to cook eggs like that. I could learn how to make eggs... well I could make my own eggs but I could try making them for you too. I'm not retiring yet because I got a lot of work to do still. So I'm not gonna make the eggs yet. But it would maybe be a good idea if you could just teach me a little about making eggs.

I could make them maybe for both of us at some point

Lorne could not cook or clean or do laundry, and was equally unable to perform any more complicated household repair than fixing a cupboard door. Their townhome did not have a lawn and Lorne had not used a mower in twenty years. In four and a half decades he had mastered only one skill. But nobody on the planet was better than he was at that one skill.

"Lorny," said Mallard, as the cleaner breezed in to start his shift. "Lorny, you missed one."

"One what?"

"Jeez, you know what."

A pause.

"Where?"

"Sixteen, west, right in the corner of a corner, Lorny. Hard to see—"

Lorne marched to the black square on the wall and stuck his head in, peering into the darkness. Then he paced the perimeter of the room like a turtle searching for the way out of a terrarium. Every now and then he rapped on one of the wall blocks. For a moment Mallard believed the news had caused Lorne to lose his head. Lorne paced around and around, tapping the wall, his face so puckered that he looked like a bulldog.

"Lorny—"

Lorne stopped and stared at Mallard.

"Lorny—"

"Jesus Christ," Lorne muttered. He leaned his back against a wall and began bending and straightening his legs, scratching his shoulders against the concrete. "Christ. Christ. *Christ.* What the *Christ.* What the *Christ!*"

"It's okay, Lorny. The super told me I should tell you."

"How many?"

"Just one, Lorny."

"Be honest, now—"

"I swear on my mother's life, Lorny."

Mallard's mother had died long ago. The swearing on her life was an old habit.

Lorne resumed circling the room, ducking behind the purple lamp, rapping on the blocks on the wall. Every now and then he muttered to himself like someone possessed. He stopped again.

"Just *one*?"

"Just the one. I promise. Nothing bad happened, nothing like—"

Before Mallard could say *like last time*, Lorne whirled on him.

"Wait—how do you know?"

"What?"

"How do you know I missed a rat?"

"Oh—"

Gliding through the ceiling above an endless stretch of cubicles on the fifth floor, Lorne peered down through a grate and saw that one of the desks was occupied. Wills sat at a computer, clicking on the mouse and listening to tinny music on a pair of headphones. To Lorne's astonishment, the man appeared to be playing Solitaire. Not mopping, or emptying wastebaskets—playing cards!

Lorne could have plunged through the grate on top of Wills, and for an instant he considered doing so. Instead, he doubled back and accessed the floor through a vent in a corner office. As he crept up behind Wills, the other man continued clicking away at his game.

Jesus, this guy.

Lorne advanced as far as the cubicle baffle directly behind Wills. The baffles were only four feet high, and he was within striking distance of the back of Wills' head. He raised his hand; he wanted the janitor to flinch when he turned.

"Hi, Chiefy!" said Wills, as if to the computer monitor. In a swift motion he swivelled around on his chair to face Lorne, resting a knee against the baffle.

"Oh—hi."

"Beauty night."

"Yeah."

Lorne's hand was still aloft. Wills glanced at it, then back at Lorne.

"Mosquito?"

He broke into a wide smile. Lorne frowned and lowered his hand.

"You sticking your nose in my business?" said Lorne.

"I'm not sticking my nose in nobody's business."

"Yeah y'are! You're climbing around in my ducts. Nobody's allowed in the ducts but me."

"They're just ducts, Chiefy," said Wills. "Ducts belong to everybody."

"Not these ducts. These're *mine*."

"Well," said Wills, leaning his other knee on the baffle, "I don't know what to tell you, Chiefy. I just do what I'm told."

Lorne bent closer to Wills. His expression was hard, but not quite angry; his eyes wandered over Wills' face as if looking for something he had dropped. At last:

"Are you a spy?"

"Whut?"

"Are you checking up on me? Did Mallard tell you to keep an—"

Wills threw back his head and laughed. Lorne, looking over both shoulders, signaled to Wills to keep quiet, as if getting caught outside the ducts could get him sent to the superintendent's office.

"Hell *no*," Wills said, smacking the top of the baffle. "I'd never be a spy for nobody, Chiefy. No way, no how."

"Then why were you in the ducts?"

"Chiefy—"

"I don't like being called *Chiefy*."

"Ah, okay, I thought you did. Well, Mr. Lorch, you got nothing to worry about. That's the first rat I found in there."

"Well no shit, you never—you never—"

Lorne froze.

"Wait—first one you found? You mean you been in there before?"

Wills shrugged.

Lorne was thunderstruck. It was as if Wills had just said *I've been sleeping with your wife, but hey, don't worry about it, it's all good!* What Wills did say was that Lorne was still *the man*, and that he—Wills—was, as Mallard had pointed out, simply providing support to Lorne, was merely his *late-inning legs*—

Lorne grasped Wills's sleeve, but did not know what to do with it, so he jerked the other man's hand towards him, as if it were a microphone he wanted to speak into.

Wills did not resist.

"I'm no spy, Mr. Lorch. You don't have to worry about that."

"Listen, guy," Lorne said, darkly, tugging at the sleeve, "let me tell you something, okay? Let me tell you something. Let me tell you something."

"I'm all ears."

"Let me tell you something—you just stick to your mop, okay?"

Wills was silent. After a moment, he slid the fingers of his free hand around Lorne's wrist and, with a smooth motion and little apparent effort, broke the other man's grip.

"I'm not a janitor," he said. "I wouldn't janit if they paid me a million bucks."

Lorne's hand hovered over Wills' arm.

"I'm gonna talk to Mallard about this. You hear that? I'm gonna tell him to talk to the super—"

"I report directly to the super, Mr. Lorch."

"I don't give a shit *who* you report to."

"Just letting you know I report to the super."

"Who gives a shit!"

"Okay, sounds good," said Wills, adjusting his headphones over his ears. He half-turned back towards his Solitaire game, but stopped, his eyes lighting up.

"Oh, hey!" he said. "I watched the lottery. Congrats, Mr. Lorch! Hope you kick Gareth's balls—"

A second later he was scrolling the King of Clubs across the screen, the Latin jazz in his ears shutting Lorne out. Lorne stood there like someone who had been splashed by a passing car. At last he left, plodding under a violet-hued night light back to the corner office and the vent and the ducts.

CHAPTER SIXTY

Scantland sat shirtless on the back of a park bench, signing autographs and posing for photos. Some of his admirers ran their hands over the tattoos on his arm and his torso while he chatted to a reporter. He did not seem to mind; at one point, he even lifted an arm so that a sixty-year-old man could get a better look at a panzer design on his flank. *I'm not a Nazi guy*, he told the man; *I just like the design of the tanks. They were works of art. My girlfriend hates Nazis, and she's the one designed the tattoo for me.*

"Beautiful, just beautiful," said the man.

"Thanks."

"What's that one?" asked someone.

"It's called a *sugar skull*," said Scantland, almost reverently. "I got one on my leg, too."

"What do sugar skulls represent, dear?"

Scantland did not answer, and it was quickly and murmuringly understood that it was not up to him to interpret his body for the masses; it was up to the masses to do their own research. He crouched on the bench and performed a series of squats. This was the purported explanation for his appearance in the park—he liked to train outdoors, he said, and he would occasionally demonstrate his workouts for the public. One woman, after watching him mount a tree branch and perform a feat that was equal parts gymnastics, trapeze, and dance, called Scantland "Batman" and walked away shaking her head. Scantland worked out more than two hours a day, and often posted videos of his sessions on Dropcuster.

A reporter from an online magazine asked him whether he was dedicating his performance at the Regatta to anyone.

"I don't know," he said, his breath growing thicker the faster he squatted. "I don't know. Bear-Bear—we know anyone in the hospital, or—?"

Bear, Scantland's girlfriend, was leaning against a tree with one ankle crossed over the other, filming him with her phone. After a long moment she shook her head. It was not clear to the reporter whether Bear was saying *No* to the question about sick fans or shaking her head for some other reason.

"Let me think," said Scantland.

He hopped off the bench and paced back and forth, collecting his breath. A young mother was nudging a stroller back and forth with one hand, trying to keep her toddler calm long enough to take a photo of whatever Scantland was about to do next. The reporter from the online magazine was surreptitiously eyeing Bear. Anyone looking at him and his pen-scratching might have assumed he was taking assiduous notes about Scantland, fishing out details about the young man's movements that escaped the other onlookers. Instead, he was writing the following:

Green eyes
Ash-blonde? Extensions?
21, 22 maybe... slight limp maybe... tat on top of foot
Sunglasses WAY too big
Shirt too big
Cheekbones YES
Skin PERFECT
Beach bunny but no good beaches around
Dropcuster prof? I should ask

"Yeah," said Scantland. "I do have someone to dedicate to."

"Okay. Who?"

"Bojangles."

"Who's Bojangles?"

"It's who I'm dedicating the Regatta to."

The reporter looked at Bear. Her green angel-of-death gaze rolled up from her phone, hovered on him for an agonizing moment, then fell back to her screen.

Later that afternoon the reporter typed up a short profile about Scantland, ending it with allusions to the cleaner's mysterious dedicatee. An enterprising individual created and sold tees and hoodies that bore a scumbly portrait of Scantland and the legend *FOR BOJANGLES, WHEREVER HE MAY ROAM*; some members of the mob who swarmed the Chunce & Chimbly on Regatta night were later identified by these shirts.

"Bojangles" was the name Scantland gave to a faceless thief who had, intermittently during Scantland's grade-eleven year, stolen food from his locker.

The thief was actually his math teacher. She noticed that he always dialed in his combination after shutting his locker door, which allowed him to simply tug the lock open when he returned. What began as a cryptic—and unheeded—lesson by the teacher on securing personal goods morphed into an addiction once she determined on which days (Tuesday, Wednesday, Friday) Scantland brought a Jos. Louis cake to eat with his lunch. The teacher had recently ended a painful romantic relationship, and the thrill of stealing snack cakes from Scantland's locker helped refresh her soul during a dark year.

A July evening, a major intersection, a foursome in yellow and purple—Xióng's colours—needling a passing trio of orange-clad Lorch partisans:

Hey Lorny Lorch—what year is it?

Hey Lorny Lorch—what's your name, Lorny Lorch?

Where's your false teeth LORNY?

Someone in orange poked someone in yellow. Loogies were exchanged. Before the walk signal flashed, seven young men were brawling in the street. One of the Lorch boys swung his fist like a hammer and popped a Xióng eardrum. Xióng's crew, in spite of their reputation for modesty and sportsmanship, used nails and teeth and made snatches at testicles. The battle was illuminated in four directions by the headlights of stopped cars. Drivers honked sporadically, though one—possibly an Aquino supporter—rapped out "Shave and a Haircut" over and over, and another, in a growling pickup truck, sounded his horn in a continuous stream.

Two of the fans ended up in hospital, one with three broken fingers. The mayor announced that any further incidents would be punished as gang-related activity.

Lou sat in the stockroom with an ankle crossed over the opposite knee and her fingers spliced over her belly.

"Again, it's just business," she said. "What part of it don't you understand, dear?"

Cricket stood in the stockroom door.

"You can't let personal interests interfere in this sort of thing," Lou went on. "You have to understand that, dear. There's nothing I would've liked better than putting it on your guy—*our* guy. But I have to be practical. I've done my due diligence—boy, have I done it. It's nearly driven me up the wall! And it was close. I went back and forth on it all night. Two nights. I barely slept. You can understand, dear, can't you? Of course you can. You can't let personal feelings get in the way of something like this. I'm not talking chump change, either. I won't tell you how much—I don't do that, it's a private matter. It'd be inappropriate, since I'm your boss. But let's just say it's not *five bucks*, or *ten bucks*, or even *twenty bucks*, Crick—"

It was in fact not even thirty bucks, or forty, she went on. Not even *fifty*. The way she said *fifty* suggested it was about fifty.

"I wouldn't put money on a stock just because I'm friends with the wife, dear. The wife of the stock—the stockbroker, or what have you. You understand *that*. This is no different. Any financial planner would tell you the same thing."

Cricket stood shadowless in the door, listening to her boss. Lou tossed her head and Cricket could hear the rattle of the beads in her boss's blue hair.

"Any planner would tell you, 'You just leave your heart out of it.' You understand, Crick. You do. You understand. There's no reason to take any of it personally; if I'm being completely honest, it's my business. It's the right thing to do. I'm being smart."

Lou unfolded her leg and leaned forward, peering up at Cricket over the turquoise frames of her glasses.

"The *Chinese kid*," she said, almost whispering. "He's the one to watch. Everyone's talking about this Scantland, but I've done my research. His stats are inflated. Just like Kravchenko's always were. It's all about building conditions. I did a lot of research, looked at lots of stats, breakdowns, sabermetrics. I know a *lot* about sabermetrics, *cleaning* sabermetrics. Do you? Have you studied sabermetrics?"

"Yes."

"Have you? Okay, dear. Then you know. You understand. The Chinese kid, in the Jumbo. It's a sure thing. I know you don't like it, and I'd be the same in your place, but that's just how it is. And—"

A tinkle of rusty bells from the front; a customer had entered the shop.

"Oh, Crick, can you take care of that, dear? I'm just finishing this—"

Cricket vanished. Lou turned to a stack of receipts and drew a finger across the touchpad of her laptop. The door jingled again, and she listened a moment, to see whether she was needed. Feet were moving slowly around the displays. A moment later a tall bald man in a Granny Smith–coloured track suit appeared in the stockroom door.

"Could I get some help out here?" he said.

"Oh—sure, sure," said Lou. She got up and followed the man back into the store space. The shop was empty; Cricket had left, had dropped her store key on the counter on her way out.

In the weeks leading up to the Regatta, Aquino underwent two massages a day by a licensed practitioner. Xióng ran four miles each morning and his superintendent arranged for a mixed martial arts instructor to oversee his hour-plus of plyometrics before work. Another young cleaner was eating nothing but protein shakes, chicken, and leafy greens and sitting half the afternoon in a sauna. Someone in the C Division was doing two hours of yoga a day in a vat of dry rice. Lorne wondered where someone could buy enough rice to fill a vat.

Leonidas put sixty dollars on his father. His wife had put a similar amount down and bought their children tiny orange coveralls with their grandfather's name stitched above the tiny breast pockets.

On the night of the Regatta, Leonidas and Arlen and the children ate a meal of eggs and olives for dinner— eggs dyed orange with food colouring—and shared KitKat bars, which Cricket had brought them from the piles fans had mailed to Lorne.

"Now you guys—you make a wish for Granddad," Leonidas told his two little children after dinner. "You make a wish that Granddad has a good night and has a fun time and nobody gets hurt, ha, ha! We want everyone to have a good time, don't we?"

Part 4

Chapter Sixty-one

Lorne smelled rats right away.

Echoes rolled across the city from outside each of the Big Nine buildings, where fans gathered in the street and sang and chanted and roared. People in distant quarters could hear the noise; the grass seemed to tremble even though there was no wind. An old emigré from France said that she had not felt a vibration like that since she was a girl in Paris in 1940, as the Germans advanced on the city limits.

When Lorne arrived, the shoulders of Sir Gareth blazed with orange lights, a colour code indicating which competitor would soon be making his way through its two kilometres of pitch-black ducts.

There he is .there's our boy

Go get 'em Lorny boy

You got this Torchy you got this

As per anti-contraband regulations, a referee in a tailored three-piece suit dressed Lorne in his coveralls. The uniform was sparkling clean. It bore no number, although the super had mulled stitching a 0 or 00 on the back; Lorne's fans had taken to doing so on their own imitation uniforms, delighting in what one writer called the cleaner's *numerical nihilism.*

"What's this—"

Lorne fiddled with a small round glass button clipped to his breast pocket.

"Your camera, Mr. Lorch."

"Eh? Am I taking *pictures* now?"

"You remember, Lorny," said Mallard, wearing a shirt and tie that looked like they had been pressed on a grinding stone. "We went over this. It's part of the protocol. Camera and radio."

"It's just for verification," said the referee.

"What channels does the radio get?"

"No, it's a two-way radio. Like a walkie-talkie."

"So—no country? No talk radio?"

The referee demonstrated the equipment for Lorne, clicking on the night-vision function and showing him the button for the microphone. Lorne held the device up to his mouth.

"This microphone business," he said, enunciating the words like a newscaster, "is even *dumber* than the camera business. Over."

His tongue and teeth, fogging up the camera device, appeared monstrously large on the referee's monitor screen.

"It's just protocol."

"Sure, just protocol."

"You can switch to another channel—this one here—if you need assistance, or want to discuss anything with your foreman."

"I won't," said Lorne. "Over and out."

Mallard glanced at the walls. He could hear the roar of the crowd in the street, which sounded like a far-off waterfall.

Once Lorne was zipped up, the referee ran his hands under the cleaner's armpits, down his sides, and over his thighs.

"Why don't you just check my ass, too?" said Lorne.

"It's just protocol, Mr. Lorch."

"What're you looking for? Cucumbers?"

"Dead rats. We have to make sure you're not carrying any into the ducts."

"Jesus Christ. Really?"

"Really."

Regatta officials milled around, all in shirts and ties and lanyard IDs. No reporters were around. A small trolley was set up with snacks, including a stack of KitKat bars, a couple of bags of pretzels, bottles of Gatorade and energy drinks, peanut butter protein bars, packages of cinnamon-flavoured toothpicks, a couple of hot towels, and a small face mirror. Nobody bothered to let Lorne know the refreshments were for him, and he looked at the trolley as if it were a display in a Christmas catalogue.

"Take a KitKat or two, Lorny," said Mallard.

"Nah. I won't be hungry till midnight—"

Lorne's coveralls bulged at the lower back with a roll of bread and butter. The cleaner had gotten a haircut, and freckles were visible through the thinning strands on his crown.

An orange-hued river was already flowing around Sir Gareth. Every window and rooftop within four blocks bristled with spectators. The fans were lusty and exuberant, twitching around in the August heat like overstrung mice. They sang a modified version of the "Olé, Olé, Olé" song featuring the following lyrics:

Lorne Lorch! Lorne Lorch Lorne Lorch Lorne Lorch

Lorne Lo-orch, Lorny Lorch

Other revellers borrowed the tune from "Ruby Tuesday" and sang:

Good-bye

Lit-tle Scantland

You might catch just one or two;

When he gets his hands on your dump

Lorny gonna school you

One fan had written out lengthy paeans to Lorne using the music of "Stairway to Heaven" and "Suite: Judy Blue Eyes" and was walking around belting them out, accompanying himself on a raspy electric guitar and a tiny amplifier that dangled from his neck. Now and then he handed out fuzzy mimeographed copies of the lyrics. The air was thick with the smell of burning hamburgers and roasting candy and beer and marijuana. A couple in their sixties wearing pumpkin-hued robes stretched a banner from one side of the street to the other; in thick letters, the banner read

LORNE LORCH CLEANING CHAMPION OF THE UNIVERSE

Vendors pushing Italian ice carts threaded their way through the crowds around each of the Big Nine buildings. Lorne's supporters ordered orange ices, Scantland's cherry. A Lorchian with a citrus allergy who ordered a neutral vanilla was booed by his comrades until he flung his ice into a sewer grate.

Lorne collected his first rat early on, just after reaching the second floor. As he had been instructed, after peeling the rat, he held its dying little body in front of the camera on his chest for verification by the referees in the control room. Outside, a couple of minutes later, the twenty-foot-high digital scoring display changed from 0 to 1. Lorne's supporters jumped up and down, screeching.

On other streets, partisans of his competitors received the news and moaned and spat and said it was a bunch of horseshit, that Lorch was getting the easiest ride of them all and that the whole contest was rigged. Inside the ducts of the Chunce & Chimbly, Lorne moved on in the darkness, his nostrils chasing a persistent scent of ice that he could not get a fix on. But it was early yet.

Leonidas sat in an old armchair, following the updates on his phone. He got up twice to carry small children to bed. Merrymakers wandered by his front window. One of them, wearing a sombrero painted in Aquino's colours—half of Aquino's fans assumed he was of Mexican descent—walked past sideways, facing Leonidas and Arlen's house, urinating on the sidewalk as he went and carrying on a conversation with a knot of friends behind him. Arlen tried to sleep but found it impossible, so she spent all evening sprawled on the couch, watching videos of great white sharks attacking seals.

Cricket knew it would be too taxing for her to loiter outside Sir Gareth with the rest of Lorne's fans. Besides, she would not have had any privacy, as she would certainly have been recognized. She paced around the little parlour, her body as rigid as steel. Her phone was not refreshing quickly enough, so she switched on a radio to listen to the tallies.

Kravchenko was one of the commentators.

"These guys," he said, "these guys—you know, they get what they get early, early—*that's* what counts. We know by midnight, half past, I'll know—once these guys do their first pass, you can know who it is. You only catch so many second time, when you come down, you guys. Right? So watch for who's in the lead."

"Any predictions?" said another commentator, a woman who did sports and weather on the city's largest AM radio station.

"Christ, too early," said Kravchenko.

No Christs, whispered the woman.

"It's too, too early."

"But you're picking Scantland—"

"We-ell, of *course*. Scantland's my boy."

"What about Lorch?"

"Oh—*next*," said Kravchenko. "No, no, okay. I love Lorny. I always say that. He might finish second. That's good. That's good—is there prize for second? But it'll be second by a mile."

Cricket snapped the radio off and resumed her pacing. She kept to a small circle in the living room. Every five or ten minutes she reversed course, and every time she did so she flicked the radio on again. Whenever she heard Kravchenko's voice, she shut the radio back off.

Much later that night she would bolt out the door in her sock feet, jumping into a cab and bawling out the driver for coming to a full stop at the curb.

Orinn, Lorne's old foreman, was providing studio commentary for one of the major networks. He sat leaning back on his stool with his arms akimbo, the old rictus smile present whether he was speaking or listening or watching.

"Where's Lorne right now?" asked the studio host. It was ten minutes past eleven o'clock.

"Probably around the twentieth."

"That means he's only halfway through."

"Yeah, but we're not halfway through the night."

"We will be soon. Where's Scantland by now?"

"Same, probably. And probably taking a picture of himself."

The mayor and her husband followed the results from her office, surrounded by twenty people: a pair of good-looking assistants, other staffers, the mayor's two teenaged children, the deputy mayor and a couple of close allies on council, and a few friends, mostly engineers and dentists. While almost every person had an eye on a phone, the mayor and her husband watched the events on a television set mounted above the non-functional office fireplace.

"The Chinese kid's looking good," said the mayor's husband. "He's up on Lorch *and* Scantland."

"Where's Aquino at?" somebody said.

"Not on the board yet."

Aquino, working the Jumbo Data Building for the first time in his life, was at that moment collecting a saucer-sized rat.

He unclipped the camera from his chest and aimed it at himself, flashing a beaming smile and a peace sign and pretending to kiss the rat as its organic light drained away. The idea of cameras had tickled him, and he was disappointed to only receive one. Moments later, when his new tally appeared on the scoreboard outside, he could hear faint echoes of whooping and hollering. Though he would not have recognized it as such, the sound was almost identical to the rebel yell of the Confederate troops during the American Civil War. The yellow his partisans wore, to match his coveralls, was so bright that a TV announcer said it made the streets glow like nuclear waste.

Outside the Westerfeldt, Scantland's faithful were marching back and forth in a sort of line dance, covered from head to toe in red and black. They sang songs ridiculing the other cleaners. One of the chants had no discernible tune:

One two three four
Lorne Lorch is on the floor

He got no ice rats in his hand
'Cause he just entered Scant-a-LAND

In these rhymes Lorne was called a drunk, an old woman, a washed-up loser, a socialist, a communist, and—ironically enough, given his wife's recent online squabble—a child molester. Scantland's fans marched and sang and produced a buzz like an ocean beginning to roil. Something about the songs and the colours and the blazing eyes of Scantland's mass of followers made some of the rooftop spectators, those who had paid thousands of dollars for their seats, uneasy.

A kilometre from the Jumbo, at the Macdonald, a skinny new cleaner named Pludder was making a hash of things in Tower 2. The streets around the complex were the colour of limes, as Pludder's growing base wore green to match the reflective construction vest he wore into the ducts. Pludder did not catch his first rat until midnight. His foreman whispered to the media that his boy had been fighting a flu, but declined to elaborate further, especially as his boy fell further and further behind.

Xióng—working in Lorne's house, the Sprill—captured three rats in the first hour. The streets around the Sprill were an unfamiliar purple-and-yellow; Xióng had a weakness for royal-looking colours, and many of his supporters wore flowing robes in those and similar shades.

A helicopter pilot, hovering high above the city, was able to make out where each cleaner was working by the various smudges of colour surrounding the Big Nine buildings. Despite his lofty perspective, the pilot was as confused as anyone a little before daybreak when he witnessed these various hues drifting towards Sir Gareth, like ants towards an apple core.

CHAPTER SIXTY-TWO

Twenty-eighth floor? Lorne thought. *Maybe.*

Twenty-ninth?

At least three, four of the bastards.

Five?

Fifteen minutes later, crawling around a joist on the fifteenth, sniffing the air:

More than five

Scantland was fascinated by the Westerfeldt's tight ducts. They reminded him of those in the Macdonald, where Kravchenko held his training camps. At no point in these tunnels could a cleaner, no matter how small, turn around without rolling into a tight ball. Scantland might as well have been burrowing deep below the surface of the earth; his lamp's beam reached only ten feet ahead of him, and beyond its pool was a pitch darkness he had never encountered before.

"Slow start for your guy?" the radio host asked Kravchenko.

"No way, no way."

"I thought he'd be ahead by now."

Listeners heard a creaking and shuffling as Kravchenko turned in his seat to look the host in the face.

"Do you say that to Usain Bolt after five, ten metres? Do you tap him on the shoulder and say, 'Mr. Bolt, you aren't in first place one second into the race, I'm sorry, you have to go home'? Do you do that?"

"No, I don't."

"No, you don't."

"By the way," said the host, "can you tell our listeners why these things our scientists call *gelucelets* you guys call *rats*?"

Kravchenko pondered a moment, rubbing his brow with his thumbtip.

"In Kyiv we called them, I guess in English it's 'cold tongues,'" he said.

"Cold tongues?"

"I like 'rats' better."

Instead of using a bag or his pockets, Xióng stowed his rats in a pail he carried with him. The *plink-plink* sound of freshly stiff prey hitting the bottom of the bucket was as beautiful to him as a Vivaldi concerto.

He never heard the rising tide of shrieks and clamour outside the Sprill. All his ears took in were those *plink, plinks*; between them there was the hiss of his breath and an occasional rush from the air conditioner. Every so often he shook the pail as if he were a street vendor pitching his wares. The noise travelled through the entire duct system. Microphones had been set up at vents in all of the buildings and amplified out into the street, and Xióng's shake-and-rattles never failed to draw a lusty response from his supporters.

Xióng's parents were watching the Sprill from an adjacent rooftop; the young man's superintendent had secured VIP tickets for them. His father spent most of the night reading a book and dozing while his mother played with an app on her phone that awarded points for solving logic puzzles. Xióng's brother and sister followed the Regatta from London and Singapore. Every ten or fifteen minutes Xióng received an encouraging text from his sister:

You got this my baby brother

You're in the lead I think, it looks like you're winning?!

On the hour, every hour, Xióng's brother texted:

Everybody can hear you jacking off

The ducts in the Sprill were as black and cramped as any in the city. Xióng moved through them without much trouble—he weighed only one hundred and eighteen pounds—but he could not believe how dirty they were compared to those of the Jumbo Data Building. Afterwards, he told his foreman that Lorne probably had "black lungs."

Plink, plink

In the Jumbo, Aquino was still mugging for his camera.

They call this place big! he said, grinning. *But it's not so big as Front Street.*

It's like BACK Street!

The cleaner who had been assigned to the Front Street Blocks, Aquino's home building, had developed the yips. It took him a half hour to peel his first rat and he got lost twice. At half past one in the morning, to prevent his suffering the embarrassment of coming in last, his foreman pulled him from the ducts.

"Crunkow's out," the TV host said. "Upper-body injury."

Orinn sat on his stool with his arms resting on his thighs.

"Where do you think he's hurt?" said the host. "Shoulder? Neck?"

Orinn made a cut-throat gesture.

"Just above the neck."

Laird, Lorne's original fan, left a gathering of Lorch supporters at a pub near the Chunce & Chimbly. The night was thick and slippery. A man in a tangerine-coloured clown costume tore the square out of Laird's pocket—an orange square, marking him as a Lorch man—and skipped away, waving it around his head like a lasso.

Someone set off a firecracker. One of the many police officers circuiting the area stomped on the cracker:

"Unless you have a permit—and you don't—you set off a cracker, I take you downtown."

Voices protested:

"We're *already* downtown!"

The officer whirled around.

"Then I drag your arses out to the sticks."

A barrage of laughter. High-fives for the cop.

Ambling through the crowd a block from Sir Gareth, nibbling on an orange ice he had purchased from a skinny sweat-covered vendor, Laird could see from the digital display that Lorne had collected four rats. Apprehension snatched at him.

Someone in the pub said Scantland had already peeled eight rats, Xióng six. Nobody had a total for Aquino, but it sounded as if he was on the board.

Laird tossed the dregs of his ice into an overflowing trash can and shuffled along with his hands deep in his pockets. The expensive fabric of his shirt clung to his neck and shoulders. It was a travesty, wasn't it? Lorne was the greatest cleaner of all time, the guy who won every title until the year they pulled the Cup for the Regatta. At last the entire country was paying attention to him and to them and to the sport. Immortality beckoned; immortality was deserved. And on this of all nights, the sport's Gretzky—its Ruth, its Bolt, its Jordan, its Phelps—its greatest legend was having a bad night; he *must* be having a bad night, Laird thought, because otherwise he was simply not keeping up. It wasn't fair to Lorny. It was an injustice. Lorne was born too early and now he was a minute late. If they had held the Regatta even a year ago—no contest, Lorne would have destroyed the field no matter what building he was tossed into. But now they said Scantland had eight rats and people were talking like it was already over. And Lorne was busting what was left of his ass in that glowing tower, up there somewhere between the silver feet and the orange shoulders, crawling, tired, fighting that weird slick metal, like an old warrior recalled to battle against an army of young men.

...But that was always the way, for many millennia that was how it had gone. Surely, Laird thought, wandering among the rabble of fans—surely if men of fifty thousand years ago had the same brains and bodies as we do, there must have been a few who missed their moment by a few years, or a few centuries. Some Paleolithic chieftain might have run faster than Bolt, or been stronger than Louis Cyr; the greatest legal mind in history may have went extinct before the ice melted, without any but the most rudimentary elements of justice occurring to it. Poor souls, yes, but ignorant of their poverty. The tragedy here, Laird reflected, was that Lorne was missing his due by just a wink, by a year, maybe even a few months. That Lorch the Torch had slowed some—that was common knowledge even diehards like

Laird did not dispute. A man in his late forties, even a generational talent like Lorne, can only do so much against men half his age.

They should have had the Regatta a year ago. They should have had the Regatta and Lorny could have lapped the others and then he could have retired, maybe, withdrawn from competition and gone out on top.

Now he's the old grey mare.

Still on the air at a few minutes to one o'clock, Kravchenko announced his retirement from cleaning. A low peal of thunder crackled in the eastern sky, but few heard it over the din of the crowd.

"I just don't have the quest in me, you know," he told the host. "I don't have oomph. You know the oomph? The quest?"

"The *drive*," offered the host.

"The drive, yes, she said it, yes, the drive. The quest. I don't return. I won't be returning. I've given all I can to the sport and now it's time for a new generation. New stars, okay?"

"Then it's a sad day for cleaning," the host said. "But well earned, my friend."

"Thanks, friend."

In the television studio, a little before four o'clock:

"What's that?"

"What's what?"

A technician peered into one of the monitors that were providing live feeds outside the Big Nine. Sir Gareth, like the fastest qualifier in a sprint final, had the middle monitor; flanking it was the Sprill and the Westerfeldt.

A production assistant, moments removed from a nap in a bathroom stall, joined the technician.

"There," said the tech.

"What?"

"Halfway up the left, there... I guess east. East?"

"So?"

"It looks shiny. Like—*too* shiny—"

"And you're full of shiny shit."

The producers were running a commercial. Orinn remained seated on his chair, holding a cup of dead coffee. When the two studio workers moved away from the monitor, he leaned forward and stared at the screen. For the first time since the day long ago that his ex-wife told him she was pregnant, the rictus smile left his face.

Lorne felt like he was strolling through a palace, or at least a fancy sewer. To him the building—Sir Gareth—was still ridiculous, but the ability to crab-walk through the ducts, rather than having to slither along on his belly, was a luxury.

A fellow could get used to this.

That smell of ice, though—it was everywhere, sometimes strong, sometimes weaker, but always around, above, below, behind, a couple of storeys higher, a couple lower. It was everywhere but nowhere...

Around the thirtieth floor he decided to stop for lunch. He happened to be halfway along one of the most spacious ducts in the building, and he slumped against its wall like he used to slump and eat Twinkies against his locker in high school. It was odd to eat sitting down. He pulled out his wrapped bundle and opened it.

"Hey," he said out loud, gazing at his lunch. "Hey, now—!"

Cricket had stuffed olives into his bread. The bread was warm and wet and misshapen from having nested inside his coveralls, but the salt of the olives hit his palate like fire.

Jesus that's good

Cricket had considered buying him an olive loaf, but knew he much preferred green olives to black.

Jesus

His nostrils were cold again. He quickly moved on, still chewing, leaving his wrapper behind. It was never found.

It struck Lorne that these ducts were not as dark as those in the Sprill. He could make out edges and corners and walls more easily than in his home building. It was as if someone a turn or two ahead were carrying a candle through the ducts, teasing him. He had no trouble tracking and spotting the strange green rats, though they were harder to see in this type of darkness than they would have been in a thicker gloom, like that of the Sprill.

He peeled two more on his way to the top. Midnight passed, then one o'clock. Down below, in the street and the surrounding blocks, in VIP rooftop sections and paid-for windows facing Sir Gareth from all directions, fans grew anxious at the lack of news from inside. Unofficial tallies showed Scantland and Xióng ahead of Lorne, and Aquino lunging from behind. Lorne reached the top of the Chunce & Chimbly at twenty minutes past one o'clock. He had seven rats in his bag. His legs were starting to ache and he took a moment to rest, stretching out to his full length along the highest tunnel in the building. If the building had been made of transparent glass, Lorne would have appeared to be hovering inside Sir Gareth's mind like an unformed dream, or like a piece of food stuck in the giant's throat.

Lying there on top of the city, he smelled ice. There were more rats. Not one or two. More.

CHAPTER SIXTY-THREE

Outside Sir Gareth, in the sticky heat of night, Scantland partisans and the orange-costumed clown tipped over an Italian ice cart and tried to set it on fire. The flavoured ices defied the partisans' lighters. Instead, they kicked the cart to pieces and urinated on the debris.

"You got any chocolate?" said the orange clown, jumping up and down on the wreckage of the cart. "Oh—excuse me—did you *have* any chocolate?"

"No chocolate," said the exasperated cartman. "No chocolate, no nothing!"

"That's too bad! Chocolate's my favourite. Yummy. Yummy."

The vandals chanted this as they circled the fallen wagon. Some of the farther-gone souls tried to eat the splattered ices off the pavement with their hands.

Yummy yummy yummy

The static and mumbling in Lorne's radio, which he had mostly ignored during the evening, grew more persistent. Descending from floors forty-five to thirty-five he did not find another rat, but the smell of them was thickening inside his nose. He shook the camera-radio, thinking a wire in its speaker had come loose. In the control room the feed bounced up and down on the monitor.

"Lorny—Lorny—"

At last Lorne stopped, held the piece to his ear.

"What?"

"It's Mallard. How are you?"

"Never better. Beautiful day."

"Seen any more rats?"

"You've seen all my rats. What do you want?"

A pause.

"Yah Lorny," said Mallard. "You got a minute?"

"For what?"

"Just a minute. Can you switch over to the other channel?"

"Why?"

"Just please switch over, Lorny."

"Christ—"

Lorne twisted the knob on the camera. Static buffeted his ear, then a snatch of someone speaking a foreign language, then laughter, then silence.

"Lorny?"

Though he spoke in a low tone, Mallard's voice came through so clear now that it startled Lorne.

"I got to keep moving, I only just hit the top—"

"We have an offer, Lorny. Scantland's team just contacted me. They're offering a draw. A tie."

"What the Christ?"

"Scantland and you. He's ahead, Lorny. He's got fourteen. Wheel of cheese territory. And I don't know"—Mallard lowered his voice even further—"I don't know how he got them all. Sounds funny to me—real funny—but he's in the lead. And the Chinese kid isn't far behind."

"Where am I?"

A pause.

"I know you're at *least* fifth—"

"No way in hell I'm fifth."

"That's what they said on TV."

"TV makes shit up."

Mallard clicked his teeth with his tongue.

"I think we should consider it," he said. "Scantland's offer."

"Why's he want a draw if he's got a thousand rats?"

"He broke his sack, Lorne."

"Eh?"

"Tore his sack wide open, on a piece of metal... almost lost a couple because of it."

"What the Christ are you talking about? Scantland cut his sack? His bag... what—his *balls*?"

"Jesus, no, Lorny! His sack—his *collection* sack, the thing he puts the rats in—"

"But what did he lose two of?"

"Lose two of—? Oh! Oh! *Rats*, Lorny. A couple of rats—when he broke his sack, a couple almost rolled down a shaft in the Wester. He didn't lose any *balls*, Lorny. His balls are okay. But nobody can carry that many rats in his hands."

"He can use his pockets."

"He's wearing a unitard, Lorny."

"A *what*?"

"A unitard. No pockets."

All Mallard heard over the radio for the next thirty seconds was the rusty sound of laughter. Lorne laughed so hard that he rocked on his hams, and had to lean against the wall of the duct. He had heard some amazing things in his time, but this was *number one*! When Cricket found Lorne in the ducts an hour later, she knew he had gone into shock, because the first thing he told her was that Scantland was wearing a unitard.

"Lorny—"

"I never knew I could have a unitard," Lorne said, guffawing, coughing. "That's what I get for getting old—"

"Listen, Lorny," said Mallard, quicker now. "The thing is the kid can barely carry them, and if he finds any more, he'll be in trouble. He's having to plow the ones he's got ahead of him, and it's slowing everything down."

Mallard had received this intelligence from Blue, one of Scantland's foremen. While Mallard had not translated everything accurately—Scantland was wearing a form-fitting pocketless suit, but it was not exactly a unitard—he got the crux of it right. At that moment, Scantland was slithering eastward through the seventh-floor ducts of the Westerfeldt, using his hands to push his catch along before him like a mother hen herding her chicks. He had tried cupping them in his hands, stuffing them in his cap, and bunching some down his uniform. Nothing worked. The discs chafed his skin raw and half of them rattled out onto the duct floor. It had taken him an hour to work his way down two floors. Xióng was catching up, having plucked three fresh rats as he descended the Sprill, and Aquino was always better in the second half of a shift. Blue had said as much to Mallard in making his pitch for a draw.

"And just how," Mallard had asked Blue, "are you supposed to fix up a tie? They'll count Lorny's rats soon's he's out."

"No, they won't. Our boy's got fourteen. Nobody's gonna get fourteen. Even the Chinese kid, he's got maybe ten. It's up there on the board. We announce we got fourteen, we say the boy's on his way down and we all talked it over and he and Lorch are neck-and-neck and exhausted, and they'll share the gold medal or whatever."

"What gold medal?"

"Oh—the cash, the money."

"Jesus—"

"Otherwise your man gets nothing, right? This way, both of them get money. People love this kind of stuff—guys laying down their swords, or pistols, or whatever. They might even find more cash."

"More cash?"

"Fifty grand apiece. I bet they'd do that. They'd bump it up—they'd have to."

Mallard's heart was throbbing.

"I don't know," he said, trapping a sob in his throat. "I don't know. The Chinese kid must be really close—"

"He's got ten, and he's almost done. He'll be out within the hour."

"I heard he had way more."

"No way. This city's reached peak horseshit tonight."

Mallard had ended the conversation and radioed Lorne.

"That's what they're proposing, Lorny. And I don't know... it doesn't sound like the *worst* thing in the world right now, okay? I think we should consider everything on the table. There's lots of money riding on this, and... hell, Lorny, you've had a good night, but we both know you're in a bum shack, the thing's rigged, it's not right. I think we need to consider it, Lorny.

"Lorny—?"

At two minutes to four o'clock, the Dropcuster feed for the Regatta reached five thousand comments. Eleven hundred of them had been posted in the previous twenty minutes.

The five-thousandth comment was:

I'm a block away now and it looks really bad—lots of people still showing up

Five thousand and one was:

At the Jumbo... one of the only ones left here everyone's leaving?? And our boy Aquino still going strong and everybody leaving???

And the next:

You got Xióng's dribble running down your cheeks into your mouth

That was the latest cut in an hour-long argument between a ten-year-old and a fifty-four-year-old.

Stay the hell away from Gareth, kids. It looks bad. REAL bad

At the television studio, Orinn had joined the cluster of technicians gathered around the monitor showing the Chunce & Chimbly. The building appeared to have grown a silver, shiny tumour low on its left flank.

In case anyone had missed it earlier, Kravchenko again announced his retirement.

Cricket got a text from Leonidas as she was rushing out the door in her sock feet:

Ah mom?

In the taxi, a reply:

Gng to your fthre

From Leonidas:

Mom don't go there it's not safe!!

The ellipses of a response appeared on Leonidas's phone screen. He waited as the ellipses refreshed over and over again. His mother, he thought, was typing a much longer answer than the circumstances required.

Jeez, Mom, you don't have to write a novel ha ha!

You still there Mom

The ellipses disappeared.

CHAPTER SIXTY-FOUR

On his way down, Lorne hit the twenty-eighth floor at 3:17 a.m. Making out the rolling echo of Regatta fans outside, he assumed it was water rushing in the building pipes. His mind was flashing like a severed electric cable. He wondered whether the entire duct system, all two thousand metres of it, was brighter than it should have been because of what he believed he was about to discover.

Two hours earlier, during his first pass of the twenty-eighth, he had felt the sweat on the back of his neck go dry. He assumed a spray of air had escaped from a seam or internal vent. He had barely noticed; it had taken his brain, working in the background, one hundred and twenty minutes to generate a hypothesis.

Now Lorne crawled back along the tunnel with his neck bent low, waiting for the building to breathe again on his flesh. He crawled as slowly as he could, moving a hand or a foot only every few seconds. His tongue was wedged in his teeth and he hardly breathed, as if he were moving over a thin pane of glass.

Yet he was thinking of other things:

...The kid broke his sack. The kid broke his sack and he's wearing leotards and now he wants to make a deal.

What kind of a man does that? What kind of a man

Making his way along the main tunnel of the twenty-eighth, he followed a turn towards the southeast corner of the building, where the duct had been diverted around a concrete beam. Even with all of his senses concentrated on that strip of skin on his neck, even as crystals formed inside his nose, he nearly passed the spot. For a second the smell of ice seemed to dissipate. He stopped, groped the nape of his neck with his hand. The flesh was still sweaty. But now he felt a chill on his lower back, a coldness that soaked like water through the fabric of his uniform.

Reversing inch by inch, Lorne stopped when the chill grazed his hair and tickled his scalp. He looked up.

You can run but you can't hide, you bastards

In the gloom he saw a thin stripe of pale green light not a foot above his head, a ghostly stria in the metal, a something where there should have been nothing. He was seeing what Scantland had only ever smelled.

The first person to spot the ice was the orange clown. At that point he scarcely knew where he was, and he was unable to understand that what he was seeing was bad. When the siren went off he ran for shelter, skipping and laughing, shouting that the Luftwaffe had been spotted high above the cliffs of Dover.

It took some wrenching and cursing. After some minutes at it, Lorne was able to thrust the panel open with hands that years of peeling had hardened to the texture of tree bark. He could not believe that neither Scantland nor any of his predecessors had ever, on reaching this lonely spot on the twenty-eighth, happened to look up. Wrestling the panel out, he leaned it against the wall of the duct; he had broken a fixture on the end, but that was not important. Slapping the grease on his hands against his coveralls, he elevated himself on his knees and raised his head into the uncovered space.

Hello boys

It was a little vertical shaft, stretching up about eight feet into a joist. The shaft did not otherwise communicate with the ductwork and was probably dead space, Lorne thought, serving no purpose, like a compartment in an old mansion that had long been boarded up. All he could see around him were glittering green stars, as if he were looking at a distant region of the Milky Way.

The shaft was studded with rats. There must have been thirty, maybe more. They were different, more elongated, than the thousands he had encountered in his decades of hunting. But he had no doubt what they were. His breath swirled in the shaft. As its warmth brushed against the rats, they flared like green fire.

Down in the control room, the monitor blazed.

"What the hell is that?" said Mallard. "Lorny—"

Light and the space-like musk of ice filled Lorne's head. For the first time in his life, he nearly swooned.

At the Westerfeldt, along the north side of the eleventh floor, Scantland lay on his back, staring up at a duct ceiling inches from his nose. Dead rats were strewn halo-style on the metal around his head. He had abandoned his torn sack somewhere on an upper floor and did not care what happened to it.

The air conditioning switched on and he felt a breeze caressing his eyelashes. He wondered what his fans were thinking.

Bear texted, again and again:

Carry them in your hat your pockets your hands

The rats I mean

Pls respond

Herding the dead rats in that cramped darkness, even with the LED light attached to his singlet, had proven as difficult as herding live creatures. The rats slid and rolled. Some were rough, some were slick, and they were all different sizes. Their hard little corpses were having their revenge. He was not injured, he was not sick, he had not gotten stuck, though once or twice he had come close. It was supposed to be the greatest night of his young life, the first cobble in a path towards duct immortality. He felt strong and healthy and could have covered the whole building, top to bottom, a second time, maybe a third time.

And yet here he was, on his back, waiting for his foreman to radio him that a broken-down old man had agreed to a draw.

What would his sponsors say about a tie? What would his thousands of Dropcuster subscribers think, the ones who even now were flooding his and other feeds bragging about how much money they had bet on him to win?

Pls respond bbe

Now his phone was vibrating in its clip every thirty or forty seconds. Bear might text all night. The sound sickened him. He had an urge to pull his phone apart or pitch some of the dead rats into the darkness or pound and scream against the metal.

Babe did you read my txt

When Scantland was nine years old his baseball team made it to the provincial championship tournament. They ended up losing in the final to a team from Richmond Hill that they had beaten the previous year. In the semi-final game, Scantland's team went up against a Windsor club. Everyone hated Windsor because they were loud. They chirped and chattered nonstop, on the bench and in the field, as if someone had mixed amphetamines into their bubble gum.

In the sixth inning, with the score tied at four, Scantland drove in what ended up being the winning run with a two-strike triple. It was the most unlikely triple he had ever hit. Unusually, he had been drawn by the Windsor pitcher's breakers into chasing a bad ball, low and curving outside. Somehow he caught it on the very end of his bat and chopped the ball to the opposite field; it was spinning so hard when it hit the grass on the foul line that it nearly skipped right out of the park. Scantland had a clear memory of rounding first base and heading for second knowing that he had done a bad thing, that he had swung at a terrible pitch, and that for some baffling reason he was being rewarded for it. He remembered a cluster of sunflower seeds Windsor's overgrown first baseman had spit onto the base path, and the shortstop's round prepubescent face howling at the right fielder to get his fat ass moving and to get the ball back into the infield. Sliding into third—nearly into his goateed coach, who was signalling at him to stop—Scantland flung his arms into the air in triumph. His teammates were beside themselves. The parents were roaring in the bleachers and the public-address announcer's grainy impassive voice had a bit of a tremble in it as he announced *TRIPLE FOR NUMBER SEVEN, SCANTLAND; OTTAWA WEST LEADS FIVE-FOUR*. After the game, Scantland's coach kneaded the boy's shoulders again and again, saying *I never saw a poke like that in all my life, I never saw someone hit a pitch like that*. Scantland himself was sheepish. He had hit a game-winning triple, but it should have been an embarrassing strikeout.

Now it was ten years later and the stakes ten times higher and he was up in the ducts in the middle of the night, lying on his back with dead ice rats haloed around his head, his phone buzzing like a hornet. Now he was trying to barter his way to victory when victory, but for a hole in a nylon sack, should have been his.

He cursed, and cursed again. He was not a natural curser and did a poor job of it. The echoes of his oaths died away in the maze of metal.

He squeezed the phone out of its clip to check whether any texts from his foremen were coming in. He could not believe the old man was not jumping at the offer. Maybe, he thought, Lorch was suffering from dementia. There were no messages from the foremen, but there were fifty new ones—from Bear, from his parents, from friends and relatives and a few random fans who should not have had his number, piling up on his screen faster than he could scroll through them.

Sir Gareth was turning to ice.

CHAPTER SIXTY-FIVE

The streets leading to Sir Gareth teemed with pedestrians, some walking, some running, some on wheels. It seemed to Cricket as if everyone on earth was converging on the same point. She jumped out of the taxi three blocks early and ran, head tilted back, chasing the illuminated summit that commanded the city skyline. Her cap must have flown off en route, because it was gone by the time she reached the block in front of the tower. She had never seen so many people in such a small space.

Is Lorny still in there?

Oh shit!

He's in big trouble, boys!

The orange clown sat on Sir Gareth's toes—the front steps—facing the crowd, throwing his arms up in the air and letting them fall to his sides. Mallard and a dozen other officials, hustling out the front doors, nearly tripped over him. The clown threw his hands up and said

Wheeeeeeee!

Rather than moving in one direction, the crowd in the street was rocking back and forth, like a wave sloshing back and forth in a bathtub. A collection of police and security were trying to evacuate the Chunce & Chimbly and at the same time prevent the orange-flecked crest of the wave from crashing into the steps. High above, Sir Gareth's shoulders flickered. A civil-defence siren, long dormant, had been activated, and it wailed, rising and falling, like the voice of an ancient god.

Looorrrrnnyyyyy

The tumour of ice stretched now from the ground floor to the eighth. Its bulge threatened the flank of the adjacent building, which was also being evacuated. The helicopter pilot arrived to pick up VIPs on the roof of the building across the street. Someone tried to grab a landing skid as the chopper took off again and was knocked from the roof, pitching twelve storeys to his death.

A police sergeant raised a bullhorn to his lips:

Please leave the street NOW and please don't run NOW

But he could hardly be heard over the skirling of the siren and the violent cacophony in the street. Thousands of mobile phones captured the wild spectacle of ice eating alive a forty-five-storey building. The ice had a ghastly greenish hue, like something escaped from a sick body.

People—regardless of affiliation, regardless of uniform colour, regardless of drunkenness—cried out in rising panic:

Lorny's still in there

Where's Lorny

SOMEBODY GET LORNY OUT

LORNY LORCH IS IN THERE

On the steps, the guards and police shot glances at one another over their bullhorns. The crowd was licking closer and closer to their feet.

GET LORNY OUT

A young man in Scantland black and red was running back and forth along the steps, stepping around the orange clown. He pounded his chest and screamed that Lorne Lorch was the biggest bastard of all time and had sabotaged the building and the whole event because he wanted to screw over the deserving champion. Bear and Scantland were having a frantic text conversation about the disaster unfolding at Sir Gareth and what that might mean for Scantland's chances of securing the Cup. The mayor was standing—twisting, in fact, after the manner of a bowler willing a ball away from the gutter—in front of the television, with phones in each hand and aides on all sides; her guests ran in and out of the office, all but dancing to get her attention but not daring to disturb her several beams of focus.

Why doesn't the damned thing melt? the mayor was thinking. *I got the damned A/C cranked in here and I can hardly breathe*

The ice was fattening itself on the side of the building. In front of Sir Gareth the street teemed with hot, drunken, confused, frightened, angry souls. A couple that could not have been younger than forty-five lurched up the steps, tore off half their clothes, and attempted to have sex five feet from the boots of a police constable. The crowd yawped with delight; the woman, slim and ginger-haired with flaring nostrils, howled along with the civil-defence siren—

YooooooOOOOOOOOOOOOOOOOOOooooooooo

SAVE LORNY

WE GOTTA GET IN THERE

And still the Scantland partisan, weaving around the guards:

Lorny did this ON PURPOSE GUYS

And at last, it was too much; at last the twig, from which the entire city was dangling, snapped in two. Whether it was the lapping tide of the crowd, or the orange clown flailing around on his back like a child, or the savage moans of the ginger-haired lover bucking up and down on her boyfriend, or the shrieking siren, or the intolerable summer air, or the helicopter chopping up the sky, a critical spring had come loose. A constable turned to a colleague on one side and a security guard on the other—

"Gents—"

And a little ball hurtled out of the crowd and through the cordon, through the doors, inside. If the constable had not seen legs, he would never have believed it was a human being. It was like a first arrow bent into the sky. The cordon collapsed like a balloon that had been pricked with a needle, leaving Sir Gareth defenceless.

The screaming vanguard of the crowd entered at seven minutes to five. As they did, the structure's lights flickered, blazed, and went dark. Most of the emergency lighting failed, and the tower stood like a block of dark matter among the nighttime luminescence of its neighbours.

Cold cold cold, shouted the ginger-haired woman, covering her breasts against the breath of the building as the mob broke down the doors.

Mr. Chimbly, Sir Gareth's co-father, followed the proceedings from Colorado, where he spent his summers. He had flipped a coin with his long-time partner, Mr. Chunce, to determine which of them would watch the event live. The coin toss had been rigged: Mr. Chimbly used a two-headed coin. Mr. Chunce guessed that Mr. Chimbly would use a two-sided coin, but he expected it would be two-tailed. He called tails almost before the coin rocketed into the air from Mr. Chimbly's knobby thumbtip.

Mr. Chunce was one of the supreme VIPs of the night and sat in the front row of a plush-lined grandstand on the roof of the building across from Sir Gareth. All night long he had sipped champagne and munched on smoked salmon and bagels. A portable air conditioner stood at his feet and cooled his ankles. At three o'clock he opened a thirty-year-old bottle of pinot noir for his guests, toasting Scantland and promising to drink from the Cleaners Cup before morning.

The two men texted back and forth until Sir Gareth started turning to ice. Mr. Chimbly tried again and again to telephone his partner. During the rush to escape the building, Mr. Chunce dropped his phone, collapsed from a heart attack, and had two fingers stamped on and broken. A ropy young caterer carried him over her shoulders down the stairs.

Aquino had finished his run, as had Pludder, Xióng, and several others. Scantland left behind his rats and was dragging himself and an unintentional erection towards the bottom of the Sprill.

When TV monitors showed the tower lights flashing and extinguishing, Kravchenko said that the "end was coming" and that he was *praying for poor little Lorny*. Orinn, watching the multicoloured masses pouring into Sir Gareth, sat forward on his stool with his elbows on his thighs, making a knickering sound, over and over, like a horse.

Leonidas was on his knees on the floor, staring at a live stream of the disaster on his phone. He felt like his insides were full of eyeballs and that someone was stabbing each one with a party hat.

Lorne knew his fingertips were moving, though he could hardly feel them.

On the day long ago that the health officials filled up the well in his backyard, Lorne had hid in the closet and not come out until the next day. His mother told his father that it was because he was sad he had lost his favourite place in the world. Mr. Lorch thought a thrashing might help the boy along, but on this one occasion his wife overruled him.

It was not until he was an adult that Lorne understood what had bothered him so much about the destruction of his well. He had never gone to the bottom. The idea had always terrified him. Yet if he had only been able to try again a year or two later, when he would have been a year or two braver, he felt he might have done it. If the rats had appeared just a few years later... He had only needed a bit more time, a bit more strength. But he never got the chance.

His eyes were shut but they were full of green phosphorescence. Or were his eyes open? Was he awake, or asleep? Was he awake—was he alive—

He was not aware that the building had gone dark. The well walls were painted with a startling bioluminescence and his lips were cold and the sweat on his neck and shoulders had curdled. His body was not oriented right. He could not move, but his hand kept scraping and scraping, and his flesh was cold under his uniform. *I have to whiz so bad*, he thought, *I have to whiz but I can't feel it—where is it?* A queer feeling took hold of him; he felt his body struggling, as if it were an entity separate from himself, controlled by something else. Tilting his head down, he saw his thighs, his knees, and his shins, but not his feet. His feet were gone. In their place was a little black pool, a pool that the freezing green glow had not reached.

No wait

... It was not a pool, that's not a pool, that's a *hole*; that's my feet gone in the dark. I can't see the dark I can't see the bottom *my hands are still moving but I'm not moving them if I let go will I fall? Am I going to fall? How far down is it is it one hundred feet two hundred what floor am I on I can't look up because it hurts my eyes but I can't see where I am Christ Almighty* and now he closed his eyes because the brilliant light and the brilliant cold watered his eyes and his feet were dangling in the black pool, exposed to whatever might be lurking in it. *Jesus Christ Almighty* Lorne tried to kick his feet and wriggle them back up the well because he could no longer remember what was beneath and he wanted to be able to see what was beneath. The swarming liquid-looking neon universe seemed to flare, as if the multitude of rats *They're called gelucelets* was breathing in and out as one single fantastic terrible organism. He could feel his feet but he could not see his feet and he was sure something below him was looking at them from the deep, was even now creeping up the stone walls, unhurried, like a spider approaching a trapped fly. He wriggled and wriggled but could not move. *I didn't mean it I just wanted three or four or five I didn't know I didn't mean to do that stop guys please stop don't be mad let me leave the party don't do that stop stop* The shaft was getting smaller and he could hear them—it—like a beating heart, like something that was not moving but was sucking all of space into itself.

Please stop you assholes I made a mistake I won't touch you again now STOP

Twenty-eight storeys; they all had to climb twenty-eight floors in the dark, because the elevators had gone dead. Lorne flailed his feet, the only part of him that could still move. He thought he could smell cedar leaves and he wanted to reach up and out and grab at them. The shaft was squeezing his body. For the first time he made out the grinding shrill of the civil-defence siren and it struck him that something incredible was happening somewhere in the city and everyone was rushing home. The wall of rats flared around him and his shoulders and thighs began to burn from the ice. He could not see. It felt behind his closed eyes that the universe of rats was jiggling and in their jiggling they were trying to communicate with him, producing a strange noise like the chanting of an invading army. The sound was wonderful and awful, rasping like a symphony of violins strung with barbed wire, shrilling into a cold, empty, blinding nothing. *Jesus Christ* He felt a pressure on his chest: the universe was laying stones on top of his body and he could not get enough air. The rats were going to crush him and devour him *No Pop I won't go in the well ever again just get me out tell the thing to leave me alone CHRIST get me out get me out of here* the chanting grew louder and fiercer and Lorne was sure he was dead, sure that the rats had killed him and were going to digest him and drag his meatless skeleton to hell and he could hear the demons wild and yelping from the bottom of the well *Jesus Christ LET GO* they were nipping at his feet and he kicked as hard as he could and expanded his body trying to break free but he only got colder and more stuck and something had his foot and he shook back and forth and his ankle joint throbbed as if the socket were about to break apart.

The things in the black pool were screaming

LORN-EE

LORN-EE

LORN-EE

He squeezed and yanked his leg

Lemme go lemme go you shits you pieces of shitty SHIT SHIT LORNY!

Down in the pool of black swallowing his feet Lorne saw an eye, then another, then a third—or maybe it was the first again; it was the evilest eye he could imagine and he squealed like a child and kicked and felt ice against his face and he shut his eyes so tight his brow throbbed.

LORNY

I GOT YOU

Below him, from the bottom of the well, a hand gripped his foot and pulled and the one or two or three eyes squinted into the unbearable green and above the roar of six hundred invading voices he heard *Lorny, Lorny dear Lorny my dear it's okay Lorny I'm here I'm here stop screaming Lorny Lorny can you move Lorny?*

Chapter Sixty-six

The siren was squalling as a cream-coloured dawn filled the sky. The tops of buildings rolled past on either side. He was staring straight up. It was noisy and ferocious everywhere but he could not see what was happening. Never in his life had he been so cold. He felt his hands moving and clawing and peeling and on one side someone was pressing their hand over his, trying to get his fingers to relax, *relax, stop, stop, it's over.* His eyes ached but he caught splashes of crimson light, first on his left and then on the right.

"Lorny—"

A blob materialized in front of his eyes, blocking the sky.

"Lorny—"

A hand brushed the chill flesh on his face, as if to close his eyes, as if he had died. The hand was warm but he could not smell it. He could not smell anything. The hand touched his cheek and his face felt like cardboard. *Who the hell,* he thought, *put cardboard on my face?* Another hand patted the top of his head, but he could absorb from it neither warmth nor cold, only a tickle as his hair mashed down, up, down, up. The hand patting him belonged to the orange clown.

Cricket's face was upside down. She was not wearing a baseball cap.

"Oh—Crick—"

The words were mangled by the cardboard.

"Hi, Lorny."

"Can you take this—this shit off my face?"

"What shit?"

"Oh, never mind... leave it. Where are we going?"

He sounded like he was talking through a pillow.

"Someplace warm."

"It's already warm as a bastard."

Before he finished saying this he realized he was wrong. The air was warm but he was cold. He was freezing. Cricket's head loomed over his, in front of the paling sky that rolled slowly past as if it were on a clothesline. Something small and wet pattered on the cardboard of his brow.

"Can you tell those jokers to stop yelling?" he said.

"I'll take care of it, Lorny," said a voice.

"Good."

Lorne recognized that he was being loaded into a vehicle, but what kind of vehicle was unknown—ambulance? Hearse? He took a lock of Cricket's hair gently in his fingers. That is what he believed he was doing, though his arm did not rise up from the gurney.

"You came back," he said.

Why does my voice sound like that?

"Yes, Lorny—"

Another patter on the cardboard, hot, this time close to his eye.

"How long did you leave me?"

"I never left, Lorny."

"I think you did."

"Be quiet, now, and rest."

"She's right," said the clown, who had nearly sobered up. "Rest, Lorny. You must rest, Lorny. You must rest, Lorny. You must rest... Lorny..."

The clown told Cricket that she, and not he, should accompany Lorne in the ambulance.

"Oh Christ," Lorne said. The gurney shivered, then floated. "Who won the damn thing? Did the kid take it? I hope none of those bastards got hurt. I hope nobody got stuck in the well. Eh, Crick? Crick? And Christ, can you take this Christly cardboard off my face?"

The ambulance pulled away, slowly, making its way around broken glass and other debris. The clown was left in the wreckage of the street. He did not wave to the ambulance as it bore away the wreckage of Lorne. Later that day, at two o'clock in the afternoon, the clown was getting married, and he needed to get home for a bath, a shave, and a rest.

Part 5

Chapter Sixty-seven

Lorne was chattering to his father on the way to the dump. "Dad—if you could be anything in the world, what would you be?"

"Deaf."

"No. If you could do any *job* in the world."

Mr. Lorch looked at his son, who could hardly see over the dash.

"There's no point thinking about things like that."

He pulled the pickup onto the access road. As the road got bumpier Lorne leaped up and down on his seat, wincing once or twice when the lap belt stung his hips. His index finger was locked into a split in the seat vinyl.

"Stop clowning."

"I'm not clowning."

"You *are* clowning."

"So what would you do, Dad? Would you be a pilot?"

"I wouldn't do nothing. I never gave it a second thought," his father said.

The front tire plunged into a dip, and the shock knocked Lorne's head against the window. His skull made a noise like a partridge thumping against the glass.

"You see what you get for clowning around?" said Mr. Lorch.

Lorne's face screwed up in pain. He did not press his hand to his temple because he did not want to give his father the satisfaction of being right. Instead he drew his shoulder up against his ear, using it to numb as many nerve endings as he could without his father noticing.

"You got that because you were acting like an idiot."

In a minute the pain began to dull. Lorne's face and shoulders relaxed. As the truck jounced along, twigs from the flanking trees grabbed at the sun-bleached green hood.

"You know what I'd want to do," Lorne said, "if I could do anything?"

"No."

"Be a wrestler."

Mr. Lorch drove over a couple more bumps and pulled into the weighing station. As he waited for the dump superintendent, who had emphysema, to come out of the shack and write out his ticket, Mr. Lorch rested his wrist over the steering wheel and turned to his son.

"What makes you think you could be a wrestler?"

"Oh," said Lorne, "it's not *real*, Dad. Wrestling. It's all fake! You don't really get hurt. You just pretend."

Lorne's hair had left a smudge on the glass, a product of his antipathy to bathing. Noticing it at the same time as his father, he slipped his fist into his sleeve and reached to polish the window.

"Don't," said Mr. Lorch.

"I was just gonna clean it—"

"Leave it alone. You'll make it worse."

The smudge was still on the window a year later, when the truck broke down.

In a closet on the first floor of the Jumbo Data Building, Xióng squatted on his heels, rocking back and forth, munching an apple. The light in the closet was out; the door was slightly ajar, throwing a narrow, broken shaft of light over the back wall. Xióng rocked on his heels and tore at the skin of the apple and stared at the vent hole he was about to squeeze himself through to begin his shift.

Footsteps approached, measured and deliberate, not the meandering scuffle of a custodian, the tread of a lone person. He rose to his feet and listened.

Xióng's Regatta had been uneventful. He captured eleven rats—one short of a wheel of cheese special, which, as he was lactose-intolerant, did not bother him much. By the time the civil-defence siren had rung out, he was already out of the ducts of the Sprill and changing into his street clothes. No scrum awaited him. He could not understand where all the reporters were, though he figured it may have had something to do with the siren.

After the Regatta, as his parents drove him home, they told him everything they had heard about the Chunce & Chimbly. Most of it was false or exaggerated.

"The whole building's *gone*?" he said.

"We don't know," said his mother.

"That's what we heard," said his father.

"But we don't know."

"That's whack," said Xióng. "That is *whack*."

"I know that. I know it."

"It's *whack*."

He was glad the whole frenzy was over, grateful to be back in his home building, the Jumbo, zipped and clipped and enjoying his pre-game apple. But footsteps approached and now the closet door swung open and he fell back awkwardly, landing against the wall and straddling a mop wagon. His foreman leaned into the closet and beckoned him out.

In the night-lit corridor Xióng confronted a group of unfamiliar men. Most were in shirts and ties. After a moment he recognized one as the official who had instructed him on the use of the radio-camera on the night of the Regatta.

"Hi, Charlie," said the official.

"Hi."

"About to get to it?"

"Yeah."

The men offered bland smiles.

"Good, good," said the official. Even in the semidarkness, Xióng could see that the official needed a shave.

"Is something wrong?"

The man shook his head.

"Not a thing, Charlie."

"Am I in trouble?"

"Not at all," said the foreman. "We have something to give you."

The official half-turned—a signal—and another well-dressed man stepped forward. Xióng had never seen this other man before, but he represented the corporation that owned the Jumbo Data Building. He carried something bulky in his arms. For an instant, Xióng guessed it was a wheel of cheese; perhaps, he thought, he had miscounted his take from the Regatta.

But the burden twinkled under the night lighting.

"Congratulations, Charlie—"

The representative handed Xióng the Cleaners Cup.

The young man gaped at the trophy; its alloyed and fluted silver had been wiped, but not polished. Scuffing and fading on the wooden base showed where the plates from previous years, all with Lorne's name, had been removed. The Cup was as light as a jack-o-lantern and Xióng held it in his left hand as the officials, one by one, shook his right. The muttered compliments had a funereal air, as if in congratulating Xióng the men were laying a terrible curse on him. Young Charlie's tongue swelled with questions—how had his rats been weighted against those caught in the other buildings? Who came in second, and by how much? Was Lorne Lorch dead?—and continued swelling until it filled his whole mouth. The queries died on his lips.

Once all the officials had taken their turns offering congratulations, they departed without another word.

The foreman, a lanky, wet-looking figure, offered to hold the Cup for his cleaner until morning. As the foreman was walking away, the great trophy folded under his arm like a table lamp, Xióng recovered enough to speak:

"Does this mean I *won*?"

The foreman turned, pondered, and tapped the rim of the Cup.

"I don't know. But you got this thing."

The officials had not said anything about the prize money or the blazer or the dinner at the upscale Irish restaurant.

The photo published by newspapers around the globe was snapped by Bear, Scantland's girlfriend, at sunset the day after the Regatta. Emergency and debris crews were still clearing the street, so Bear had to take her picture from half a block away, stealthily, leaning around the corner of a building. By accident she took the photo in black and white, which added to its starkness.

She caught the first thirty floors of the Chunce & Chimbly, which looked as if they had been encased in a giant, amorphous diamond. Strewn along the street, among the shadowy figures of the workers, were chunks of ice and stone and brick and metal. Less than a day earlier, this rubble had formed the top fifteen floors of the building. The top third—Sir Gareth's head, neck, and chest—had peeled away and crumbled to the ground late in the morning.

Scantland hated the picture. He said it made the disaster look worse than it was. Bear replied that, if anything, it made the disaster look *better.*

It didn't matter, Scantland told Bear. Lorne Lorch, he believed, had purposely destroyed the structure.

"Why would he do that?"

"You ask him. Only he knows."

Scantland was still in his singlet.

Now I don't have a place to play," he told Bear.

"You will. You know you will."

Buildings all over the city, including one whose existing cleaner had competed in the Regatta, were already offering Scantland contracts—two years, three years, eight years. The superintendent of the Front Street Blocks reached out to Scantland via Kravchenko, as Aquino, his long-time cleaner, was threatening to hold out for higher pay and more benefits. But in Scantland's mind the Blocks, and every other structure in town, was too small; none was even half the size of the Chunce & Chimbly.

"Size doesn't matter," Bear said.

"I should send a thank-you card to the old simp for wrecking my life."

"You should give the poor man a break. It was probably an accident."

"No way in *hell* an accident like that happens to *me*."

Lorne wanted to read the mail people sent, but Cricket would not let him. He assumed people were writing to wish him a speedy recovery. Yet more than half was hate mail. Many people—some of them Scantland supporters, some not—accused him of sabotage. He knew he was going to lose, they wrote, so he did something, *something*, somehow, to torpedo the event.

"It's just dumb stuff, Lorny," Cricket told him. "Most just want to know what happened."

"Christ. Me, too."

Then:

"Any KitKats?"

The only bars that arrived had been pre-licked or crumpled up or urinated on. One had a nail driven through it. Cricket had Leonidas bring over a handful of KitKats that she told Lorne were from his fans. She had to peel the wrappers off for Lorne because he could not do it himself.

The scientist telephoned Lorne after he was out of the hospital, and he gave her an account of what had happened. He left out his panicking and screaming because he had no memory of it. Describing the mass of green fire he thought would be the last thing he saw on earth, he said it was like *a bunch of the little bastards bred like little whores of rabbits faster than anything I ever saw!*

The scientist had him repeat the story over and over as she took notes. That the rats Lorne found were of different shape from the standard fascinated her. How long had they existed in the dead shaft without migrating, or without freezing anything outside of their nest? When Lorne attacked the colony, did the rats act individually, or in concert? Were they—was it—trying to flee, or was it offering a defence? Elongated shape aside, were these *little bastards* the same species as the traditional rats? Were they something new?

"It makes you wonder," she said, mostly to herself, "how many more of them might be hidden around the city. And beyond the city."

"Hopefully none," said Lorne.

That afternoon the scientist called her grown children and told them she was thinking about returning to work. Her grown children tried to talk her out of it, since they relied on her for babysitting.

The Sprill offered Wills Lorne's job. Wills held out for more money and a seven-year contract and a signing bonus that was equal to six months of Lorne's salary. When at last the superintendent—now wearing more muted polo shirts—agreed to the demands, Wills announced he no longer wanted the position.

"I want to be a dentist," he told Mallard.

"Nobody wants to be a dentist!"

"I do."

Mallard asked Wills if he knew how much dental school cost.

"Doesn't matter to me," said Wills.

The Westerfeldt was paying for Wills' tuition and housing. In exchange, upon graduating, Wills was to serve three years as its cleaner.

Lorne put on a shirt and tie every day even though he rarely left the house. One morning Cricket put all of his button-down shirts in the laundry, and he sat beside the washer and dryer with a tie around his naked neck until the load was done. He wanted to help out around the house, but there was still too much cardboard on his skin. Rather than turning him grumpy, as Cricket had expected, his helplessness made him feel heavy, like a wet towel. Now and then she caught Lorne sitting on the step outside the back door. Once in a while she could not find him at all; yet if she waited long enough, and was quiet enough, she would hear an unmistakable sigh or a low mumbling in the ceiling.

Cricket went back to work a couple of months after the Regatta. Lou attempted to lure her back, telephoning and saying that the money she had won betting on the *Chinese kid* was not worth the loss of a "fine employee and best friend."

"No chance," Cricket told her.

"I need you back, Cricky. I'll double your store discount."

Cricket replied that she had never used her discount, since she never had anything that needed framing.

"You need money," Lou said. "You can't keep going without—"

"We have money."

"It won't last. Mark it."

"Marked."

Rather than return to the framing world, Cricket found a job in a store that sold party supplies. It did not pay well, but it had more to look at than the framing store. Her direct supervisor was a nineteen-year-old woman whom Cricket never saw on her feet, even though company policy forbade employees from sitting in view of customers. The store sold oversized animal costumes, and one of Cricket's only joys in those post-Regatta months was to don a giant panda head and tap her supervisor on the shoulder and watch her jump off her stool.

Some of the rooftop VIPs who attended the Regatta passed the hat and scraped up the skeleton of a pension for Lorne. They did so without any fanfare, aware as they were that half the city—half the country—blamed Lorne for the Chunce & Chimbly's annihilation, as well as for the three deaths and the injuries to dozens of fans and rescue workers who rushed into the building when it started turning to ice. The mayor was one of the pension subscribers. The superintendent of the Sprill was another. A couple of NHL players donated autographed sticks.

He can't eat sticks, boys, the superintendent told the players. *But are they game sticks?*

I don't know, said one player.

That one there isn't my stick, said the second. *But that's my signature.*

A few dozen diehards sent money and gifts, which Cricket shared with Lorne even as she discarded the hate mail. One fan sent a letter telling Lorne he should go straight to hell, and then mailed him fifty dollars and said he was sorry.

Lorne said he would send a thank-you note to every person who wrote, regardless of whether they had sent money. He asked Cricket to bring him home some stationery. At the party store she found some surplus Halloween cards and envelopes and brought those home for her husband to use. But despite having little to do during the day, or the night, he could not quite get around to writing. On occasion he fell asleep at midnight or one o'clock and got up at seven, and before Cricket left for work he would say to her

Gonna get at those thank-you's.

And Cricket would bite her lip at seeing her husband, for so long a nocturnal creature, a man who toiled in dark places at dark times so that the world would not turn to ice, creeping his way towards diurnality, dullness—ordinariness.

CHAPTER SIXTY-EIGHT

Leonidas asked Lorne to take his children fishing.

"I haven't fished since I was two years old," Lorne said.

"Ha, ha! Oh, the kids won't know the difference, Dad. They don't even like fish."

"Then why in hell do they want to go fishing?"

They went to a bridge not far from Leonidas's house and cast lines for half an hour before nightfall. Lorne leaned the two children over the guard rail and held them fast by the backs of their sweaters. After ten minutes the granddaughter caught her hook on something under the bridge.

"You probably caught a tire," Lorne said. "We'll have to cut you loose."

"Maybe it's a dead dog," said his grandson.

After a while the grandson wandered a few yards up the sidewalk, circling around with a faraway look on his face.

"Are you taking a shit?" Lorne asked him.

"No!"

A wind blew up, flapping the collar of Lorne's jacket. A dying sunset glowed orange behind him, but a bank of purple clouds was marching in from the east.

"Time to haul ass," he said.

Lorne gathered the rods and tackle together onto a toy wagon and plunked his granddaughter, carrot-coloured stockings and all, on top of the gear. When he glanced at the spot where his grandson had just been idling, it was deserted.

"Jesus—JESUS—"

A horrible idea occurred to him, but he would have heard a sound, a splash. He bent over the railing anyway, looking for ripples in the water. Then he hustled up the sidewalk, yanking the wagon behind him, his granddaughter sliding forwards and backwards on top of the load. He called out his grandson's name. The last rays of the sun were dissipating. He could feel cool air on his back.

He bellowed his grandson's name and his granddaughter began kicking and yelling:

"Stop, Grandpop, *stop*—"

She nearly toppled out of the wagon. Lorne halted, wheeling around, a curse rising to his lips. The little girl was tipped on her side, her yellow boots kicking back and forth, and she pointed into the ditch they had just passed.

"There—"

Lorne bolted down the decline of the ditch and nearly stomped on the head of his grandson, who was peering into a drainage pipe.

"What the *Christ*—you're getting your pants all dirty, boy—!"

"I saw a frog—"

"You never saw no frog! Now look—your pants're all shit-covered—"

The boy wanted his grandfather to frog-chase with him, but Lorne hauled him up to the wagon and dumped him on top of the pile with his sister and told him not to by Jesus move a jeezly muscle. The granddaughter fell asleep on the way and the grandson lay sprawled over her, looking up at the purple clouds. Lorne tugged them the five blocks home, the wheels of the wagon groaning over the paving stones. The party arrived just as it was getting dark.

"Did you catch anything?" Arlen asked Lorne, hoisting the limp form of her daughter over her shoulder with one hand and twisting off the little yellow boots.

"I think little miss snagged a whitewall," he said.

"Was it in season? Ha, ha!"

"Not much biting tonight. We'll try another place sometime."

Lorne's hand was already on the door handle.

"Tea, Dad? Beer?"

"No, no. Want to get home before it rains."

"Ride home, Dad?"

Lorne was already out the door. Leonidas waved at his father's head as it floated past the kitchen window.

Scantland got offers from buildings in Montreal and Vancouver and New York and one in Abu Dhabi. He announced that, before he made any decisions on the next stage of his career, he was taking three months off. He was physically and mentally exhausted, he said. No one could possibly understand what he had been through. He told Folknall the Regatta had nearly killed him.

Folknall wrote a short column about the disaster, predicting that there would be another Regatta next summer and that Scantland would *mop the floor with the competition (no pun intended).* It was not clear which pun he intended. Scantland ended up moving to Los Angeles and cleaned a glass skyscraper for eight months, until homesickness overcame him. He returned in the spring. Rumours of another Regatta abounded, and Scantland vowed to Bear that he would take the Cup for keeps.

Xióng left the business and took a job at his uncle's seafood shop. Skinning and fileting did not pay as well as hunting ice rats, but it allowed him to work during daytime.

Lorne was awake. Rain splashed against the window. He rolled out of bed as lightly as he could, watching Cricket's sleeping form twitch as his weight left the mattress.

He still smelled like the river. In the kitchen he pulled on a raincoat and boots and one of Cricket's ball caps. It took an effort not to cough. Without noticing, he had donned his wife's boots rather than his own. He did not bother lacing them. There was still too much cardboard on his hands.

The rain was heavy and loud and it surprised Lorne that a sky could be that violent without lightning or thunder. He hurried at first, thinking he could reach his destination without getting too wet; when that became impossible, he slowed to a canter. The rain roared upon the street and the grass and the trees.

He was months from his fiftieth birthday. As he crossed the beams cast by streetlights, he saw his shadow flickering across the pavement, and in the cold wet darkness it moved like something much older than himself. Cricket would understand. His nose never rested and it would not sleep. It was impossible to sleep. His nose was always awake.

It took him an hour to reach the river. The bridge—the same one he and his grandchildren had fished from earlier that night—was darker than the surrounding night. Only one streetlamp stood near it, and the bulb was blown. The sky was the colour of dead violets.

Smells good

Cricket's boots were soaked and her cap was sodden. The rain penetrated Lorne's thinning hair and ran in jagged meridians down his face.

It smells good here

Cedar; he could smell wet cedar. A few feet from the bridge he squatted on his heels and listened. A furious battle was taking place between the rain and the river.

I forgot to tell Leo the boy shit himself—

Now he mumbled, or his mouth started mumbling, as if the mumbling were a stray thought slipping into his mind as he fell asleep. Still squatting, he crab-walked on his toes, reaching out his hands and feeling the cold wet blanket of grass on either side of him. The grass sloped down and he followed it until he felt a fresh chill on his feet and knew they were under water. It was so dark that the purple sky above him seemed to glow. Lorne moved another step forward and the chill rose above his ankles.

Or did he shit? Maybe he didn't

Icy, indifferent cold crawled up his legs. He was still crouching and the water bit at his haunches. His eyes were closed.

Okay now—

Drawing his chin to his chest, he gave the air a mighty snuffle, carving his head up as he did so, with a noise like that of an air compressor. He snorted until his head was tilted back and facing the sky.

I knew it I knew it

Splashing, cold, ice: he had fallen over, fallen back, but he paddled to his feet again and stuck his head inside the drain, the same pipe in which his grandson had seen a frog. He lowered his head and thrust it into the mouth of the pipe. For a moment he huddled there in the ditch, headless, like a strange creature from a fairy tale, soaked to the soul, with nostrils as wide as the sky.

I knew it

The rain swelled and the river frothed. In the next instant, he was gone.

Acknowledgments

Thank you to a number of people:

Chris Needham and NON Publishing for taking a chance on an unpublished writer. Chris made the process eerily—even suspiciously—low-stress, and from day one handled this neophyte with generosity, kindness, and professionalism.

Frances Boyle, who provided encouragement and support in the exciting and terrifying days after the story I'd been plugging away on during the pandemic found a publisher. (Frances also recommended writing an Acknowledgements section for this book when I was on the fence about it, and that alone secures her a mention.)

Acquaintances, former colleagues, and random writers I approached either in person or by email who shared their experience and advice and assured me that publishing and promoting a book usually does not, as had been my impression, tear one's soul to pieces. These kind individuals were either happy to help or did an excellent job pretending.

A family like no other. Despite their many foibles and eccentricities, we're as tight as a New Orleans jazz band. Decades of love and support get you mentions by name: Ron, Deb, Sean, Kat, Jack, Henry, Jessi, Owen, and Isla (not to mention a fantastic batch of relatives). On that note, equally cherished is the finest set of in-laws anyone could imagine: Keith, Marlene, Jon, Erica, Blake, Kiernan, Callie, Abby, Jordan, Ellie, Magnus, Shauna, Tim, Kaleb, and Annie (and ditto on the relatives-in-law).

And last but most: Signi, the warm bright oxygen of my life, and our son, the most interesting chap I've ever met.